# PROMISES
## BOUNTY HUNTERS 2

# A.E. VIA

*Promises – Part Two*
*Bounty Hunters*
Published By: Via Star Wings Books
Copyright © March 2016
Edited By: Ally Editorial Services
http://allyeditorialservices.weebly.com/
Cover Art By: Jay Aheer of Simply Defined Art
Formatting & Illustrations By: Fancy Pants Formatting
http://www.fancypantsformatting.com
All rights reserved under the International and Pan-American Copyright
Conventions. No part of this book may be reproduced or transmitted in any form or by any means, electronic or mechanical, including photocopying, recording, or by any information storage and retrieval system, without permission in writing from the author, Adrienne E. Via.

No part of this book may be scanned, uploaded, or distributed via the Internet or any other means, electronic or print, without permission from Adrienne E. Via. The unauthorized reproduction or distribution of this copyrighted work is illegal.

Criminal copyright infringement, including infringement without monetary gain, is investigated by the FBI and is punishable by up to 5 years in federal prison and a fine of $250,000 (http://www.fbi.gov/ipr/). Please purchase only authorized electronic or print editions and do not participate in or encourage the electronic piracy of copyrighted material. Your support of the author's rights and livelihood is appreciated.

# Trademark Acknowledgments

The author acknowledges the trademarked status and trademark owners of the following trademarks mentioned in this work of fiction:

7- Eleven: 7-Eleven, Inc.
Adidas: adidas America Inc.
Atlanta Falcons: NFL Enterprises LLC.
Berluti: BERLUTI
Busch Gardens: SeaWorld Parks & Entertainment, Inc.
Chevy Suburban: General Motors
Dolby: Dolby Laboratories
F350: Ford Motor Company
FedEx: FedEx
Food Network: Television Food Network G.P.
Hanes: Hanesbrands Inc.
IHOP: IHOP Restaurants LLC
Johnnie Walker: Imported by Diageo
Kenneth Cole: Kenneth Cole Productions, Inc.
Keurig: Keurig Green Mountain, Inc.
Lifetime: Lifetime Entertainment Services, LLC, a subsidiary of A+E Networks.
Macy's: Macy's, Inc. (formerly known as Federated Department Stores, Inc.)
Marlboro: PHILIP MORRIS USA INC.
McDonald's: McDonald's
Mercedes: Mercedes-Benz USA, LLC
Mickey Mouse: Walt Disney Productions
Mustang: Ford Motor Company
NFL: NFL Enterprises LLC.
North Face: The North Face, A VF Company
OnStar: OnStar, LLC.
Prius: Toyota Motor Sales, U.S.A., Inc.
Range Rover: Jaguar Land Rover North America, LLC
Stetson Cologne: Coty, Inc
Subway: Subway IP Inc.
Tide: Procter & Gamble
TMZ: EHM PRODUCTIONS, INC.
Trader Joe's: Trader Joe's
Uber: Uber Technologies Inc.
Velcro: Velcro Industries B.V.
YouTube: Google Inc.
Jeffrey Osborne - "Yes I'm Ready"

# CONTENTS

Acknowledgements ................................................................7
Chapter One ..........................................................................9
Chapter Two.........................................................................15
Chapter Three.......................................................................23
Chater Four .........................................................................29
Chapter Five.........................................................................37
Chapter Six...........................................................................45
Chapter Seven ......................................................................53
Chapter Eight .......................................................................59
Chapter Nine .......................................................................69
Chapter Ten..........................................................................75
Chapter Eleven .....................................................................81
Chapter Twelve ....................................................................89
Chapter Thirteen .................................................................97
Chapter Fourteen...............................................................105
Chapter Fifteen...................................................................117
Chapter Sixteen ..................................................................127
Chapter Seventeen..............................................................133
Chapter Eighteen ...............................................................139
Chapter Nineteen...............................................................147
Chapter Twenty..................................................................155
Chapter Twenty-One..........................................................161
Chapter Twenty-Two ..........................................................167
Chapter Twenty-Three .......................................................175
Chapter Twenty-Four .........................................................185
Chapter Twenty-Five ..........................................................193
Chapter Twenty-Six ............................................................203

Chapter Twenty-Seven.............................................................209
Chapter Twenty-Eight............................................................215
Chapter Twenty-Nine.............................................................225
Chapter Thirty ......................................................................233
Chapter Thirty-One ...............................................................239
Chapter Thirty-Two ...............................................................247
Chapter Thirty-Three .............................................................251
Chapter Thirty-Four ..............................................................257
Chapter Thirty-Five...............................................................263
Chapter Thirty-Six ................................................................271
Chapter Thirty-Seven ............................................................281
Chapter Thirty-Eight .............................................................289
Chapter Thirty-Nine ..............................................................295
Chapter Forty ......................................................................307
Chapter Forty-One ...............................................................313
Biography............................................................................322
Also by A.E. Via...................................................................324

# ACKNOWLEDGMENTS

I'd like to thank everyone that helped me put Quick and Cayson's story together.

My family
My team
My friends

Loves
Adrienne

# CHAPTER ONE

*Quick*

Quick slid out of his Range Rover, squinting up at the light breaking through the dawn. He loved this time of the day. Quiet, peaceful. Before the hustle and bustle of the laborers in the city began their day. Atlanta in the winter was beautiful to him, January and February being his favorite months. Most of the leaves had fallen from the trees, and as he walked, he enjoyed the loud crunch they made under his black, steel toe boots. He let his long hair hang for a while, the still-damp strands sending a pleasant chill through him. Propping himself against the large Magnolia tree next to their modest one-story building, he inhaled the smell of nature before it was time to pick up Atlanta's trash . If he still smoked, it'd be a great time to inhale a few drags to calm his mind. But, since he didn't, inhaling the big city air would have to do. It was probably just as toxic.

He saw that Duke's midnight black F350 was already in its usual spot, closest to the side entrance. *He's sure here early.* His friend had begun to sleep in on some mornings, he'd been on two brief vacations, and Quick had lost count on the unscheduled days off Duke now took at will.

Duke wasn't only his best friend since they were still young enough to chase tail; he was also his business partner – and almost son-in-law. Yep, they were a typical American family. It'd been a couple months since Quick's one and only son confessed his love for his best friend and saved his life by giving one of his kidneys to Duke while he was on his death bed. Now the two were connected in a way that was immune to destruction and disgustingly sweet.

Regardless, Quick was happy for his friend. His son Vaughan had always been a levelheaded, determined individual. Though Vaughan was ten years younger than Duke, he had to admit that they were perfect together. Quick and Duke were both in their early forties, but the new pep in Duke's step made him look younger and more striking every day. It was about time one of them got their happily ever after. Duke had always been more romantic than him, though. Quick was accustomed to his comfortable, isolated life. He went to work, caught bad guys, kicked ass, hung with buddies here and there, and then went home… alone. He could do that for the rest of his life. Adding another person into the mix only complicated shit.

"Rome! You going to work today, or not? Out here sight-seeing at nothing." Duke's deep voice yelled from the open door.

Quick threw up his middle finger before pushing off the base of the massive tree and making his way up the bricked walkway. "Can't a man have a few minutes of peace?"

"Not on my fucking dime, he can't. Now get in here, we have two skips today and Dana is heading over to Fulton to do a bond." Duke was rattling off the day's business, already in full steam ahead mode. His energy level through the roof at five a.m. *Pfft. I wonder why.*

Quick's steps were heavy along the all-wooden floor. He made a beeline for the still-dripping pot of coffee and poured himself a large cup, not caring about interrupting the flow. He'd slept like shit last night. Although Vaughan hadn't lived with him very long after he returned from law school, he'd still liked the idea of cooking for two again, of sitting on the patio and discussing his day with his son while they drank a few brews. That had actually been pretty cool. But Vaughan had moved in with Duke fairly fast, so Quick found himself arriving earlier for work than usual and was typically the last to leave.

Duke was going on about where they were headed, but Quick only had one ear tuned in, his other was on… well, anything besides Duke. He dropped down into his chair and spun until his back was to his friend and he could focus on the serenity of the morning outside the large window.

"…Should be a clean pick up. Brian and Ford will be here any minute and we'll roll out." Duke finished up, and Quick nodded, still facing the window. He liked going out with the two brothers. They were efficient, sharp, and most of all, strong as oxen. It didn't even bother him that Brian had yet to speak a word to any of them, still using sign language as his means of communication. Quick's head jerked up when he heard the door open, expecting it to be the towering brothers. It wasn't.

"Vaughan, what are you doing here?" Quick stood and hugged his son. They'd just seen each other the night before for dinner, but a hug was their customary greeting. Quick looked his son up and down, frowning at his attire. Noting that he was again dressed like a model, not a lawyer. His blue suit matched the light gray dress shirt he wore under a white and gray vest. No tie and ridiculously expensive gray suede shoes.

"Hopefully he's here to see me," Duke said, leaning casually against his office door. Vaughan completely forgot about answering his father and made his way over to his lover. Quick turned away when he saw their lips connect almost violently, cringing at the sounds that emanated from them.

"Damn, Duke, don't you have enough spit of your own?" Quick grumbled.

The sound of laughter was his okay to turn back around. His son was wiping his mouth, staring at him like he'd ruined the best kiss ever. "I was on my way downtown and thought I'd stop in and—"

Vaughan was cut off when the door burst open again, another gust of cool air rushing in along with the two brothers. Since they were going out in the field on recoveries, they wore all black, including thick leather pants and coats to protect them if they had to scuffle with anyone. When you were a bounty hunter, the bail skippers didn't always come willingly. Underestimating how badly someone valued their freedom could result in you being critically injured or in death – something Duke had experienced when he was practically beaten to death by some strung out drug addicts who would rather kill than go back to prison. Duke and Quick had been bounty hunters for almost twenty-five years, they knew this business, and they were the best. Not only did Duke have his own bail bonds business, but he also did bail recovery for other companies, while their other business partner, Judge, ran the private investigations office.

There was plenty of work to go around and to keep Quick's mind off other things. Quick watched as Duke walked his son to the door, his large hand at his back, his mouth close to his ear. Spinning his chair again, he noticed that Brian was staring at him with an amused look on his arrogant, handsome face.

"What?" Quick barked. Knowing Brian wouldn't respond – like always – he got a soft shrug, but no words. Working together for the last few months, they'd quickly become comfortable with each other

Ford came in from their small break room, which consisted of a couple tables, a forty-two inch television, a microwave, and refrigerator. Most of them still ate at their desks because they were constantly communicating and exchanging information. Duke was the only one with an office. The rest of them had large desks placed throughout the open space. Dropping down into his large, executive-style chair, the mechanisms groaned and squeaked at the sheer weight and bulk of Bradford King.

Out of the corner of his eye, Quick saw Brian's hands move in a quick series of gestures and his brother snorted at whatever was communicated to him. "You sure you're okay with your son dating Duke?" Bradford asked, his grin barely there.

"That's a stupid question. Vaughan saved his life. They're in love. Case closed," Quick mumbled, still not making eye contact with his colleagues. He fired up his computer so he could have somewhere to direct his attention other than on the speculative glances he kept getting.

Brian's hands moved again. If you blinked, you'd miss it. Ford responded, "You're right Brian. He didn't answer the question."

Quick rolled his eyes, but decided to stay hidden behind his monitor instead of delving further into the topic. He wasn't bothered that Duke and his son were together. He was upset because he'd thought he and Duke would eventually be grumpy old men together. It was stupid, but it was the truth. He could admit it to himself, if no one else. When Duke and Vaughan first sealed their commitment, Quick was actually happy. Duke was a damn good man; he knew his son's heart was safe. That's what every parent wanted, right? But some of their long-held traditions began to change pretty quickly. Instead of going out for beer and darts after a hard bust, Duke opted to go home and be with Vaughan, leaving Quick to unwind by himself or with the King brothers. Duke used to come over for dinner at least three or four times a week, now Quick was lucky if he came over once. Who could blame him? Vaughan was an even better cook than him. Duke and he used to laugh at couples who went to dinner parties and game nights with other couples, but now his friend bragged about being the king of Win, Loose, or Draw among Vaughan's lawyer friends. Friends Quick wasn't asked to meet. Even his internal quarrel made him feel like a jilted bitch.

Quick simply needed to find something to do with his free time. Or at least with the time he used to spend with Duke.

# CHAPTER TWO

*Cayson*

"What is it that you're so afraid of, huh? Did you have a bad experience? You can tell me. Then maybe we can work through this." Cayson's voice was shaky when he spoke up again. He wanted to pretend what Joe had just done wasn't degrading and humiliating, but it was difficult to hide his feelings. He couldn't ignore the simmering heat he felt on his cheeks and the sweat beading along his hairline as he picked up the tossed bottle of lube from the foot of the bed. When he'd tried to give it to Joe to get him prepped, the man had damn near thrown up on him before slapping the thin, clear bottle from his hands.

"No! No, I didn't have a bad experience! I just don't want to play with your asshole, Cayson! Why is that so hard to understand? Not all men are into anal." Joe was already throwing his legs over the edge of the bed, stuffing his feet into Cayson's leather slippers. "Now I've lost my dang erection."

Cayson squeezed his eyes shut when Joe closed himself inside his bathroom, slamming the door hard enough to make him flinch. *Why do I even bother?* Cayson and Joe had been off and on since they'd first met in the OR at Piedmont Hospital, three years ago. Joe was – and still is – a deeply closeted anesthesiologist. At fucking forty-two years old, he was still afraid of his grandfather, a big name in the hospital's administration. Joe had even gone as far as taking a job at a hospital on the other side of town when Cayson started wanting more and had begun winking at him in the halls or in the lab. Now they only saw each other periodically. It definitely was a friends with benefits type of thing, but Cayson always screwed up when he started to want more. Joe would never give him more than what they had. Cayson was his uncomfortable little secret.

They typically had a good time between the sheets, when Joe relaxed enough. There was a lot of stroking, kissing, and sucking when they got their hands on each other, but Joe still considered it fucking, even though he wouldn't penetrate Cayson, or let him do him. He thought he couldn't be labeled as gay if he didn't actually fuck Cayson in the commonly accepted definition of the word. Frowning again at the absurdity, Cayson stood and began to pull some clothes out of his dresser. He heard the bathroom door open, but didn't bother to turn around. His cock still ached, so did his ass. It clenched in anticipation, only to be rebuffed again. He was so done with this. *You said that the last three times.*

~~~~~~~~~

"Dr. Chauncey, your three o'clock is here," his nurse called through his speakerphone.

"Thanks, Nania, send him in."

Cayson smiled while he straightened a few papers on his desk and closed a couple of strewn files. Duke and Vaughan had become more than just his patients; they were considered friends now. Although he *was* still waiting on his invitation to football night or something, anything. He thought he knew why they were keeping him at bay for now. Cayson had an overwhelmingly sinking feeling it had a lot to do with Quick. Cayson was the attending surgeon and Nephrology case manager for Duke and Vaughan's kidney transplant. He'd been so blown away by the love and dedication the men had for each other that he couldn't resist doing everything in his power to give them a real chance. He didn't think he'd ever worked so hard on a case.

It made Cayson believe that miracles were real. If a man as sensual and stunning as Vaughan could swoop in like a comic book hero and save a man like Duke – who was no spring chicken, but gorgeous all the same, then there had to be some kind of hope for a decent human being like himself. He pushed his hand through his dirty-blond hair. He'd been letting it grow a little more on the top since Joe had mentioned that he thought Cayson's longer hair was sexy. Hating where his mind had gone again, he jerked his head up at the sharp knock and the twist of his doorknob, telling the two lovers to come in.

He stood and came from behind his desk. He hugged Duke first. The contact was strong and sincere. The man didn't look a day over thirty. His fit body filled one of the two large client chairs as he eased down into it. Cayson noticed Duke's careful movements and made a mental note to ask about it. But, first, he looked Vaughan up and down, giving him a friendly look of approval. Duke blushed a little when Vaughan sat close to him and ran his hand over his thick mop of black and silver hair, which lay waywardly all over Duke's head. But damn if it didn't work.

"So what have you two been up to?" Cayson smiled, loosening his green and silver necktie. Vaughan grinned and nodded at the gesture, and Cayson just realized that it was the tie Vaughan gave him for his birthday a couple months ago. It was his favorite. With a light chuckle, he smoothed down the silky fabric before continuing looking through Duke's chart. "Work got you staying busy?"

"Me, or…?" Duke asked, letting the question trail off.

Vaughan gave Duke what looked like a reprimanding glare, but the look was returned with heat and passion. Cayson had to loosen his tie a little more as he waited for the two men to have their moment. Vaughan finally spoke up first. "He tumbled down a flight of stairs with a three hundred pound man. His ribs took a beating."

"How come I wasn't notified of this?" Cayson aggressively fingered through a couple previous pages to see if he missed an ER visit documented in Duke's file, but he hadn't. "You didn't get any X-rays done? What the hell, Duke?"

"I told you he'd be mad." Vaughan whistled low, giving Duke a look of pity.

"Oh, shut up, troublemaker," Duke groused.

"On the table, Duke." Cayson got up and went over to the far right side of his office where he had an exam table and sink. When Duke hesitated, Cayson threw in a forceful, "Now" for emphasis.

"It was just some bruising. No big deal. I've had cracked ribs before, they were way worse than this. Besides, Quick took the real beating. I was on top of the pile. He's the one all fucked up."

Cayson's hands froze while lifting Duke's shirt. *Quick. Is he hurt? Is he okay? Did he go to the ER?* Duke noticed Cayson's pause, his dark brow raised slightly in amusement. *Great.* Cayson could feel his face heating. *Not now.* Anytime Duke mentioned Quick, all Cayson could think about was how he'd embarrassed himself by flirting with an obvious straight stud who was so far out of his league it was ridiculous. Quick had shot him down so fast it'd made his head spin, and Cayson hadn't fully recovered before he was thrown out of the man's home like the filthy slut his behavior resembled.

"You okay, Doc?" Duke asked, reclining on the table and lifting his black t-shirt. Vaughan stood on the opposite side, absently stroking Duke's large biceps with one hand while his other hand flew across the keyboard on his phone.

Duke smiled shyly. "Lawyers, huh?"

Cayson smiled, but was still distracted as he pressed a few tender spots on Duke's abdomen before working his way over his ribs. Duke was right. They most likely weren't fractured, but the man needed to be careful out in the field. He may look gorgeous, but his body was still its age and it had taken a hard setback last year. Vaughan and Duke both took great care of themselves and exercised regularly, but he worried about the aggressively physical nature of Duke's work.

"Duke, I need you to be more careful, man. If the bruises weren't already healing, I'd have you downstairs getting some images taken, but I'm pretty confident you're just bruised." He palpated a few more areas, which Duke seemed fine with, then told him he could get up. All the other tests and bloodwork were good on both of them. Life after a transplant could be difficult if you didn't have a good case manager to watch for signs of trouble. It'd been almost nine months since the surgery, and Cayson couldn't be happier with the results. He'd hate for all his hard work to be undone because of a perp who skipped bail. But that was Duke's life.

"I promise, Doc. More careful, and no more dancing with men bigger than me." Duke pulled his shirt down and climbed off the table.

Although Cayson's back was to them, he heard their kiss and whispered promises to each other before they rejoined him. Settling back behind his desk, he tried to play uninterested when he asked, "So, um. Roman got hurt. Did he see a doctor?"

"Yeah, right. Since there were no protruding bones or visible blood, he felt no need. But, personally, I think his ribs might be worse off than mine. Stubborn bastard took on three men, ignoring my call to pull back."

Cayson squirmed in his chair. Thinking of the big, bad bounty hunter caused reactions in his body that he had no control over, often leaving him embarrassed and ashamed. But Quick fighting three men, that sounded like damn good jerk off material. There was no denying the exceptional amount of lust that snaked through him when it came to Quick, no other way to describe it. It wasn't love. He didn't know him well enough for that. But it was electric, for sure. Facing Roman, especially going to his home again, wasn't a good idea at all.

"I would feel more comfortable if he got it checked out. His cheek is still swollen, too." Vaughan nodded, agreeing with Duke. Cayson peered at booth of them over his paperwork. "I can recommend someone."

"Quick would never agree to that."

"I doubt he'll agree to me treating him, either." Cayson focused on keeping his expression blank, even though saying that out loud hurt like a bitch. It was how he showed himself, how he shined. By caring, healing. It really was the only thing he was good at. But Quick hadn't let Cayson touch him since he'd stitched up the gash in his arm, months ago. Cayson tried to pour as much care into that menial procedure as he could, but Quick had still left the ER without as much as a "See you later," or "I'll talk to you soon." He got nothing but a canceled follow-up appointment.

"Dr. Chauncey, please go check on him. He's as stubborn as the day is long, but I don't think he'd react the same way he did before." Cayson knew what Vaughan was referring to. He groaned and closed Duke's file, digging the pads of his thumbs into his dry eye sockets. He checked his watch. It was almost four. Duke was his last appointment, but they didn't know that. He could make up something. Only thing was, he was a terrible liar and his gut gnawed at him to go check on the big man.

"He's probably not home," Cayson said quietly, checking his watch again.

"Yes he is," Duke and Vaughan said, in perfect unison.

*Damn these two.* Cayson hadn't been able to resist either one of them since they'd barged into his life. Looking into Vaughan's concerned eyes; he sighed and reached for his intercom button. "Nania, are you still here?"

"Yes, doctor. Just getting ready to head out. You need something?" She sounded tired. Cayson had a hectically full schedule. He was one of the managing board members of the Nephrology transplant team in addition to being a well sought out surgeon. Not to mention the number of hours he volunteered in the ER to let the doctors who had families have some time off.

"Do we have a radio portable available to check out?" His question was met with curious gazes from across his desk while he waited for his nurse to respond. *Those things are never available.* The hospital only had four of the tablet-style portable X-ray radios, so the odds of him....

"We actually have two available, Dr. Chauncey. Do you want me to check one out for you?"

Cayson cleared his throat in surprise. "Yes, please. Thank you, Nania. You can go on home now."

"Good night, Doctor."

Cayson stood and began packing a small bag with supplies he thought he'd need from the cabinet behind his desk. He even got a heat wrap, maybe Quick would let him massage some of the strained muscles he must have. *Wishful thinking.* He'd grab the radio tablet on his way out.

"I really appreciate this, Cayson."

He didn't know what to say to Duke or even how to look him in the eye. Did he tell him how scared he was to face Quick? Particularly an injured Quick. Tell him that he wasn't sure he could control himself, or his bodily fluids? His fucked up whatever the hell it was with Joe was becoming increasingly silly and immature. All the humping and grinding made him feel like he was a nervous virgin, too scared to go all the way. He needed to be touched, loved, fucked hard up against the wall. Didn't he deserve that as much as the next man?

"We'll walk you out." Vaughan stood and buttoned his jacket. Cayson watched Duke appreciatively scan Vaughan's entire six-foot frame before he stood himself.

Feeling the warmth from the men in his office, his jealously was there, riding him, making him edgy, quick to get upset and cop an attitude, because he knew he was deserving of the same treatment Duke was getting. Where the fuck were all the men like Vaughan? Cayson tried to remain calm as he threw a couple files still on his desk into his vintage cowhide messenger bag. He wouldn't act like a ridiculous child with these great men and piss on their picnic basket. He just needed to find his own picnic.

He tossed a couple more files in, just in case Quick threw him out on his ass again, giving him time to do some work at home. The thought made him want to change his mind. He was done with the mistreatment – if it meant being alone, so be it – but no more allowing men to walk all over Dr. Cayson Chauncey. *There. Oath to self, made.*

# CHAPTER THREE

*Quick*

Quick finished his long shower. He'd let the scalding hot water beat on his back and side for as long as he could stand it. His ribs screamed in protest any time he turned too fast, squatted or bent over, and he was beginning to think he may have fractured a couple. His chest ached when he breathed, but again, he self-diagnosed, contending it was only tenderness… nothing more. He reached into his top chest drawer and pulled out some boxer briefs, but when he thought of bending twice to put on his underwear and pants, he opted for his thin cotton lounging pants and no shirt. Lifting his right arm, he gingerly touched the black and purple bruises all along his torso. *Fuck me.*

What had he been thinking? What was he trying to prove? Watching Ford and Brian toss men around and beat them like it was a sport had Quick wanting to show off his shit, too. He was martial arts trained since he was a teen. Three fuckin' men were barely a challenge, but he always had to remember to keep his anger from rising to levels that caused him to act without considering the consequences. He'd easily taken the first two, kicking one in the nuts while he held the other in a tight chokehold. Then the third scared bastard had slammed into him from behind, sending all of them crashing down the apartment building's concrete stairs. Those damn steps had to be what had done the most damage to his body. But, still high on adrenaline, Quick ignored Duke's orders and got back on his feet, stomping bodies until he reached their bounty.

Now he was home hiding, because Duke was pissed off at him for taking unnecessary risks, which he no doubt had told his son by now, so he knew without checking what all the missed calls and angry texts from Vaughan were about. It'd been almost five days since the bust, and he couldn't ignore his son or his best friend forever. However strong he considered himself to be, there was no way he was going back into the field right now. A few more days of recovery were definitely needed.

He'd just tied his still-wet hair back in a loose ponytail at the base of his neck. Rubbing on a thin layer of deodorant and a little aftershave, he was slowly making his way downstairs when he heard a firm knock on his front door.

"Oh, no," he grumbled, not in the mood for Vaughan or Duke's antics tonight. He frowned when the knock became louder and more persistent. It couldn't be them. They would've used their key after the first knock. He couldn't run down the stairs, so whoever was at the door had better be patient. That thought wasn't even done before there was another knock… more like a banging.

"Stop knocking on my damn door like that!" Quick shouted from the second landing. He was trying to navigate the short distance between him and the front door, but was moving slowly. Using his leaf blower in the yard earlier today probably wasn't a great idea, but he'd never been one to sit around and wallow in pain. He came from a long line of tough men. His father worked their farm through every ailment he ever got, so did his grandfather. Surely, Quick could do the same.

When he unlocked the bolt, he twisted the knob and was almost knocked back off his feet when he saw Dr. Chauncey – um, Cayson – standing there on his porch with his large medical bag at his feet. He had on a puffy, mid-thigh, black North Face parka with the large hood trimmed with tawny brown fur. He looked adorable all bundled up and rosy cheeked from the brisk temperature.

"I'm sorry. I didn't mean to knock like I'm the police. I got a little worried when it took a while. I came... um... Duke told me... he said maybe I should come by. Totally his idea. I promise I'm not just swinging by. As a matter of fact, I think it's rather rude to stop by unannounced, but Duke said—"

"Cayson, would you like to come in and get out of the cold for a bit?" Quick smiled, pulling the door open wider. The man was blabbering like a silly fool. But Quick new exactly why Cayson was nervous about coming into his home again. He'd make sure the man felt welcome this time.

He wasn't typically an asshole, especially to nice doctors who saved his best friend's life, but damn if Cayson didn't catch him off guard that afternoon he'd come home to find the sexy doctor in his personal space. He was supposed to be there to check up on Duke and Vaughan's recovery, but Cayson was examining everything but his patients when Quick had come in wearing his bounty hunting gear. Those focused, blue eyes brazenly surveyed him like he was a piece of USDA prime rib in a butcher's window. He could see Cayson's chest rise and fall with his elevated, lustful breathing. But to do it right in front of his son and Duke, that wasn't cool. He was a private man. If the doctor was interested in him, then he should've approached Quick privately and asked him out like a real man, not used trickery.

He'd been attracted to men in the past – very deep past – but he'd married a woman and had dated a couple more after the divorce. Now, this handsome, sexy, slightly nerdy in a charming way surgeon was rapidly igniting embers that hadn't burned in a long time, and Quick had handled it badly, scaring Cayson off. He'd promised Duke and Vaughan that he'd fix it. He'd call the doctor and apologize, make things right, but he hadn't. He'd copped out. Nerves. Anxiety. Maybe even fear had gripped and held him fast.

"Actually, I wouldn't mind coming in. Thank you." Cayson took a breath between ramblings and hefted his large bag to step across the threshold.

Quick immediately noticed Cayson scanning his chest as he walked by, but he didn't take offense this time. The man was a doctor and Quick was riddled with bruises. It was clear Cayson had been sent by his son or Duke to check him out. "I already know why you're here. Thank you for coming."

Cayson was in the process of pulling off his thick coat. He looked a little shocked, and Quick suppressed a grin. Seeing the doctor confused and uncertain was quite entertaining. "I thought I'd have to wrestle you down to examine you." Cayson closed his eyes and grimaced at his choice of words, but this time, Quick couldn't hold in his chuckle. "That's not what I meant. I just… I thought… I wasn't sure, I mean, if you'd let me examine you. I swear I can be professional. I won't make you uncomfortable. I really think we got off on the wrong foot last time I was here."

Quick went into the living room and didn't stop until he was standing close enough to the doctor for him to smell his aftershave. Cayson hastily diverted his eyes from Quick's, like he was being extra careful how he looked at him, and he began to nervously dig in his bag, coming up with a device that looked like a twelve-inch tablet.

"And that is?" Quick hadn't moved. He knew he was flustering the doctor with his proximity, but he had a purpose for doing it. He hadn't called Cayson because he wasn't sure the man would be willing to forgive him for being a massive asshole, especially after everything he'd had done for his family. However, he was here. He'd come, regardless that Quick had yet to apologize.

Cayson was doing everything to keep from looking directly at Quick. Now he was desperately searching for an electrical outlet for his machine. "This is a radio portable X-ray. It uses digital imaging technology to compact the images so I can immediately see any broken bones, fractures, or whatever other abnormalities may be there. It's very accurate and eliminates having to go and wait in the radiology department. Or for patients who can't get to a hospital."

Quick smiled. Damn, the man was so smart and sweet. "You brought this over here for me?"

"Well," Cayson said slowly. "I brought a few things. I wanted to be sure to check you over real good." Cayson's cheeks flooded with color when the words left his lips. He scrunched his brow and waved his hand in the air. "You know what I meant. Would you mind lying down in your recliner? It'll be easier for me to move around you… unless you were busy… like about to put on more clothes or something."

Quick's smirk was fuckin' sinister before he slowly walked over to his large, brown leather recliner, which was positioned in front of his big screen television, and pulled the handle until he was lying almost flat. He could easily sleep in his chair. He lifted his arms, making sure his biceps flexed along with the movement, and linked his fingers behind his head. "Nope. I'm all yours. Examine away."

# CHAPTER FOUR

*Cayson*

*What the fuckin' fuck?* Quick was practically naked. Okay. What kind of game was this? Screw with the horny, gay man's willpower. Did Duke know that Quick walked around his house like this? In various stages of undress? Why wasn't he warned? Fuck the fact he wasn't wearing a stich of underwear under those thin-ass cotton pants that hung low enough to show his enticing trail of damp, sandy brown hair along his stomach and above his pubic bone, but he was shirtless and still smelling heavenly from the shower Cayson must've interrupted. Even Quick's long hair was still dripping small beads of moisture. Oh, but that large chest was so hard to ignore. Muscles, bulges, and vibrant tattoos were everywhere, and damn if the bruises didn't make Quick look like the bad boy Cayson had heard he was.

Damnit, now he was getting hard. He knew better than to ogle Quick like that. Did he want a repeat of the last time he was here? *Shit, shit.* "Um. I'm gonna go wash my hands." Cayson darted down the hall, making a hasty retreat behind the bathroom door. He washed his hands three times before splashing cool water on his face. He needed to calm down. He just wasn't sure how. He had a walking, talking, wet dream waiting for him to give him a complete exam. He counted backwards from twenty twice while he composed himself. He noticed that Quick had changed the wallpaper in his bathroom since the last time he'd been there. It was good that Quick took so much pride in his home. If Cayson had ever been officially invited, he'd probably feel more welcome to explore the nice space, but he didn't get that feeling when he was here. He wasn't quite sure what welcome even felt like. He definitely wasn't welcome at Joe's house.

The portable X-ray device was already fully charged, but Cayson had plugged it in anyway, to put some much-needed breathing room between him and his new patient. *That's right, be professional. He's a patient, not a lover.* He could do this, right? He could professionally examine Quick as a favor to a friend. He'd done countless favors for others. This was no different. He'd performed mouth to snout on a dog before; surely, he could handle this. Cayson unplugged the tablet and shook his head at his own weirdness. *Where's the correlation between helping a dog and fawning over Quick?*

Huffing softly and sending up a fast prayer for strength, he powered up the device and stood next to Quick's outstretched chair. He cleared his throat a couple times before he was able to speak. "You can put on a shirt if you want. The device can be used over several layers of clothing, actually." Cayson tried to appear unfazed, but he had a feeling he was failing, because Quick wasn't budging to cover himself.

"Nope. I had a really hot shower, so I'm trying to cool off," Quick said easily.

"Oh, okay. Of course. You should be comfortable in your own home." Cayson cursed under his breath and turned around to let the device finish booting up the software. He noticed the tablet screen moving annoyingly as he tried unsuccessfully to punch in his identification and password. He was shaking. *Shit. Stop it. Stop it. Be cool.* Otherwise, he'd find his ass back on the curb again. Roman "Quick" Webb was just another patient. The thought was barely formed before Cayson was telling himself how much of a lie it was.

"I'm not making you uncomfortable, am I?" Quick asked, running his large hand across the top half of his chest, his nipples responding immediately. That voice. *Fuck*. Deep and sensual. He imagined Quick whispering in his ear. That decadent, gravelly baritone could probably bring him to the brink of orgasm without him even being touched. How he'd love to test that theory.

"No. I'm fine," Cayson lied, swallowing a huge lump of nothing in his throat. He dropped back down and fumbled through his bag again. *Gloves!* He'd put on gloves to limit the skin on skin contact. *Start with the basics.* Still urging himself to stay calm, Cayson took out a traditional blood pressure cuff and slid it up Quick's corded forearm and over his tattooed biceps. The cuff was barely large enough. Cayson probably squeezed the bulb harder than needed, but he appreciated the distraction for his hands. The Velcro crackled and popped as it inflated, but Cayson masterfully adjusted the valve and was able to get a good reading on the gauge. He recorded the numbers and jotted a couple notes down on a small pad. He'd record the details properly in a file later.

Back down on one knee next to Quick's plush armrest, Cayson continued his thorough exam. With his stethoscope secured around his neck and the ear pieces snug in his ear canals, he gently placed the diaphragm over Quick's lungs, applying a little pressure on the bell. He whispered softly, "Breathe deep for me, Roman." Sharp green eyes focused on his every move as Quick's chest rose and fell with his breaths. He usually didn't mind being scrutinized, he was too damn good at his job to be nervous, but Quick's undivided attention had him shaking like a leaf. Cayson listened for any wheezes or crackles, satisfied after a minute or so that Quick didn't have any constrictions or fluid in his lungs. He listened longer to the lub-dub sounds of Quick's heart, noting no murmurs. Last was his abdomen.

Cayson angled his face away from Quick's eyes and tried to calm his hands, but when he moved down Quick's torso, he became too aware of how sexy his body was. *Just examine him like normal*. Cayson gingerly placed the bell of his stethoscope over the fine, straight hairs covering Quick's rippled stomach. Even through his gloves, the hair was silky and smooth to the touch. Cayson groaned inwardly. No matter how much he tried to avoid touching, his wrists and forearms continuously grazed Quick's belly while he listened. He needed to focus on the distinctive gurgling of the stomach, not how much hair was below that low-riding waistband.

Cayson closed his eyes and took a deep breath, trying to will his erection to stop growing, because when he'd braved a look further down Quick's body, he noticed a pretty prominent bulge through those thin pants. *What the hell?* Was Quick fucking with him so Cayson would slip up and then Quick could throw him out again? Deciding to ignore it, Cayson yanked off his stethoscope and moved on to the X-ray tablet. He needed to get this exam over with. He'd make sure Quick wasn't dying and then hightail it out of there before he got his feelings hurt… like usual.

Scribbling hastily in his notepad, Cayson picked up the tablet and pushed the necessary keys to start the imaging. He slowly moved the tablet over Quick's chest and stomach, paying extra close attention to the clear images on the screen. He noted each bone in his upper torso. Glad his mind was fully focused, Cayson quickly found the small, hairline fractures on ribs seven and eight, but no other signs of breaks or floating segments. That was a very good thing. Duke and Vaughan could rest assured that Quick would heal and be on his way to kicking ass again in no time. He wanted to tell him to be careful. Don't take stupid risks. There was a shortage of gorgeous, older men in this world, and it'd be a damn shame to lose him or Duke.

Cayson removed the latex gloves with an audible snap before he asked Quick to roll over onto the side without the fractures. He palpitated the area around some significant bruising, but

Quick didn't make a sound. "Any tenderness here?" Cayson asked, pressing a little more firmly around Quick's kidneys.

"Nope."

"Are you being honest?"

"Of course, I am. I wouldn't lie to you, Doc." Quick's voice was muffled by the thick cushions of his recliner, but the tone was suggestive. Cayson couldn't have been imagining this, but he wouldn't take the bait. He couldn't trust Quick, he was confusing and unpredictable.

He moved up and around Quick's spinal column with both hands, observing Quick for a painful reaction or sound. Instead, all that came were grunts of what sounded like pleasure. Cayson was nervous to even ask. What kind of exam was this? He should've been asking more questions, but goddamn Quick's voice and that long expanse of beautiful tan skin along Quick's back.

"Any soreness along your spine?"

"No. Just on my side." Quick pointed right to the fractures.

"Yeah. You have a couple simple fractures, sometimes called hairline fractures, right there where you have your hand," Cayson informed him.

"That's explains why it hurts some when I take a deep breath," Quick said.

"Yep. I know you've had them before, so you know the pain will subside with time. No additional treatment is necessary. But I'd say you've got about a good couple weeks of tenderness." Cayson was still rubbing up and down Quick's back while he spoke softly, carefully grazing over the bruises. He didn't even realize what he was doing until he heard Quick exhale slowly before moaning a rough, masculine sound. Pulling his hands away as if Quick had burst into flames, Cayson tapped him on the shoulder. "You can turn back over."

Why'd he say that? When Quick was flat on his back again Cayson couldn't't've stopped the gasp if he'd been forewarned. Quick was full-on hard. His cock spiking a massive teepee in his pajama pants. *Fuck. Fuck. Fuck.* Why was this happening to him? He was trying so hard to be professional. This shit had to be a joke, but he wasn't laughing. He stood all the way up and tossed his few tools back inside his bag. Swallowing the saliva pooling in his mouth, and fighting his wood again, he couldn't help but chance another inconspicuous look at... at... *Oh, god.* There was plenty of hair around that hard cock. He could see it as clear as those X-ray images. Quick had to be at least eight or nine inches of mouthwatering firmness. Cayson's hole clenched with need. He needed all that firmness pushed deep in his—

"As you can see, the equipment still works fine," Quick whispered, winking at him as he uselessly pushed his hand on his own cock in an effort to force it down... but it didn't work. It kept springing back up like a proud soldier.

"Fuck you," Cayson murmured, confident he wasn't heard since his back was still to Quick as he closed up his bag. He saw the syringes and knew he still needed to take a couple vials of blood to test that all Quick's organs were functioning fine, but he was actually fighting doing the right thing. He wanted to say screw it and leave Quick to be responsible for his own health care. Cayson always had everyone else's best interest at heart, constantly neglecting his own. It was his life story.

His whole life, people made him the brunt of very bad jokes and pranks, but this took the title by far. He was here as a favor. Taking time out of his life – never mind that it was boring as fuck – to do an exam for free outside of his work hours, and this is how they treated him. It was such an unoriginal storyline. Straight hunk tempts the lonely gay man into confessing his feelings, only to take offense to it right after. Classic one. Ignoring the rising anger inside him at his own inability to even come close to compromising his oath, he took out the tourniquet, syringe, an antiseptic wipe, and two vials. Putting another pair of gloves on, cursing himself for touching Quick's bare skin in the first place, he knelt down next to Quick's still-reclined chair, doing everything in his power to avoid the large tent in the room.

"You gonna stick me with that? Will it hurt?" Quick asked, amused, but Cayson failed to see the humor.

Keeping his eyes downcast, his cheeks burned with humiliation. His cock was still half-hard, despite his irritation, and that made him angrier still. As he fought his most basic desires, tiny beads of sweat began to pop up on the back of his neck, dampening his hairline, before they ran down his spine, causing him to squirm uncomfortably. He saw Quick push at his own dick again, drawing Cayson's attention to the action. Couldn't have been Cayson making him so aroused.

He hurriedly tied the tourniquet and wiped the alcohol pad across the crease in the middle of Quick's arm. He opened the needle – and like always – took a calming breath before he stuck his patient. He wouldn't be an ass and stick him hard, when Cayson knew how to do it without the patient feeling the slightest pinch. Instead, he angled the syringe like he'd been taught during his pediatric internship and gently pushed the tip, easily breaking the skin and entering the vein.

"Wow. I didn't even feel it."

"Mmm hmm," Cayson replied halfheartedly, staying focused on the job. He clicked on the couple of vials, filling them just enough to run the tests, before removing the needle. He handed Quick a gauze square for him to put over the pinprick. He knew his tone was forced and clipped, but he couldn't help it anymore. "Hold it here for a few seconds."

He was hurting now. Still not bothering to look Quick in the eye, Cayson pulled out the three-container storage unit and properly placed the labeled vials in the container. "I'll have the test results by tomorrow afternoon. If I don't call, that means everything is good. No news is good news from a doctor." Cayson finally rose to his feet and made sure he had the dock charger for the X-ray tablet in his bag before he closed it. He didn't bother saying anything else. He had Quick's email and mailing addresses. He'd send him some pamphlets on healing ribs later. Right now, he had to get the hell out of there before he lost it. He was embarrassed, sweating, and he felt like a fool. He knew he was on rocky terrain with Quick, but he'd at least thought Duke and Vaughan were his friends. *Guess I was wrong. Again.*

"I think you should call anyway," Quick grunted, sitting back up. Quick slammed the recliner down and stood up, stretching his long torso, in turn making those loose pants slide down to an obscene level. As soon as Cayson's eyes diverted, Quick noticed it and chuckled at him. "You like?"

Cayson narrowed his eyes and just barely refrained from taking a swing at Quick. He was furious, not suicidal. But, that bastard. Did he like? Was he serious? Cayson had showed his "like" before and Quick had a shit fit that time. What the hell was going on now? "You know what. Grow up, Roman." Cayson hefted his bag on his shoulder and raced for the front door. He was across the spacious living room and yanking on the door handle by the time Quick realized what was happening and called out to him, but he wasn't stopping.

"Cayson, wait! Don't leave. I wasn't—" Quick couldn't move as fast as Cayson because of his tender ribs. "I'm sorry."

Ignoring the words, Cayson was so happy when he was finally outside Quick's playhouse and safe. It wasn't until he shivered trying to get his key in the car door that he realized he'd left his good parka behind. He looked up and saw Quick wearing a confused expression. Probably wondering why his trap didn't work. Fool him once, shame on you.

# CHAPTER FIVE

*Quick*

Quick watched Cayson burn rubber out of his driveway in his little Prius hybrid, his face a mask of anger and betrayal through the thick windshield. Closing his door on the bitter cold that was beating against his flushed skin; he locked both locks and leaned until his forehead was against the smooth wood surface. *Now what did I do?* Walking back through his living room, he looked through the blinds to see if maybe Cayson had circled back around, but of course, he hadn't. Had Quick come on too strong? He couldn't help that his cock took interest when the sweet doctor took off those gloves and began to lovingly caress his back. That wasn't a fuckin' exam. He'd had plenty exams, none ever felt like that. Feather-light fingertips just barely grazing his body, hot breaths blowing against his moist skin. And Quick didn't miss the doc's erection, either. No matter how hard he tried to hide it.

Disgusted and tired, Quick picked up his cell phone off the breakfast bar. Damnit. Now he knew exactly how Cayson had felt when Quick had shot down his advances before and thrown him out. Sighing in frustration over blowing his last chance, he called his best friend. When it began to ring, he switched to speaker while he powered up his laptop to order his dinner, too tired to make his preplanned chili.

"Yo." Duke's rough voice came through his cell speaker.

Quick rubbed his still aching head, not even sure how to start this conversation.

"Quick? What up, man?"

"Duke. I thought you said the doc was interested. What the fuck, man? He flew outta here faster than a felon on a revoked bond."

Duke chuckled lightly, but Quick wasn't laughing.

"What happened, Rome? Oh, never mind. I'll be there in ten."

Quick frowned when he realized Duke had hung up. He was coming over. Meaning he actually had time for him. Quick rolled his eyes. He felt like an idiot. How could a man feel good about himself when he was feeling sour because his son ran off with his best friend? It was absurd. Quick's food hadn't even arrived yet, and Duke was coming through his front door, using his key. He had on a no-name pair of sweat pants and a thick Atlanta Falcons hoodie. When he yanked it off, his black and silver hair stuck up in various directions. His cheeks were covered with dark stubble, but Quick could easily see the redness from the cold underneath it.

"Where the hell is your coat?" Quick grumbled, turning down the volume of the Food Network. "You wanna get pneumonia?"

"It's in the car," Duke huffed, blowing on his hands. He flopped down on the couch, sparing a quick glance at the television before looking back at him. "It is getting cold as hell. What is it, forties tonight?"

"Yep. It's like negative ten in Chicago and we're complaining about forty degrees."

"We're spoiled. We're not used to cold. We're tropical now." Duke smiled, still looking at Quick.

"I'm from Buffalo, Duke. I'm far from tropical," Quick mumbled, staring back at the muted television as the chefs scrambled to get their dishes on the plates before time was up.

"This what you wanna talk about, bro? Geography. The climate."

He tried to ignore Duke's dark glare for as long as he could, but he knew why his friend was there and exactly what they were going to discuss.

"So. You gonna tell me?" Duke leaned back, draping one arm along the back of his couch.

"I could've told you on the phone. You didn't have to waste time coming over here."

Duke sat straight up. "Whoa, whoa. What the hell is all this 'waste time' bullshit? When have I not come over when you needed to talk?"

All Quick could do was shrug. He didn't want to have this conversation. He didn't want it to appear like he was whining. "You got Vaughan's stuff to deal with now; you don't need me adding—"

"First of all," Duke cut him off. "Vaughan doesn't have any stuff. Unlike us, he has his shit together. Probably always will. It's usually *me* bringing my shit to *him*. So I'm wide open to accept yours."

Quick believed what Duke said. His son had always had it together. He truly was one of the luckiest parents in the world. If it weren't for his son always trying to impress Duke his whole young life, he wouldn't have been as focused and determined to become such a great man. He guessed he owed that to his best friend. Vaughan didn't do anything unless he thought Duke would approve and praise it. "You just seem…."

"In love." Duke sat towards the end of the couch, looking hard at Quick. "That's all, man. I'm in love, but I'm still your best friend, you idiot. Nothing could change that. Sure, I want to be around Vaughan a lot, but I miss your big, ugly face." Duke smirked, picking up one of the small pillows and throwing it at Quick's chest. "All these reservations you have about hanging around us are in your own head. I've always showed you respect when you're around. I don't grope your son in front of your face."

"No you don't, and I appreciate that."

"Nope… I wait until he's in my bed to do that." Duke laughed hard when Quick threw the pillow back at him with significantly more force. "Just joking, man."

Duke's good mood was infectious. Quick was actually feeling lighter. This was the relationship he and Duke had. *Have*. And he'd been missing it. Maybe the hesitation was his own doing. They'd invited him over or out plenty of times where he'd refused, not wanting to feel like a third wheel. Maybe his friend had been missing him, too.

"Cayson was here," Quick said, lower than he meant, but he was sure Duke still heard him.

"I'm not going to ask how it went, because your call clued me in on that, so tell me where it went south."

Quick got up and started pacing. His ribs yelled at him to sit his big ass back down, but he ignored them. He didn't need to worry about being overly careful anymore, since he was sure everything was okay in his old body. *Thanks to my sweet doctor*. "Heck if I know, man. He was smiling when I opened the door. I made sure I was smiling. I was surprised, but still happy to see him."

"You were… happy?" Duke's full lips rose in amusement.

"You know what I mean! I wasn't mad, okay," Quick barked, and Duke threw his hands up in apology, so he kept talking. "I um… I'd um… just finished… finished—"

"Finished what? Jerking one out?" Duke asked, confused.

Quick twisted his face up like he'd just sucked a lemon. "No, man! Jesus, Duke. I'd just finished showering, so I was a little underdressed."

"You were naked."

"No, not fully. I had on these pants, but they were slightly damp at the time and maybe a little see-through, but I didn't have this shirt on. I thought he'd...."

"Get excited, again. Like last time."

"Yeah, man," Quick huffed, carefully sitting back in his chair.

"He got turned on by your chasing gear… the leather, remember. Not your nakedness. Maybe you intimidated him or something."

"This is stupid, Duke. I'm not doing this anymore. He doesn't like me, and all I do is make him mad whenever I'm around."

"Rome. He wouldn't have come, man. He brought all that equipment to your house. What doctor would do that for a person who's not even technically their patient? No doctor I've ever encountered. The idea of you getting hurt bothered him. I could see it before he was able to school his expression."

"He did seem pretty nice when I got nicked by that bullet and he stitched me up a few months back," Quick said softly, grasping at straws, needing to cling to a sliver of hope.

"Okay, then," Duke said excitedly. "You deserve someone, Rome. I thought it'd be a woman, but I think this would be real good, man. To at least explore a little. Vaughan and me both like Dr. Chauncey, too. If he stirs something in you that's been dormant for years… don't fight it. The doc is a solid guy, and since you hate going to the doctor so much, or getting checked out when you're injured, don't you think it'd be a good idea to date a surgeon?"

"Everything doesn't work out all the time, Duke. We all don't get a happily ever after ending. What? Did you think we were all going to double date and eventually do a double wedding, where we all go down to city hall in cheesy ass tuxes and get our gay marriage licenses?"

"I think it's just 'marriage license,' no need to add 'gay' before it." Duke ducked and rubbed the back of his head, trying to hide his smirk.

"Shut up. No joking. Just tell me what to do, then. I asked him if he liked what he saw and… he told me to… he told me to grow up."

Duke was trying so hard not to laugh, but after a few horrible hiccups, the laughter burst through. "You mean he didn't fall at your feet with smooth lines like that?"

"Shut up, you asshole. I thought men liked to be direct and straightforward. So that's what I was aiming for."

Duke only laughed harder. Quick was two seconds off Duke's ass when his doorbell chimed, alerting him his takeout Thai was there. Although Quick wanted to put on a pair of boxing gloves and spar a few rounds with his smart-mouthed best friend, this is truly what he'd missed the most. Him and Duke shooting the shit and talking trash while ribbing the hell out of one another.

After sharing half his dinner, Quick and Duke got off the subject of football and got back to a topic that was more pressing. "You still didn't say what I should do."

"Well. In my opinion." Duke wiped his mouth with a napkin. "I think you should go big or stay home. You know the saying, right?"

"Yeah, I know the saying. Go big, but big like how? I mean, I know what women would want as big. Jewelry, quality time, compliments, candy, whatever. I don't think the doc would go for that. So big like… fifty yard line tickets or something?"

His best friend was looking at him like he'd just said the stupidest thing in the world. "You wanna get him football tickets?"

"Sure, why not? That's fuckin' huge. Those seats are hard to get. I'd be grateful as hell if someone got those for me."

"I know that, but that would probably benefit you more than him. Do you even know if he likes football?"

"All men like football," Quick said confidently.

"Stop being ridiculous."

"You're the one being ridiculous. You think just because he's gay that he might not like football."

"I'm not saying that at all, I just think you might want to go a different route before you buy those tickets, bro. Get to know the guy a little better. Hey, he might not even be an Atlanta fan."

*True. Not everyone makes good choices.* "Okay. Then give me some suggestions. It's obvious I'm going to have to apologize and atone for how I treated him in the beginning, or he'll stay skeptical. I gave him the impression that I was a bigoted, heterosexual homophobe and now he won't take my advances seriously. You've been dating the past few months. Without grossing me out or being too detailed, what's something nice you've done to apologize for a screw up?"

"Don't know. I never screw up." Duke shrugged simply.

Quick stood up, throwing his hands in the air. "You're really annoying me, Duke."

"Alright, alright." Duke was so good at ruffling his feathers. He'd been doing it for over twenty years. "Being completely honest. Vaughan was pretty pissed about our last bust. He said I wasn't being careful with my health after I'd promised I would."

They all took their promises very seriously. Quick kept quiet, intrigued to hear how Duke made up for a broken promise.

"That was the first night we didn't go to bed at the same time."

"Duke," Quick warned on a snarl.

"Easy. I'm simply saying he was really mad. I thought he was gonna sleep on the couch, and I felt like shit." Duke looked up at him, like he was sharing a big secret. "So the next day I took him some flowers to his office."

"Flowers?" Quick reared back, surprised. *Only women want that type of thing.*

Duke's cheek colored slightly but he kept his head up. "Yeah, man. Flowers. Nice ones from a florist, not from the damn 7-Eleven gas station. I brought him a dozen roses… yellow ones. Yellow means you care."

"You know what flowers mean?"

"I wish I could add botanist to my repertoire, but no. The florist told me. All rose colors mean something."

Quick grunted again, but he was paying attention.

"Maybe you should go there and ask her which ones mean 'I screwed up my first shot but please give me another.' If flowers are mostly for women, then there have got to be ones that mean that." Duke laughed and Quick joined right in with him.

Touché.

# CHAPTER SIX

*Cayson*

"Nania. How many times do I have to ask for the Jamirez file? Cayson let the intercom button go with a hard snap of his wrist, immediately regretting it. He shouldn't be taking out his frustrations on his innocent nurse. She was surely moving as fast as Cayson could bark. And boy was he barking today. Had been all week.

"I apologize, Dr. Chauncey. Here you go. It was downstairs, since it's over five years old, and they tried to stall me down in records."

"I'm sorry too, Nania. I just..." Cayson removed his reading glasses and rubbed at the tiredness in his eyes. "...haven't been sleeping well."

Regardless of his lack of sleep, his surgery rotation was still very demanding. If he didn't get himself under control, he was going to have to exclude himself from surgeries. It'd be the first time in ten years. The last time he'd had to be excused from seeing patients was when his mother died.

"Maybe you should take some of your vacation time, Doctor. I've been here six years and I've never seen you take a break, holiday, leave, or anything. It's not healthy to be so consumed with—"

Cayson couldn't hear any more of this, so as politely as he could, he cut into her concerns. "Nania. I think I'm good for the day. It's after three. I'm sure your grandbabies would love to see you earlier than usual. Why don't you take the rest of the afternoon off?"

"Why don't you, Doctor?" On that final note, she closed the door and left him alone in his large, silent office.

He researched the file he'd requested for about thirty minutes, his photographic memory immensely helpful in his efforts to get reacquainted with the old case. The Jamirez file was one of the many he was looking at to help him with a potential clinical trial he wanted to assist on. Anything that would consume his every waking hour. His personal cell phone buzzed on his hip with a text notification. He already knew who it was, since he didn't get many calls.

*How about you make me dinner tonight? Say 6ish. I'll even be open to an apology if you get on your knees.*

Cayson scowled when he read the text. *Ugh, god.* He wanted to smack himself. How could he let himself be used like he'd been doing? Joe came to him to get his rocks off and that was it. Oh yeah, and dinner. There was no love or sentiments. Cayson was his good time guy. The thought made him want to vomit. What had he done? He decided there and then that he was no longer being a doormat. If love came, then it came, but he was done looking for something that frankly just wasn't in the stars for him.

He heard a soft knock on his door.

"Nania, I told you to go home," Cayson yelled before he could stop himself.

The door eased open and when Cayson saw the tip of a black boot, he knew immediately it wasn't his secretary. Quick's head peeked around next. "I'm not Nania. There was no one out there, so I decided to just knock. Can I come in?"

Cayson sat there behind his desk, staring dumbfounded for a couple seconds, debating whether he should follow his new rule of not being a doormat and kick Quick out of his office and onto his beautiful, sexy ass. Of all the thoughts that swirled around in his mind, "What the hell are you doing here?" was what actually came out.

"I felt bad about the other night so I thought—"

"Thought what?" Cayson had to at least know why he was there. This was a little far to take a joke.

Quick finally stepped inside his office and Cayson immediately saw the large bouquet of orange roses in Quick's other hand.

"These are, um. For you. I wanted to apologize for coming on so strong the other night. I thought you were attracted to me, but I didn't mean to jump to conclusions. I let my best friend and son talk my head up sometimes." Quick looked slightly embarrassed while he handed over the big bush.

It was already in a very masculine but pretty brown and tan vase that fit Cayson's office décor well. He took the heavy arrangement and set it on the low mahogany file cabinet in front of his window. He couldn't help but stare at the flowers.

"The florist said that orange roses represent desire and enthusiasm, so after I told her my story, this is what she recommended." Quick shrugged like it meant nothing, but Cayson could see the thought he'd put into the gift, not to mention, men didn't bring other men flowers very often.

He wanted to show his appreciation to Quick, but he wasn't going to drop to his knees to do it. Those days were gone. Cayson ran his hand over his sweater vest, wishing he'd worn the tie with it, but he hadn't expected company. He sat back in his seat and gestured for Quick to sit across in one of the cushioned chairs. The man towered over everything.

"You h-have a real nice office. Lots of um, books." Quick shook his head and squinted like he'd regretted what he'd just said. "Duh, of course you read a lot."

"Yes." Cayson laughed, the sound alien to him. "I do read a lot. Have to." Cayson was shocked at Quick's discomfort, his stuttering and stammering were really eye opening to him. It gave Quick the appearance of vulnerability.

"Of course you do." Quick fidgeted in his seat and Cayson finally looked at him. He had on dark black jeans that squeezed in all the right places, the black t-shirt with the Duke's Bail Bonds logo over the right pec, and damn, did all that muscle stretch out the lettering. Quick kept on his leather coat and Cayson licked his lips, wondering if Quick had a lot of weapons hidden on his body. He wouldn't mind searching him from head to toe and checking... *Shit, shit, shit. Stop it.* He had to stop thinking so sexually when no one wanted *him* that way.

"Look, Doc. I'm not good at this, okay. I'm not as good looking as Duke and I'm not smooth like my son. I like you and I have no clue on what I'm supposed to say to get you to believe me or forgive me for being an ass before. I hope the flowers helped, though." Quick was nervously tapping a couple fingers on his knee while he spoke. "I, um. I was married before to a woman. I was lying to myself all through my senior year in high school, and then next thing I know my beard girlfriend is pregnant, so I did the right thing. I never got a real opportunity to explore the other side of my sexuality. Everything was all about Vaughan when he was born."

"Why are you telling me this?" Cayson asked. He hoped it wasn't rude, but he needed to know.

"Because I'm sorry and I'm trying to get another chance." Quick's brow turned down determinedly. "I don't know how to date a man – what to say, what not to say – so I was hoping you'd cut me some slack. Obviously, I wasn't saying the right things before and surprisingly, there was nothing on YouTube to really help me."

"No. No, you weren't saying the right things," Cayson agreed before wrinkling his nose. "I'm sorry... did you say YouTube?"

Quick waved his hand like he wanted Cayson to disregard that. "Forget YouTube. I really am sorry for doing that to you the other night. It wasn't intentional."

Cayson shot him an incredulous look.

"Okay. *All* of it wasn't intentional. I really had just taken a shower. I had no clue you were coming over. Duke didn't warn me at all. But then you were there... and... so I thought—"

"So, you thought you'd play with me a little bit." Cayson nodded like he suddenly understood.

"What? No! No, I wasn't playing around with you, Cayson!" Quick said hurriedly.

"I thought maybe you guys wanted to be friends. But I see exactly how it is." Cayson got up, slamming his hands on his desk. "You need to leave now."

Cayson wanted to hold his chest, because it hurt like someone had punched him hard. All he'd wanted was to make some friends, maybe have a date. As soon as Cayson got this asshole out of his office, he was going to send a fast "Fuck you" reply to Joe's text and then he was going to see if anyone wanted a night shift covered. So he hadn't slept more than a couple hours at night for a while. He could gulp an energy drink... or two.

~~~~~~~~~~

Quick gritted his teeth and released a low growl of exasperation. He ran his hand over his hair in frustration. *It can't be possible. Are men harder to please then women? No way. Not possible.* "Cayson, please sit back down."

Cayson walked the short distance from his desk to cross his office, pulling the door open and waiting for Quick to get up.

"Fuck. Now what did I do?" Quick complained tiredly.

"I'm done being fucked with." Cayson dropped a heavy palm on his creased forehead like he was fending off a migraine. "Don't you eventually get tired of screwing with people's feelings?"

"Hey!" Quick barked, standing to his full six-foot-three, aggressively demanding the doc's attention. "I've never screwed with anyone's feelings a day in my life."

Quick walked over to Cayson and softly closed the door. He wished he had even an ounce of his son's swagger, but unfortunately, he didn't. Vaughan must've gotten his moves from his mother, because Quick didn't have a clue. He'd never got a chance to perfect pickup lines to get a date before he became the groom in a shotgun wedding. Then life happened. We all know the story.

Careful not to push, he very gently cupped Cayson's chin in his palm and lifted until those pretty blue eyes were on him. To his surprise, the doctor didn't fight him. *Damn. Has he always been so handsome?* He had to; otherwise, Quick wouldn't lose his shit every time the doc was around. "You don't call me Quick. I'm pretty sure you hate that name. You can call me Rome or Roman."

Cayson stood stock still while Quick touched him. "Why are you doing this, Rome?"

That name sounded much better to him, but the hurt in Cayson's eyes was more than he could handle. Quick had several inches over the doc, but he loved his height advantage. Couldn't wait for Cayson to put his chin on his chest and stare up at him. "Will you give me one chance? I'm trying to ask you on a date, but for some reason I keep screwing it up."

"A date." Cayson blinked owlishly.

"Yeah, a date." Quick tried not to sound like he was begging, but if it was good enough for the Temptations, then he could do it. He would do it. "Please, Cays. One more chance."

"And you're not fuckin' with me?" Cayson swallowed hard and Quick's hand slid down to that bobbing Adam's apple. He wanted to apply a little pressure but refrained… for now. The sharp intake of breath could hardly be missed and Quick felt a small surge of victory. He definitely still had an effect on the lonely doctor.

Quick's dick was so hard and confined behind his closed zipper he knew he'd have track marks on his shaft, even through his briefs. He had to be a gentleman. Dry-humping Cayson wouldn't help anything, or redeem his reputation in the man's eyes. What term did Vaughan always use… oh, yeah… a classic man. Quick eased back, giving the doctor a little breathing room. His large frame could be intimidating. That's not what he wanted the doctor to feel. "Is that a yes?" he asked.

"I… I'll think about it, okay. But I have to get down to the ER and help out. Night shift is the worst."

"What time do you get off?" Quick was getting concerned. Cayson looked exhausted. His usually smooth ivory skin was paler than normal, and he had dark smudges under his naturally vibrant blue eyes. He'd hoped he'd caught Cayson at the end of his day and he'd be able to drive the doctor home, but that didn't look like it was gonna happen.

"Not until the morning shift comes back. At seven."

"Seven!" Quick fumed, glancing a look at his sports watch. "That's fifteen hours from now!"

Cayson dipped his head to hide his smile. "You add fast, Rome."

"I'm not joking. Why are you beating your body into the ground like this?"

"You should talk."

"Are we arguing again?"

Cayson slumped against the hard door. "No. I'm just… just—"

"Exhausted. Drained. Tired. Is that what you were going to say?" Quick filled in.

"If that's concern I hear, save it. I'm fine."

"Will you trust me for just a few minutes?" Quick was asking, but he'd already clasped the doctor's hand and led him to the loveseat against the wall next to a large ten-shelf bookcase.

"I suppose." Cayson complied warily, but Quick had the feeling he didn't have energy to do much else.

# CHAPTER SEVEN

*Cayson*

Cayson sighed loudly before clamping his lips shut. Quick was giving him a shoulder and neck rub to rival the best physical therapist in the hospital. He sat with his back against the arm of the loveseat, Quick standing over him, kneading the knots and tension that had built up over the last few… years. His hands were so big and strong. Large enough to handle him. He was trying so hard not to think sexual thoughts. He named every bone in the leg before moving to the foot. Popping an erection could earn him some attention he didn't need.

"That feel good?" Quick asked, his voice melting over top of him like late evening sunshine. Quiet and breathtaking.

Cayson wanted to respond, but he kept a lock on his mouth, otherwise he'd be moaning like a whore on payday.

"You don't have to say anything, Cays."

Quick must've gone down on one knee, because his mouth was there next to his ear. Feeling so wonderful. *He's calling me, Cays.* He tried to tamp down his knee jerk reaction – which was to thrust his groin upwards. Cayson needed like nothing he could explain. So much want, which had built up over way too much time. Never having taken a lover who cared about *his* needs: in or out of the bedroom. He wouldn't set himself up for disappointment by thinking Quick was any different. He was just damn good at massages. So Cayson tried to focus on the pain that was in his neck, and not the tingling that was in his nuts, or the throbbing around his hole.

"Stop thinking so hard. I can only imagine how much brilliance is in that pretty little head of yours, Doc. Beauty and fuckin' brains. Always has been a turn-on for me," Quick whispered.

Cayson was stunned, stunned into instant lust. What the hell kind of test was this, now? He clenched his teeth in an effort not to squirm, but Quick had to know he was getting to him. *Is that sweat dripping?* His collar felt damp and his brow was covered with a fine sheen of perspiration. Cayson took in a deep breath and blew it out through his nose, but that seemed to make him even dizzier. *What's he doing to me?*

"Relax. Stop fighting."

*Oh, fuck.* A voice like he'd never heard. Rome wasn't even talking like the normal Rome. Normally, Rome's voice was deep with a touch of grit in it. No. Blowing over his ear and down his throat into his moist collar was a voice that was comforting, but powerful. Sensual, but stern. Cayson had sure picked a fine damn time to develop some dating morals, because he wanted Quick to body slam him on his desk and take him like the bad motherfucker he was. Unleash every ounce of strength he was sure Roman Webb possessed. *Not now.* Cayson was getting hard. *Of course, I'm getting hard, I'm thinking of being slam-fucked.*

"Feels good, huh?" Quick said, while kneading his thumb into a particularly tender spot at the base of his neck. "No need to talk. Just listen to my words."

*Yes.* Cayson was glad for the distraction. His thoughts or words were not safe at the moment. Though Quick's massage voice was ten times more dangerous. Answering questions shouldn't be too hard. But, as soon as Cayson's lips opened to answer, a rogue moan escaped him.

"Mmm," Rome moaned right along with him, the cockiness in his voice evident, but not in a nasty way. "That means yes."

Rome was quiet for a few minutes, or maybe it was a few seconds. Hell, he wasn't sure; he'd lost all concept of time. He also missed the hell out of that voice. Wanted it back. Wanted so damn much. Could Quick give him all that he needed? He sometimes felt like he didn't ask for much, but when he thought back on past guys… *they* damn sure thought he did. He hadn't dated much early on, because of his grueling school schedule, but the few he did ask out had their own selfish agenda. Not one guy wanted to go out in public with Cayson on his arm… would Quick really be different? He'd have to figure out if he wanted to trust Quick to take him out when the guy had just admitted to being limited-lover-challenged… plus, a gay virgin to boot. It was a lot to think about, but he couldn't do it with Rome's magical hands all over him.

He had to clear his throat like five times before he could speak without moaning before each word. "This was really nice. It felt great, thank you. But, I really must be getting downstairs to see if they need some help."

"Whoa. What do you mean – *see* if they need help? Are you saying you're not scheduled or whatever to work down there right now?"

Cayson sat up higher, wondering when he'd slouched down that far. He rotated his neck a couple time and was amazed at how much better it felt. Less stiff and angry. "Well, technically, no. I just try to be courteous and give other doctors some time off with their families. I don't have anything else to do… so. Ya know what I mean?" Cayson looked up into Quick's handsome face. "No, of course you don't. I'm sure your social calendar stays booked up." Cayson sounded like a jealous nerd who was bristling because he wasn't in the cool crowd. Which was absurd. Cayson was knocking on forty. He really shouldn't be feeling so alone.

"You'd be surprised. No one wants to hang out with me," Quick corrected him.

"Don't lie." Cayson got up and grabbed his white lab coat from off the coat rack. "I doubt you have a hard time finding company, Rome."

"I'm not lying. I'm home every single goddamn night. Just like when you came over the other night. I was home… alone. Did I look prepared to entertain a crowd? Did I look like I was about to go paint the town? No. I was about to make some chili." Quick caught the crook of Cayson's elbow when he tried to walk by him. He brought them face-to-face, well – face to chest. Cayson looked up at him. "*Was* about to make chili, until someone left me in such a bad mood that I didn't feel like cooking."

"My apologies." Cayson smirked, trying to ease back. His cock was still half-hard, any closer and he'd be stabbing Quick in that thick thigh of his.

"If you don't *have* to go down to the ER then don't go. You're tired. I just wanna drive you home, maybe feed you a little dinner. I'll be a gentleman, I promise. No more coming on to you like an overzealous frat boy. I'm tamping it way down. I just want to be in your company for a little while. Is that okay?"

*I think that's the best ask out I've ever had.* Not that he'd had many to compare it to. Cayson already knew he was going to say yes. One evening on his own turf wouldn't hurt anything. He'd be safe there. And Quick promised to be considerate. He hoped not *too* considerate. He chewed on his bottom lip, his eyes shut tight in thought.

He felt the rough pad of Quick's thumb tug at his lip, freeing it from its torture. He was sure he'd gnawed the plump flesh until it was practically red instead of pale pink. Cayson drunkenly opened his eyes to see Quick's green gaze trained on his mouth. He rubbed more of the moisture across his tender flesh. "Such a sexy mouth. Pink and perfect. Shouldn't treat your lip like that, Cays."

Quick leaned forward, his knees bumping Cayson's as he got down to good position. Cayson thought Quick was going to kiss him, but instead he aimed for his ear. "I want you to hang that white coat back on the hook, turn your office light off, and let's go, so I can take care of you. So you can believe and know for sure that I'm not playing games. I'm forty years past games, gorgeous. I want you to drop your walls just a bit, enough for me to show you a few things. I mean, I'm not as debonair as Vaughan, but this old dog's got a few tricks."

"I don't want you to *act* like Vaughan," Cayson finally responded. Quick caressed down the side of his cheek. He was looking at him like Cayson hung the stars and the moon. Was he so desperate that he was imagining all this? But Quick said he wanted to take care of him. Him. He'd be crazy not to see if there was any way Quick could give him what his body deserved. What it craved. "I'm also not concerned with tricks or seduction. Just show me you, Rome. I'll be able to see through an act. I've had enough men *act* a certain way to get a certain something. I'm done with actors. Promise you'll be real." No more guys acting concerned, acting in love, acting… straight. He needed… wanted a real man.

"And in exchange for that promise, you'll give me one evening?" Quick's smile was boyishly hopeful and too damn cute.

"Yes. One promise. One evening."

# CHAPTER EIGHT

*Quick*

"So, do you mind if we swing by the grocery store first? I want to make a little something for you. I got my truck." Quick put his skullcap on and pointed to his Range Rover in the far end of the visitor's parking lot.

"No. I don't mind." Cayson smiled. Genuinely smiled for the first time, and it made Quick want to turn and smash his mouth against those soft-looking lips. "What are you going to make?"

Quick leaned to the side, putting his mouth close to Cayson's temple. "It's a surprise."

Cayson looked at him suspiciously.

"Skeptic, huh?" Quick used his key fob to unlock the door. He hurriedly moved to open Cayson's door, hoping he'd see it as chivalrous and not emasculating. First, he pulled out the parka Cayson had left at his house. The pretty rose color that appeared suddenly on Cayson's cheeks was priceless.

"You left this. I've been riding around with it in my truck." Quick slung the thick coat around Cayson's back and assisted him with sliding his arms in. Quick bent and connected the zipper, snuggly encasing his sexy doctor inside the warmth. "There. That's better. Don't want you catching a cold."

Cayson smiled bashfully. Finally, Quick felt like he was on the right track. If he could just keep him smiling like that, Quick's life would be complete.

Quick pulled into the Trader Joe's parking lot. "I'll only be a minute. Do you wanna wait here?"

"Yeah, I'm good. I'm gonna make a phone call."

Quick ignored the feeling in his gut that the phone call was personal and climbed out of the warmth of his truck. In the store, he moved past the large display of Valentine's Day decorations and made fast work of getting his meat and easy minute-rice. Not knowing what type of spirits Cayson had in his house, Quick grabbed a rich cabernet sauvignon and two small vanilla scented candles that were close to the register. When he got back in the truck, Cayson was tucking his cell phone back inside his coat pocket, a disgruntled look altering his usually soft face.

"Everything okay?"

"Yep," Cayson replied a little too fast.

"Good then." Quick dropped his bags in the back seat. "I'm going to make something easy, but comforting, since it's getting late."

"It's only five or so. I got enough energy for dinner."

*Is that all you have energy for?* Quick bit his tongue at his initial response, remembering how well behaved he was supposed to be. Instead, he focused on driving.

"You know where I live?" Cayson asked when Quick turned onto his street without direction.

"I find and catch people, Cays, it's what I do."

Cayson looked at him with a weird expression.

"That sounded a little creepy, huh?"

"Yeah, little bit."

"Sorry. But you *are* listed. You do know that, right?"

"Oh. Yeah, I do."

"Cayson Chauncey, MD, your phone number is listed too. You don't see that too much these days."

"Might as well." Cayson shrugged. "It's a piece of cake to get anything on line anyway."

"Very true." Quick parked a couple houses up. Cayson lived on the East side of Atlanta, in the historic Inman Park, in a Victorian style home that had been renovated into a duplex. It was naturally beautiful. The light was fading quickly, and the temperature steadily dropping. Quick glanced a look around him, a lifelong habit, before turning to face Cayson. "Something you want to tell me, Doc?" Quick asked, gently pushing down the thick collar of Cayson's parka to touch the skin on his throat.

Cayson's gulp was loud in the silence of the truck. Quick didn't know why he was so fascinated with Cayson's neck, but he'd figure it out soon. In the meantime, he had what he hoped was a minor situation. "Are you expecting company already?"

Cayson frowned in confusion. "What?"

Quick nodded towards Cayson's front porch.

When Cayson turned and focused his eyes, Quick saw the recognition in those baby blues first. So, Cayson knew this man. Then he saw aggravation spread like wildfire across Cayson's warm features. Quick now knew the stranger wasn't welcome company and Quick was, so – situation solved.

"Um, Rome. Can you wait in the truck for a moment, please?"

"Um, Cays. No, I can't," Quick answered easily, but with a charming smile attached.

Cayson smiled and shook his head. "Fine. Come on. He's a friend who didn't get the message. I'll send him away."

Quick grabbed the grocery bags then closed and locked his vehicle. The man on Cayson's stoop was not near as tall as him, but not short either. He looked like a professional, maybe a colleague, but what type of co-worker was coming over at this time of evening. The scowl on his face as they approached said he was feeling the same way about Quick's presence as Quick was feeling about his. There was no need for Quick to flex his muscles… yet. As long as the guy left peacefully.

Cayson turned to face Quick when they got to his security gate. He took out his key and unlocked the door in the four-foot brick wall surrounding the property. He turned and scooped the bags into his arms. "Rome, wait right here, please. I'll be right back."

Quick nodded once and stepped back, letting the gate shut and lock behind Cayson. There was no reason for him to act like a Neanderthal. Besides, it was *his* date. This guy was getting ready to get the brush off. He pretended not to listen, but he was nosy, so what the hell. After a couple minutes Quick's hackles rose when he heard the visitor's voice growing louder.

~~~~~~~~~

"Dr. Joe, what are you doing here?" Cayson said through clenched teeth. He needed to keep his voice down because he really didn't want to have this conversation with Quick a few feet away, looking on. He said a silent prayer that Joe didn't get too upset with him and blurt out anything personal that should remain between them. Cayson dropped the bags at his feet and turned to face the man who he'd thought he wanted a relationship with. But how could he, when he wasn't even allowed to call the man by his first name? Since Dr. Joe is what everyone else called him, Cayson had to also use it. Otherwise, someone could get suspicious of their relationship.

"I texted you an hour ago and said I'd be over. Why'd you make me wait in the gosh-darn cold for thirty minutes?" Joe frowned when he looked over in Quick's direction. Cayson wasn't surprised when he saw Quick's gaze aimed dead-on at them. "Who is that?"

"He's a friend. Dr. Joe, please go. I responded to your text."

"What?" Joe yelled. "Fuck off! That's your response to me? What has gotten into you Cayson? When'd you starting using explicit language? Are you… are you seeing that thug?"

"Okay, stop right there. First of all, you have no clue who that man is, so don't call him names. Secondly, I don't know why you're here and upset. We don't have a relationship." Even as Cayson finished the sentence, Joe was looking around, terrified that someone may be lurking in the bushes with a voice recorder. "That right there. I'm done with that, Joe. You'll never be out. I'm done with being confined to your closet. For some reason, I've compromised my morals and values and settled for less than I deserve."

"Excuse me?" Joe said sternly, inching in closer. "'Less than?'"

Cayson took a small step back. "Joe. You were always honest. I can't fault you for that. You said you'd never be out and—"

"Is there a problem?" Quick's voice was full of confidence and it made Cayson startle when the hard bass of that brusque tone carried to them.

Cayson put his hand up to signal he was fine, but Dr. Joe wasn't smart enough to shut the fuck up. Could he not fully see what Quick looked like? Maybe all the large trees blocked his view. Quick just didn't look like the kind of guy you picked a fight with.

"It's none of your business. You can go now," Joe said condescendingly. Like Quick was the grocery delivery guy.

"Joe. Keep your mouth closed." Cayson looked at Quick. The expression he wore was equal parts scary, dangerous, and sexy.

"Did you lock the gate?" Joe asked Cayson, his eyes still on the hulking figure throwing death glares at him.

Before Cayson could nod, Quick took a half step back, braced one arm on the top of the gate and shot his large body over the fence in a single leap. He made it look effortless. Surprisingly, his huge boots made little sound when he landed on the other side, his leather coat flying up in the air behind him like a goddamn cape.

"My gosh. He's not a thug, huh?" Joe crossed his thin arms over his equally thin chest, looking overly arrogant. The entire

Wellington family had patented the look-down-your-nose-at-people face. Why had Cayson been so blind to it? Better said, why had he ignored it?

Cayson gritted his teeth. This was going bad fast. He dug his key into the lock and threw his front door open. He made a mental note to get his gate key back, too. Dr. Joe made to step inside, but Cayson put his hand on his chest, holding him in place. As soon as Quick was on the porch, it was almost comical the way both of their heads tilted up to look at him. It looked like a unanimous salute. He knew that Joe was assaulted by the same delightful smell of leather and wild that seem to embrace Quick's body. Hiding his amusement at Dr. Joe's surprise, Cayson ushered Quick through the front door with the grocery bags.

"Roman, the kitchen is straight back. I'm sure you'll find everything easily. I'll be right in." Cayson didn't let Quick respond; instead, he let his storm door close and waited for Quick to walk away.

"Are you crazy?" Cayson asked Joe, who was still standing and glaring inside Cayson's door.

"Is this all because I won't have your kind of sex with you?" Joe inquired, louder than Cayson would've have preferred. Joe was making him sound like a sexual deviant, like he'd asked his bed partner for something disgusting. *What does he mean, "My kind of sex?"* Cayson didn't need elaboration right now. He didn't want his seventy-year-old retired neighbors to know that he was a sexually repressed man.

"You'd take this drug dealer over me, just to have sex? Come on, Dr. Chauncey, you can't be that stupid. Do you know what I could do for your career?"

Cayson was mad now, but he still kept his voice to a stern whisper. "You fuckin' snob. Don't talk about Roman anymore, and don't talk about me. There is no us. And for the record, my career is fine without the help of you or your daddy."

"Cayson, don't be a love-sick fool. We could help each other, benefit from each other. Have an arrangement or—"

Cayson had to unclench his teeth to form his words. "I deserve better than a goddamn arrangement. Rest assured, Joe. I would never tell anyone your secret. Ever. I swear that to you. Go on, Dr. Joe. Go home."

"You can't be serious." Joe scrubbed his thin fingers over his forehead like he was warring with something in his mind. Not in a million years did Cayson expect him to say what he did next. "Okay. Fine, Cayson. I'll penetrate you in the ass. Will that end all this mess you've caused?"

"Oh, god." Cayson jolted so hard he may have thrown up some in his mouth. *Please tell me no one heard that.* Cayson was so offended he couldn't move or speak.

"Leave. Now." Quick burst through the front door and was in Dr. Joe's face, fast and furious. He barked the orders more than spoke them. His voice was rough and full of venom. It was a sound Cayson found turned him on, but he was too mortified for his body to react. Humiliation trumped lust.

Quick's chest bumped Joe's hard enough to cause him to windmill off the top step, falling hard onto the cobblestone walkway. Quick crossed his bulging arms over his chest, succeeding where Joe had failed to make that gesture look threatening. "You won't like how I remove you if you don't go voluntarily."

Cayson's hands were still covering half his face, hopefully the part that was aflame with shame. "Dr. Joe, I won't tell anyone. I promise," Cayson muttered as Joe scurried out the gate.

"I have no reason to promise anything, so you'd better get the fuck out of here. I'm terrible at keeping secrets." Quick sneered and Joe turned a disgusting shade of green as he scrambled to dust off his black slacks while he walked.

Cayson didn't like the look in Joe's eyes. It was a look he'd seen before, but he couldn't say where. It unnerved him more than anything. It was a look that promised—

Quick gripped Cayson's shoulder and kissed him on his forehead before he could finish contemplating that look. He turned them to go inside the house and Cayson went obediently, feeling shocked at having his dirty laundry tossed all over his yard.

"Roman," Cayson whispered. "I wish you hadn't said that to him. He's really nervous about being outed. His parents are really important people in the Emory Healthcare Administration and in the state government."

"Yeah?" Quick hung his own leather coat on some large hooks mounted on the wall behind the door before pulling off Cayson's coat. "What the hell does any of that have to do with me?"

*Hell*. Joe wasn't going to let this go. Cayson had a horrible nagging feeling in his gut. That's what he couldn't deal with right now. He needed to think. He needed to go into hiding for a few days. "Would you mind leaving me alone for a bit?"

"Not at all. I'll go fix your dinner while you go up and take a long, hot shower. By the time you come down, it'll be ready, then you can show me the rest of your place." Quick smiled softly.

"No. I meant would you—"

"I know what you meant." Quick cut him off. "I'm not leaving you alone. It appears that's what most people do to you. But I'm not letting that pompous pussy steal the date I begged to get."

Cayson actually chuckled at the crudeness of Quick's language and what he'd called Joe. Of all the things Joe had called Quick, none had been accurate. But Quick called Joe one name and it was spot on.

"Don't take my chance away because of that prick. I can see he's put you in a mood, but you don't have to stay that way." Quick stepped closer to Cayson. "Damn that guy."

"Are we gonna confront the elephant in the room?" Cayson asked, maintaining eye contact with Quick, even though it made his retinas burn. But this was best. Get it out and over with.

"Elephant?"

"Roman," Cayson huffed.

Quick inched in closer. "I like that sound you just made." Quick rubbed his roughened hands up and down the thin sleeves of Cayson's dress shirt, making him drop his chin to his chest. The touch warmed him and irritated him. Was this pity? He couldn't be sure. He hated how unsure he was lately. He was supposed to be changing things in his life. His breathing was coming faster and faster. Quick smelled like outdoors and man. A fragrance most women probably wouldn't like, but it had Cayson's dick perking up with interest the closer Quick got.

"If you want to talk about him, fine." Quick held Cayson's biceps and crowded into him until his back was against the wall where his television hung. Quick didn't appear mad, but his movements were dominating and his tone was sharp. "I heard everything that asshole said to you. I wasn't snooping, but I couldn't walk away."

"So you heard him say—?" Cayson choked on the words. He couldn't even say it. It was too deplorable. A grown man not good enough to fuck. Joe revealing that fact only confirmed that Cayson was his dirty secret and all Joe allowed him to do was get on his knees for him, that Cayson took whatever scraps he was thrown. He grumbled deep in his throat at the humiliation. He was glad Quick was so close, that way he could keep his face buried in Quick's armpit. Inhaling the virility. He wanted his head to stay buried there, like an ostrich… as long as he didn't have to see anyone, then they couldn't see him.

~~~~~~

"Yeah. I heard him," Quick confirmed, his tone steely. His mouth was a firm line, his grunts commanding as he nudged and chased Cayson out of his hiding spot with his chin. His eyes had taken on a darker, more alluring hunter green while he stared at Cayson and tried to get a handle on his control. He only had a second to make his decision, and he did. He bent and licked gently at Cayson's bottom lip – asking permission – before he sealed their closed mouths together. Cayson moaned prettily, but Quick didn't take the bait. He could easily lose his control around the guarded man. If he wasn't careful, he could scare him away again… possibly for good. The bitch-assed doctor Cayson had been sneaking around with had done enough damage. More than was probably on the surface. Quick briefly wondered if he had what it took to make Cayson forget past exes and focus on him. More importantly, not make him pay for their shortcomings. When Cayson melted into Quick's chest, sighing his reprieve… he had his answer.

Quick pulled back and tilted his head, directing Cayson in the other direction with his palm while he deepened the kiss. Cayson gripped the material of Quick's t-shirt, pulling him closer like a drowning man would a life raft. Quick was already making him forget. He'd do it until he was all Cayson could think about. He may be new to the team but he wasn't new to the game. He was going to heal Cayson from the inside out.

*But first things first.* "Why wouldn't he have sex with you?"

# CHAPTER NINE

*Cayson*

"Quick." Cayson grimaced.

Quick had asked the million-dollar question now that Dr. Joe had let the ugly cat out of the bag earlier than he would've liked. Cayson had fully intended to tell Quick about all this, but in his own time.

"In a nutshell," Cayson drawled and tried to put some distance between them, but Quick wasn't having it. He kept him wrapped tight in his strong arms. "Um. Long story short. For the past few years, I've had a friends with benefits arrangement with Dr. Joe, but he was extremely stingy with the benefits. Hell, who am I kidding? Okay, very few of my love interests wanted to be with me, even fewer wanted to fuck me, or date long enough to even get to that point with me." Cayson took another deep breath, because he was aggressively fighting the moisture building up in his eyes. His state of loneliness was bordering on too much. If he let those useless tears fall right now, he thought Quick would probably turn on his heels and make his way to the door, too. The big bounty hunter wouldn't be interested in dating a whiny, sex-desperate pansy. It'd take a confident, sure man to hold on to someone as handsome and strong as Roman Webb. But when he thought of Dr. Joe's proposed arrangement, his stomach knotted hard enough to make him double over.

"Listen to me." Quick held Cayson's face with both large hands. His wide fingers covering practically his entire face. "I want you to go and wash off all the poison your haters have sprayed on you today, and I'll be right here when you come down."

"Sure," Cayson whispered, turning to leave, fighting to keep his head from hanging low. Before he was out of range, Quick's hand shot out and gripped him by the back of his neck to yank him back against his hard chest. Cayson hit with a hard thump and he hadn't had a chance to collect himself when a thick, possessive tongue was down his throat. Cayson whined softly and opened wide enough to take it all.

Quick released his mouth when he was damn good and ready. He leaned in low and nipped Cayson's neck, scrubbing his coarse goatee along Cayson's smooth skin. "You won't have to worry about being made love to anymore, Cays. Now, go."

Cayson wasn't sure if he was supposed to be able to walk upright after that statement or not. Right now he was frozen. The thought of Quick wanting to fuck him was beyond what Cayson could believe at the moment. Pity and regret were still words bouncing around in his soul. He wouldn't take Quick's pity. Even though his aching hole begged for attention, he wasn't jumping onto the first flat surface with Quick. If Quick wanted him, he'd better damn well prove it. No, he was going to earn it.

As soon as Quick heard water running, he looked up for the first time, noticing that the entire upstairs was open. He could see a sliver of light across the ceiling. Was it all Cayson's bedroom? He wanted to go up and explore, but he'd have time for that later. That's how he'd win the war to gain Cayson's trust. Time. Patience. He wouldn't rush him.

Quick yanked out his cell phone and called Duke, switching the speaker on so his hands weren't tied up. He'd needed to know what to do for Cayson to change his mood. While the phone connected, he hurriedly foraged through Cayson's very organized cabinets. He had the skillet and a pot already out when Duke's voice blasted through his speaker.

"How'd it go? Did you call him?" Duke said instead of hello, which was fine because Quick had limited time.

"Even better, bro." Quick smiled while filling the pot with water for his rice. "I went to his office with…" Quick huffed a laugh, preparing for his best friend's reaction. "I took the flowers."

"Oh, snap!" Duke cheered. "And did it work?" he asked after eventually calming down.

Quick was grinning ear to ear. "I think so. I'm at his house."

"No shit!" Duke laughed hard.

"Yeah. He's in the shower, I'm making him dinner."

Quick had to hurry and adjust the volume on his phone since Duke was yelling and cheering like a crazy ass. Cayson was going to be able to hear them at this rate.

"Duke, shut up," he scolded with a harsh whisper.

"You are the man, Rome! I knew it! I knew you two would be good together!"

"Whatever," Quick mumbled, still having a hard time concealing his pleased smile. "There may be more to it than I thought." The boneless pork chops were already sizzling in the skillet in some olive oil and a few sprinkles of flour to make a gravy.

"Meaning?" Duke's voice had dropped some of its humor.

"Meaning he has a boyfriend."

"What?" Duke yelled again. "But he seemed so—"

"Lonely… yeah, I know. Okay, wait… he's not technically a boyfriend." Quick groaned and shook his head tiredly. "We'll discuss that more later. All I know is the guy is a massive fuckin' tool and he was here waiting for Cays when we arrived."

"'Cays'," Duke teased. "Nicknames already. Is he calling you 'Romey'?"

"Duke, I swear to god."

"Okay, okay. I'm just happy for you, man. Alright. Being serious now."

"Thank you." Quick flipped the pork chops. The wonderful aroma quickly permeating the first floor. Hopefully it'd reach upstairs soon and tempt his date back down. "He said some really fucked up shit to Cayson and I threw him off the porch and he scrambled away. But he—"

"Shit." Duke's voice hinted at amazement and disbelief. "I said go big, man, but goddamn. I didn't say go fuckin' hulk, Rome."

"Dad, are you over there acting like a barbarian in front of Dr. Chauncey?" Vaughan's disappointed voice came through the speaker next.

"He deserved it," Quick barked defensively. Why were they ganging up on him without the whole story?

"Dad, come on," Vaughan snapped. "You know better."

Sometimes Quick wondered who the parent was between the two of them. It'd been like that since the boy could talk.

Quick walked to where the ivory linoleum in the kitchen met the plush rug that covered the dining room floor. He peered upward and listened. There was a brighter light on and the water had stopped. Quick took his phone off speaker and nestled it in the crook of his neck and shoulder. "Look you two; he's almost finished with his shower. I need to relax him. Y'all just don't know what an asshat that guy was, and if you'd heard what he'd said to our friend, y'all would've been all over him, too."

"Sorry," Vaughan murmured right along with Duke. They were all extremely protective of their little makeshift family, so they knew what he meant.

Quick dropped a couple bags of instant rice in the pot of boiling water and put a lid on his almost finished pork chops. Quick's voice softened. "I want to make him feel better."

"Nice." Duke chuckled.

"Not that damn nice. I want him to feel better about himself." Quick shook his head, getting exasperated. "What do I do, Vaughan?"

"Dad. You are a great guy. Just be you and he'll relax. Cooking for him is the best idea. You're an awesome cook. What are you making?"

"Pork chops. What do I do after dinner is finished and he's ready for me to leave?"

"Do you wanna leave?" Duke asked first.

"No. That guy was a first rate jerk. His eyes said he would catch Cays when I'm gone."

"Are you for real?" Duke's voice was serious. They never took threats lightly. Whether spoken or implied. He and Duke hadn't made it as bounty hunters for so long by underestimating desperate people.

"I wouldn't joke about that."

"Then do whatever you have to do to stay with him. Make up anything. Improvise."

"Uh-oh." Quick wasn't the best liar. Grown men didn't have to lie. It was man up or shut up. "Alright guys. Well you've been... you've been very little help. Thank you for nothing."

"Hey, man. I'm the one that said get him flowers. Obviously it worked, because it got your big foot in the door, so take that back," Duke complained.

"Quiet, Duke. Dad. See if he has a music player. Turn on something nice. And I don't mean The Rolling Stones. Something jazzy and mellow. Fix a couple of cocktails and try to work a massage in there. That'll help him relax and he'll see that you're all about making *him* happy... and not yourself."

"Got it. Thanks, Vaughan."

"You're welcome. Good luck, Pops."

"And Duke...."

"Yeah, buddy?"

"Go to hell."

Quick hung up, not giving Duke a chance to respond. Knowing his friend, he was probably still looking at the phone. He laughed to himself while he checked the doneness on his meat. *Perfect.* Letting the meat sit and simmer in the gravy, he washed his hands again and went in search of plates.

# CHAPTER TEN

*Cayson*

Cayson's body felt so much better after the long shower. He could hear Quick talking to someone, but he couldn't fully make out the conversation. Probably because his stomach was growling too loud. The smell of seared meat was easy to detect as soon as he stepped back into his loft-style bedroom. It was the largest and best renovation he'd made to his home. He looked around the large space, wondering if he should pull the sheets up on his bed or cover up the pile of dirty laundry waiting to be tended to. He let the bedspread fall from his fingers. *No. Quick isn't getting in my bed, not even in my bedroom, so I don't have to waste time on this.* And with that newfound determination, Cayson chose to put on a pair of worn cargo pants and a soft, white Hanes t-shirt. He was going for comfort. Besides, he wouldn't get his hopes up just yet. He'd been with guys who talked a good game.

As soon as he turned the corner, Cayson's mouth dropped open in surprise. Quick had not only set the table rather nicely, with scented candles, wine, and water glasses, but the food was already on the plates, steam rising from them along with the heavenly aroma. Quick was hastily whipping something in a small plastic bowl and when he turned, he nodded at Cayson to sit down. However, Cayson didn't miss the appreciative glances Quick was throwing his way as he walked across the room and sat at the table, still at a loss for words. He was trying to remember the last time anyone had made him a home cooked meal.

"Feel better after the shower?" Quick went in his refrigerator like he lived there and pulled out two small bowls that already held salads.

"I'm better, yes. Thank you, Rome. This looks fantastic," Cayson said, in awe as he watched Quick set the salad in front of him and drizzle the homemade dressing he'd been making on top. "How'd you learn how to cook?"

"Well, Vaughan's mother and I decided to call it quits and stop fooling each other after Vaughan got old enough to understand. So when he came to my place on weekends, I had to feed him, not to mention myself. Pizza and Chinese got old pretty quickly. Since I believe a man can learn anything he needs to on YouTube, I watched a few tutorials and managed to produce a couple of edible meals. Food Network and a couple food clinics later… Viola! I'm a pretty decent cook."

Cayson laughed and followed Quick's lead when he sat, too, and began digging into his salad. "YouTube, huh?"

"It's true. I started looking up basic recipes and following along. Next thing I knew, I was starting to enjoy it. It became sort of a hobby. Playing around with and destroying some creations really took my mind off missing my son, missing…."

"Companionship," Cayson filled in after Quick trailed off. "I get that."

"I have to ask." Quick wiped his mouth after chewing a hearty chunk of his pork chop and took a sip of his wine. "How in the hell did you end up with a first class jerk like Dr. Stuck-up? He doesn't seem like your type at all."

"And you do?"

"More than that asshole."

"If I recall. You were a real ass—"

"Yeah, yeah. I know. Thank you very much," Quick said hurriedly, his sexy quirk of his lips showing Cayson a playful side. "At least it wasn't the norm for me. I was nervous and unprepared for you, Doc. That's all. I'm far from an ass, and I think deep down, you know that. That other guy seems like he embraces the title."

Cayson had eaten most of his tender pork chop by the time he finally got around to coming up with an answer that didn't make him look desperate. "Well. I always knew he was deep in the closet and wasn't coming out. So he never led me on in that respect."

"But the not touching you."

"He'd touch me," Cayson said sternly, before softening his voice. It wasn't right to project his frustrations on Quick, especially after he'd cooked him such a nice meal and made a gallant effort to make him feel better. "He just wasn't keen on touching—"

"Where you needed to be touched." Quick's voice was smooth and calm when he said it.

Cayson knew his face was as red as the wine in his glass and hotter than the food on his plate. No matter how many ways he tried to word it or justify it; it was embarrassing to have a fuck buddy who wouldn't technically fuck you. Who was too disgusted by you to even touch you. Cayson felt so much shame wash over him. He didn't want to consider these feelings right now. He knew he wasn't grotesque. Joe had serious emotional issues regarding his sexuality and Cayson didn't have the correct initials behind his last name to try to understand them. Nonetheless. This was the third male acquaintance – couldn't technically call any of them boyfriends – who wasn't interested in Cayson intimately, and especially going out in public with him. "I'm not most men's type, I guess. Maybe I should leave well enough alone. There are plenty of single doctors who never marry or have a family. It happens. They're married to their craft. I'll maintain on my work. That should keep me busy until I die."

Cayson had barely heard the growled "Goddamnit" leave Quick's mouth before his table was pushed to the side and a seething, angry date was advancing on him. Cayson was frozen to his seat. Not scared… but startled. Cayson felt like if he bolted and ran, Quick would walk him down and catch him like in those scary movies. He hadn't understood what he'd said or what expression he wore that had Quick reacting like this, but he kept his mouth closed when he was swept up out of his chair and pulled tight into a solid chest. Hot, moist lips were on his and Cayson moaned, letting his arms drop down to his sides while Quick held him up by his biceps.

"It's difficult to listen to you put yourself down, Cays." Quick only pulled back slightly to annunciate his words, his wine-tinted lips still brushing lightly against his. "You keep saying you're not most men's type, but I'm standing right here, and you're doing your damnedest to convince me that I'm not going to like what I find in you."

"N-no I'm—"

"You are," Quick snapped, refusing to let him get a word in. Cayson ducked his head. He *was* doing that. He'd had too many losers and now he couldn't recognize a winner. "Look at me, Cayson."

Quick's grip loosened on his biceps as his firm hold became a soft massage. "I don't know what else to tell you to convince you. I'm not sure what the perfect thing to say is."

Cayson liked the flustered, not-so-sure-of-himself Roman, too. Confident Roman was sexy as fuck, but so was this one. "I'm not interested in perfection… there's no such thing as perfection in existence. Anything that we do as humans, we can call it perfect, but it isn't, really. I just want to…."

"Want to what? Ask me. Whatever it is… I'll say yes," Quick assured him.

Cayson was still being held tight against Quick's chest, and it was hard for him to think clearly. His sentences were choppy and his thoughts weren't complete. Damn, he could even smell the fragrance of Quick's deodorant. He needed to retreat to solitude and get his bearings before he offered his ass up on a platter like that mostly eaten pork chop. "Rome." Cayson's voice was coarse and strained as that one line floated back to his head before making a beeline to his ass. *You won't have to worry about being made love to anymore, Cays.* Cayson locked his knees to keep them from buckling. Just the thought of Roman fucking him. Oh, god, Roman.

"Say it, Cays." Quick's reply was like a hushed groan, since his voice was way too deep to fully accomplish a whisper.

Fuck. Quick's vocal sounds were like a soothing balm to his tortured soul. So calming, yet demanding. And damn if he didn't talk with so much conviction. Cayson wanted to believe him, wanted to eat up every word and let them satisfy him just like his dinner had. He cast a brief look at his four top table, which had been shoved almost all the way to the wall. *Fuck. He's strong.* Quick's sheer bulk was enough to assure him of that, but Cayson wondered if he would be as rough with his heart as he was with his furniture. "I think I'm gonna turn in."

Quick looked taken aback and disappointed, but he slowly stopped caressing Cayson's neck and let those wonderfully calloused hands fall to his sides. As soon as they were gone, Cayson busied himself pulling the table back over. Quick helped him and even pushed in all the chairs, but Cayson didn't like how quiet he was now. His eyebrows were drawn down, causing a few wrinkles to form in between his eyes. He looked fed up. Damn, had he given up already? *Why am I not worth the fuckin' effort?*

When the table was righted and the dishes were stacked in the sink, Quick finally spoke again. "I'll just take care of these few dishes."

Why that annoyed Cayson a little, he wasn't sure but it was lame. Dishes. Whatever.

"I'll walk you out."

# CHAPTER ELEVEN

*Quick*

He didn't want to go. Cayson was clearly upset and Quick didn't want to go. Every fiber in his body was telling him to stay, because he had a bad feeling about Cayson's so-called friend with benefits. The guy was a spoiled, over-achieving, self-righteous bastard, but he was a desperate bastard. Desperate, and with one helluva secret that Quick now knew. How was this Dr. Joe going to react? Actually, Quick already knew. He was in the desperate-acting-people business.

Just when Quick was begrudgingly heading towards the front door with a dawdling Dr. Chauncey behind him, his best friend's voice slapped him in the back of the head. *Then do whatever you have to do to stay with him. Make up anything. Improvise.* Damn, he didn't want to leave, but he didn't want to come off as a pig like probably most of the men Cayson had been with. Insisting to stay the night was basically the same as begging to get a little taste. At least that's what it used to mean. And this was their first date. Shit. Quick rolled his eyes. How was he supposed to make this sound honorable? He really wasn't trying to sleep with the doc. He had some YouTubing to do first. He wanted to make it good for Cayson, of course.

As soon as he reached the door, Quick turned, snapping his fingers. "You know what. I think it's probably best if I just stay the night." Quick placed a couple fingers over Cayson's lips as soon as he opened them to object. "Not stay the night, like that, but stay and make sure you're alright."

Cayson moved around Quick and unlocked the door. "Really, Rome. I'm good."

Now what? "Um. Um." Quick was at a loss. He really wasn't a good liar. "I think I'm real low on gas and it's dangerous to pump gas so late at night, ya know? I think they mentioned that on the news a while back." Quick could've kicked himself. How in the hell would a brilliant man like Cayson believe that he was cautious about being out late? Didn't he hunt down society's dangerous people for a living?

"It's only a little after eight, Rome. I think you'll be just fine at the gas station." Cayson smiled, handing Quick his heavy leather coat. When he cracked open the door, the cool night air burst in completely uninvited. Quick refused to go out into it.

"It's still dark, though. Bad things happen at night. Especially at shady gas stations. You can't trust those people who loiter around there all the time." *Argh! What the fuck am I saying?*

Cayson was wearing a full-on smile now and it was hard for Quick not to smile, too. "I don't think anyone will try to start trouble with a big man like you, Rome. Day or night. Now, good night."

Cayson was inching Quick further and further out the door and he wasn't putting up a fight. He liked Cayson's expert hands pushing on his pecs. But when he was almost on the porch, he dug his heels in. "Seriously, Cays."

Cayson sighed wearily. One palm was still lightly pushing on Quick's chest, the other propped against the doorjamb. He looked so sweet and tired, and Quick just wanted to hold him close. Protect him from all the bad in the world, the shit that Quick saw on a regular basis. Protect him from the bad that had been on Cayson's porch when they arrived. He needed to stay.

Cayson said good night for the second time and was gearing up to close the door, but Quick stopped him again. Only the truth would work. He held Cayson's wrist, careful not to apply any real pressure. "Okay. Truth, Cays. I want to stay because I don't like the situation that happened earlier."

Cayson scoffed. "Are you talking about Joe? Please. Joe is harmless."

"Cays look at me." He tilted Cayson's face up to his, hoping he could see that he wasn't joking around, but was dead serious. "What I saw in that man's eyes was not harmless."

"I think that look was directed at you, not me."

"I think it was, too, but I don't question men with motives. Any man with a secret that big, one that could possibly devastate him if it got out, is going to do all he can to protect his future by any means necessary."

"You really have seen some terrible stuff, I'm sure. But, what is it you think Joe's going to do? Come back in the middle of the night and staple my mouth shut while I sleep?"

"Possibly. But if he does… I'll be right here waiting for his ass."

"Oh, goodness," Cayson moaned like Quick was being unreasonable. "What're the chances of you going and getting in your truck right now and going home?"

"Slim to none."

"I figured." Cayson turned around, leaving the door slightly ajar. Quick took the silent invitation and bounded back through the door and past the dimly lit foyer.

Quick hung his leather coat back on the rack. "So. Got any good music?"

"Not happening." Cayson dug inside his closet just off the foyer and pulled down a thick fleece blanket. "It may be early for you, stud, but I'm exhausted. No music, no television, no more wine. I need sleep. I have a partial nephrectomy at seven and if I still have these black rings under my eyes, the family might be a little hesitant to let me operate."

"No problem. I have a bond hearing I need to sit in on at eight, so works fine. You go on up and get in bed. I'll be up soon."

"Um, wait."

Quick reared back and laughed, the hearty sound permeating the large living room. "I'm just joking. I'm more than fine with the couch. Although, I hear it's bad for the back. I have been having a few issues with it."

"I'm sure you'll survive one night." Cayson smiled on a yawn. As soon as he turned to take the stairs up to his open bedroom, Quick pulled him back to him.

"How'd you like our first date?" Quick said softly. He really needed to know. He didn't think he aced it, but he couldn't have flunked.

"It's the nicest time I've had in a while, and definitely the best dinner," Cayson admitted.

"Good. Very good. Did I redeem myself?"

"Yes," Cayson murmured.

"Can I have a good night kiss, since my date is over?"

Quick stood still and let Cayson close the small distance between their mouths this time. He didn't always want to be the aggressor. It was a soft, chaste kiss. Nothing to make your toes curl, but enough to make Quick heat up. He wasn't sure how long it'd been for the doctor, but it'd been at least a couple years since he'd gone all the way. His few dates had ended before he was even able to get to third base. But now that he thought more about it, maybe he didn't want to get too far with those women, knowing all along that it was a man he desired. His job was a pretty big turnoff, as well, with regards to having something long-term. No one liked the danger inherent in his work.

"That felt good." Quick closed his eyes and licked the last lingering taste of Cayson from his lips. He kept his hands by his sides, otherwise he would be tempted to take both his hands and grab himself a couple handfuls of Cayson's sexy ass. What the hell was wrong with Dr. Joe? He never hit that? Didn't want to? Was he blind? The ass on Cayson was mouthwatering. Curved, not flat, and probably a bit of soft hair dusting those plump cheeks. Blond hair over a pale ass. Fuck. Heaven. Be patient.

"Yeah, it did. Good night, Roman. And thank you again for dinner."

Quick hated for Cayson to leave and end their evening so soon, but the man clearly needed a full eight hours of uninterrupted sleep. So Quick took Cayson's hand and linked their fingers together before he turned their joined palms and gently kissed the back of Cayson's hand. The shy smile he received was worth an uncomfortable night's sleep on a couch. "Sleep well, handsome."

"You too." Cayson turned and slowly made his way up the stairs, almost as if he didn't want the night to end either, but had ruled against his own desires.

"Yes. I'll be fine. Don't worry about me and my bad back on this couch," Quick yelled, knowing Cayson could hear him. Quick was pulling off his boots when he looked up and saw Cayson's head peeking over the thick guardrails with one bemused brow raised.

"I'm not worried. Good night, Roman."

"Night, baby." Quick winked and smiled when Cayson ducked back into his room. Quick couldn't wait to be invited up there... he wasn't going up a second before he received an invitation, either.

Quick waited until he finally heard light snores filtering down to him before he got back up. First thing he did was move his truck around the corner so it wasn't obviously visible. If Dr. Prick was coming back, he wanted him to think that he was gone. Closing the front door as quietly as possible when he returned, he looked around on the interior wall and noticed the absence of a security system. To Quick, it meant that night after night Cayson slept completely unprotected. For fuck's sake. He hoped the guy at least had a gun or some type of weapon.

Opting to keep on his jeans, albeit unbuttoned, he removed his shirt and boots. After perusing Cayson's bookshelf, his CD collection, and his DVDs, Quick made a few mental notes of what Cayson liked. He also made a note to tease him about the Lady Gaga CD he found way down on the bottom rack.

Quick shook his head. He had a warm feeling in his gut that he and Cayson could possibly have something. That is, if the doctor didn't think him too much a roughneck. He may not be as educated and refined, but he was an honest, successful business owner. Surely, that gave him some bonus points.

He was thinking of where he'd take Cayson on their second date when Quick heard a faint noise – sounded like right outside the window – and went to look out the blinds. The view was a mess. *Well let's rephrase. If you are keeping a lookout, the view was a mess.* Large trees lined the sidewalk, and Cayson's neighbor really needed to prune back her bushes. He could barely see if someone was approaching, they'd practically be right in front of the house before he spotted them. He bet Cayson had a good view from one of his bedroom windows, but Quick had made himself a promise. He wasn't going up until he was beckoned.

His eyes scanned back and forth over Cayson's front yard. He clenched his teeth, wondering if Cayson ever gave that bum a key to his place. He hoped not. Parting the blinds a tad further, he looked as far as he could, but he didn't see anything, more accurately: anyone. He'd stay on high alert, regardless. *I hope you come back, motherfucker. I'll show you a damn thug.* Quick recounted the feud again for the hundredth time. Problem was he'd heard every nasty word that prick called him, and if he hadn't been trying to impress his distinguished date, he would've put Joe on his self-important ass.

After determining that the noises he'd heard must've been an animal, Quick checked the clip in one of his all-black 9mm handguns and tucked it under the couch cushion where he'd laid his head. He checked his watch. It was going on eleven. Still early, so he stretched out, linking his fingers and tucking them behind his head. All that bulk and muscle looked comical on the standard length couch.

Quick closed his eyes and thought about Cayson. Usually at this hour – if he wasn't working – he'd be on his patio, sipping a brew and trying to relax. He imagined Cayson reclining between his legs on his outdoor chaise lounge after they'd both had a long day. Quick could see himself burying his nose in Cayson's neck and murmuring sweet words of encouragement while his lover told him all about his stressful day. He wondered if they could be together, find something special between them, like his best friend had found. Wondered if he'd found the one who would make his heart soar. Duke was the happiest guy he knew, now. But a year ago, he was as big a mess as Quick. Wanting a friend, a lover, and a partner. Quick wanted it all. He wanted it with his sexy surgeon, who in his opinion had single-handedly saved his son's and best friend's lives. And the man was gorgeous.

Beautiful blond-brown hair with a few sprinkled grays along the edges. Quick had more grays than the doc, but his was long and usually pulled back at his neck. Clearly, Cayson was a man who took care of himself, because his body had very little fat on it. He wasn't packed with muscle, but his toned frame was a big turn-on for Quick. But, nothing did it for him more than when Cayson was in his white lab coat wearing his nerdy, gold wire-rimmed reading glasses. Quick closed his eyes and relived their first date to keep himself from drifting off to sleep too fast. Cayson was in such an affluent neighborhood, Quick didn't hear any police sirens, helicopters or any other big city noises. Behind his closed lids, Quick pictured their kiss, their hug, pictured the way Cayson had hung on to him, like he'd shatter if Quick let him go. He most definitely wasn't leaving. It'd been years since Quick felt this alive. Cayson stirred feelings deep down inside of him, feelings which he'd thought had been suppressed too long to arise again.

The time crept by, but Quick used it to think and brainstorm. He knew how to devise a plan. He'd need one to deal with Dr. Joe, especially since he couldn't move in to protect Cayson.

While he thought, his eyelids dropped lower and lower.

# CHAPTER TWELVE

*Cayson*

Cayson was deeply asleep, finally getting the much-needed rest he'd been seeking, when a sharp knock made him bolt upright, scaring the shit out of him. It took only a second for him to gather himself when another knock fell and was forceful enough to rattle the few pieces of art Cayson had on the walls downstairs. What the damn hell?

"I know you're in there. I either want a full apology or give me my stuff, Cayson! Right now!"

Cayson rubbed at the stress quickly building behind his eyelids. Glancing over at the clock on his nightstand, his eyes widened. It was after midnight. "Why isn't anyone letting me sleep?!" As soon as the complaint left his mouth, he jumped up, remembering Quick.

Cayson was out of bed and yanking his robe on as fast as he could. He'd just cinched the tie at his waist, and Quick rounded the corner of his stairs and was in his bedroom, pulling him protectively closer with one arm, while the other hand held a scary black handgun.

"Are you okay?" Quick asked him sternly, checking his watch.

"Yes. I was just on my way to the door," he said, sounding annoyed. Taking a step back from the embrace to make sure his robe was tight; he looked up and almost came all over himself and his imported oriental rug. Quick was shirtless, with only his jeans on. They were unbuttoned and the zipper was partway down. Cayson could see the black briefs Quick wore underneath and wanted to drop to his knees and bury his nose in the dark cotton covering that glorious cock. But it was the tattoos. Goddamn, they were everywhere. Some bright and vibrant with color, some black and gray. He was dying for a chance to get up close and personal with them. No matter what was happening at any particular moment, the sight of Rome bare-chested would always make him pause and drool. Roman's name truly fit him to a T.

BANG! BANG! "Are you in there, Cayson? You big idiot! Open up, I have something to say!"

"He's gonna wake the damn dead," Cayson grumbled, moving quickly down the stairs with Rome close on his heels. He didn't see this ending well. What the hell was Joe doing screaming outside like that? It was a sure way to draw unneeded attention. In his quiet neighborhood, surely someone had already called the police. Cayson needed to hurry and get rid of him before Joe was arrested and charged with disturbing the peace.

Fact of the matter was Joe treated Cays like a business arrangement, not a partner. So if Joe's feelings got bruised because Cayson no longer wanted to be his doormat, well now that was Joe's problem, wasn't it? Cayson wasn't going to give Joe much of his time.

"And Roman, please put that gun away, for Pete's sake." Cayson shoed him back further against the wall behind the door, so when he opened it, Rome couldn't be seen. He didn't need his huge date overreacting. "Dr. Joe has a very sensitive ego, so I guess he's trying to save face. Don't worry, I'll get rid—"

BANG! BANG! BANG! "Right now, Cayson! I want an apology."

The last word sounded slurred now that Cayson was right at the door. *Oh, god, please don't be drunk.* Cayson hesitated before opening the door. If Joe was out of his mind from having his pride wounded, was it a good idea to let him in? His first thought was no, but he began to unlock the bolt lock anyway.

He tried his best to put on his groggy, sleep-roughened voice, hoping he could convince Joe to do this some other time. "Joe, w-what are you doing here at this hour?"

"Le'me in so we can talk," Joe demanded on another slur, but this time a slight belch followed the command. He had on the same clothes as earlier, appearing as if he'd been at a bar this whole time, getting shit-faced. Cayson could smell Joe's rancid breath through his storm door. There was a permanent frown marring his brow, like he'd made an angry face and it got stuck that way. No. This wasn't Joe. Wasn't the prim and proper friend he'd made years ago. This crazed man wasn't the distinguished anesthesiologist who refused to even check his mail if he wore anything other than a fully pressed suit. Joe's hair was all over his head and his severely wrinkled shirt was untucked. Cayson had never seen Joe like this. Especially not drunk. Being drunk and disorderly was uncivilized.

"I have a real early day." Cayson's tone was light and held not even a trace of meanness. "We can talk tomorrow if you want, okay? Sit there on the steps. I'll call you a cab."

"Don't need a damn cab. Now, let me in."

"No. Joe, I'm really tired."

Joe scoffed, his lip turned up in repugnance. "I just bet you are, Cayson Chauncey. So did you finally get screwed the way you wanted? Are you finished acting like an ass?"

"First of all. It's none of your business. You're drunk, Joe. You're going to find yourself up shit's creek without a paddle if you don't stop all your yelling and banging on my door. I'm sure you've woken everyone on this street." Cayson glanced up and down the street and noticed that Quick's truck wasn't where he'd left it. He'd obviously moved it for this reason. He'd been right. Joe came back, just as he'd predicted.

"Then I want my stuff. Now!"

"Shh. Quiet, daggonit… and what stuff?" Cayson was trying to keep his voice down, but was losing patience faster than a compulsive gambler losing his rent money.

"You know what!"

Before Cayson could even think what Dr. Joe was referring too, he'd pushed hard on the door, knocking Cayson backwards. The door probably would've slammed into the wall from the momentum, but Quick was there to stop it. Joe didn't even notice. He wasn't accustomed to noticing things like that. He wasn't a man who'd ever had to watch his back.

"Joe, what the hell? Get out of my house. I told you not to come in."

Joe ignored him and stumbled further into the room, only glancing around before making a wobbly beeline to his closet. How the man didn't notice the largest pair of black boots Cayson had ever seen lying next to the couch and the black t-shirt slung over the arm was beyond his understanding.

Cayson knew what was about to happen the moment he saw the front door in his peripheral vision slowly shutting to reveal Quick's very pissed off posture. Joe's back was to them while he dug through the closet. Cayson had no clue what he was looking for, but he pleaded with his eyes for Quick to stay calm. One look at Quick, and he knew that wasn't about to happen.

"I can't find it!" Joe screamed, his head still buried. "I know I left it here. I can't find it at home, anywhere."

"Find what, Joe?" Cayson left the front door open, Joe wasn't staying much longer.

"My gray and white Berluti cardigan," Joe said, his voice muffled by the coats he dug through.

"Joe, there's nothing like that in there. I don't remember you ever leaving anything here. You don't even stay the night except for maybe once every couple of months." Cayson sighed when

Joe started throwing things out of the closet, burying himself deeper inside it. How ironic. "Now, for the last time – leave."

Quick's hand was on Cayson's shoulders, massaging and rubbing the tension that had settled there days ago and refused to move out. It was becoming more and more painful to watch, as Joe became a huge mess. He was on the floor, digging and pulling things all over the place. Both he and Roman looked on in disbelief and sadness.

"Do you want me to get rid of him for you, Cays? Because I will. Whatever you need me to do. Just ask." Quick stood closer now. Looking large and damn sure in charge. It gave Cayson a warm feeling deep down that Quick wanted to help him… protect him. He spoke like it'd take an army to move him, to get close enough to harm Cayson. The big bounty hunter stood so close that his groin was pressing into Cayson's hip. Of course, their height difference put what Cayson really wanted to feel a little off target, but everyone was the same length when you laid down in bed. The coarse hairs above Quick's lips brushed the shell of Cayson's ear as he spoke in that soothing tone. It hadn't failed to have a profound effect on Cayson, and he ended up loosening his robe for a little extra room.

He wanted to turn into those massive arms and let Quick make it all better. He hurt. He hurt everywhere. He was a compassionate man. He hated for people to go through pain, but self-inflicted pain was the worst to watch, because all that Joe had to do was be honest with himself. Obviously, he was waging an internal war. Maybe even wanting to have something more with Cayson, but too afraid. Too fucked up. Too steeped in his family's traditions to start his own. Not man enough to stand up to his old man, when Joe was damn near an old man himself. Forty-two was too long to hide your sexuality. Forty-two was too long to still be controlled by your upbringing. Forty plus years of bathing in misery and dining with anguish. Cayson felt for him, he truly did – but he couldn't let Joe hold him back from what he deserved.

"He's still here?!"

The shouted question yanked Cayson out of his thoughts and away from the encouraging rub he was receiving. Joe had finally noticed Quick standing behind Cayson like a bodyguard, equipped with a dark death-bringer in his right hand. He felt Quick tense behind him – like he was ready to act – but he didn't make a move. He was sure Quick knew tons of moves, but hurting Joe was not an option in Cayson's mind. He was hoping Quick would stay cool. "I'm calling him a cab. I'll be upstairs, but I'll be watching." Quick had lowered his voice, but surely not low enough that Joe didn't hear him from only a few feet away.

"Thank you, Rome," Cayson whispered, almost shyly. He hadn't had someone dote over him in a long time. It felt good.

Quick moved from behind him, running his big hand along Cayson's back as he stepped in front of him, his next words specifically for Joe. "You put your hands anywhere on him and you'll regret it. I promise."

That was all Quick said, then he was taking the stairs three at a time, his long ponytail swaying slightly with each long stride. Cayson watched until neither Quick, nor the black gun now tucked against the small of his back, were visible.

"A gun!" Joe shrieked. "He has a gun in your house! Did you see that?" Joe was hysterical and still way too fucking loud for midnight. "You hate guns, remember! Guns kill."

"No. I never said I hated guns. And guns don't kill people, Joe. Ignorant people with guns kill people. And of course, Rome has a license for that weapon. He's in law enforcement… sort of." Cayson didn't need to give Joe any definitive information about Quick. The less Joe knew, the better, because he and his family had plenty of money and power. He didn't need them to stir up trouble or make Quick's life hard.

Joe looked like he was going to burst into flames. Cayson was shocked Joe could turn that damn red. But when Quick was out of sight, Joe changed from wild, to livid, to achingly sorry, too fast for Cayson to keep up. Next thing he knew Joe was sobbing, leaning heavily against the wall next to the closet, his head pressed into his fist. "I can do better, Cayson. I can, if you give me some time. I just need a little more time. I-I can't come out, but I can do better by you, I promise I can."

Cayson placed his hand over his chest. This was going to burn both of them. But Cayson knew it was the absolute right thing to do. With his eyes closed, he started speaking slowly and concisely, so there was no mistaking his intentions. "Joseph. I can't do that. You've made lots of promises before, and I don't think you've kept even one. It's time we both move on. Our season is over, good friend. Our friendship doesn't have to end. I don't want it to end, because we still have to work together. But any romance that was between us ends here and now, Joe. I'm sorry. But this is it for us in that capacity." Cayson shook his head. Damn, even the way he ended their *arrangement* sounded like a contract being terminated. All technical and no emotion.

# CHAPTER THIRTEEN

*Quick*

Quick wasn't even going to pretend he wasn't listening. He was in full-on guard mode. If Joe acted like he wanted to hurt his sweet doctor, then Quick was going to stick the entire barrel of his pistol in his mouth and make him deep throat it like the pussy he was, then he'd pistol whip him with it. Yep. That was Quick. Fuck with someone he considered important, and a side of him no one wanted to meet came out. A fierce bounty hunter who had trained masterfully in several styles of martial arts since he was a boy. Joe would be absolutely no competition for Quick. He didn't need the pistol, he was a warrior, but the gun was his bottom fucking line. Hopefully, Dr. Joseph was smart enough not to make Quick cross it.

When Quick hung up after calling for the cab, he peered over the railing, and though Dr. Joe was groveling, he was keeping a safe distance. Quick looked down to the floor. How fast could he get to Cayson if he needed to? He could jump over the railing, but he'd land on the dining room table, his brawn shattering it. He shrugged. He'd jumped further and landed on worse. The table was replaceable... not so, Cayson.

Quick sat gingerly in the chair in Cayson's room that was closest to the railing. He debated sending Duke a text, but thought better of it. He could handle this alone if things took a turn for the worst. When Quick had threatened Joe if he touched Cayson, he almost wanted to frisk the man before he left the room, but knew that would escalate things. He decided to just keep an eye on them. If Joe appeared to reach for something nestled in his waistband, then Quick was going to reach for his first. He'd win that old-style Wild West standoff, too. He was too quick to let a man get the jump on him. Hence the name.

Now, Joe was crying for another chance, promising Cayson he was going to change and be good to him. *Shit, fuck, goddamn you, you sneaky motherfucker.* Quick knew the asshole was gonna come back, but he didn't know he'd come like this. Joe came equipped with a different kind of arsenal, one that Quick was yet to possess, regarding Cayson. Knowledge and longevity. The two men arguing downstairs had a long history of friendship, and Dr. Joe knew how to pull Cayson's heartstrings perfectly. Could read him and play off the kind doctor's emotions. Joe would know how to get Cayson to fold and accept his apology. Quick hoped Cayson was strong enough to see past the bullshit. He didn't know Cayson very well yet, and he didn't fully understand the two doctors' relationship to know how this was going to end. He couldn't help but think that any second now Cayson would come upstairs and tell Quick he was going to give Joe another chance. That they had too much invested to throw away. It would really do a number on him, but he'd bow out gracefully.

After a few more minutes, Joe finally stopped whining long enough to let Cayson get a word in. When his sexy doctor did speak, he declined Joe with sincerity and gentility, and it made Quick the happiest man in the world right then. Hopefully, it was because he'd given Cayson such a nice evening that he wasn't ready to stop seeing him.

But Joe heard that no and the evil, I'll-get-you-back stare was aimed right at Cayson. It was time for Quick to make his presence known again. The conversation was over and there was a car horn honking out front.

"Your ride's here," Quick said with a rough finality, standing midway down the stairs. Crossing his arms over his chest. His

9mm now tucked securely in the front of his jeans. Faster access. "It's time for you to leave. If Cayson's wants you back… he'll call you."

Cayson plopped down on his couch while he and Joe had their stare-off. Quick never blinked, and neither did Joe. Quick nodded once. Challenge received and accepted.

~~~~~~~~~~

Cayson was pretty quiet while he and Quick walked around the corner to his truck the next morning. He was still upset about Joe. The guy had been a mess when he finally left. Although he told the cab driver Joe's address, he hoped his old friend made it home safely. He wasn't going to call Joe. Right now, they needed distance. His friend may have his issues, but Cayson couldn't deny Joe's immeasurable intelligence. When he calmed down, he'd see that Cayson was right. They had no real future together.

Quick opened the passenger door first, before jogging around to the driver side. "I wish we'd had time for me to make you breakfast, but I thought you'd like to sleep as long as you could. I can swing by an IHOP and get something to go if you want." There wouldn't be enough time for anything else.

Cayson placed his messenger bag on the floor at his feet and fastened his seat belt. "No. I'm okay. I'll grab a muffin or something from the coffee cart. I don't like to perform surgeries on a full stomach, anyway."

"Okay, then."

Cayson was in a sour mood and he picked up that Quick was trying to bring him out of it. He appreciated the effort, but the wound was still very raw. He'd lost a friend last night. He was sure of it. Cayson wasn't ready to give up on Quick, or even the smallest chance that he could be loved, just so Joe could have an arrangement with him. It didn't take his thirteen years of college and graduate school to know who held the better chance at keeping Cayson's heart safe.

"I haven't even checked my schedule for today yet," Cayson said absently. He pulled a tablet out of the front flap of his bag and began tapping. Quick was focused on the road, the traffic starting to pick up. It was only about fifteen minutes from Cayson's house to Emory Hospital. Quick opted to take Briarcliff instead of Lullwater Road, and while Cayson waited for his schedule to load, he watched the cars whizzing around them, everyone with somewhere they were supposed to be.

The chime on his tablet alerted him that his first appointment was only an hour away. The rest of his schedule looked pretty light for a Friday, and he felt instant relief. Hopefully, by three at the latest, he'd be leaving. He needed time to process everything that'd happened. No covering in the ER tonight, either. He had a total of three checkup appointments, no names were listed, but he knew Nania would have a detailed schedule on his desk when he got there. Only two surgeries. The last was an incisional biopsy – no sweat – with monitored anesthesia. Oh, no. Please, no. But a quick flick of the screen and… fuck me! Cayson groaned. Not Dr. Joe.

"You alright, Cays?" Quick asked.

He only managed a slight curve of his mouth in reply.

Cayson pinched the bridge of his nose, his head lowered and his eyes squeezed shut, he couldn't imagine his luck being so bad. Joe was employed by a network of hospitals, so he could show up in anyone's operating room in any of the four hospitals within that network. He went where he was assigned. However, Cayson hadn't had Dr. Joe in his OR in almost two months, and of all the times, he was paired with him after what'd just gone down between them. Cayson would be professional. He was certain Joe would, too. He wouldn't dare risk anyone whispering about him, spreading rumors that he was behaving erratically in an OR. Joe's surname had to remain untainted. Besides, it was a general rule not to bring your personal bullshit into anyone's surgery. It meant life or death for the patient.

"I have a great idea!" Quick's jovial voice broke into Cayson's exhausting thoughts.

Cayson smiled a little brighter. *Of course he does. I hope he's full of great ideas.* "What's that?"

Quick rounded Clifton Road and pulled into a reserved parking space for physicians at the main entrance of the hospital, killing the engine. Quick turned in his seat, giving Cayson his full attention. Quick just watched him for a few seconds before he leaned over the large center console and kissed Cayson gently on the lips. "Good morning." He beamed. Those gorgeous green eyes gleaming with all kinds of delicious mischief.

Cayson fully laughed this time. It felt good. Real good. "Good morning, Roman," he replied breathlessly, absently licking his lips. Quick tasted just as good in the morning as he did at night.

"Duke texted me a moment ago. We have a bounty this afternoon. Usually I go and unwind somewhere after we're finished, but I'd like to unwind with you... um, wait." Quick's eyes widened slightly. "Not unwind like that... you know... like I want in your pants... unwind, ya know... like go to a—"

Cayson put his hand on Quick's hard shoulder, still chuckling at the big man's fumbling. "I know what you meant."

"Good. I'm still trying to redeem myself with you. I know last night was a clusterfuck."

"No, our date wasn't. The dinner was special to me and I enjoyed it very much. What happened with Joe was not your fault at all. Besides. You were right. He came back, pissed off and out of control. Things may have ended differently if you weren't there. Joe wouldn't've left. Not without a police escort."

"I wasn't concerned with being right. I was concerned about you."

Cayson's head swam with emotions. Was Quick really for real? He hoped so. But he'd already hoped for so long. He needed to be about the actuality. Meaning, he would judge on actions alone. No more fancy words or empty promises. Walk the talk or get the hell out of his face was his new motto. It seems Cayson thought of a new slogan each day. The fact of the matter was, Quick had been there for him. Told him he would be and then he came through for him. "Thank you for being there."

"No thanks needed."

"Yes, there is." Cayson was feeling lightheaded and slightly tired, but at least he'd gotten five hours of sleep thanks to Quick, so he'd make it through the day. Thank god, it was Friday. He needed a couple days of reprieve.

"Well then, you can have dinner with me tonight as thanks, since you insist." Quick slowly kissed the inside of Cayson's palm while looking up at him through his dark brown lashes. No man ever did that to him. What did Quick see in Cayson's hands anyway? It was the second time he'd done that. As if he read his thoughts, Quick spoke.

"These hands saved my best friend's life. My son's life." Quick turned Cayson's hand over, and began to sensually kiss and flick his thick tongue at each fingertip. "So soft," he whispered, massaging Cayson's palm now.

If Cayson didn't leave soon, he was going to walk into the hospital with a mad hard-on that wouldn't be concealed behind his dark gray slacks. But he swore that if he'd had no appointment scheduled right now, he'd probably be eyeing the space capacity of Quick's backseat. Shaking away his lust, he responded to Quick's request, when he finally remembered what it was. "You want to cook again?"

"No."

"Well, I'm a terrible cook. I might can boil water, but who knows. Never had time to learn," Cayson confessed.

"Of course, you didn't. I couldn't imagine that much college," Quick admitted.

"So you want to come back to my place?" Cayson offered begrudgingly. This conversation brought up all the times he'd wanted to go out but Joe didn't.

"I was actually hoping to take you to a little place I love downtown. It's quaint. Nice atmosphere, terrific food, and they have live music on Friday nights. It's a hidden gem I found a while back." Quick ran the backs of his fingers down Cayson's freshly shaved jaw. His eyes clouded with doubt. "What d'ya say, huh? You want to go out on the town with an uncultured ruffian like me?"

Cayson was ecstatic. Out! Out on an actual date? He kept his poker face, he refused to gush, and blush like a teenager. The way Quick worded his last question, Cayson didn't feel right beaming in the man's face when he looked to be doubting himself. Did Quick honestly feel he wasn't good enough for Cayson? It was nuts, because Cayson had been thinking the opposite. It was a boost to his ego, especially after Dr. Joe had demolished it mere hours ago. "Sure. I'd love to go out with you. That sounds like a real nice place."

"You like jazz, yes? I saw your collection, it's impressive."

"I do." Cayson smiled. "I love it. The collection's kind of a hobby."

Quick looked at his watch. Cayson needed to go and Quick had work to do, too. "Great! I'll pick you up at home around six. That work?"

"Perfect. Yes." That'd give Cayson time to get home and get a little shuteye before going out. Cayson opened his door, but turned when he felt a tug on his elbow. He hid his surprised smile. Quick wanted a kiss goodbye.

This time the kiss wasn't chaste. It was full of sensual, smoking hot promises. Quick tasted like strong coffee and

Cayson slowly dragged his tongue across Quick's moist palate, seeking his unique taste, sucking his tongue hard enough to make the big man groan. But Quick yanked back like he'd been tazed, leaving Cayson blinking and wondering. Wondering how he could get just a bit more.

"I look forward to tonight, Cays," Quick said breathlessly, his eyes pinched closed like it'd taken a lot of willpower to end that kiss.

With his own eyes slightly hooded, Cayson nodded. "Me, too. Be careful today."

Quick winked. "I'll be extra careful now."

Cayson starred at Quick for a few seconds, trying to understand what he meant. When the silence had stretched into awkwardness, Cayson gripped his bag tightly and got out the large SUV before he screamed something stupid like, "Take me here! Take me now!"

# CHAPTER FOURTEEN

*Quick*

Quick pulled his court duty, but it was as annoying and probably equivalent to a police detective having to pull traffic detail. They rotated that assignment because it was cruel and unusual punishment to make one person do it every day. Whenever they returned bonded defendants to jail on a revoked bond when they hadn't shown up for court, the bail-skipper would get another hearing, and it was necessary for the bonded agent to be there. They also had to be sure to get their money back. The only thing that helped Quick pass the time, as the judge droned through the morning docket, were his thoughts of Cayson and their upcoming date.

Finally, it was lunchtime, and thankfully, the court had gotten to his last case right before it recessed. Quick was in his leathers, ready to get this last duty fulfilled so he could finish planning his date. Vaughan gave him a few pointers on topics to discuss, foods not to order unless you wanted dragon breath, how to be a good giver not just a taker, and of course: what he should wear on his first date with a man, you know, the things a typical father and son talk about. But, as soon as Vaughan hinted at discussing sex, Quick cut him off. He had to draw the line somewhere, and sex tips from his son were miles over that line. He was on his own there… well… he still had YouTube.

Quick was in the office, waiting on the guys to get there so they could recover a perp they'd been trying to find for almost six weeks. He was a two-time loser about to get his third strike, and they all knew what that meant. So the punk went into hiding.

Only, the guy didn't know how damn good they really were, and the King brothers could find an ant in a scorpion hive. There was nowhere to hide.

With his boots propped up on his desk, he enjoyed the peace and quiet while he surfed the web. First, he made reservations for his date, even though the woman who answered the phone at The Foxhole said it wasn't necessary. But Quick wanted a certain table, so: yes, it was. Then he'd shock the shit out of his date with a very special outing after dinner. Sure, it'd been Vaughan's idea, and Quick was nervous as hell to execute it perfectly. He'd certainly give it his all. He just hoped he wasn't being too presumptuous. This was getting so exciting that he fought to drop the persistent smile which had been affixed to his face since he'd made the final preparation for their night out.

Quick craned his head back and looked out the window into the small parking lot to see if anyone had pulled up yet. With nervousness flittering in his stomach, he opened his YouTube app and typed in "gay sex," his eyes widening to twice their size as soon as the results popped up. All varieties and flavors right there at the tips of his fingers. Taking another glance out at the parking lot, the coast still clear, he clicked on "hottest alpha males sex." That directed him to a whole new site.

Quick didn't feel like he had a specific type, but he knew enough to know he liked a man who behaved like one. Quick wanted a partner, not a headache, and certainly not a passive lover. While Cayson was intelligent and strikingly handsome, he was a tad timid, but Quick had noticed over the course of the time that he'd known Cayson, that the man had straightened his backbone significantly. And Quick found it very attractive. The way he stood up to that pretentious doctor, even though the man had delivered a brutal blow to Cayson's pride. His doctor held his head high. Confidence was an important trait for him to see in someone when dating. He didn't want to have to constantly build someone up, not at his age, anyway. That's why he loathed this Dr. Joe character.

His gulp was audible when he saw the models for the alpha males site. Big men fucking other really big men. They were all so damn handsome and strong. Like him. Like his sweet doctor. Cayson may not be bulky, but he wasn't small. It was obvious he took care of himself. His golden brown hair was cut in a sexy, but conservative, style. Enough on the top for Quick to run his fingers through. Quick groaned when he thought of Cayson naked and spread out for him like one of the models in the picture he'd clicked on. The video played for three erotic minutes before a pop-up appeared on his screen. If he wanted to see more, he had to put in some personal information. There was a seven-day free trial before they would charge his credit card twenty-five bucks. He should be able to get a sense of technique within seven days. He'd learn what to do to please Cayson if it killed him.

"What you working on so seriously, Quick?"

Quick startled so hard at Ford's deep voice that he'd comically wind-milled in his chair to keep it from falling completely backwards when he tried to clear the screen before the brothers could make their way to him. How the hell hadn't he heard the door open? Kicking himself for being so stupid, he vowed to use his home computer for research from now own. The backlash he'd get would be nonstop if any of his team found out he was trying to learn how to fuck online. If Ford or Brian saw what he was looking at, he'd be the object of their ridicule for the next six damn months.

Ford paused at Quick's theatrics, raising one thick brow in question. Quick tried to wave it off as nothing, diverting his eyes back to his computer, feigning deep concentration. He blinked, noticing he was staring at the blank screen. "Um, just research on that um… um… you know what case. The case."

Ford continued to stare Quick down, Brian's Special Forces-trained eye twitched like he sensed something was off. Quick glanced up and noticed him smirking while signing something to his brother that looked like a crude gesture. Fuck. Brian couldn't've seen what Quick was looking at, his computer monitor faced away from the back door.

"Maybe so," Ford confirmed. He and his brother were clearly sharing a private joke at Quick's expense.

Brian suffered from a unique form of PTSD and had difficulty communicating with anyone other than his brother. While he was physically able to speak, he mentally could not. It was a sad story. One that was littered with words which were mostly military acronyms for something horrible: MIA, POW, AWOL. Frightening words that we, as free Americans can't fathom, but nonetheless, it's Brian's story and only his to tell when he's ready to do so.

"What did he say?" Quick growled at Ford, only making the brothers laugh harder.

"Ahh, nothing. Brian said you look like you just got caught jerking off to porn."

Quick rolled his eyes and threw up his middle finger at Brian. He didn't know sign language, but he knew the universal sign for fuck you. That's all he needed to say to the enigmatic man. Quick continued to try to appear unfazed, but goddamn those perceptive ass military men. Just when Ford's eyes bulged at the truthfulness of his brother's signed words, Duke barged through door with Dana behind him. Phew, saved.

"Everyone set?" Duke said. They all began to check their weapons as soon as Duke spoke. "We go in ten, brothers. Be ready."

Duke closed himself in his office while they suited up. Wearing leathers was hot and a little uncomfortable, even in the winter, but it was a necessity. Quick sure appreciated them when he was rolling around on asphalt. They prepared themselves in silence. No one talked or joked. A retrieval was serious business. All a person had to do to be able imagine the danger of a bounty hunter's job, was picture how hard you'd be willing to fight to keep your freedom. That's the type of aggression and desperation they faced every single time they went out.

They all knew their roles. Duke and Quick remained together and were the lead. Brian and Ford stayed on their six, making sure no one snuck up on them from behind, and of course, provided plenty of extra muscle. Before they'd hired the brothers, Quick and Duke used to fight back to back, but with the huge King brothers protecting them, Quick could concentrate on threats in front of them, knowing their asses were covered. Dana was the watch hunter. He was to keep communication open and alert them to any immediate or potential threats coming from the outside. He was a good hunter and a skilled marksman. They'd come to trust Dana over time, he was a solid addition to the group. As soon as they got to their location, Dana would take up a perch somewhere outside or in, depending on where they were.

Quick locked up his computer since he wouldn't be coming back to the office. After the seize he planned to drop Duke off at home and continue to his place to handle a few tasks before it was time for his date. Quick triple checked his 9mm handguns before he holstered his weapons at his sides. He had a blade in his boot and one hooked to his belt. Both were necessary and had saved his life on more than one occasion. His utility vest held a silencer in one pocket, lock picking tools, police-issue pepper spray, and a couple other cool gadgets Ford had gotten from his military contacts. The grenades, they left locked in the safe at the office. Quick never laughed as hard when he saw Duke's reaction when Ford opened up the box, revealing three real military hand grenades. "When the hell are we going to have to use those, Ford?" Duke hollered, shaking his head frantically. It was quite a sight. Duke threatened Ford's life if he got them in trouble for possessing illegal military contraband. However, there was a seize in Buckhead about four months ago where one of those grenades would've come in handy.

Standing in their spacious building, each of them reflected on what was important to them as they prepared not just their weapons, but their minds. They were a band of brothers, an army. When together, their defense was impenetrable.

After their final moments of silence, Ford asked for everyone's attention while he unlocked the bottom cabinet of his own desk and pulled out something that looked like a storage box for cigars. *Oh, boy. Here we go. What is it today?* Live mines to put around the building, perhaps? When Quick moved in closer, he noticed what was in the box. Eight of them. Masculine identical wrist watches. Quick didn't know why, but they looked rare and expensive. They were similar to any higher-end sports watch, but there was no brand name.

"These are military grade. Can't get them anywhere," Ford said proudly.

"You got them." Quick smirked.

Ford was a man of few words. He responded by methodically lifting the cover like the contents were poisonous and held out one of the watches to Quick. He took it, shaking his head. "I like my own watch."

"I'm sure you do. But this one can save your life."

Quick was more interested now. "How so? Does it shoot poisonous darts?"

Ignoring him, Ford pushed a button on the side, and the face glowed bright orange. It had all the important components of a regular watch, including the crown for adjusting the time, but there were three buttons on the opposite side that didn't belong.

"Top button alerts and dispatches emergency services to your exact location. Think of OnStar. Kinda works like that.

Middle one is linked to all of us. If you press and hold for three or more seconds, our watches will alarm with your exact location. It will also relay back to you when we receive your message. The last button you can program to do whatever you want. It can link to any one time piece or to any registered cell, land, or secure line."

"Damn. That's wild as hell, Ford. How did you get these gadgets, man?" Dana asked, taking his own watch off and fastening the one Ford handed to him securely around his right wrist.

Quick did the same. The wide strap of black leather was pulled tight while he surveyed the features. The center of the watch was a typical dial with ivory watch hands and a recessed dial that was a mother of pearl etching of the world. It was classy as fuck, but the leather band would match the expensive piece with any possible outfit.

As soon as they all had their own, each of them familiarizing themselves with the new gadget, a shrill alarm pierced the room, making all of them instinctually reach for their firearms. Ford had pushed his alert on his watch.

"You're an ass," Dana yelled over the noise, holding his hand over his chest. The shrill ring sounded like a firehouse alarm. There was no way to miss it or ignore it.

"This is what it will sound like if you push the button to alert anyone in the team," Ford explained, continuing his short demonstration. "You can contact one of us or all of us at the same time. We're talking state of the art, boys. This thing can get tossed into the deepest parts of the ocean and still work." He showed them a few other interesting features, including web and some phone services. Quick was tech savvy enough that he was able to catch on fairly easy.

Quick saw a map display on the face of his watch, the time now flashing a digital display at the top. A red dot pulsed over the map, then the address to their office appeared a millisecond later. This thing was the fucking truth. It was basically a GPS tracker that also told the time. Maybe it would come in handy. He'd need two, though.

"Let's roll, men," Duke said, coming out of his office, in his full-on leather and bulletproof vest. He took his watch from Ford as well, telling all of them that it was now a permanent part of their uniform and must be worn at all times. As business boomed, they found themselves taking more bonds and accepting contracts from other bond agents who didn't do their own retrievals. If any of them got in a jam, this gadget could be extremely beneficial.

Quick noticed Duke was implementing a lot more security measures. First the earpieces and now this. He could only imagine how much these watches set them back. Whether purchased legally or not. Even for the lower risk seizes, Duke was triple careful. Quick wasn't mad about it. His best friend had something special to live for. Quick hoped he did too. He tightened the straps on his own vest and fell in line behind Duke as they filed into the vehicles. Brian and Ford in the middle, and Dana drove the truck that was designed for transporting their detainees.

Duke pulled into the McDonald's parking lot off of Queen Street. The other Suburban, driven by Brian crept past them, circling around the block, getting in position to take up the rear. Dana was the last to pull in. He parked the truck behind the dumpster, since it was the only vehicle that said Bail Bonds on the side. Quick noticed the warehouse across the street had too much activity going on in the parking lot for Dana to get on the roof unnoticed. They watched as Dana hurriedly scanned the area before he walked quickly towards the McDonalds.

"Is he really about to get on the McDonald's roof?" Duke laughed.

Quick laughed a low rumble. "Looks that way. Luckily, there are hardly any customers. Should be fine if we're fast."

They waited until Dana was ready, his rifle assembled and aimed in the direction of their skip's last known address. It was the defendant's girlfriend's house. Brian had been scoping out the house for weeks, when he finally confirmed that RayBud – as he was known on the streets – was back there again.

The intel these brothers provided was the best. Quick was sure it was all due to their military background, about which was little known, but their methods weren't a topic the brothers liked to discuss, so they typically didn't.

"We're in position." Brian's voice came through their earpieces.

Duke and Quick were out of the truck and jogging up to the front door just as Brian and Ford came around the rear, keeping watch on the back door. Trash littered the yard, everything from old car parts, to beer cans, random trash, and a shit load of cigarette butts overflowed out of an old flowerpot. Duke had been informed that no children, elderly or other relatives lived there. Across the street, he ignored a couple of old men looking on from their porch as they got into position.

"Dana?" Duke inquired quickly, mindful to keep his voice down.

"All set, Boss. Looks good from up top. Perimeter is clear."

"Copy that." Duke turned to Quick and got his nod, confirming he was ready. He flicked his head in the direction of the door, asking if Quick wanted to do the honors. Without missing a beat, Quick banged on the door, simultaneously yelling, "BOUNTY HUNTERS! OPEN THE DOOR OR WE WILL BUST IT OPEN!"

Technically, they didn't have to knock or announce themselves, but why destroy someone's door if they were willing to open it? Quick knocked hard once more and stepped back, ready to kick it down, when a woman cracked open the door, just enough for them to see her mouth.

"Open the door, ma'am. We're here for RayBud," Duke said, flashing his identification. His bounty hunter star on one side and his bonds license on the other. He pulled the revoked bond order from his back pocket and waved it in the woman's line of sight. "We have a right to enter without your consent, ma'am."

"He's not here. He's at work," she lied, still keeping the front door open only a couple of inches.

"He's out the back, Duke!" Dana yelled in their ears. With the woman completely forgotten, Duke and Quick both busted through the front door, careful to watch for any hidden threats as they vaulted through the dark living room. Quick pushed on the sliding glass door, but it was locked. Not caring about preserving the doors anymore, he picked up one of the wood dining room chairs and slung it with all his might. He and Duke both put their leather-clad forearms in front of their faces to block the majority of the shattering glass.

"You assholes! You broke my door! I'm calling the police!" the woman yelled, throwing cups and anything else she could find at their backs as Quick and Duke raced through the backyard. They already knew there was no fence or gate, so they doubled their speed.

"Don't let that fucker get away, Brian!" Duke yelled out, the sound of his deep voice deafening in their ears.

The brothers were in the lead – Brian was faster than Ford – almost a half block ahead of them. Goddamn if they both didn't have the build and physical stamina of NFL linebackers.

"Which way?" Quick heard Ford huff through their earpieces.

"North on Ralph.

"Is he armed?"

"Unknown at this time," Dana said, his watchful eye tracking everyone's movements through his scope.

"Copy that," Ford confirmed.

"Proceed with caution," Duke reminded.

No sooner had they rounded on Ralph Boulevard, Quick saw Brian's massive frame go airborne and crash down on their perp's back, sending them rolling across the unforgiving asphalt. Brian ended up on the bottom. Quick and Duke were closing in fast, but Ford got there first, and Quick knew it wasn't going to be pretty. Ford lost it anytime someone touched his baby brother. Never mind that he was military trained as well, and was capable of taking care of himself. Ford, still running full speed, dove head first, knocking RayBud off his brother. This was why they wore the leather. Otherwise, Ford and his brother would have a seriously nasty case of road burn.

RayBud was yelling his surrender, but Quick still had to pull Ford off the scared man. Duke dropped a hard knee onto their skip's back, making him yell out in anguish. "Someone help me! Record this! Police brutality!"

"Shut up. You shouldn't've run, idiot," Duke grumbled as he secured their perp's hands and feet with zip ties. They weren't required to Mirandize their detainees because they weren't cops, they only had one sentence to say, everything else could be handled by the authorities. "Your bond has been revoked, Raymond Jones, for failure to appear in court." Duke pulled RayBud up and began to walk him past the small crowd that'd gathered to gawk.

Brian was up now, brushing the gravel off his clothes. His brother looking on with a watchful eye. Quick asked Brian if he was okay, and of course, he got a dismissive wave. If any of them were hurt, they'd deal with it later.

Dana pulled up to the curb with the gutted out truck and helped Duke frisk their skip before loading a still screaming

RayBud into the back. There were a few people standing back with their cell phones raised high, recording their every move, but Quick didn't give a damn. That was a regular occurrence. RayBud was a coke dealer who didn't mind that ninety percent of his clientele were high school kids. Now he was off the streets. They deserved medals. Let them shoot their cell phone video; he'd love to star on the six o'clock news.

Speaking of six o'clock… Quick checked his new hi-tech watch. It was a little past one. Dana had transport duty today, so Quick's day was officially over. He'd drop off Duke at the office and then he'd handle a few things before he picked up his date.

Quick waited for Duke to check on Brian and Ford. They confirmed they were both alright and said they'd head back to the office to handle the last of the paperwork. Real team players.

When Dana pulled away from the curb, Duke and he made the short trek back to his vehicle. "Back to the office."

"Um. Drop me off at the hospital," Duke said, now checking his own timepiece. "I'm a little behind."

"Hospital? Why?"

"I'm cool. It's just a checkup. I had planned on rescheduling, but Vaughan wasn't having it."

Quick's mood rose even higher. "Oh, no problem. I'll take you, even walk you inside."

"I think I can manage, buddy."

"No. I insist."

"I just bet you fuckin' do." Duke laughed.

Quick didn't care that he and Cayson already had plans to see each other later. He missed him. He'd only admit that to himself right now, though.

# CHAPTER FIFTEEN

*Cayson*

"Dr. Chauncey, your two o'clock is here," Nania's professional voice echoed through his intercom.

Thank god. Last appointment until Monday. Cayson smoothed down his light blue tie and waited for Duke to come in. There was the sharp rap of knuckles on his door before it opened. As soon as Duke cleared the doorway, Cayson greeted him with a sincere smile, but it soon turned megawatt when Quick followed Duke in.

He stood and shook Duke's hand before hugging him briefly in greeting, like he always did. "Good to see you, Duke. I see you brought company." Cayson gave Quick a personal wink and got a charming one right back. He wanted to lean in and kiss Quick, and maybe even rut on his thigh for a few seconds. There was something about those guys when they walked around, towering over everyone, like they were gods of the universe, in all that black with weapons hanging off of them. You'd think the apocalypse was right outside the safe confines of the hospital. The large, bold white letters, spelling BOUNTY HUNTER across their chests made you want to never miss a scheduled court date if they were going to send men who looked like Duke and Quick to get you.

With one final look of approval thrown Quick's way, Cayson overcame the urge to touch the big man and walked back behind his desk. Duke was here in a professional capacity, so he'd act as such. He gestured for Duke and Quick to get comfortable. Duke sat down in his usual chair in front of Cayson's desk and Quick sat on the couch, crossing his leg and resting his boot on the opposite knee. Yes, the same couch he'd been reclining on just last night when Quick rubbed the tension from his shoulders. Blinking, he cleared his throat, not wanting his hard dick to get to the point of painful.

"I hadn't planned on bringing company, Doc, but someone insisted on tagging along." Duke didn't look behind him, so he didn't notice Quick's middle finger aimed at the back of his head. He really was a roughneck. Cayson didn't mind the character trait at all. He made it feel so right to do something bad and wrong. True, Quick was a law-abiding citizen, but dressed like he was, Cayson felt it okay to indulge in a few fantasies.

Cayson was able to get through Duke's appointment quickly since they were only going over his lab results from his last visit. The man was in his prime and extremely healthy. His kidneys were functioning well, and looking through Duke's journal, he saw very little documentation of any complications. He was supposed to document any pain or even twinges he felt during his everyday routine. Cayson squinted at one particular entry, two weeks ago. "Are you still experiencing numbness in your right leg, Duke?" Cayson asked.

"No. I think it was a onetime thing. I may have been sitting too long."

Cayson watched Duke for a moment. "You sure?"

"Yeah. I'm good. I haven't felt it anymore, and even then, it only lasted a few minutes."

"Alright, then." Cayson closed the worn notebook and gave it back to Duke. His was a classic fairy tale story. Vaughan swept in like a white knight and saved Duke's life, in hopes they'd have a future together. Cayson was glad he'd got to be a part of that. It made all that time in isolation at medical school and residencies worth it. "If it happens again, please call. Don't wait until your next appointment. I'll want to get another MRI and see if there are any new developments."

Duke stood and clapped his hands once. "Sure thing, Doc." He turned to Quick. "Ready to go, buddy?"

"Sure." Quick stood and stretched his back. "I'll meet you out front."

"Good to see you, Duke. Everything looks fine. Make sure you see Nania to schedule your next appointment. You know the drill."

"Sure do."

When Duke closed the door behind him, Quick didn't waste a second before he had his arms around Cayson's waist, pulling him into him. Quick held him, caressed his back, his neck, dipping down, he placed a sugary sweet kiss on Cayson's cheek. "How'd your surgeries go this morning?"

Cayson adored that question. Smiling in the safety of Quick's arms, his cheek pressed against the hard steel that was Quick's chest, while he recalled his day. He absently fingered the gold bounty hunter star clipped to Quick's thick belt. He was enjoying their current position, so he took his time answering.

"It was good. It was routine, no complications."

"My brilliant surgeon." Quick kissed his forehead in praise, continuing his light massage.

"I-I actually had Dr. Joe as the anesthesiologist for my biopsy."

Quick stiffened before he pulled Cayson back, concern etched all over his gorgeous face. "What happened? Did he hurt you? Did he say some shit to you?" Quick wasn't yelling, but his posture shouted how upset he was.

"Nothing happened. No, he didn't hurt me; he didn't utter a word. Matter of fact, Joe acted like he'd never seen me before. I think he was more terrified than anything."

"Terrified?"

Cayson rubbed his hand over his chin, thinking about Joe's abnormal behavior. He should've known Cayson wouldn't out him. For years, they'd been civil, but mostly friendly colleagues. "Uh-huh. He came into the OR looking pale and sick. I gave him a curt nod, ya know. Kinda saying hey. But he ignored me and turned around. He kept his back to me for the entire forty-five minute procedure."

"Fine. As long as he doesn't step out of bounds, I don't care how silly he acts." Quick pulled Cayson back to him. He loved how Quick used touch to express himself. Cayson was the same way. He loved being embraced, moved, and even manhandled. Quick tilted his chin up. "I thought about you today."

"You did?" Cayson grinned. Hell. He really shouldn't be that happy about such a very broad statement. Quick could've thought anything about him, and here he was prematurely celebrating. Straitening himself he asked, "What did you think?"

"Well, I made the preparations for our date tonight, and I couldn't help but picture you happy and leaning into me all night while I wine and dine you." Quick's smile was amazing. Behind those full lips were pretty white teeth, although the bottom ones were a little crowded. Cayson felt it gave Quick more character.

"I can't wait. I'm looking forward to it." Cayson looked Quick in his eyes and said honestly, "I thought about you, too."

Quick didn't ask what about, like he'd done. Instead, his bounty hunter leaned in and let his tongue do the talking. Cayson groaned as soon as Quick's tongue met his. Oh, god, he tasted wild and new. Cayson linked his hands behind Quick's neck and let him take the reins while he enjoyed the exciting new ride. His stomach rose and fell as if he were on a rollercoaster at Busch Gardens.

"Taste so damn good," Quick murmured against Cayson's mouth before he delved in again.

Cayson knew he needed to put a stop to this. This wasn't the time or place for intimacy. He knew of several doctors who fucked in the hospital – albeit nurses – or spouses who showed up in the guise of simply bringing a surgeon dinner, all the while, they're naked under their long cashmere coats. Cayson had class, if nothing else. He wouldn't be caught bare-assed, bent over his desk. He was the one to break the kiss next, but Quick wasn't having it.

"I'm not done," he said in his roughened tone, pulling Cayson back in. His lust and passion flowed off him in waves, filling a huge void within Cayson. He wasn't done either, not by a long shot, but he needed to have this exact moment in his living room, not in his office with his nurse just outside the door.

"I don't want you to be done, either. But can we continue a little more of that tonight?" Cayson blushed.

Quick clasped both of Cayson's hands and removed them from behind his neck, placing a quick couple kisses on his knuckles before releasing him. "You can have whatever you want tonight. I promise."

Cayson was starting to become fond of Quick's promises. At least it wasn't just verbiage, or a common term he threw out on a whim. Quick meant it. If he promised, it'd be done. Quick was a confident, sure man. Just the type of man he needed in his life. Had always wanted, but didn't find. Quick may have gotten off to a rocky start, but Cayson couldn't keep holding it over the man's head. He'd accepted Quick's apology, now he needed to forget about the past and focus on a future. He wasn't over the hill. He had a lot of good years left. Years he didn't want to spend alone, no matter what pep talk he gave himself. He needed to be positive. He wasn't going on this date with animosity in his heart. He wanted to give him and Quick a real fighting chance.

Quick hugged him tight one last time before he let his hands go.

Cayson took off his white lab coat and hung it on the coat rack behind his door and grabbed his blazer and his parka. He was done for the day, and he chuckled at Quick's surprised smile when he noticed that Cayson was leaving with him.

"You're done for the day?"

"I am." Cayson flicked off the light switch and closed his door, double-checking it was locked. "Finished the last of my rounds right before you got here."

Duke was standing there charming Nania while he waited patiently for Quick. Cayson only made brief eye contact with a smug, slightly amused Duke. It was as if the man saw through the reinforced steel that was his office door and watched him tongue down his best friend.

"All set?" Duke looked back and forth between them.

Cayson sucked his kiss-swollen bottom lip into his mouth, trying to hide it. It was useless. He'd been kissed until he was gasping for breath, and there was no hiding that. Cayson released his pink lip and gave Duke a wary smile.

"We're outta here," Quick confirmed.

With Quick's steady hand on the small of Cayson's back, he plucked the two pink message slips from Nania's inbox as he bid her a goodnight.

"Goodnight, Dr. Chauncey. Have a good weekend. And come back on Monday as happy as you were today. Whatever you took this morning worked wonders for your mood." She laughed loud, making Cayson blush.

Of course. Cayson could fell the warmth all over his neck and at the tips of his ears. Quick walked alongside him, and looked down to wink his appreciation at what he'd heard. There was only one reason Cayson was so happy today, and it was because of his hearty dose of Roman Webb right before it started.

Duke nodded at Quick and put his hand up for a high five, then left his flat palm up for Cayson too. "Bout damn time you guys got that party started. Put it up, Doc." Cayson laughed, but he slapped Duke's hand anyway. He felt like one of the guys. At least that's how he felt on the inside, but the outward appearance – him walking with two huge bounty hunters down the hall – made him look like he was being escorted to jail.

"Where are you parked?" Cayson asked Quick. Remembering the man had insisted on driving Cayson to work instead of letting him drive himself. It was okay. Cayson could've gotten a ride home with anyone. He wasn't far away at all. Walking distance if it weren't so brisk out.

"I'm in visitors' parking."

"Let's cut through the ER, it's faster. Not interested in the scenic route today," Cayson said, trying to avoid the busy main lobby.

When Cayson came through the ever-swinging double doors of the emergency room, he was met with quite a few curious, but mostly shocked stares from the nurses and a couple over-worked doctors.

"Dr. Chauncey. Everything okay?" Renee asked him. Standing to get a better look at his large escorts. That woman was the biggest gossipmonger. She wasn't concerned for him; she wanted scoop to talk about on her lunch break.

"Yes, Renee. I'm fine, thank you." Cayson kept his stride, and only managed to get another twenty feet before he was blocked by the ER's security guard. Cayson was familiar with the stout man, but couldn't say he knew him.

"Is there a problem?" he asked, jutting out his chest, his shiny silver badge gleaming in the harsh fluorescent lighting as though he polished it every night.

Duke scoffed at the guard and Cayson elbowed him in the arm for it. "I'm not being arrested, they're friends." Cayson stood in front of Quick to sort any confusion, and Quick eased in right behind Cayson and placed a protective arm over his chest. The security officer was fast to get the hint and moved aside.

"Dr. Chauncey, introduce us to your *friends*," Renee purred, leaning over the nurse's counter, eyeing Duke and Quick like they were on auction. *Why did I come this way, again?* Renee not so subtly licked her lips, and Cayson almost busted out laughing. If she only knew.

Cayson was known as a really nice guy in the hospital. All the nurses loved when he came down to help out. He may not have had Joe's last name, he wasn't a Wellington, with medical-administrative-clout flowing out of his ears, but he was a highly sought after nephrologist. He'd been flown all over the country to give consultations or second opinions. Despite what Dr. Joe thought, Cayson was doing just fine on his own. Most everyone enjoyed working with him, simply because he respected them. He didn't bark at the nurses, and the doctors didn't mind that he'd cover for any of them in a heartbeat.

"Hey, you. In the red tie, behind that computer. Don't I know you?" Cayson craned his neck, looking at Quick to see who he was talking too.

Following Quick's line of sight, he spotted Dr. Joe, practically hiding behind one of the computers in the HUB. "Roman. Don't," Cayson admonished seriously, but Quick was ignoring him.

"Is that him?" Duke whispered, oblivious to Cayson's pleading. He'd had a feeling Quick would tell Duke about Joe and what happened last night, but he didn't think they'd gang up on the man.

"That's him, alright." Quick wasn't loud, but he wasn't quiet, either. They now had the attention of the entire damn department. Everyone turned and looked at Dr. Joe, wondering what Quick was referring too. Intrigued. Trying to figure out the relationship between the four of them.

Quick snapped his fingers as if he was really contemplating. "I have seen your face somewhere before, haven't I?"

Dr. Joe looked as sick as the patients, his usual peach coloring rapidly leaving his face, making it appear transparent and gray. Joe shook his head in mortification, looking around at all the eyes now trained on him. It was Joe's biggest nightmare come true – he was going to be outed. There was no way Cayson was going to let that happen.

Cayson put his back to the staff and looked up at Quick's eyes, hoping he'd pay attention. "Don't do this, please. Leave him alone. If you have any respect for me. Don't do this," Cayson begged on Joe's behalf. Sure, Joe had done him wrong on more than a few occasions, but this wasn't the way to get even. The game Quick and Duke were playing with Joe wasn't going to end well. Everyone would lose.

Quick finally looked down at Cayson. "Stop it. Stop, now."

Duke flicked his head in the direction they'd been walking. "Let's go, Rome. That's not who you think it is."

Quick held Joe's eyes, putting his huge arm protectively around Cayson's shoulders. Now Cayson's own face was blooming bright with color and embarrassment.

"No. You're right." Although they were talking to each other, Duke and Quick kept their hunter eyes on Joe. Whatever private cryptic message they were trying to relay to Joe, Cayson didn't think he got it. "That's not him. Sorry man. Thought you were someone else."

As soon as Cayson got outside, he walked off in the other direction, leaving a laughing Duke and Quick to themselves. If they thought that was funny, Cayson wanted nothing to do with them. If that wasn't a form of bullying, he didn't know what was. Joe probably would've preferred they stuff him in his locker than embarrass him in front of his peers.

# CHAPTER SIXTEEN

*Quick*

"Uh-oh." Duke pointed at Cayson's retreating back and Quick spun around, his laughter dying fast, replaced with confusion. He wondered where his handsome doctor was rushing off too, and without him. He told Duke to get in the truck, while he jogged up the sidewalk and caught up with Cayson.

Quick hooked Cayson's arm and spun him around to talk to him. The look he got felt like a slap across his face. Lowering his head, he knew already why Cayson was mad, and decided to let him have it.

"If you are going to humiliate me in my place of business, then I'd prefer you not visit, Roman." Cayson put one hand on his hip, the other he pointed back towards the ER's doors. "What was that in there?"

"I wasn't trying to humiliate you, babe. I was giving the good ole doctor there a dose of his own medicine. I'm sure it was a very hard pill for him to swallow." Quick rubbed Cayson's shoulder, inching in closer to him. He lowered his voice, hoping to hurry up and diffuse this bomb before it exploded and got out of hand. "Cays, I sure don't recall Dr. Joe, or whatever, feeling this bad when he yelled out your secrets to your entire street. Did he even bother to apologize? No. Instead, he treated you like nothing again today."

"None of that concerns *you*. That's my business. Not yours. I didn't ask you to fix this, Rome. I don't need you to!" Cayson argued.

"I apologize. It was juvenile and unnecessary. I was only thinking of you, and that makes me do crazy things. It makes me overprotective. Makes me want to right all the wrongs done to you." Quick chuckled mirthlessly. "I thought you'd want to see him squirm a bit, for a change."

Cayson turned his head, but Quick caught a glimpse of that lopsided grin. He'd only wanted to show Cayson he was on his side and he'd pay back anyone who hurt him. But, Cayson was right. He was a well-liked and respected man at work. He would never want him to lose any of his colleagues' admiration. Next time he encountered Dr. Joe, he'd make sure it was in a territory he controlled. Revenge is a dish best served cold. Meaning completely unexpected and not so much immediate. He'd speak with Duke and Ford about this later. Surely they'd come up with something fitting for Joe's crime against someone they admired.

"Come on. Don't walk. Let me drive you home, okay?"

Cayson looked reluctant to agree until Quick gripped the back of Cayson's head and pulled him in for a kiss that showed him just how truly sorry he was for upsetting him. He felt the doctor's hands on his waist, drawing him in even closer until their stomachs and chests were flush together. Quick heard Cayson's moan and it went straight to his nuts. He regretfully released Cayson, not wanting to start anything lewd in a surveillance-monitored parking lot. "Unless you really want some admin problems, I think we should continue this kiss later, too."

"You know, kissing me isn't going to get you out of hot water every time," Cayson said defiantly, leading them back towards the truck.

Quick smirked smugly. Loving that Cayson was speaking of them in the future tense. "But did it work this time?"

"Yes."

Duke was already in the driver seat, so Quick opened the passenger doors, helping Cayson into the back of the large cab.

After they fastened their belts, Duke took off in the direction of the main road. Quick could see an impish grin on his best friend's face out of the corner of his eye and knew he was ready to start in on him with some good-natured ribbing. "Should we stop by the florist on the way, Rome?"

"Fuck off," Quick snarled, turning and giving Cayson a look that promised payback, since he thought Duke's joke was so hysterical. Duke was laughing so hard, Cayson right along with him; he could barely give Duke the directions to his house in Inman.

When they pulled up to Cayson's fence, Quick was the first one to see the large gold box on Cayson's doorstep with a huge yellow bow tied around it. "What the hell?" Quick and Duke were out of the truck at the same time. It was amazing how tuned in to each other they were. Years of a partnership, devoid of any romance, only pure trust and loyalty to a brother, made them a dangerous duo.

"From him, you think?" Duke asked, hopping the locked gate just as easily as Quick did.

"Why do you keep doing that?" Cayson wondered. Pulling his keys out of his messenger bag and unlocking his gate. "It does open, ya know."

Quick picked up the box, ripping the card from where it was tucked inside the ribbon.

"Um. Do you mind?" Cayson raced up the steps and snatched the card from Quick's hand, flipping the blank envelope over while unlocking his front door.

"Does good ole Joe have a key to your place?" Quick hated to ask that question, dreading an answer he didn't want to hear, but it was necessary.

"No. He doesn't. Only to the gate."

"Get it back," Quick ordered.

Cayson looked at him like he'd lost his damn mind and Quick rushed to back-pedal. Cayson didn't need to be told what to do; he'd probably gotten enough of that from previous partners. "I'm sorry. Too much. I mean, he doesn't need his key anymore, right?"

"Right," Cayson confirmed, letting Duke and Quick in behind him.

Quick looked around, satisfied that no one had been inside. Everything was exactly how they'd left it that morning. Cayson's half-eaten bagel and Quick's coffee cup sat side by side on the kitchen island.

Duke set the obvious flower box on the living room table, standing back from it. Quick and Duke's eyes met over Cayson's head while he opened the box, revealing two dozen long stem red roses. More expensive than the bouquet he'd purchased. Cayson opened the card, and Quick was shameless when he leaned forward to read the almost unintelligible penmanship over his shoulder.

*I've changed. I miss you.*

*J.*

"Motherfucker!" Quick bit out. He was well aware now that red roses meant love.

"Calm down, Quick," Duke said cautiously. "Nothing wrong with a little friendly competition."

"I don't want competition," Quick grumbled.

"Not up for the challenge?" Cayson asked nonchalantly, tossing the entire box of flowers in the kitchen trashcan along with the note.

"I don't mind putting in the work, Doc. But I won't be made a fool of."

"Fair enough," Cayson agreed.

"Duke. Can you wait for me in the truck?"

Duke nodded and left after saying a short goodbye to his doctor.

"Cays. Come're." Quick took Cayson's hand and led him back over to the couch. He was going to wait to give this to Cayson after their date but it suddenly felt appropriate right now. The unease he felt in his stomach was his instincts. Hair didn't raise on his neck or arms when he sensed danger. No. Quick felt it in the pit of his stomach. Apprehension about leaving Cayson right now felt like lead weight in his belly. He couldn't treat his doctor like a child. He was a man. A man who could handle his own affairs. As his hopefully future boyfriend, Quick's job was to back him up, not push him aside and take over his life for him. Obviously, he'd done fine all this time without Quick. If he wasn't careful, Cayson would continue on without him.

Quick pulled out the military sports watch and showed it to Cayson.

"Are you giving me a watch?" Cayson was smiling, but he looked confused, too.

"This watch is exactly the same as mine. It's a tracking device."

Cayson blinked incredulously. "Excuse me?"

"Easy. Let me explain." Quick put a calming hand on Cayson's thigh, rubbing absently while he explained all the features.

"I'm not trying to keep tabs on you, babe. I just want you to have a way to contact help immediately, if you need too."

"I can simply call."

"Emergencies don't always happen around a phone."

"I've never needed anything like this, Rome. I have no enemies."

"Are you sure?"

"Well, if you're thinking of someone in particular. I'd still say no. I'm not afraid of Joe."

"Being careful doesn't have a damn thing to do with being afraid. We all have the same ones on our wrists." Quick unhooked Cayson's elegant watch and replaced it with the new one. One he hoped he'd never have to use. If Quick was nothing else, he was cautious. He refused to take second chances. Not with Cayson, he wouldn't. He couldn't.

"The last button here only alerts me. If you push and hold it, your location will flash across my watch. If you push this one, you'll have five men barreling in your direction within seconds."

"God, no. Okay, so never hold that button down. I'm only wearing it because it's kinda James Bondish. I like the pearl and gold. But I know I won't need it."

"That's all I want." Quick hooked his arm around Cayson, their thighs pressed next to each other. Quick dipped down, seeking out Cayson's mouth. "I gotta drop Duke off and get home to change. I'll be back in a couple hours." Quick spoke against Cayson's temple, kissing him gently there and on his forehead before he stood and walked back towards the front door.

"Okay," Cayson replied softly.

Six o'clock couldn't get here fast enough to suit Quick. He needed uninterrupted time with his new man. Time to show him how much better life would be with him at his side. Someone that'd be proud to show him off. Dr. Cayson Chauncey was too wonderful to be someone's secret lover.

# CHAPTER SEVENTEEN

*Cayson*

He didn't even take the watch off when he showered. Quick told him to make it a part of his skin, and since he couldn't take that off, he wouldn't take off the watch, either. He was too wired to nap, so Cayson turned on the radio in his room to a classic rock station. He loved all kinds of music, but when he was in a really good mood, he wanted to hear some Tom Petty, Steve Miller, or someone equally good. He wasn't much of a dancer, but he could bob his head to the beat.

The music buoyed his mood tenfold, and he got more and more excited as six grew nearer. He was showered, shaved, and dressed in under an hour. He opted for dark blue jeans and a white and tan collared shirt. He left it untucked, throwing a camel corduroy blazer over it. Not knowing how much walking they'd do, he chose his comfortable, tan casual shoes. He hadn't worn cologne in ages, but he still had a few dusty bottles in his bathroom drawer. Working in a hospital, it was courteous to the patients not to wear overpowering fragrances. He was so out of date. Checking the names of each one, he froze when he saw Stetson fading sadly on one of the bottles. Not that it was a bad fragrance; it was just so damn old. Cayson had the original one with the cowboy and horse on the label. *Jesus. I bought that bottle in college.* There was no way Cayson was putting any of that on. He'd probably have to treat himself for chemical burns if he did.

He yelled, "Ah-ha!" when he picked up the Kenneth Cole cologne giftset with aftershave that he'd got from the Pollyanna his nurse made him participate in last Christmas. Right now, he was so happy she did. He gave the cologne a sniff before he sprayed a fine mist around his collar. That was plenty. He walked around with a glass of Port in his hand while the Red Hot Chili Peppers screamed through his Dolby speakers about giving it away now. He startled slightly at the sound of his doorbell. It was only five forty. Quick was early. Thank goodness. Because, if Quick was even one minute late, Cayson would already be nervous about being stood up.

Cayson opened the door without even a who is it? Jerking to a pause when he saw Dr. Joe standing there, looking nervous and uncomfortable.

"Did you get my flowers?" Joe asked quietly, anxiously looking around, like someone was in Cayson's hedges with a long-range mic and a TMZ camera. "Can I come in?" Joe finally asked after Cayson just stared at him through his storm door.

"I was just getting ready to leave, Joe. This isn't a good time."

Joe finally got a good look at Cayson, narrowing his eyes with realization. "Are you going out with him?" Joe said the word "him" like some would say the word "shit." With pure disgust.

"That's none of your business." Cayson stepped out onto the porch and closed his door behind him. There was no way he was about to get caught in the house alone with Joe when his date would be there any minute.

"It is my business. You are going to get yourself in a world of trouble, Cayson. Traipsing around with those two thugs at the hospital this afternoon. Are you trying to lose your license?"

Cayson barked a sad laugh. "You keep using the word thug to describe my friends – one of whom is my patient – and I don't appreciate it." Quick had been sticking up for Cayson; maybe it was time Cayson did the same for him. "They are bounty hunters. Didn't you see their uniforms?"

"That's just a cover occupation for hoodlums who want to fight and hurt people legally."

"My gosh. Joe, you do know bounty hunters put criminals back in jail when they try to evade going to court? I mean, that's common knowledge. I would hardly say they're hoodlums. I sleep better knowing there are occupations like that out there to keep people safe."

Joe shook his head pityingly, as if Cayson were the most naïve person in the world. "You always have been too trusting, Cayson. But I'm not going to keep giving you chances," he said harshly.

"I didn't ask for a chance at anything, Joe."

"I mean it, dangit!"

"Joe, settle down. I don't understand any of this." Cayson took a step back; needing distance between him and a man he thought was his friend. That was the only thing Cayson had ever been naïve about. Joe was turning that frightening shade of red again, and Cayson noticed his fists were balled up and shaking at his sides. Joe was being completely irrational, and Cayson hated to admit it, but he was nervous. He wasn't afraid. He and Joe were rather equally matched in size and weight. Cayson actually had a few extra pounds of muscle, but he wasn't a fighter. Violence only begat more violence. Wasn't that taught in grade school now?

Joe got right in Cayson's face, making him rear back to keep their mouths from being too close. Joe stabbed a long, accusing finger at Cayson's chest. His old friend's fury was palpable, and it choked Cayson, gripped him, and tore at his conscience. There was no way he could give Joe another chance. He wasn't a glutton for punishment. He realized then that he was slowly but surely losing a friend, and all Cayson could think about at the moment was where in public Quick was taking him.

Spittle flew out of Joe's mouth and landed on Cayson's chin as he hurled more insults and fired off threats. "I'm not coming back if I leave this time!"

"That's a promise I'm going to make sure you keep."

Quick's voice cut through Joe's fussing, and the tone he used sounded like he already had a short leash on his anger. The gate was still open, and Quick was through it and at Cayson's side in seconds. Damn, the man looked fine as wine. Dressed casually, but still very handsome. Dark slacks and a dark gray ribbed turtleneck under his jet-black pea coat. Cayson was stunned stupid because it was the first time he recalled seeing Quick's hair loose and flowing across his shoulders. He looked like Cayson's Renegade Highlander fantasy come to life.

"I'm talking to Dr. Chauncey, not you." Joe stood his ground in front of Quick, but he'd lowered his voice.

"Leave. Now. Or else I'm going to show you just how thuggish I can be," Quick said. His teeth clenched as he spoke, as if he were trying not to raise his voice.

"I'm not scared of you, meathead. You thought you were so cute in the ER today, but I can play dirty, too," Joe threatened uselessly. Cayson didn't think Quick was the kind of guy who scared easily, and his non-reaction proved it.

"You sure you want to dance this dance with me, Ana?"

Joe tightened his eyes at the name, and Quick laughed right in his face. "You're an anesthesiologist, right? Thought I'd call you Ana for short. And since you act like a bitch." Quick over-annunciated the last word. "I thought it fitting."

Cayson couldn't stop the abrupt laugh that escaped his mouth, but tried to disguise it with a cough.

"Fine. Have your fun, now." Joe looked around Quick's large frame, throwing his next threat at Cayson. "This isn't over."

Maybe Joe shouldn't have said that, because Quick went from zero to a hundred in a second. When Joe moved to leave, Quick grabbed him by the lapels of his suit jacket and pulled Joe so close to his mouth that to anyone watching on from a distance, it looked like they were getting ready to share a passionate kiss. Joe was up on his tiptoes, trying to pry himself out of the hold. Quick's mouth was close to Joe's ear, stating something that Cayson couldn't make out. Only the squinting of Joe's eyes told Cayson that whatever Quick was saying to him, Joe didn't agree with or appreciate at all. He finally jerked himself out of Quick's tight grip and hurried down the rest of the stairs and out the gate. He looked back for a second, and Quick nodded before Joe turned back and got in his Mercedes S Class and carefully followed every traffic law that applied when he pulled away from the curb and drove exactly the speed limit out of Cayson's neighborhood.

"Dumbass," Quick grumbled. "Can't even make a threatening exit. Who puts on a blinker to pull away from a curb?"

Quick turned and looked Cayson up and down as if ensuring he was alright. Slowly lifting his right wrist, Quick pulled up Cayson's sleeve to see if he had the watch on. "Why didn't you call me?"

"You said this was for emergencies. I had everything handled." Cayson smiled. He was too excited to be going out on a date to worry about what'd just transpired between his new beau and his old friend.

"What did you say to him just now?" Cayson asked, running his hand mesmerizingly through Quick's soft mane. It looked so full and beautiful, like he could've starred in a hair conditioner commercial. It was such an erotic, refreshing change from Quick's usual ponytail.

"It's of no consequence. Now get inside, I want to get a good, long look at you." Quick's eyes turned hazy with his hunger and Cayson wanted to tell him to cancel all reservations and take him upstairs and not let him out of bed until he could barely walk.

As soon as they were back inside, Quick had Cayson's back against the door and his hands all over his body before he could ask another question.

"Damn, you smell good... and you look... fuck, Cays. You look so fuckin' beautiful." Quick fingered Cayson's pale pink bottom lip with the pad of his thumb while he kissed him.

# CHAPTER EIGHTEEN

*Quick*

When Quick pulled up to the curb and saw Joe up in Cayson's face, he had to count to ten before he could get out of his truck. He was a shoot first; ask questions later kind of guy, especially when he felt threatened. Quick growled low in his throat as he watched his man lean away when Joe advanced. Damnit. This guy was like butt fucking without the lube. A straight pain in the ass. Couldn't the bastard take a hint?

After he'd said his piece, Quick had been fine to let Joe leave. He was ready for his date to start, so he wasn't going to provoke the already scared man. But when he hurled that last threat at Cayson, Quick's leash broke and his anger came out full force, like lava bursting from an awakened volcano.

Before he knew it, he had Joe in his grips and it felt amazing. He wanted to lift him and throw him off the porch again, but decided on something even better. Something to make Joe think the rest of the night.

With his mouth close to Joe's ear, Quick made sure his voice was low enough that Cayson couldn't hear what he said. "You're a real idiot, Ana. Cayson is mine now. You let him slip through your little bitch-scared hands, now I've got him." Quick's voice was rough and deadly. If the devil spoke aloud, he'd probably sound like Quick did at that moment. "Rest assured. I'm gonna fuck Cays so good, and so hard, he's going to forget all about you, Ana. I promise you that."

Joe thought he'd yanked himself out of Quick's grip, but he'd let the man go when he was finished. He wanted Joe to go stew over what he'd just said. While he had no intentions of trying to sleep with Cayson on only their second date, Joe didn't have to know that. But, hell, the way Cayson was sucking on Quick's tongue right now, he wasn't one hundred percent sure how the night was going to end. Both of them seemed starved for a little intimacy.

Cayson moaned boldly, writhing against Quick's body like a wolf marking its mate. "You look really nice, Rome," Cayson said breathlessly. "I'm trying not to attack you."

Quick laughed. Now, that would be a sparring match he'd happily volunteer for, if it was in the bedroom.

"I told myself I'd be good, but you are making it very difficult." Quick bent even lower and chanced his luck, hoping he didn't get a hard shove in retaliation. He ran both hands down Cayson's sides and around to the small of his back. Quick kneaded the taut muscles there first, before he worked his hands over the thick mounds of Cayson's ass. The loud gasp made him chuckle softly in the crook of Cayson's clean neck. "Feels good?" Quick murmured.

"Yes. God, yes," Cayson hissed while Quick continued massaging his ass.

"I want you. I want all of you, Cays. Not just behind closed doors. I want everything I've been missing for so long." Quick wasn't scared to claim what he wanted. He was a grown ass man, and he knew who and what he was. A bisexual man who was too old to act like he didn't know his own mind. He'd been married for seven long years before he decided his wife deserved a man who could give her what she deserved... and so did he.

"Damn, it's been a long time." Quick dragged his middle finger up Cayson's seam, mimicking the video he'd watched earlier. But Cayson's response was so much better than the man on camera. The reaction was genuine longing and yearning from deep down in his doctor. It pulled on Quick's heart and his resolve. How dare that prick starve Cayson of this? For what? Quick could see the plea for more in his sweet surgeon's blue eyes. *I'm right there with you Cays.*

"Jesus Christ you taste so good. Before I get ahead of myself, let's go to dinner. I need to talk. We need to talk." Quick waited while Cayson turned everything off in his home and locked the front door. With his hand tightly clasped around Cayson's, he made sure the coast was clear of Ana before he walked them to his truck and headed for downtown Atlanta on a Friday night.

~~~~~~~~~~

If it wouldn't've looked silly, Cayson would've been bouncing with anticipation while he rode with Quick to The Foxhole. A night out on a real date. He didn't count the times he'd been invited to men's homes, or they asked to come to his place. He didn't count the secluded groping sessions on the far outskirts of the town where he went to college. None of those were dates. A date was what Quick was giving him now. And it only took him god knows how many damn years. Quick parked at 14th and Piedmont, telling Cayson it was a good night to walk. The Foxhole was on the street parallel to Piedmont, so he was glad he'd chosen to wear his comfortable shoes.

Quick held his hand out for Cayson, and he gladly took it.

"Is this okay?" Quick asked, flicking his head at their joined hands when he began to walk towards the main road.

"Absolutely." Cayson hid his smile as he and Quick walked amongst all the other date goers. They got a few glances at their closeness, but Quick was oblivious. He looked as if he hadn't a care in the world. Cayson supposed growing up the biggest and strongest, you didn't worry about being assaulted because of your orientation. Quick maneuvered them around people, while he kept a protective arm over Cayson's shoulders. "I hope you're hungry. This place has the best food," Quick said, kissing the top of his head. He slowed down when they got to a wooden door, painted to look like a foxhole. A petite lady in dark stockings and a pretty, short black dress addressed them politely when they approached her hostess stand.

Quick spoke confidently, "I have reservations under Webb."

The woman looked down and flipped through a couple pages before replying, "Yes, sir. We have you all ready." She gave them a huge smile through her bright red lips and pointed in the direction of a roped off booth. Quick followed right behind the hostesses, still clasping Cayson's hand.

The atmosphere was perfect for a first date. The restaurant was dark, with only a few recessed lights dimmed low above their heads and two votive candles on the table. It was plenty enough light to set a romantic mood. Cayson was pleasantly surprised when they were shown the best seat in the house. It was towards the back, against the wall in the far left corner. A beautiful rock garden fireplace was built into the wall next to their table, and Cayson sighed, welcoming the warmth. He removed his heavy coat, keeping his blazer on and slid into the horseshoe-shaped booth, Quick easing in right next to him, picking up Cayson's hand and kissing his palm before he released it to take the menus. The restaurant was small, but warm and cozy. Several four top tables were spread throughout the minimal space, but Cayson loved the coloring. All dark reds and earth tones. There was a small musical trio nestled in the corner of the tiny dance floor. A violinist, a keyboard player and a saxophonist serenaded the diners with soothing melodies like you might hear in a spa. When Quick said the place had live music, Cayson thought it was going to be something like a Hall and Oats cover band, or similar to that.

"James will be your server this evening. You gentlemen enjoy." The lady reached up and pulled a privacy curtain, closing them off from any curious eyes.

"Oh, nice." Cayson grinned. "We need privacy?"

"I thought it'd make you more comfortable when I did this." Quick held Cayson's waist with one hand, the other palm cupped his cheek while he kissed him on the corner of his mouth, before moving down his jaw to his sensitive neck. "I love how good you smell. Mmm, how good you taste."

He was so glad he chose the Kenneth Cole instead of the Stetson. Cayson closed his eyes, nuzzling closer to Quick's large body. He felt so good, he could barely keep a lid on his emotions. The privacy curtain didn't offend him. It only made him blush more, because he had a feeling people knew what was going on behind that partition. Quick didn't hesitate to show everyone in the restaurant that they were there as a couple, not buddies.

"Thank you, Rome. This is really... really nice. I'm overwhelmed," Cayson said softly against Quick's lips.

"Why are you overwhelmed?"

Cayson didn't get a chance to answer, because just then their waiter tapped on the side of the booth and waited for Quick's okay before he pulled the curtain back just enough for him to speak to them.

"Good evening. I'm James. Welcome to The Foxhole. Can I get you started with something to drink?"

Quick had his arm draped over the back of the booth, making it so easy for Cayson to lean into his side. "What do you want to drink, babe?"

*Babe.* "I'll have a water and a scotch on the rocks." He felt like being daring tonight. He always kept a fine bottle of scotch in his liquor cabinet, but rarely indulged. For Cayson, tonight was all about the adventure. He'd do all the things he normally didn't. It was a long time overdue for him.

"Is Johnnie Walker, okay, sir?" The waiter asked, scribbling in his notepad.

"Perfect."

"I'll have the same. And I'd like the stuffed mushrooms to start as well." Quick ordered and Cayson nodded his head in agreement, he loved stuffed mushrooms.

"Would you like me to leave the curtain open?" James asked, not the slightest bit offended by their closeness. This was a world Cayson never knew existed. Acceptance. Tolerance.

Quick sweetly caressed Cayson's jaw, looking into his eyes when he answered the waiter. "Closed please."

"I'll be back with your drinks in just a moment."

As soon as the waiter left, Quick was on him again. He hadn't made out with a man in quite some time, and it made him feel sexy and desirable. Joe wasn't a fan of kissing. He'd do it, but it was obvious he felt like it was a chore. With Quick, it was as if he used his mouth to say what he couldn't verbalize, and Cayson was okay with that. Very okay.

When they came up for air, Cayson had one hand tangled in the long strands hanging down Quick's broad back, his other pressed firmly against his chest. When Cayson bit Quick on his jaw, he was rewarded with a sensual growl, which had a tantalizing effect on his balls. Pausing their kiss, Cayson had no other choice but to confess. He simply couldn't hold it in anymore. "I want you, Roman."

"You can have anything you want." Quick kept his arm behind Cayson, but his other hand was beneath the table, slowly sliding up Cayson's inner thigh towards his aching nuts.

"Fuck. I'm trying to do this right." Cayson grimaced. He wasn't supposed to be inviting Quick to his home. Not right now. He was worth the wait. If Quick really wanted him... he'd wait.

"Tell me what you're thinking? It looks serious."

"Well. I was thinking that—"

"Your drinks, sirs. And your appetizer," their waiter announced, removing their items from a tray balanced on his shoulder. When he had placed their drinks in front of them, he asked if they wanted to hear the specials.

"Sure," Quick replied for both of them.

After they'd heard the specials, the trio started playing a tune that was soulful and mellow and Cayson found himself swaying to the relaxing sounds. He watched as patrons went up to the tiny stage and dropped bills into the big bowl, which served as the band's tip jar.

"How's the pasta sound to you, sweetheart?" Quick asked, still surveying the menu.

Cayson turned back to Quick, reeling inside at the terms of endearment he'd used right in front of the server. This was such a unique experience; Cayson had to keep telling himself to lighten up. He was turning into a mushy, lovesick mess. Sweetheart and babe? Really? He used to hate when he heard people refer to their spouses or partners like that. Now he realized he didn't hate it, he was simply being a hater. A jealous hater.

Quick didn't appear worried about being out in public with him. This was what he'd been waiting for. *Just relax and enjoy it.* "Pasta?" He loved linguine. Throw in some fresh seafood and he'd love it even more. "Yeah. Good choice." Handing the menus back to the waiter, he confirmed their order before closing the thick, red curtain back.

Quick turned his body back towards him as if giving Cayson his full attention. "Talk to me."

Cayson smiled at Quick's bluntness. "What do you wanna talk about?"

"You."

Cayson bit his bottom lip, wondering how much he should really disclose on a second date.

"Unless you want me all over you, I suggest you let that bottom lip go and stop teasing me." Quick looked so serious that Cayson was nervous with excitement. Just the thought of what

Quick could do to him had him clenching his ass right there in the booth.

"Okay, then." Cayson let his lip slide from between his teeth. "Let's talk."

Quick reached out and popped another mushroom in his mouth, chewing loudly and talking with his mouth half-full. "You start."

Cayson laughed. His Quick was certainly rough around the edges, but he didn't mind. They weren't eating at the Savoy in Vegas, so Cayson put down his fork and started using his hands, too.

"There really isn't much to me, Rome. I'm rather boring, to be honest."

"I'm not bored. Matter of fact, it's been nothing but fireworks from you since we met. So knock off the 'boring' crap," Quick told him, using air quotes.

# CHAPTER NINETEEN

*Cayson*

Cayson let Quick place another decadent mushroom on his tongue. The way he watched him chew made Cayson squirm, made him feel like he was next on Quick's menu to devour. Those sexy green bedroom eyes would be his undoing.

"Exactly what kind of doctor are you?" Quick asked, jump-starting the conversation.

"I'm a surgical nephrologist."

"Kidney doctor."

"Exactly. Any and everything regarding the kidney."

"What made you choose that field?"

Cayson thought about it for a moment. "Well my mom passed a while back. A bad car accident. No siblings. So it was just my dad and me after that. My father did his best, but he was struggling with heartache. He adored my mom; she was everything… everything to both of us. I tried to be there for him, but I was never able to fill that hole created inside him when she died, because I had my own holes. She was the glue that held us together. She planned the vacations, the dinners, the outings. When she left, unfortunately, all that fun stuff we used to do as a family left with her. So, my father and I didn't talk or discuss our days. I went to school, he went to work, and then we came home and coexisted. Did that for years, until I went out of state for graduate school.

"Instead of letting all that depression consume me, I threw myself into school, and then medicine. I did nothing but academics and studying. Having to be the best at everything was my excuse for not socializing at all. That made for a lot of quiet, lonely nights. I'd become quite used to it, honestly. While I was in med school, my father was diagnosed with RCC, and I became obsessed with knowing everything there was to know about the kidney and its cancers. I was going to cure him myself if I had to. I knew he was all I had left. At that time, I wasn't able to accept the possibility of being completely alone."

Cayson released a sad sigh when Quick began to massage his neck. It was just what he needed to finish the story he'd kept to himself for so long. He wanted to be honest with Quick, but most of all he wanted to be honest with himself.

"What's RCC?" Quick asked, his voice back to the sweet, melodic baritone Cayson loved.

"Renal cell carcinoma, kidney cancer. By the time I could convince the stubborn old fool to fight it… it was too late."

"When did he die?"

"Six months ago," Cayson said softly, taking a long drink of his whisky. "I think he wanted to die, though. He was tired of fighting, I suppose, and lonely. I was gone, but even when I was there, I was a recluse." Cayson leaned in further when Quick placed a soft kiss on the side of his head, whispering how sorry he was for his loss. A part of this conversation seemed so silly and outdated, but another part felt cathartic. He'd not told this to anyone. Never had a chance to release those emotions. His father had been cremated and his ashes spread over the park where he'd married Cayson's mother. He coughed a fake laugh because it was better than letting the tears form. "It was a rough time. So, just like when my mom passed, I threw myself into medicine. Taking crazy hours to keep my mind off of personal things… off of being alone."

"You're not alone now, Cays. Can you handle that?" Quick was looking at him like he'd just asked the most important question of his life. He made sure Cayson was looking up at him before he spoke again. "Are you ready to be happy?"

He sat quietly, fully absorbing Quick's question while the soft sounds of the violin sang to his lonely soul. He wasn't lonely by choice. He had simply gotten used to it. Dating or having a normal social life for a medical student were practically unheard of, anyway. There was simply no time. A fast one-off here and there was the most that could be afforded. If you wanted to be the best, that is. Cayson wasn't the type to skate by, either. He graduated top of his class and went on to study with the best Nephrology department in the country at the University Hospital of Columbus and Cornell. Sowing wild oats didn't make him the successful doctor he was today. But it did make him the most desolate.

It didn't make much sense, that of all his life, it was at his age now that Cayson was craving a physical and emotional connection with someone. Hiding and sneaking around with Dr. Joe only made Cayson continue to feel like that young man who used to hide his problems and insecurities away in a medical journal. That guy was gone. There was Dr. Chauncey, the professional, who had everything he needed. Prestige, intelligence, and patients who adored him. All he'd worked so hard to achieve. But that left Cayson the man. A part of him which had been ignored and pushed to the back for far too long. Quick would be just for Cayson.

"Yes, Roman. I think I am ready."

~~~~~~~~

Quick listened intently while Cayson got increasingly comfortable and opened up to him. Vaughan told him not to bombard the conversation with a bunch of talk about himself. Quick's job was fun and full of excitement, but that didn't mean he should only tell his stories. The more Quick listened to Cayson over their entrees of seafood pasta, the more fascinating his doctor became. The things he knew and could do with his hands was awe-inspiring. All Quick could do was fight really well. What could he possibly have to offer the brilliant man beside him?

*Don't sell yourself short, Dad. You can give Dr. Chauncey something no one else has, that no one cared enough to give him.*

*What's that, Son? Please, do tell, because I'm at a loss here.*

*Romance, Pops. The doctor needs romance and you can give him more of that than he can handle.*

*But how?*

*Just do exactly what I say.*

*God help me.*

Quick let his son's words fade to the background. Their dinner was over and Quick had something planned for Cayson that he hoped didn't embarrass the shit out of both of them. He'd told Vaughan it was a little over the top for a private guy like him, but Cayson had dealt with privacy for long enough. He needed a bold lover. Quick could understand that, so he'd listened to what his son had to say. That was why he made sure to keep close contact with Cayson, so he didn't think Quick was embarrassed by him. He used nauseatingly sweet endearments, even when others were around; showing this great guy that there was nothing he wouldn't do to make him feel cherished and special.

Quick had given the small band a ballad to play for him and his date. Quick didn't know what the song was, but he trusted his son. This song had lyrics, so when Quick had spoken with the trio's manager yesterday, he confirmed that their piano player knew the song and could sing it better than the original artist could.

Quick's heart beat wildly in his chest when the waiter came to clear the last of their shared dessert. The waiter gave Quick a discreet nod, when the keyboard player pulled the microphone closer to his mouth and began to speak in a Simply Red raspy tenor. "This song is for a couple celebrating a very special night."

He didn't say anything else, didn't blurt out their names or anything equally mortifying. Instead, Quick stood and held out his thick palm, saying a two-second prayer that Cayson wouldn't refuse, and humiliate him in front of the entire restaurant. But the gleam of surprise he saw in Cayson's gorgeous eyes immediately put him at ease.

"Dance with me?" Quick asked assertively as the man began to sing the song Vaughan had picked and deemed as their song.

*I don't even know how to love you*
*Just the way you want me to*
*But I'm ready to learn*

(Listen to Quick and Cayson's song here: https://goo.gl/AmHsuH)

When they reached the small area of smooth wood that was allocated as the dance floor, there were two other couples already there, and it made it a little less awkward that they weren't the center of attention. They may have had company, but this song was specifically picked for them by Vaughan for a reason.

Quick wrapped one arm around Cayson's waist. With the other, he held Cayson's hand and tucked it close over his aching heart. Cayson laid his head on Quick's chest, his arm wrapped around Quick's neck, stroking the long, silky hairs there. He so badly wanted this man to be his. He leaned lower and ducked his head, putting his mouth just above Cayson's ear while they slowly inched side to side. He wasn't the best dancer, but he could manage that. The song was slow, and the lyrics were almost spoken instead of sung. Like a promise or confession set to music instead of a love song.

"Vaughan picked this song for us," Quick admitted. He was glad he did when Cayson looked up and placed a gentle kiss on his chin.

"I see why." Cayson laughed and laid his head back where it fit perfectly.

So did Quick. The words were beautiful… and very fitting for both of them.

*I don't even know how to hold your hand*
*Just to make you understand*
*But I'm ready to learn*
*Yes, I'm ready to learn*
*To hold your hand, make you understand*

Holding Cayson tight to him, they both closed their eyes and let the words settle into them.

*I don't even know how to kiss your lips*
*At a moment like this*
*Oh, but I'm going to learn how to do*
*All the things you want me to*
*Oh, but I'm ready*
*Yes, I'm ready*
*Are you ready?*
*Yes, I'm ready*
*To fall in love*
*Right now.*

When the song was over, Quick tucked Cayson close to him and walked up to the small band and dropped two one hundred dollar bills into the tip jar. The guy nodded his head in thanks and began to play a comforting instrumental while everyone cleared the dance floor.

"You ready to go?" Quick asked, walking back to their table.

"I am." Cayson squeezed Quick's thigh under the table while he pulled out his wallet to pay the tab.

"Did you like the song?"

Cayson palmed Quick's cheek this time and drew him forward. He kissed him with so much passion and warmth, Quick had to take a few deep breaths before he was able to stand again. They walked back towards his truck and Quick was mindful to hold Cayson close on the crowded street.

"Want to see what movie is playing, or I was thinking of walking in the garden, but they have a big Valentine's Day thing going on there. I didn't want to appear too presumptuous. I was never really a Valentine's guy, but I heard it might be nice out there tonight."

"Yeah, like what?"

Quick closed Cayson's door and jogged around to his side to finish what he was saying. "It's supposed to be all decorated and lit up nice. More music, dancing, and food."

"Well I'm stuffed, thanks to that delicious dinner, but the lights and garden sound nice."

"It does." Quick smiled, not able to keep himself from leaning over and going for Cayson's soft, pink lips again. "So, you do wanna go check it out? You don't think it's too cold out?"

"You'll keep me warm, right?" Cayson smiled seductively against Quick's mouth.

# CHAPTER TWENTY

*Quick*

Quick held up his date so he could pull the keys from Cayson's pocket. He hid his smile while he unlocked the gate, as Cayson hummed parts of their song in his ear.

"You're a real lightweight, you know that, Doc?" Quick let Cayson practically drape his entire upper half over his back while he stumbled up to the front door.

"Who can refuse free wine?" Cayson sing-songed, and Quick hurried him through the door before the man woke his neighbors. Hadn't they had enough of a show starring the two of them?

Quick was still holding his hand and Cayson spun around in his arms just like he'd spun him on the dance floor at the Gardens, while the aromatic smell of chocolate and orchids drifted around them. He loved seeing Cayson this carefree. The Atlantic Botanicals was beyond beautiful and sickeningly sweet. Hearts, balloons, and chocolate fountains overflowed in abundance. Cayson and Quick did a private tour, so they were able to stop to kiss and fondle whenever they wanted too. They slow-danced and nibbled on cheese and wine samples, basking in each other's company until Cayson's several glasses of wine caught up with him and he became a little too touchy feely on the dance floor. Like now.

"I think you'd better go on up and get ready for bed, gorgeous," Quick murmured, yanking a drunk Cayson back to him. "You're in no condition to pull off what you're offering."

"Let me be the judge of that," Cayson slurred. One hand already inching down the front of Quick's pants and the other hand fisted tightly in the front of his shirt. "I need you, Rome. I want it. I want you."

"You already have me, Doc," Quick confessed. Holding him close, Quick noticed Cayson was putting more of his weight on him. He shook his head affectionately when he heard the soft snores and felt the hot breath through his shirt while his doctor laid there and napped. Quick scooped down and caught Cayson behind the crook of his knees and hefted him in his arms. His still-healing ribs barked an angry "What the fuck are you doing?" Because Cayson wasn't a small man by any means, but he ignored it and took his drunk date to bed.

He removed Cayson's clothes, piece by piece, until he was in nothing but a pair of white boxer briefs. Quick wanted to bury his face in the mound protruding from the front of Cayson's underwear, but he wasn't a pig. He'd wait. *God please give me the strength to wait.* Quick pulled up the covers and leaned down to give Cayson a lingering kiss on his cheek before he reached up and turned off the bedside lamp, submerging them in darkness. Quick went back downstairs and locked up everything, because Cayson's safety came first.

He watched the block for about an hour before his own eyelids began to get heavy as well. He pulled down the blanket from the other night and dropped it on the couch. He took off everything except his pants, and stretched out on the uncomfortable couch.

~~~~~~~~

With both hands tucked under his pillow, Quick was easily awakened by the sound of hesitant footsteps on the stairs. He didn't make a move, being sure to keep his breathing even. He could smell Cayson the moment he got to the foot of the couch. The lingering traces of his subtle cologne made it difficult for Quick to control his cock's reaction. The mind could play games, but the body couldn't lie. When Cayson didn't speak, he wondered how long he was going to stand there.

"I'm not so easy to sneak up on, Doc," Quick said, finally opening his eyes.

"I didn't think you were." Cayson's sleepy voice made Quick's cock rise up higher to listen.

"Come're," he said, pushing the covers off and holding his arms out. Cayson came to him as easily as a baby going to a bottle.

They both groaned when their bodies aligned and Cayson melted into Quick's huge frame. He wrapped his arms behind Cayson's back and began to rub him there, as was becoming his habit.

"You feel okay?"

"I'm good. A little embarrassed. I didn't think I could get drunk that easily."

"When you're not a regular drinker, you can." Quick ran his hands through Cayson's hair, enjoying the softness.

"I only had three glasses of wine, though."

"Something like that. And two whiskeys at the restaurant."

"Oh, yeah."

Quick chuckled. "Be glad you don't feel sick."

Cayson shifted on top of Quick and sucked in a sharp breath when their hardening erections bumped against each other. "No. Sick isn't what I'm feeling right now."

Quick gripped Cayson's hips tightly, moaning when he started grinding his pelvis down onto his. "You don't have to do this now. I can wait." Quick breathed harshly.

"But I can't." Cayson shuddered. "Do something, Roman."

"Fuck," Quick groaned. He wanted this so badly, but he was more than a little inexperienced. He'd watched a couple videos, but nothing in detail. He knew the fundamentals and he knew what Cayson had been denied. So, he figured he'd start there.

He'd watched one act in particular, slightly longer than he wanted to admit, all the while wondering if Cayson would enjoy it.

Quick dragged his hands up Cayson's back and massaged his neck while staring into those crystal blues. Eyes that were naked and open. Showing Quick all that he needed and wanted. They kissed for a long time, kissed until it became its own powerful language, kissed until one of them had to wrench away to breathe.

With their eyes still locked, Quick slowly ran his hands down Cayson's smooth back until he got to the top curve of his ass. Cayson's pupils dilated to twice their size, which Quick took as a very good sign. Not wanting to feel the cotton of Cayson's underwear, he lifted the waistband and eased both hands inside and over the softest, most luscious ass cheeks he'd ever felt.

Cayson whined in his ear, his face buried in Quick's neck. "Ahh, god, Rome. Your touch feels so good."

Quick ached, too. Not from the lack of sex in his own life, but for Cayson. He had no clue when the man had last been touched or cared for the way he needed it most, but his wait was over. "You can have anything you want." Quick applied more pressure, kneading Cayson's ass in his controlling grip. When his doc began to writhe on Quick's thigh, he used his middle finger to tease the crack of Cayson's ass, not quite giving him all of what he begged for. This was their first real intimacy. They weren't about to rub off a quickie on the couch. With newfound determination, Quick pulled Cayson from out of hiding and ordered, "Upstairs."

Cayson slowly got up and Quick was close behind him, taking the steep stairs that led to his man's bedroom. Quick let his pants fall to the floor, as he watched Cayson climb onto the bed, and turned to face him. Quick absently pulled on his pulsing length. Cayson made such a breathtaking sight. His beautiful, pale body spread out on his royal blue sheets. Waiting for Quick to take all his stress away, like a good partner is supposed to.

Quick stalked up Cayson's body, starting at the foot and licking his way up until he got to his mouth. No skin was left untouched and Cayson was an absolute mess by the time Quick reached his lips. His hair was rumpled and askew on top of his head, and his hands reached and grasped at Quick's strong arms while he held himself over top of him.

"Turn over." Quick's voice had turned dark and frightening, but it excited the hell out of his impatient doctor. Cayson flipped over, pushing his long, hard cock between his legs, giving Quick quite an erotic show. He wanted Cayson to be comfortable with him, so he had to appear as if he knew what he was doing. Basically, he did. He was doing what came natural to him, what had always been natural to him.

He started at the base of Cayson's neck and began to kiss his way back down. His own cock was hanging heavy with neglect, but he was going to stay focused. Pulling up the images in his head from the porno, Quick flicked his tongue inside the dents on the sides of Cayson's ass, driving him crazy with anticipation.

"Rome," Cayson begged. His smaller fist reaching back and clenching anxiously in Quick's long hair.

"Shh." Quick cupped and caressed one soft, lightly furred ass cheek, slicking down the fine, golden brown hairs with his tongue while he worked his way to the center. Both of them were moaning loudly by the time Quick parted Cayson's ass and went after his unloved hole.

# CHAPTER TWENTY-ONE

*Cayson*

All he could do was moan. Cayson buried his face in his pillow to stifle his cries of ecstasy while Quick tenderly laved at his hole. *Oh, my fuckin' god, has it been that long?* Cayson knew he was going to come any minute. It felt too good, too stimulating. He wanted more already.

"Please fuck me." Cayson sounded like an unsexed slut. He knew he promised to play hard to get from now on, but Quick had more than proven himself. The public affection, the special song, the dancing, and then the garden... What more did Quick have to do to prove he really did like Cayson?

"I'm not gonna fuck you right now." Quick rubbed and licked at Cayson's ass while he spoke, his hot breath fanning over his moist hole made him clench with the need to be penetrated.

*Not now? Why the hell not?*

"Try to relax. I want to do something to you first."

"Okay," Cayson said shakily.

"Where's your lube?"

"Top drawer." Quick's hand shot out and yanked the drawer hard enough to send a certain secret flying to the front. Cayson hid his face when his jet-black eight-inch dildo rolled into view. "Kill me now," Cayson groaned.

Quick didn't laugh, but amusement was all over his face. He pushed it back further in the drawer where it belonged. Cayson felt solid muscles pressed against his back – and just that fast his shame was gone. Quick pumped his hips and talked Cayson right back into an aching, quivering mess.

"I want to watch you fuck yourself with your toy, one day. I bet you'll look hot as fuck, pushing that in your ass while you look at me," Quick murmured thickly.

Cayson didn't admit the last time he'd used that thing Bush was in office. He never felt fulfilled by it. Most people used toys like that to spice things up in their bedroom. Cayson had used it to make up for the lack of anyone in his bedroom.

"I'm going to take real good care of this beautiful ass, Cays. And as soon as I feel I can control myself, I'm going to fuck it until you're begging me to stop."

"God," Cayson gasped and clamped down on Quick's thick finger as he pressed inside his heat. His body began to tremble and Quick wasn't even up to the first knuckle.

"Easy baby. I got you." Quick was lying next to him, while Cayson lay flat on his stomach, eagerly accepting what was being offered.

Quick pumped the tip of his finger, and Cayson flinched when he felt more lube run down his seam. With their faces only inches apart, Quick leaned in for a kiss. "Does that feel good?"

"Mmm hmm." Was all Cayson could articulate.

"I need to hear you, Cays."

Quick sank his blunt finger in inch by inch until he hit Cayson's gland, making his hips rise off the bed of their own volition. "Ohhh, fuuuck." His goddamn prostate. He'd begun to wonder if it still worked.

"That's it. I wanna hear you." Quick climbed back on top of Cayson, slowly fucking his ass with one finger, while he bent down and sucked the head of Cayson's dick, which lay, red and throbbing, between his thighs.

He thought Quick was new to this, but the man ate his ass and fingered him like a pro. His big hunter was a natural. Cayson humored himself to think Quick was made just for him, since no other man ever had him. Well, he had no intention of letting a man like Quick get away if he could help it.

"Turn around," Cayson gasped, his orgasm so close to the surface he had to stop and take a few gulps of air. Quick was making him feel so good. By the time he pulled his head out of the clouds, he realized that he was taking all the pleasure for himself. Just because he'd had selfish lovers in the past, it didn't mean he was one. He wanted to taste Quick so bad. Make him yell for him – make him come undone.

"I don't need anything," Quick said huskily. "I just wanna please you."

"Then let me taste you," Cayson said, rolling to his side.

Quick slowly pulled his finger from Cayson's ass and turned and brought his pelvis closer to Cayson's face.

"Are you sure, Cays?" Quick asked again.

He loved that Quick was being a respectful gentleman, but he really didn't need to keep asking him that. Cayson was more than sure, especially when Quick's cock was knocking against his chin. First thing that caught Cayson's attention was Quick's appealing masculine smell. It made him push his nose up under those heavy balls and breathe in a deep gust of that wonderful fragrance, wanting it all over his body and his bedding.

It took a little maneuvering for them to get in the classic sixty-nine position, but as soon as they did, Quick tucked Cayson into his chest and went back after his hole. Cayson shook as he licked at the wide, blushed crown of Quick's thick cock. It was a decent length, but it was the girth that made Cayson's mouth water. Opening as wide as he could, Cayson took in as much of that wide cut cock his mouth would allow, hollowing his cheeks and sucking hard when he pulled off. Quick's body jerked on the bed and his ass-eating technique faltered, but it only made Cayson work harder. His sounds were obscene as he licked and slurped nosily around the base, his nose twitching against the wiry hairs there.

"Cays, fuck! You're gonna make me come."

"Yes," Cayson moaned, and filled his mouth again.

Quick spit around Cayson's hole and plunged his finger back inside while he did the exact same thing to Cayson's dick that he was doing to his.

"Gonna come," Cayson gasped. He jerked Quick a couple times, feeling the shaft expand in his fist. "Oh, fuck. Oh, fuck."

Quick pushed hard on the spongy gland buried in Cayson's channel, making him come harder than he ever had in his life. "Rome! Ahh, god!"

The first jet of hot come burst from Cayson's cock so fast and forceful, he almost bucked Quick off of him. It must've surprised Quick, too; because he pulled off Cayson's dick and pumped his shaft as the rest of his come hit him on his chin and his chest. It looked so damn erotic. His come coating his lover. He'd just barely finished, his orgasm still wrenching tiny spasms of pleasure from him, when Quick yelled his own warning before he flooded Cayson's mouth with his essence. However, Cayson didn't let a drop get away. He wanted all of Quick for as long as he could.

~~~~~~~~~

"Goddamnit." Quick grunted again, when the last of his tremors wracked his big frame. His head spun like he'd just gotten off his favorite ride. He guessed technically he did. Now he needed Cayson's mouth. He squirmed, reared, and twisted until his feet were back at the foot of the bed and he and Cayson were kissing and murmuring to each other again. Their noses bumped and nudged while they went at each other from every angle. The eagerness of their connection was gone now that they were sated, replaced by delicate, slow fingertips fleetingly dancing over flushed skin. The gestures were so loving and comforting that Quick was fully relaxed in a lover's embrace for the first time in ages.

"Sleep," Quick said after a few minutes of just hugging.

"Okay." Cayson got up and went to the bathroom and Cayson watched that sexy, pale ass sway naturally all the way until the bathroom door closed. *Joe, you are one dumb ass motherfucker.*

Quick took the time to go downstairs and double check the doors. He took his 9mm from under the pillow on the couch and brought it upstairs. That showed how much his head was completely focused on Cayson, because he'd never left his gun anywhere. He hurried back upstairs when he heard the water shut off, anxious to sleep in Cayson's comfortable bed instead of on that couch. He pushed the weapon under the pillow closest to the stairs. If Cayson was used to sleeping on this side, he was going to have to get used to sleeping on the inside. If anyone came into his doctor's home, they'd have to get through him to get to him.

Cayson ignored what side Quick was lying on and climbed over him to settle in. With one arm tucked under his pillow, keeping his burner close, he let Cayson curl into his side. He leaned down and kissed the top of Cayson's head. "Night, Cays."

Cayson's reply was music to his ears. "Mmm. Night, Rome."

# CHAPTER TWENTY-TWO

*Quick*

Quick hadn't slept so soundly in a long time. He peeked an eye open just enough to see it was daybreak. It was definitely early, because the warm, orange glow from the sunrise was filtering through the blinds. His internal time clock told him it wasn't even six yet.

"It's Saturday, go back to sleep," Cayson mumbled against Quick's pec, where his head had remained the entire night.

Quick rumbled a content agreement in his chest and Cayson snuggled up closer. He threw his leg up higher on Quick's body, bumping his morning wood.

"Well." Cayson chuckled sleepily. "Good morning."

"See what you do to me," Quick said, rolling into Cayson's warmth.

"I'm pretty sure that would happen whether I was here or not."

"True. But I don't usually do anything about it."

"Are you saying you want to?"

Quick hugged Cayson. "Nope. I just want to lay here with you a little while longer. That's all I need."

"What if I want to?" Cayson challenged cheekily.

"Then I'm all yours."

"I'll be right back."

Quick propped one knee up, the sheets pooling and tenting between his legs. He put his hands behind his head and reclined back to wait. He'd wait all damn day. He had a mind to pull out his phone and go back to the YouTube channel where he'd found that porno, but shook his head. He was going to do whatever felt good. He knew the important stuff. Be considerate, use a condom, lots of lube, and stretch Cayson properly before he dared to penetrate him.

Damn, if Duke wasn't with Vaughan, Quick would be throwing questions at his best friend like a ninja threw knives, but it was too awkward. Through the whole conversation, he'd be too busy to take notes, because he'd be consumed with trying not to picture Duke doing those things to his son. So it was just him and the World Wide Web.

Quick's dick was still rock hard, as if it knew it had a job to do. He grinned to himself thinking about what he and Cayson could do today. He hoped the man wasn't ready to send him home yet. Quick didn't want to wear out his welcome – as his grandfather used to say – but they still had a lot of learning and talking to do. Quick hadn't wanted to broach the subject of his rough childhood or his job too much at dinner. Some of the details could be scary, so he'd taken Vaughan's advice and tried to be a good listener. He'd only told Cayson why he became a bounty hunter, and then he moved off that topic as fast as he could. Quick heard the shower turn on, and groaned, mildly annoyed. "You already smell fine, Cays." Rolling his eyes, he slid his jeans on over his bare ass and fought to shove his erect dick inside the confined space as well. He was thirsty and in need of caffeine. His mouth was dry and tasteless from the scotch last night, and the thought of nasty morning breath had him up and in search of some flavor to coat his cottonmouth.

He wanted to put on a pot of coffee, but noticed Cayson had one of those one-cup machines just like Duke and Vaughan. "No one appreciates a good ole fashioned coffee pot anymore. Maybe I want more than one cup. Ever thought of that, Keurig people?" Popping a k-cup in the top, Quick's head jerked up in surprise when Cayson's doorbell rang, disturbing his rant on modern kitchen appliances.

"Who the fuck? At this time of morning?" Quick left his coffee and went toward the front door. Chancing a look up at Cayson's room, he could hear the water running in the bathroom. He took a peek through the side window and saw Dr. Joe standing on Cayson's porch with two cups of coffee in a drink carrier and a bag of donuts from a bakery Quick recognized. A place that he'd deemed too expensive and bougie for him.

Quick flung the door open, wanting to give the prick a good look at his appearance. No shirt, no underwear, sleep-rumpled hair. He knew the anesthesiologist was smart enough to put two and two together.

"What are you doing here?" they said in unison.

"I was invited," Quick said fast, his anger rising slowly, but steadily. Couldn't this guy take a hint?

"Where is Dr. Chauncey?"

Quick smiled a devious smile that would rival Lucifer's. "He's in the shower."

Dr. Joe turned his lip up in disgust as he eyed Quick up and down. "You know you're really starting to get on my nerves."

"Good," Quick countered. "Because you're already on mine."

Joe squinted and stared at Quick. "I know who you are, Roman Webb. I know your business. Your business partners. Your son."

"Are you trying to die?" Quick asked Joe, moving his head from side to side, the sound of the joints cracking in his neck were loud enough to be heard next door, but remarkably, it didn't intimidate Joe.

"You going to kill me, bounty hunter?"

"I will if you mention my boy again." Quick stepped outside until he and Joe were only inches apart. He had to say he was pretty surprised that the considerably smaller man didn't back down or advert his dark brown eyes. "I've been giving you the benefit of the doubt, Ana, because of my respect for Cays. But make no mistake—"

"Why do they call you Quick?" Joe cut in smugly. "That's not a reference to your stamina in the bedroom, is it?"

"Nope. And if you don't believe me I'm sure Cayson could answer that question better."

"So, why Quick?" Joe almost raised his voice, his composure dwindling right along with Quick's willpower.

"Because I'm quick to whip a motherfucker's ass if he fucks with me or anyone I love."

"Love?" Joe scoffed. "What would a thug like you know about love?"

"What would a scared-ass-too-fuckin-old-to-be-a-daddy's-boy like you know about it?"

Joe huffed an agitated breath. "Cayson and I make sense. You and Cayson don't. Leave him alone so he can think clearly, if you really like him. You're nothing more than a huge distraction for him and a threat to his prestigious career. Do you think he could show up with you on his arm at the Physician's Annual Gala?"

"Can he show up with you?"

Quick liked Joe's reaction to his last jab, because the closeted man knew his answer was no.

"Enough bologna," Joe said through clenched teeth, his nostrils flaring wider than an enraged bull. "How much?"

"Excuse me?" Quick asked, surprised at those words. There was no way this guy was going to do what Quick thought he was.

"You heard me, you over-sized brute. How much? How much to make you disappear? My family is very rich. I could make you rich, too."

Quick wondered if Cayson knew what type of jerk he'd been calling a friend all this time. Shaking his head in complete dismissal, he answered Joe the only way he knew how to keep a lid on his anger. He used humor. "It's too hard being rich in America... taxes, ya know what I mean? Am I right, Ana?"

"Stop calling me that, and I'm not joking!"

"I'm not, either," Quick growled.

"Cayson is mine, he belongs to me. It's my name that has helped his career."

"I beg to differ, because last night." Quick crudely adjusted his dick and nuts. "He was all mine. It's funny how your name never came up."

Quick could see that Joe was on the edge and it was too early for a showdown. "Leave, now. Me and Cays still have all morning to enjoy each other."

"If you touch him!" The doctor pushed Quick as hard as he could – it would be almost comical if it weren't so pitiful – but Quick didn't even lose his balance. The man was weak in more ways than one.

"If you wanted to touch my chest, all you had to do was ask." Quick laughed in Joe's face. "Is that what's going on? You want me for yourself? Sorry, I'm already taken by a real doctor, Ana."

"I AM A REAL DOCTOR!" Joe yelled.

"No you're not, Ana. You put people to sleep. Big fuckin' deal," Quick snarled. "I can do that."

He heard Joe take a deep breath and pause before blowing it out, like he was trying to gain back his composure. He guessed the man had realized he obviously couldn't best Quick with physical strength, so he returned to the one method of negotiation he'd mastered. Money.

"I'm talking cold, hard cash... Quick." Joe said his name so snidely, that Quick surprised even himself by not taking a swing at the guy. "That's usually what gets you hoodlums' attention, isn't it? Five hundred thousand sound fair? Imagine how many guns you could buy with that amount."

Quick was almost to his breaking point. He wasn't sure how much longer he could hold it together. His hands ached from being clenched in fists for so long and his body began to heat as if his blood really did boil with rage. His fury could consume him if he let it, or if he was really provoked. So Quick gave one last warning. "You'd better get the fuck out of here before I hurt you."

"That's all you can do is fight, huh?"

Damnit. Now that stung. But the truth always did. Fighting *was* all he knew. Martial arts was the only thing he'd studied since high school. He didn't have years of college under his belt. But he did have an eighth degree black belt. It was equivalent in years of study to a college doctorate, but no one cared to know that. It was all just fighting to someone on the outside looking in. He was honored and called a Grandmaster by lower degree belts and he was damn proud of it. But, now, Dr. Joe was trying to make him feel like he was inadequate, and Quick couldn't have that. He knew who he was and what he'd become.

He'd come so far from the angry little boy who was raised by his grumpy, homophobic father and even grumpier grandfather on a small farm in Clarence City, NY, just a half-hour outside of Buffalo. His mother had called it quits on all of them when he was just a boy, leaving him to fend for himself against his two angry older brothers. It wasn't an easy childhood. He had difficulty reading and was forced to wear hand-me-down clothes that didn't fit properly, which earned him an ample amount of teasing and bullying in school. It became harder every year to take so much abuse. But eventually, Rome got sick of the teasing, the beatings. He was tired of getting so angry he'd black out.

That was when he walked off the street and into his master's dojo. He'd been fighting and was beaten and bruised by gang members in his neighborhood. His master must have seen something in him, because he became a student that same evening… for free. It was Master Yung who taught him to control his rage instead of letting it control him, and to channel it into something constructive. That's when he met Duke and his father. They took him in, and taught him the bounty hunting business and how to use his fighting for what was right.

Any man can hurt someone, but a real man can heal. It took a while for Quick to know his master wasn't talking only about medical healing, because Quick wasn't a doctor, but about emotional healing. Quick had the power to do that. Even though Cayson was the doctor, he was the one who needed healing. Quick had wasted enough time on this conversation; he needed to get back to Cayson before he came out of the bathroom to an empty bed. He told himself he was more than good enough for his guy. He'd grown into a smart, respected businessman, a loyal best friend, and a good father. He was hoping to soon add a good boyfriend to that list of accomplishments. That's more than a lot of men can say for themselves in this world today.

"One million dollars!" Joe blurted, immediately yanking Quick's attention back to him. "Yeah. I thought that would get your attention. All you have to do is forget Cayson exists. One million dollars cash, today. My final offer." Joe looked so damn confident, but Quick was stunned to silence not by the number he was offered, but that the man truly believed Quick could be bought and Cayson was a prize at an auction.

"You son of a bitch." Quick poked one finger into Joe's chest, hard enough to leave a mark. "I'm going to go back inside and make love to my man. When he's relaxed and feels appreciated, I'm going to tell him just what type of unbelievable animal you really are. Now, this is *my* final offer. Get the hell out of here, before I forget why I haven't laid you out on your ass yet!"

Joe sighed and rubbed the trimmed hairs on his long chin. He looked like he hated to do what he was about to. "I tried to give you a chance to leave. But you have to do things the difficult way."

"Looks pretty easy from where I'm standing."

"Well, let's hope you stay vertical, Roman Webb."

"Meaning."

"You aren't the only one with friends you can call."

"Duly noted, Ana. Are you done? Because this is ten minutes of my life wasted."

"Yeah. I'm done," Joe said casually, turning to leave.

"Wait a second," Quick hurried to say before Joe walked down the few steps.

"What?" Joe barked.

Quick reached out and yanked the bag of donuts from Joe's hand, his fast reflexes shocking the hell out of Dr. Joe. He held up the delicious smelling bag. "I'm taking these. That's for disturbing my morning."

Quick turned and went back inside, slamming the door for effect and locking it behind him. Dipshit. He looked at his watch. *Good thinking, you were smart to do that.* He'd recorded the entire conversation. Although Joe had pissed him off, he was intrigued to see Cayson standing there by the window, laughing his head off.

"What's so funny?" Quick smirked.

"I can't believe you took those donuts like that."

They continued to laugh while they ate their confiscated donuts and drank their single-brewed cups of coffee.

# CHAPTER TWENTY-THREE

*Cayson*

When Cayson came out the bathroom, fully groomed and prepped, he heard raised voices outside his upstairs window. Since Quick was nowhere to be seen, he knew it had to be him, but who the heck was he yelling at this early in the morning? Peeking out the sheer blue curtains covering his window, he saw Joe on his porch, red and angry about whatever they were discussing.

He was beyond angry himself. Not only would Joe never make love to him, but now he was cock-blocking him getting any action elsewhere. Why the hell was Joe fighting the end of their agreement so hard?

Cayson threw on the first clothes he found on top of the dresser drawer and hurried downstairs. Instead of opening the door wider, he stood off to the side and listened. Listened to the man he thought was a friend offer up a half a million dollars if Quick would leave him. The thought that Quick would take the money never entered his mind. He was quickly learning the kind of loyalty and honor Quick and his friends believed in. Although Cayson had been skeptical in the beginning about Quick's intentions, he'd more than proven himself these past couple days. But now... now... he'd turned down a million dollars to be with Cayson. He was even more convinced than he'd been last night that Quick could be good for his heart. Just the person he'd been looking for to protect it.

He'd been watching with a serious but nervous eye as he witnessed Quick getting more angry. A large vein bulged out the side of his neck, and all the way to the tips of his ears, his usually tanned skin burned a dark shade of crimson. He was fuming. But when Quick snatched Joe's donuts, Cayson thought he was going to fall over, that's how funny it was. When Quick came back inside, he pushed a couple buttons on his watch before noticing him.

They were still laughing while they ate their breakfast, deciding to make light of the situation for now. But he knew they'd have to discuss the possibility that Joe just might be a potential threat. Cayson cleaned up their mess before he walked up to Quick and slung his arms around his neck, kissing him hard on the mouth. "That was good. I'm full on sugar."

"I'd like to be full on something else," Quick grumbled, his thick palm snaking down and cupping Cayson's left ass cheek, yanking him hard against him.

Cayson was mad at Joe, livid honestly, but he refused to give Joe anymore of his energy or attention when Quick was here in front of him, deserving his full focus. "That sounds good, too." Cayson laughed quietly, as Quick walked them backwards towards the stairs, his tongue messily lapping at any exposed skin. Cayson's dick was already half hard, but when he felt a thick tongue sucking on the sensitive skin behind his ear; he was harder than freezer meat by the time they got to the top step.

Last night, Quick took the lead, making Cayson feel desired and cherished, but it was his turn in the driver seat. He wanted Quick to long for him, to crave him, and need him the way Cayson had yearned to be needed for so long.

Cayson stepped out of his sweats, his cock bobbing freely. Quick licked his lips when Cayson stroked his cock, squeezing a clear bead of precome out of his slit. He heard a low groan reverberate through the room, but Cayson was so turned on, he kept up his show. Still holding his cock firmly in his right hand, he took his left hand and dabbed at his essence, dragging his finger along his tongue, tasting himself. He hadn't realized he'd closed his eyes, until he felt himself being yanked onto the bed.

"You think you can tease me and I'll just stand here and take it?"

"No." Cayson smirked, still rubbing his dick.

Quick looked down between their bodies. "I'm gonna let you fuck me with that long cock, Cayson. But for now...."

Cayson fought his nerves, oh, how he needed to be fucked hard. He thought he was going to take charge, but he'd guessed wrong. Quick yanked his pants down to his ankles and hurriedly kicked them to the floor. Quick climbed back up Cayson's body, nipping and flicking his tongue over areas that'd gone unattended for quite some time.

Cayson wove his hands through Quick's long, thick hair. "Damn, I love your hair." Cayson gasped when Quick buried his face in Cayson's balls, aggressively trying to suck both of them into his mouth. "Fuck!"

"You like that?" Quick huffed, coming up for air. Cayson was in bliss. Quick may lack technique and experience, but Cayson could tell he was trying to do anything he could imagine would make him scream. Cayson didn't disappoint when Quick sucked hard on the head of his cock. He cried out into the semi-darkness of his bedroom. His blue curtains helped to block out the small amount of daylight, casting the room into shadows. It looked like late evening, not early morning. The coloring and peacefulness added to the romantic feel of their first coming together.

With both knees up, Cayson let his thighs butterfly open – giving over all of himself. Trusting Quick to make this good, amazing.

"You ready for me?" Quick murmured, his deep voice sending enticing vibrations through Cayson's groin.

"I've been ready," Cayson answered. He was trying not to yell at Quick to fuck him already. His goal was not to appear too needy, but when he heard the snap of latex, his body pulsated all over, his skin warm and over-sensitive. "Please, Rome."

"I know," Quick whispered, lubing up two fingers.

Cayson didn't need any more stretching; he'd had enough of that last night. He tried not to huff in annoyance when he felt the blunt tips of Quick's fingers at his opening instead of his cock. But when Quick pushed in one finger to the knuckle, Cayson bucked his hips up, seeking out more, and Quick was fast to give it to him.

"God, you feel so tight." Quick looked like he was in a haze of pleasure, eyeing Cayson's cock as it leaked heavily onto his stomach.

"I'm ready, Rome," Cayson grunted, rotating his ass shamelessly on Quick's fingers, clenching his muscles around them.

The pillows had all been tossed on the floor from Cayson's thrashing, and Quick had pushed the comforter to the foot of the bed. It was just their hot, naked bodies on a thin fitted sheet. For the first time in a long time, Cayson wasn't worried about his body being on display. Wasn't concerned about grossing anyone out. He was in decent enough shape, but he spent all his time in the OR, not in a gym. His stomach was flat, but it lacked the definition that Quick's had. His arms were lean, but not toned. He was just him. But Quick caressed him like he was the most beautiful man in the world.

"I can't wait any longer. I need to feel you."

"Yes. God, yes."

~~~~~~~~~~

Quick tried to get himself under control, so he could give Cayson the best loving of his life. But his nerves were riding him hard. He hoped that his shaking was perceived as anticipation and not something else. He didn't want his special doctor to be uncomfortable.

With his eyes locked on Cayson's glazed-over blue ones, he lined up his dick and clenched his hip muscles as he pushed in, trying to be careful not to hurt Cayson. He'd used so much lube that it dripped down Cayson's ass, making a mess on the sheets. He'd rather be sure Cayson was comfortable and didn't have a moment of pain than worrying about the bedding. When his broad head pushed through that tight ring of muscle, they both gasped in surprise.

"Holy fuck," Quick grunted, stilling his hips, not sure how to proceed. His cockhead was in a vise grip. Did this feel good to Cayson? He tried to maintain eye contact but they were both failing at that.

Cayson's eyes fluttered closed. "More. Give me more, Rome."

Quick's hair fell around their faces and his arms shook with exertion as he entered Cayson, inch by inch. "Goddamn, Cays." He struggled to be cautious, but the way Cayson was pushing his ass up to take more, while digging his heels into Quick's thighs and pulling him closer, he knew his resolve would crumble any minute. He heard Cayson growl into his mouth, gripping Quick's biceps hard enough to leave marks.

"I'm okay, Rome. Take me. I need it hard, I do," Cayson begged prettily.

Quick hissed when he felt Cayson's muscles tighten around his shaft. Did he do that on purpose?

"Come on, Roman. Show me what you got."

He was taunting him. What the hell? This was a first for Quick, but he was going to enjoy it. He reached beneath them and squeezed Cayson's ass while he hoisted his leg up on his shoulder. He'd seen this position in one of the videos he'd watched, so he hoped his man enjoyed it too.

Quick eased out to the tip, pulled Cayson's ass cheeks apart, and dove back in with a little more force, testing Cayson's bravado.

"Yes, that's it! More, Rome."

He'd thought he'd gone overboard, but his doctor surprised the hell out of him by wanting more. He ached to give Cayson exactly what he'd missed, so Quick set a fast pace, making sure his own groin ground against Cayson with every thrust. He turned his face and licked the crease behind Cayson's knee, sucking a mark there when Cayson called out his name. Quick's hair was all over the place while he concentrated on hitting a spot that he knew would drive Cayson wild. He pulled Cayson's other leg up on his shoulder, equal parts surprised and turned on that Cayson could handle the position, Quick practically had him folded in half. He pounded his doctor's ass, the loud sound of skin slapping spurring him to leave an impression, to let Cayson know who owned him. Cayson may not be ready to admit it, but Quick already knew. After this, Cayson was it for him. He'd found home.

"You feel incredible," Quick confessed, kissing Cayson's neck and jaw, panting with each stroke. He had to slow down just a tad so they could catch their breath. He wasn't ready for this to be over, but his balls screamed to let go of his release.

"You're gonna make me come, Rome," Cayson groaned, arching his back. "Oh, god. You feel so good. Fuck, it's been so long."

"You don't have to want anymore." Quick let Cayson's legs fall back to the bed while he gave his starved doctor all he had. He braced both hands on either side of Cayson's head, while sweat ran down his face from his exertion, a look of seriousness etched across his features while he concentrated solely on Cayson.

"I'm 'bout to come so fuckin' hard." Cayson's eyes slammed shut, and Quick had the urge to make him open them and watch their union but he let his man have his way. Let him buck himself on his cock and claw and dig at his hips to pound harder. Quick laced their fingers together and pinned Cayson's hands against the wooden headboard, while he rammed his cock against Cayson's prostate.

Cayson went still and rigid for a split second, and Quick thought he'd done something wrong until Cayson yelled out his name with the first gush of pearly liquid from his cock hitting just above his navel. With nothing touching his dick, they both watched in amazement as Cayson spurted more and more come onto his stomach.

Quick used one hand to keep Cayson pinned and the other he swiped through the warm jizz pooling between them. He gave it an experimental taste, not hating it, but it didn't taste like pineapples, either. It tasted like Cayson. He leaned down and drove his tongue deep in Cayson's mouth. Sharing with him.

"You taste good," Quick confessed after another taste.

"Let me go. I wanna make you come," Cayson said lazily. He sounded drunk and Quick smiled, loving that he'd put that look on his beautiful face. It'd been years, and no one else had bothered to learn what Cayson needed. If this was all it took to make him so blissed out, then Quick had everything handled from here. He let go of Cayson's wrists, gently kissing each one.

His cock was still rock hard, his balls aching and tight, but he was a patient man. This wasn't about him at all. He'd let Cayson take the lead for a little while.

"Lie on your back."

Quick ran his hand through his damp hair, pushing it behind his ears while he got comfortable under Cayson's sweat-slick body. He was so perfect. So sweet and full of compassion. Inside and out. There wasn't a sum of money on earth large enough to make him walk away from this man.

Cayson climbed on top of him and grabbed his stiff length, placing it against his hole. He lowered himself slowly, throwing his head back, exposing his long throat, sinking all the way down. "Fuck I'll never get used to that."

Quick grabbed Cayson's thighs, enjoying the feel of them flexing under his palms while Cayson gyrated on top of him. He kept it slow and sensual. It gave him a completely different feeling than the fast fucking. This made him feel loved. Made him want to love in return. The warmth flooding his heart was overwhelming.

"That's it, Cays. Nice and slow… Ohhhh, fuck. So good. S'good," Quick cursed, his eyes narrowed as he watched Cayson destroy him from the inside. How in the hell this felt so good, he'd never know. No one told him. He'd known he was a bisexual man, but he'd never got to enjoy this side of himself. He had a feeling he and Cayson were getting ready to really make up for lost time.

"You like it slow, Roman." Cayson wound his hips back and forth and Quick shot upwards, throwing his arms around his doctor's waist, pulling him down, and gripping him tight to his chest.

"Fuck, yeah." Quick didn't have to thrust up into Cayson, because his doctor had his knees spread wide when he sank down on him, his soft ass cheeks rubbing against the coarse hairs on Quick's thighs. He was so fucking deep inside him. The passion, the intimacy, the sheer connection between them was unlike anything he'd felt for anyone. It was too much. Cayson held him around his neck, using his hot mouth to suck up dark, wet marks all over his throat, whispering sweetly against his Adam's apple. He felt his orgasm barreling towards the finish line.

"I wanna feel you come. Come for me, Rome."

Quick grunted and cursed when Cayson lifted up, and fell down hard. He was doing that thing again, squeezing the muscles in his already too-tight channel, choking Quick's cock until he gave it up. He threw his head back and groaned, low and deep, as he filled the condom buried deep inside his man. His man.

"Mmm. So warm," Cayson moaned, holding Quick tight, while he came down from the best orgasm of his life.

"Damn, baby." Quick was panting, his chin tucked into his chest while he rested his head against Cayson's heart. "You just blew my mind."

Cayson chuckled lightly, softly fingering Quick's long, damp waves. It was another few seconds before he finally rose off his softening dick, flopping back down beside him in exhaustion. Quick wasted no time scooping Cayson into his arms. There were no words. What could he possibly say that would give justice to how Cayson just made him feel?

# CHAPTER TWENTY-FOUR

*Cayson*

Cayson walked through the busy halls of the hospital, eager to get his emergency call answered so he could get back to Quick. He could still feel him inside him right now. Could feel the indent that thick cock left in his ass. It felt wonderful. They'd just finished their shower together, where Quick had washed every inch of him before he let him out. Although their sex had been life altering, they still had a dark cloud trying to cast a shadow over their sunshine. They had to talk about Joe. No sooner were they dressed to head over to Duke's office to discuss it, when he was paged. One of his patients was presenting the start of an infection, so he had to postpone. Quick understood and said he'd be waiting for Cayson at his place when he was done. He looked forward to going over there and hopefully spending the night. That way, they were sure not to have any disruptions. Cayson smiled, thinking about making love in Quick's house, and ended up drawing a giggle from a couple nurses when he walked onto the floor.

"You look awfully happy to be called in on your day off, doctor." One of the charge nurses commented through a cheeky grin.

"Hi, Debbie." Cayson waved. He ignored her comment, shaking his head as he stood at the nurse's station and read over his patient's chart. His smile was still firmly in place, and the more the nurses ribbed him for details, the more red and flushed he became. It was so obvious he'd been well fucked. As soon as he left, he'd be the focus of their dinnertime gossip, while they tried to figure out who was giving it to him good. All they had to do was call down to the ER and ask; surely, they had a clue regarding who had rocked his world. Duke and Quick left a lasting impression anywhere they went.

The nurses toned down their teasing when Cayson began to order up tests for his patient. It looked like post-op pneumonia, but he was going to be sure. He asked Debbie to start his patient on an antibiotic while he waited for the test results. "I'll be in my office. Let me know when the results are back."

"Sure thing, Cayson."

He never minded the nurses using his first name. He was so familiar with them that it felt too formal to expect them to call him Doctor Chauncey. It was these women who made his work life bearable. He never understood why some doctors mistreated nurses. He unlocked the door to his department and walked past Nania's empty desk, opening his office door. He put his coat on the rack, and with his nose still buried in his patient's chart to make sure he hadn't overlooked anything, he didn't notice the large box on his desk, wrapped in beautiful gold paper with a large white bow, right away.

He dropped the chart on the corner of his desk, grinning wide, wondering what Quick had sent him now. He picked up the card, ripping it open excitedly. As soon as he saw the handwriting, his smile dropped.

*Dear Cayson,*

*I tried to deliver this to you personally today… but you had company. I'm not blaming you for falling for that man's tricks. Now that it's over, this is just the start of our new relationship. I love you. I do. Here's something to prove it.*

*Love*

*J.*

Cayson felt bile rise in his throat, the nasty acidic taste making him gag. What the hell did Joe mean by "Now that it's over"? Nothing was over with Quick. And was he insane? Joe didn't love him; he'd just tried to buy him for the going rate of one million dollars. Cayson wasn't even calm enough to call Joe yet, and now he'd gone and pissed him off even more. Lifting the lid off the box, he was knocked off his feet. It was a 24K gold, premier edition stethoscope. He had it marked in a catalogue under his coffee table. How'd Joe find it? It didn't matter. He couldn't buy Cayson and he damn sure couldn't buy his way into his heart.

Running his hands down his face in frustration, he groaned when he thought of having to tell Quick. He couldn't keep this a secret. Joe was acting irrationally, and he honestly had no clue what they were dealing with. All he wanted was a chance to be happy. Joe needed to grow the fuck up. This was getting crazy. He yanked up his receiver and punched the number for Joe's cell phone. He answered on the first ring.

"Hi handsome. Did you get my gift?"

Cayson scoffed. "Are you for real? Have you lost your mind, Joe?"

"Why are you mad?"

"Why am I mad?" Cayson lowered his voice, although no one was around. "You tried to buy off my boyfriend this morning, now you—"

"Wait! Boyfriend? He's not your goddamn boyfriend. I am!" Joe yelled, loud enough to make Cayson pull the receiver away from his ear. He'd never heard Joe yell or swear like this. "This has gone far enough, Cayson. Are you in your office? I'm on my way."

"No, don't—"

Joe had already hung up. What's he thinking coming up here? Was he trying to get outted? Shit. Cayson wasn't sure if he should call Quick, or not. He couldn't run to him to fix all of his problems. Cayson was a grown ass man and he wasn't scared of

Joe. He was going to stand up to him, once and for all. How dare he, or anyone, think they could control his life?

He made rounds on a few of his other patients while he waited for the lab results on his post-op patient. He needed to stay busy. His smile was gone, now replaced with concern and nervousness. He went back to his office when he had nothing else to do. He opened his door to find Joe standing in the far corner of the office, in the dark. He had on black slacks and a black turtleneck. If he weren't such a rat bastard, he'd look quite handsome in his own regal way.

"You left the door unlocked," Joe admonished.

"That wasn't done intentionally." Cayson gritted his teeth. He couldn't yell. Although his door was closed, you never knew who was lurking. "You should leave… and you can take that with you." Cayson pointed to the expensive gift still in the box on his desk.

"You wanted it, didn't you? I saw you looking at it. Don't you like it?"

"The question is: would you have bought this for me if Roman wasn't in the picture?"

Joe shrugged. "Who knows? Maybe. Probably." As he moved closer, Cayson took a few backwards steps. Joe looked predatory, his dark brown eyes shining bright with his intent. Cayson would've loved to have seen that look on Joe's face a few months ago. Now it was too little, too late.

"I want you to know that I understand why you were traipsing around with that man." Joe waved his hand dismissively. "I'm not going to even ask, because I don't want to know. I'm going to make sure you never want for him again."

Cayson shook his head. He didn't know what was happening. He was still trying to understand why Joe was being so persistent when he'd made Cayson feel like nothing but a nagging housewife while they were involved. Anything he suggested for them to do, especially if it included going out, Joe would look at him like he'd sprouted horns.

It wasn't until Cayson heard the rattling of Joe's belt buckle that he snapped back to focus. "What are you doing?"

"I'm going to fuck you." Joe sneered. The look on his face was a mask of anger and revenge.

"Excuse me?"

"I know you already let him fuck you. I accept responsibility for allowing you to get so desperate that you'd pick up a thug off the corner and let—"

"Get out!" Cayson thundered, oblivious to where he was. Joe made him so furious he was having a difficult time not punching him in the mouth, so forget about keeping his voice calm. "I wouldn't fuck you if my life depended on it."

"Maybe it does."

Cayson froze in place. Joe's words were sort of frightening, but they were delivered in such a nonchalant tone that it was confusing him. Was that a threat? Cayson thought about what Joe had said to Quick before he left that morning. Told him this wasn't over. Maybe he should push his panic button. Feeling for his watch, he realized he didn't have it on. Fuck! He'd had such a relaxing morning after he and Quick made love that when he'd gotten paged to come in for a patient, he'd left hurriedly so he could get back to learning the big man who was smoothly working his way into his heart. He remembered taking it off last night, thinking that he didn't need to be wearing it while he was with Quick. He'd made a mistake, and Quick was not going to be pleased.

Joe ignored Cayson's incredulous look, steadily unzipping his pants. His cock was actually hard, his uncut meat pressing forcefully against the thin black cotton of Joe's briefs.

"I'm not having sex with you, Joe. We're in my office. In the hospital! Where someone could see you… hear you. Are you ready to come out?"

"There's nothing to come out about."

"Your head is completely screwed up, Joe. You need help."

"I need your ass."

"That ship has sailed."

"Did he fuck you that good?"

"Yes," Cayson quipped right back. He wanted to make Joe hurt. Wanted him mad enough to get the fuck out of his space.

"He's not as good as me." Joe looked around. "No one can see in here and I'll make sure you stay quiet." Joe laughed, but Cayson knew he wasn't joking. He had to get out of there. "I'm going to make you forget him. That's for sure." Joe squeezed his dick, moaning Cayson's name. "I know what to do to make you mine."

"Nothing," Cayson hissed.

"Stop fighting this. It's what's best for both of us. You know you can't be serious about that guy. You're a professional, Cayson. Are you trying to end your career?"

"Leave."

Joe was on Cayson in a heartbeat, pushing him against the bookshelf behind his desk. Joe smelled and felt so different from Quick. He was so much smaller, his chest was frail and bony, where Quick was thick and firm with muscle. Joe reached down and grabbed between Cayson's legs, clumsily aiming for his balls. Cayson swore and grunted, closing his thighs tight, trying to push Joe's hands off him. It made him sick to his stomach. He didn't want Joe's grimy hands on him. Ever again.

"This is sexual harassment," Cayson said, finality in his voice and his actions as he pushed hard against Joe's chest, putting some much-needed distance between them.

Joe's eyes were wide as he began to zip up his pants as if he was being watched by Candid Camera. "Harassment, Cayson?" Joe's mouth was in a firm line, his neck turning redder the more he righted himself. He angrily shoved the hem of his turtleneck back into his slacks. "It was just last month you were begging me to take you, any way I wanted. Now you're yelling sexual harassment. Fine. You and your hoodlum can live happily ever after. I'm done trying to help you."

"Thank you for your blessing."

Joe's eyes narrowed to slits. "No one embarrasses me."

"I'm not try—"

"Save it!" Joe barked startlingly; loud enough to make Cayson jump in the quiet office. Joe flung the door open hard enough that it bounced off the arm of the couch. "You'll regret this," Joe said in parting.

*I think I already do.*

# CHAPTER TWENTY-FIVE

*Quick*

"Let's be sure to stay alert. Don't assume anything and don't underestimate this guy. Money is power and he has a lot of it," Brian signed, his brother translating for him.

"He's a spoiled brat who's used to getting his own way," Quick huffed.

"The rich ones usually are," Duke confirmed. "Damn, how old is he?"

"Like forties. Fuck if I know. Too damn old to be pulling bullshit, Mickey Mouse stunts like this," Quick scoffed.

Brian was reading over some information on Dr. Joe's family while his older brother, Ford, spoke with Quick about their next move. "Let's wait and see, Quick. If he wants you bad enough, he'll come get you. We don't want to be the ones to initiate anything."

"You just be ready," Duke added.

Quick was always ready. He looked at his best friend, making eye contact, trying to relay his concerns without actually saying it out loud.

Brian signed something and they all waited for Ford to say it aloud. "Brian wants to know what the look was."

Brian's hands moved in another series of jerky motions. He was saying something for his brother, but Duke and Quick watched carefully. It crossed Quick's mind then, and not for the first time, that they all needed to learn a little ASL, so the whole team could communicate without Ford having to interpret. The King brothers were becoming an important part of their business, and it just made sense. After a few more seconds of Brian signing, Ford ran his hand over his buzz cut before speaking.

"Brian thinks we should put a tail on him."

"Why?" Duke frowned. "What do you see in those papers?"

Brian shook his head. Looking down at the papers, his forehead creased in concentration, he signed while Ford rattled off all the business ventures that the Wellingtons were involved in. It wasn't just hospital politics. They were connected with the governor and a couple federal judges last names were Wellington. "There appear to be Wellingtons serving in several branches of the federal government."

"Anything shady or underhanded?" Quick questioned.

"Some things look sketchy, but they're good at covering their tracks," Brian signed enthusiastically. "Looking at it from this angle, I don't see much that appears illegal. But, I'm sure I could find it if I dig hard enough."

"Fine. Dig deeper." Ford agreed with his brother. "We may need our own leverage if it comes down to it."

"In the meantime." Quick quirked his brow.

"In the meantime, we're on Defcon Four."

Duke rolled his eyes. "Civilian talk, please, Ford."

"Meaning we're going to increase our watch and tighten up on security."

"Well, hell. If that's what that means, then we're always on Defcon Four." Quick checked his watch; it was after five. Surely, Cayson should be ready to leave work by now.

"We're talking about you and your guy's safety," Ford chided.

"I know. I'm on it." Quick stood, ready to conclude this meeting. He wasn't being honest with himself, or his team. How did he touch on this subject again? He hadn't had to deal with losing control of his anger in a long time.

"Something else you want to say?" Ford asked.

"If I get my hands on this guy, I'm not sure what I'll be capable of."

"We're all well aware of what you can do. Hopefully it won't come to that." Duke clapped Quick on his shoulder on his way by. "Let's not worry if we don't have to."

"Keep this from Vaughan," Quick said to Duke's retreating back.

"I keep nothing from Vaughan," Duke responded, not bothering to look at Quick as he closed himself in his office.

Whipped prick.

Quick didn't have time to ponder the what-ifs, because as soon as he sat back at his desk, the front door opened. He was so consumed with his thoughts that he didn't notice Cayson until he was standing over him.

"Hope I'm not interrupting," Cayson said softly.

Quick stood up and wrapped his arms around Cayson like he hadn't just seen him that morning. "Hey you." Quick placed a delicate kiss on Cayson's neck while he bent low and soaked up all the warmth Cayson could give. His meeting with the guys had gone well, but whenever Quick talked about his anger or fighting, it made him anxious. Cayson showing up right now was exactly what he needed. "This is a nice surprise. I thought I'd meet you at my place."

Cayson looked nervous, clearing his throat before he could speak. Looking around the office, Quick saw that all eyes were on them in the open space. He didn't want Cayson to feel uncomfortable or be afraid of them, especially since any one of them would lay down their life for the other, and that now included him.

With his hand on the small of Cayson's back, he ushered him over to the brothers. "Cayson, this is Brian and Ford King. Fellas, this is Dr. Cayson Chauncey."

"Cayson is fine," he corrected, holding his hand out to shake. Both of the men had a solid, forceful grip. "It's nice to meet you both."

They both nodded, but Ford was the only one to speak. "It's good to finally put a face with the name."

Cayson looked back at him, a slight smile ghosting over his beautiful face.

"Yep. I talk about you all the time."

"We were just taking about you, actually." Duke came out of his office, offering his hand to Cayson. "To what do we owe the pleasure, Doc?"

"The pleasure is mine. He's here to see me… finally." Quick laughed, pulling Cayson close to his side.

"Well, um." Cayson shifted. He looked so uneasy. What was going on? "I'm kind of here to speak to all of you."

Quick looked concerned, as he bent down to look Cayson in the eye. "Did something happen at work, Cays?"

~~~~~~~~~

Cayson didn't expect for all of Quick's coworkers to be in on a Saturday afternoon, but he guessed they didn't work normal business hours. He looked around the room, astonished at how much smaller he felt around them. They were huge, military trained, and very serious.

"Cayson! Where's your watch?" Cayson didn't realize that Quick was holding his hand, his face showing just how upset he was, no matter the excuse for his bare wrist.

"I left it at home by mistake this afternoon. I was kind of distracted." Cayson hoped Quick could accept that one. However, his sharp green eyes focused back on him, his teeth clenched together, as if he was trying not to yell.

"What's going on, Doc? It's okay to tell all of us, because we can't have secrets between us. If Quick needs us, he's going to tell us anyway," Duke interrupted Quick's glare.

"Well. When I got to work, there was a gift on my desk." Cayson looked at Quick expectantly, telling him yes, it was Joe. "I called his cell and fussed at him. Next thing I know, he's in my office, pushing me around."

"He touched you." Quick's voice was low, deadly. If Cayson hadn't been looking at him, he'd have sworn a demon had spoken.

"Rome," Duke said Quick's name, sounding like a warning.

Cayson watched as Quick closed his eyes and took a couple deep breaths before he opened them again. It took a lot for him not to gasp at the startling green of Quick's irises, his pupils contracted to tiny pinpoints, showing just how livid he was. No matter how he tried to calm himself, if he was angry, his body would react and no words could disguise it. He didn't really want to know what Quick did when he was this livid. How he fought for a person he cared for. Cayson had a feeling it wouldn't end well for the other person. Now he was regretting saying anything at all. Was he about to seal Joe's doom?

"Cayson, why don't you sit down here and tell us from start to finish." Duke guided him to a chair in their makeshift lobby, all the men crowding around to hang on his every word. Quick stood behind Duke like he needed someone to hold him back.

*Fuck. What am I doing?*

When Cayson had finished, none of the men said anything for a while and he assumed they were digesting it. He'd conveniently left out the part about Joe grabbing his crotch. He said Joe shoved him... that's it, but regardless, Quick's body language was screaming at him. As if they could all hear it, Brian was the one to place a hand on Quick's shoulder in an effort to settle him.

"All right. This guy has just upped the ante on us," Duke said first, and all of them nodded their agreement.

*Wait! What the hell are they agreeing to?*

"Cayson, are you okay staying with Quick for a few days until we figure out this guy's intentions, or at least until he calms down?" Duke asked, his voice calm and comforting like he was trying to soothingly trick Cayson into saying yes, he needed a babysitter. No freaking way. And that melodious voice may work on Vaughan, but Cayson was immune... mostly.

"I'm not going to impose on Quick." They'd just started seeing each other. He wasn't about to live with him, he wasn't an adolescent. Cayson had to do what was logical. And running to hide out at Quick's didn't sit well with him rationally or physically. They still needed their own space, or shit would go south.

"There's no imposition," Quick finally spoke again. "I have a guest room, if that's what's bothering you. This is only about safety."

Cayson stood up, his hands out in front of him. "I think we may be going overboard. And I may have overreacted. Joe isn't dangerous. He's a mediocre anesthesiologist, for Pete's sake." Cayson didn't know why, but for some reason he wanted to appear as strong and fearless as the men surrounding him. Even without all the black and leather, they still looked vicious. They looked like trained killers. Cayson puffed his chest out a little more. "I'm not scared of him, if that's what y'all think."

"No one thinks anyone is scared. Safety has little to do with being scared. Plenty of men have met worse fates, all because they 'weren't scared'," Duke said around air quotes. "You wanna know what's on their gravestones? 'Here he lies dead, but he wasn't scared.' No one gives a fuck if you're scared or not, but you will be safe." Duke stood to his full six-foot plus height. "You've been telling me what to do for almost a year, controlling my health. Now you're in my house. I assume you came to us for advice, and this is it. You're going to stay with one of us... I don't care who you pick. You'll be under our protection while this jilted ex gets some act right about himself. When I'm confident he's not a threat to you or my guys, then everything can go back to normal. Until then. Defcon Four. Am I clear?"

"Clear," Quick and Ford called out in unison, Brian slinging up a gesture too fast for Cayson to catch.

Duke turned on his heels, leaving them to the details. The two brothers stood up, gripped Quick in a one-armed hug, and nodded once to Cayson before leaving together. Cayson looked around, slightly confused. *That's it? Duke says clear, and like in the OR, everyone raises their hands and scatters. What the hell? I didn't agree to anything.*

"I'm not staying with you, Rome," Cayson said, while Quick went about straightening his desk.

"Then who are you staying with?"

"No one. I'm going home. Well, after our date." Cayson smiled ruefully. But Quick failed to see the humor, if his dry expression was any indication.

"Fine." Quick locked his desk drawer and pointed to Duke's closed door. "Go in there and tell that to him. I'm warning you though; Vaughan's been out of town for two days, so Duke's not a happy camper."

Cayson rolled his eyes. He had no doubt Quick was right. He didn't want to piss Duke off while he was missing his man. "Okay. One night, since I'd planned to stay, anyway." Cayson approached Quick slowly where he leaned against the side of his desk. Enough of the dreaded ex talk. He needed Quick's hands on him, especially after Joe had unwantedly touched him. Quick watched him, his face still unreadable, and it almost gave Cayson pause, but he kept advancing. Quick wanted him. He had a gut feeling, and when he was close enough, he ran his hand up Quick's hard stomach and over his pecs. Cayson smiled when the muscles flinched beneath his touch, the tight material of his t-shirt, stretched over his broad chest could barely conceal all that firm flesh.

"Touch me, Rome." Cayson moved in until there wasn't an inch of room between them. Quick still had his hands clenched tight at his sides. "Are you mad at me, or just sulking a bit?"

"Neither," Quick answered, smoothing his hands up Cayson's thighs to his waist. He closed his eyes, enjoying the touch. Relishing the way Quick held and controlled him. It made his cock come to life. "I want you to be careful is all. I'm not trying to take over your life."

Cayson tilted his head back, looking up into Quick's ruggedly handsome face. He hadn't shaved this morning and his beard was full enough to cause a pleasant burn on Cayson's face if he could get Quick to devour him with his mouth again. He'd agree to just about anything right now. "I promise. I'll be safe."

Quick yanked Cayson hard against him. He grunted and took the punishment, loving where this was going. "You can't just say those words, you have to mean it." Quick bit down hard on the spot beneath Cayson's jaw, making him hiss and moan at the same time.

"I'm not just saying it. I'll be careful."

"No more calling him," Quick added, sucking a hot passion mark beneath the collar of Cayson's dress shirt. He was busy concentrating on giving Quick all the access he needed, so whatever he was agreeing to was irrelevant, as long as this big brooding man kept touching him. He wouldn't admit it yet, but he felt completely safe in Quick's arms. He felt like nothing could touch him. Quick was the first place he'd thought to go when he left work. He did feel out of control when Joe became aggressive, but he wouldn't be caught off guard next time. Maybe Quick or Duke could show him some basic defense moves… never know. Damn, thinking about rolling around with Quick on the floor while he showed him various submissive moves had him wanting to leave immediately.

"I won't call him, talk to him. Nothing."

"You notify me if he corners you again."

Cayson was quiet. Quick held Cayson's chin and tilted his head back to look at him. "If you're worried what I'll do to him, then call Duke, or Ford… as long as you call someone. I think the more people who get involved, the faster he'll tuck tail and run. He's still in the closet, so unless he wants an early coming out party, he'd better leave you alone. My patience is wearing thin when it comes to him."

"Did you tell Duke about the bribe?"

"Yep." Quick flicked the light off, leading them to the front door.

"And what did Duke say about it?"

"He said I should've taken the money and kept dating you."

Cayson laughed. That sounded like Duke. "Hey. Thank you for not throwing your hands up. I realize you didn't expect to have to deal with this."

Quick pecked Cayson on the mouth as he walked past him into the dark parking lot. He caught him by his biceps and turned him so he could crowd in close. It was an erotic contradiction the way Quick could look so rough and raw but kiss so tenderly. He made Cayson feel cherished, just in the way he looked at him. One more sweet kiss on his cheek and Quick whispered against his warm skin. "I'm not close to done with you, Cayson." Quick looked like he wanted to add something else to that, but chose not to.

"Hey, maybe we should invite Duke over tonight," Cayson said on his way to his car. Quick stopped next to his truck like he was thinking about it.

"Naw. Vaughan will be home sometime tonight. Duke will work in his office until it's time to pick him up from the airport."

"Okay, then. It's just us."

"I'll follow you to your place so you can get a few things."

Cayson rolled his eyes, but got in his car and pulled out of the parking lot with Quick's dark Range Rover close behind him. His own personal bodyguard.

# CHAPTER TWENTY-SIX

*Quick*

Quick tried not to squeeze his steering wheel so hard, but it was taking every breathing exercise he knew to tamp down his rage. How dare that fucker think he could just own Cayson? And where did he get the audacity to put his hands on him? He knew there was more to Cayson's story, though for some reason he chose not to voice it at the office. But he was going to find out what else happened after he cooled down.

*He that is slow to wrath is of great understanding: but he that is hasty of spirit exalteth folly.*

A small tilt of his mouth was all he could manage when he thought of the many proverbs his sensei recited when Quick got mad. All of them had made sense. Cayson would trust him with more as soon as Quick had shown he was worthy of it. If all he did was fly off the handle, he'd loose his sweet doctor, and the thought of that hurt already. He was trying to get used to the fact that he may not have to live out his life alone, watching everyone settle down around him. If he reacted like a small-minded cave man, that behavior would push Cayson away. His man wasn't a fighter – he was a healer. Quick couldn't start laying men to rest because they posed a threat. As much as he wanted to retaliate, it would serve no purpose.

Quick turned onto Cayson's street, half expecting to see Joe standing there, but released a relieved breath when he saw no one. Now wasn't the time to see Joe. Although the man had fired the first shot, Quick would bide his time.

*There are two kinds of idiots. Those who don't act when they're threatened and those who think they're acting because they've issued a threat.*

"Yes, Sensei," Quick said under his breath before he got out of his truck and caught up to Cayson.

Before he could unlock the door, Quick noticed Cayson's neighbor was waving to get his attention. He hurried over to her, pasting a bright smile on his face. "Good evening, Mrs. Maven, I hope I didn't disturb you."

Quick chuckled when the older women squeezed her paisley house robe in front of her chest when she peered over to get a good look at Cayson's company. "No, you're fine. I wanted to tell you a package was delivered for you today that need a signature and since you weren't home, Davis signed for it for you."

Quick gritted his teeth when the woman pulled out a long, slender box wrapped in black and silver wrapping.

"Oh, boy," Cayson said under his breath, making his way over to his fence to get the gift. "Thank you Mrs. Maven, and thank your husband for me, as well. You have a good night."

"Night, doctor." She slowly made her way back to her porch, turning the light off after she'd closed herself inside.

"Nice lady," Quick said when Cayson opened his door.

"She is." As if it were nothing, Cayson dropped the box on his coffee table in the living room and kept moving, going upstairs. Quick wanted to open it so badly, but knew better. That piece of shit was still buying his man gifts. Cayson made it sound like Joe was giving up by telling them to have a nice life, but it appeared they interpreted that phrase differently. When Cayson came back down with his messenger bag and a small duffle bag that couldn't contain more than two days' worth of clothes at the most, he wanted to argue for him to go back up and get more, but held his tongue. Cayson could walk around naked in his house for all he cared, as long as he was with him.

"You going to open it?"

"Nope."

"You just gonna let it sit there?" Quick leaned against the front door, his arms crossed defensively over his chest.

"I don't care what it is. It's not important. A label is still on it. I'm going to drop it at the post office and write return to sender on it."

Quick didn't like that idea, but it was Cayson's choice. He wasn't one hundred percent convinced that Cayson was over this man. He could think of no reason not to take Cayson at his word. He'd trust him until he gave him a reason not to. He liked that Cayson had changed out of his dress clothes and was wearing a pair of worn jeans and a green polo shirt with the sleeves pulled up. Quick beamed when he saw the watch back on Cayson's wrist.

Cayson smiled at him, holding up his wrist. "Better?"

"A little. Not enough." Quick growled as he looked hotly at him. "I don't like the thought of his hands on you. Come're."

Cayson dropped his bag and was in Quick's arms faster than he thought he could move. Those strong hands rubbed up and down his back as Quick feasted on his mouth. He needed to erase everywhere Joe may have touched and replace the memory of it with his own mark. The coarse hairs on his beard brushed deliciously over his cheeks and Cayson moaned deep down to his toes when Quick sucked hard on his tongue. "Damn. I need you."

"Say it again," Quick demanded, unbuckling Cayson's belt.

"Fuck. I need you, Rome. Just you. Need you inside me."

It took a lot for him not to rip off Cayson's clothes and pound his ass until he screamed Quick's name, let everyone know who owned him. He'd own this man's heart, he'd earn it the right way, and not by trying to purchase it like it was on sale at Macy's. It was a much-needed revelation that his doctor wasn't concerned with anything Dr. Joe could put into a box. Material possessions. So easy to buy and return them like they're nothing. Because in actuality, that's all those empty gifts were – things. Quick could already tell that Cayson wanted something that couldn't be bought, that wouldn't fit in a neatly wrapped box. Cayson wanted a love of epic proportions, he wanted a man's heart, and Quick wanted to give him his. It was Quick that Cayson wanted, it was the man, not the stuff. Quick's presence was worth more and valued higher than any present ole Joe could find in a catalogue.

Feeling like he'd won another round, Quick spun them until Cayson's cheek and chest were against the door. He pushed in hard against him, using his bulk to pin him down while he massaged the hell out of Cayson's ass. Not concerned with gentility or subtlety. He hoped he wasn't turning Cayson off, but this was him, it was who he was. Sometimes, he needed to be in control of the situation. It fed his dominant urges and soothed his beast. He needed to handle Cayson like he needed air to breathe. Needed to possess him. There was something about the handsome genius that called to Quick on every spiritual and sexual level. He had no words to describe it, or lengthy explanations. The man just did it for him. He'd been around long enough to know when it was right.

"Need some stuff," Quick bit out. His body was overheated, his hands burned to hold Cayson down, his cock weeping to be confined in his doctor's warm channel. Cayson was maneuvering his pants just below his ass, spreading his legs as far as the restriction allowed. Oh, fuck. They didn't have time to get naked, no time for foreplay, or even to find a solid horizontal surface. It was happening right here, right-the-fuck-now. This was going to be fast and raw. "Cays," Quick groaned, pumping his erection against Cayson's plump ass; that act alone making him want to shoot.

"In my bag. Front pocket," Cayson finally managed.

Quick pushed his palm against the center of Cayson's back. "Don't move," he ordered.

While he dug around in Cayson's bag, he kept one eye trained on his man, pleased that he'd done what Quick said. He'd been a natural dominant from the moment he'd discovered who he really was. He hadn't been able to explore much of his forceful side while he was married, since Vaughan's mother was pretty conservative. He hoped he could try out all his fantasies with Cayson. Starting by taking him hard against the wall.

Quick tore the condom open and snapped it on his aching cock, wincing as he rubbed the lube up and down his shaft. He took two fingers and brushed them around Cayson's hole, applying a little pressure. The tight flesh clenched and released under his touch as if it was talking to him… begging for more. "Your hole is so fuckin' hungry."

"Starving." Cayson gasped when Quick pushed in the tip of his middle finger.

"I don't need stretching. I'm still good."

Quick smiled, burying his head in the soft, dark blond strands of Cayson's hair. He inhaled deeply, because his doc always smelled so good. Like aftershave and his office, always so clean.

"You sure you're ready, because I can't hold back." Quick swore as he got a solid hold on Cayson's hip with one hand, the other he used to guide his cock towards heaven.

"Fuck, yes. Show me what you can do, Rome. Don't hold back."

As soon as the head of his cock was inside, they both choked on the intensity of coming together again. Quick took in several gulps of air. He hoped Cayson was ready, because he didn't try to contain himself when he pushed the rest of the way inside Cayson's body, not stopping until his pelvis was pressed against that supple ass.

"Jesus! Fuck, Rome!" Cayson cried out into the dark open space of his foyer. His hole was clamped around Quick's dick, pulsing and tensing around him. His voice only a hoarse whisper. "So goddamn full."

Quick waited a moment while Cayson fell apart in his arms. He held him tight around his chest to keep him close to him, and with his other hand on his smooth hip; he slammed Cayson back into him. He kept his thrusts to a minimum, instead making Cayson do exactly what he wanted. His eyes rolled behind his closed lids when Cayson braced both hands on the wall in front of him and used it for leverage as he thrust back onto Quick's thick cock, taking it deeper each time he shoved hard into him.

Quick's cock surged inside Cayson, while his quiet surgeon talked filthy to him. His doctor was a professional in his office and a complete freak in private. An aggressive bottom. Not afraid to take the cock if he had to. Quick was stunned and feeling ten degrees past incredible. "That's it. Ride my dick, Cays." Quick leaned over Cayson's body, still holding him tight to him, only allowing Cayson enough room to buck his ass back against him. Quick pushed his hair behind his ear and turned Cayson's face towards him so he could whisper against that soft pink mouth. "Ohhhh, fuuuuck. Take this dick, Cays. Goddamnit. Take it."

# CHAPTER TWENTY-SEVEN

*Cayson*

"Hurt me, Rome. Make it hurt so good." Cayson pushed back as hard as he could, impaling himself on Quick's thick rod. God, he didn't know it could be like this. It was like Quick was consuming him, taking everything Cayson had and telling him that it was enough. He was satisfied. No matter who Cayson dated, he was never enough. He was simply him. And by the time he'd reached thirty, his self-esteem had been shot to hell. No one wanted him, needed him. Not until….

"Damn, you're fuckin' tight. Gonna make me come if you keep squeezing me like that."

Cayson could barely register what Quick's rough timbre was saying against his cheek, in his mouth, behind his ear. He felt like he was immersed in Quick's deep sensual voice, listening to him in surround sound. His mouth was everywhere, his hands all over him. The dirty words coming from his bad boy were making Cayson crazy with lust. He could hear gut-wrenching moans, could feel sweat pouring down his brow, but he didn't know if it was his or Quick's, their bodies were fused together so perfectly.

It felt like his lover's strength was stuttering as his orgasm grew nearer. Cayson tried to voice something, but it came out sounding like a whine, a cry for more.

"Fuck you're driving me crazy with those sweet noises."

Cayson leaned his head back, craning his neck for a deeper kiss. His ass was full and hot, throbbing around Quick's dick until it became rock hard.

"You're so damn hard. Filling me up, Rome."

"You better stop talking like that," Quick warned, pulling Cayson flush against his chest, while he panted for breath.

Cayson wondered how far he could push before Quick snapped. He didn't know he could talk so dirty, didn't know he could writhe on a dick like a professional tramp until Quick put his hands on him. Cayson's heart rate kicked up higher at the thought of tempting this big man. "Are you going to punish me Rome? Huh? Make me pay?"

"You're playing with fire, doctor," Quick hissed. Cayson's eyes widened when Quick reached around and grabbed a handful of Cayson's balls, kneading them roughly before pulling his sack hard enough to make Cayson slap the wall. Every one of his senses was being stimulated. He didn't know what to do, who to curse, or how to prepare for the most violent orgasm of his life. He could feel it. The all-encompassing feeling starting at the heels of his feet began to snake its way up through his already quivering legs. He fought to hold them both up. Since Quick's moans had risen higher, he was bearing down harder on Cayson's body, putting his massive weight behind each punishing thrust. His ass screamed for mercy, and Cayson loved that feeling. Loved being pushed to his breaking point.

"Oh, yeah," Cayson grunted, and pushed his ass back to meet Quick's pounding. "Show me how strong you are, Roman."

Damn. Where was all this coming from? Cayson didn't know he could be so dirty and flirty, didn't know he wanted to until Quick threatened him in the most tempting way.

"You want me to punish you?" Quick pulled out to the tip and slammed his hips back into him hard enough to make Cayson yell out in pleasant surprise. "Can you take it hard?" The broad head of Quick's dick was digging at his prostate every time Quick bottomed out. He was going to blow hard any minute, any one of those thrusts was going to put him over the edge, and he couldn't wait. He would let Quick know his ass was his. There was no getting better than this, no greener pastures. The alluring green of Quick's irises was all he needed. They stared at each other for a few seconds, both of their chest heaving and taking in air – when Cayson felt the connection he'd been dreaming of click into place, as easy as a seatbelt locked into its anchor.

"Rome," Cayson whispered in awe. Looking into Quick's bedroom eyes, he knew he felt it too.

Quick pulled out slowly and Cayson thought he was going to lose his mind. His orgasm was so close, his body at the point where it demanded it. "Don't stop." Cayson's voice was almost gone. His body was Quick's for the taking.

"Not yet. I'm not gonna stop until you've come all over me."

Cayson slammed his eyes shut and gripped the base of his dick. Fuck yes. He wanted to spray his load all over that rock hard stomach, rub it into his skin like lotion. Quick turned him, pushing Cayson's back against the hard door. It took a little fumbling for Cayson to get one of his pants legs off so Quick could hold his leg up on his hip. The position wouldn't let Quick go as deep, but the way he was able to maneuver and control Cayson's body sparked a whole different kind of heat in the pit of Cayson's balls. Quick stood towering over him, his body completely shadowed by all those muscles, even Quick's long, beautiful hair cascaded around them, blocking out the world. He felt like life was going on around them, and Quick had managed to freeze time, just for him.

Quick's hips were unmoving for too long, his cock poised at his entrance like he was awaiting permission. "You like this don't you?" Quick pushed in to the hilt, the change in angle causing dramatic shivers to wrack Cayson's body. "You like me covering you, protecting you." Quick stooped lower, hooking Cayson's leg higher on his forearm, giving a few warning thrusts before he went back to fucking Cayson hard enough to bang his back against the door. If Quick let him go, he'd keel right over from the pleasure. It felt like they'd been fucking for hours when it'd been a few minutes.

Cayson nuzzled in the warmth of Quick's chest, pulling up the hem of his shirt to get to all that tanned skin. He stroked his cock, throwing his head back at the rush of euphoria, the spike of adrenaline as he erupted on the inside, his essence spilling over his palm and coating Quick's rock hard abs. "Ohhhh, ohhhh," Cayson cried with each gush of come, oblivious to what he was saying or how he sounded.

"Fuck, Cays. You look so beautiful when you come like that."

Cayson wondered if this is what it felt like to be high. He'd never done illegal drugs, but this had to be close to it. He was floating, his body felt both heavy and free at the same time. He couldn't move a muscle and yet he felt like he could run a marathon. It was such an amazing rush. "Rome," he said tiredly, his eyes struggling to focus on Quick's face.

~~~~~~~~~~

Quick leaned down and kissed Cayson with all the care he could conjure at that moment, his man's tight body was slowly milking his cock, stealing his orgasm before he was ready to let it go. He wanted to stay just like this forever. The endearing words tumbling around inside his mind made his head spin and his heart soar. He was positive at that moment that Cayson was his. No matter what situation came, they'd handle it together.

Quick closed his eyes and stumbled backwards, trying to hold on to Cayson and his emotions. He felt so good all over that the feeling shocked him. Scared him, too. Was this love? Was he in love? He knew twenty-seven ways to kill a man with his bare hands, maybe he should figure out how to love one. His head whirled, trying to come up with an answer, nerves made his heart pound inside his chest, but his body was oblivious to his inner conflict as it convulsed from the pleasure. He was going to blow.

He was in love and making love. He never thought he'd see this day. *I'm in love.* Quick shook his head like he was confused, lost the rhythm of his lunges as he held Cayson's thigh tight to him, keeping him impaled on his dick while he pulsed inside of him. "My sweet doctor." Quick's mouth dropped open, his mouth a wide O, his eyes sealed tight. Quick hardly recognized his own voice when he spoke again. His confession sounded painful, but it was anything but. "I'm coming, Cays." Quick slammed in hard one last time and flooded the tip of the condom. "You're all mine, Cayson. All of you."

Cayson appeared to still be coming down from his release, and Quick was whispering slurred innuendo while his hot cock throbbed deep inside Cayson. They stood there, leaning on each other and catching their breath. Quick didn't want to move, but he wanted to get Cayson to his home and in his bed. Maybe a bath before that. That'd probably be a good time to tell Cayson he was having deep feelings for him. He just hoped the sentiment was reciprocated. He wouldn't stop working on them until it was.

He slid free of Cayson's heat, his eyes fluttering at the over-sensitivity of his cock. "I want to get you in my bed. Come on."

Cayson obeyed – again. They straightened their clothes; neither of them saying much, simply letting their blissed-out expressions say it all.

# CHAPTER TWENTY-EIGHT

*Cayson*

It wasn't a long drive to Quick's place, but he'd kept his hand on Cayson's thigh for the short duration. When Quick got to the last stop light before his neighborhood, he turned to face him, but Cayson was looking straight ahead, afraid of what he'd see if he looked at Quick.

"What's going on? Are you okay?" Quick asked, tightening the squeeze on his leg.

Cayson nodded his head.

"You are? Because you're awfully quiet."

"Just thinking," Cayson said solemnly.

"Care to share?"

"Not particularly."

Quick laughed under his breath. "Okay, then. Can I ask something?"

"Shoot."

"Is it bad thoughts… or good?"

Cayson finally turned to look him. His bright blue eyes were radiant even in the darkness of the truck. "It's good mostly. And part terrifying."

Quick turned into his driveway, pushing his remote to lift the garage door. He shut off the engine, and before Cayson could go for the door handle, Quick clamped a hand on the back of his neck to stop him. The touch was hotter than a brand, but he still closed his eyes and leaned into the hold.

"I think I know what you're talking about." Quick stroked Cayson's firm jaw with his thumb while he kept up the light massage. "Why don't we just let things progress naturally? However slow or fast that is, we just go with our gut. Do what feels good."

Cayson nibbled on his bottom lip, thinking that over, and next thing he felt was Quick leaning in and sucking his tender lip into his own mouth, giving it his own assault. Quick ran the tip of his tongue along the opening of his mouth, teasing and flicking at him to open wider. It only took him a second to do what Quick wanted.

"You don't have to worry, Cays. Not about me hurting you." Quick's voice was low and husky, like he was struggling keeping his own fears at bay.

"We haven't discussed anything serious, Rome. Or exclusivity."

"I already told you… you're mine."

Cayson stared at him, waiting to see deceit or malice. But there was none there. He prayed Quick was old enough to know what he wanted, because he didn't have time for games. It was unfortunate that games were all Cayson had experienced in the minimal amount of time he'd had to date, but he hoped Quick was ready to show him the way romance was supposed to be. Just like their song said. Quick told him he'd married right out of high school, so he probably hadn't carved a ton of notches in his headboard, but he didn't need to sleep with a bunch of people to know how to treat someone he cared about. Right?

Cayson finally smiled, and Quick inched in for one more kiss. "Now. No more worrying about what ifs, okay."

"Okay." Cayson opened the door and pulled the seat up to grab his bags. He had Sunday off but he usually went through his upcoming cases. He'd need to borrow Quick's office for a while. He blew a tired sigh. He had to stop fretting over nothing. Quick had practically forced him here, so he should accept that he wasn't an imposition. Especially since he'd only just gotten there.

Maybe Quick would enjoy him in his house as much as Cayson liked having the big lug in his space.

Quick opened the door which led into his laundry room. He had a newer model washer and dryer, and some products sitting on top of the machines. On the rows of shelves lining the opposite wall, were canned goods and other pantry items. Lots of green vegetables. So, he preferred Tide laundry detergent and had a thing for canned spinach. He was already learning so much about Quick and he'd only gotten ten feet inside his home.

"I like it when you smile. If it weren't for the stubble, you'd almost look pretty." Quick eased Cayson's bag off his shoulder and took his hand, leading them through the long hallway into the living room. "Let's put your stuff in the guest room and then we'll decide on dinner."

Quick was definitely a take-charge man and he found it easy to listen to him, do as he said. Joe had been annoyingly, unattractively bossy. Quick was the epitome of an alpha male, the one in the relationship who took out the trash and fixed the toilet. Cayson would bet his cable package consisted of all the sports channels and he was the kind of guy who never had a hand towel in his bathroom. Quick was the kind of man he'd stayed away from in high school and college. He guessed his neat khakis, collared shirt and wire-rimmed glasses weren't a huge turn-on back then, and didn't scream jock. What Quick saw in him, he wasn't a hundred percent sure yet, but he did believe, now. That he turned the man on to some degree. He wasn't as pessimistic as he'd been in the beginning.

"Dinner sounds good. Then after, I was thinking…." Cayson's words trailed off as he stood at the entrance to the door of what he assumed was the guest room, because Quick placed his bag on the bed and turned on a green porcelain lamp on the night stand. He had to admit he was shocked by the warmth. Even the curtains matched the duvet. Warm, earth tones surrounded him when he stepped farther inside. Deep greens and dark brown furniture coordinated nicely in the large space. A decent-size television sat inside a dark oak credenza, and Quick pointed to two drawers at the bottom.

"Those are empty down there. Feel free to use them." Quick turned and opened the door closest to a double-paned window. "Your own bathroom. There's a few toiletries already in there, mostly stuff Duke left, but I can get you anything you need."

"Duke used to stay in this room?" Cayson looked confused.

"Only when he was too drunk to drive home after a game night or something, but that went for any of the guys." Quick shrugged, turning on the light to a walk-in closet. "You'll see at the next game night, which I'm hosting this coming week. There'll be guys sprawled all over the floor and on any free space."

Goodness. Quick talked like Cayson had just moved in. Since Quick was looking so comfortable and sure, he choose not to make any negative comments. Besides, game night sounded like fun. But he wasn't moving in with Quick. Bottom line.

"You were saying something a second ago." Quick stood in front of him with one hand on his hip, and the other curved around Cayson's neck, pulling him closer to him. Oh, he smelled so good. Even though he'd showered hours ago, he could still smell his soap and shampoo in Quick's long hair. Not thinking about it, he sunk into Quick's embrace and ran his hand through his hair. The long, gray strands mixed with the dark brown made him look like a mature model. He hadn't ever seen a grown man with hair that luxurious. "Why do you like your hair so long?"

Quick's head jerked back in surprise. "You don't like it?"

"You know I love it. I'm just wondering if I'm going to go to work one day, come back, and it's all gone and you're sporting a buzz cut talking about how you wanted a change."

Quick laughed down in his belly. "No. That probably won't happen. In fact, I'll probably be one of those pathetic men who have a huge bald spot in the middle but are too stubborn to cut off the few long strands left hanging around the perimeter."

Cayson had a good laugh in Quick's arms. It felt so wonderful to laugh with a lover. "I won't let you do that to yourself."

"Promise." Quick beamed down at him, his light, carefree smile transforming Cayson's world right before his eyes.

"Promise." Cayson's voice had dropped low, his smile sliding off his face, replaced with a feverish seriousness. He went up on his toes and aimed for Quick's mouth, wondering if he'd ever get tired of kissing him. Despite his ass being sore from only an hour ago, it was still greedy. He wouldn't mind taking that cock one more time before bed. He had all day tomorrow to recover. Or maybe... *Maybe I can top him.*

Quick groaned and pulled Cayson higher in his arms. He drove his tongue deep enough to taste all of Cayson's nasty thoughts, and he couldn't stop from grinding his erection on Quick's solid thigh. Hissing, he stilled his hips, licking a path across Quick's rough cheek. "Mmm. Rome. Why do I turn into such a slut around you?"

Quick's laugh was sultry, a quiet rumble. "I'd be a little disappointed if you didn't." Quick said, squeezing a handful of Cayson's rising cock.

"Fuck."

~~~~~~~~~~

"Later, maybe." Quick held his fiery doctor to him. He needed to get himself under control and not hump all over Cayson like an unneutered dog. He didn't want to scare him away. Although, he was having a time peeling Cayson off his thigh. He smiled the entire time, loving that his sweet doctor was full of surprises, and not so sweet behind closed doors. Fuck yes! "After dinner, you want to watch a movie?"

Cayson massaged Quick's large pecs, licking his lips as he stared straight ahead. "Well. I thought maybe you could show me a few moves."

"Moves?" Quick frowned, not sure what moves Cayson wanted to learn.

"Yeah. You know. So that if I'm pushed against a wall again, I can get…" Cayson began to turn an embarrassing shade of rose as he shook his head. "Never mind. That's stupid. I was thinking stupid."

"No, wait." Quick pulled Cayson back to look at him. "Did he do more than push you around?"

Cayson's mouth probably resembled a fish out of water. He closed and released his pursed lips as he tried to think of something to say. Quick was standing so tall, towering over him, his brow pinched and his massive hands balled into alarmingly sizeable fists at his sides. "I don't want you to be upset. Or fly off the handle."

"Cayson, tell me! What else did he do?" Quick yelled, just lower than a dull roar.

Cayson jumped, startling back out of Quick's space. He hadn't meant to yell that loud, but at least Cayson didn't look scared. That's not what he was going for. He closed his eyes and recited a couple of his favorite proverbs from his sensei, all the while Cayson stood off a ways, watching him.

Quick did his breathing and thought of a calming place. Not mindful of how many seconds passed, he opened his eyes, blinking as if he were coming back to reality. When his head pounded and his skin heated to the point he felt like he'd combust, he knew he was losing composure. It was terrifying and alluring when he crooked his finger, beckoning Cayson back to him. He wasn't even sure what he was going to do or say. All he did know was that Cayson was going to tell him the whole truth. Did Joe do anything more beside push Cayson?

Cayson still hadn't moved and Quick hurried to show him he was in full control. He felt a cocky grin play across his face as he began to walk slowly towards him. Cayson looked like he was going to bolt, and how much fun that would be. "If you run. I'll catch you," Quick said darkly and Cayson shook his head, finally smiling back at him. He'd backed him up to the wall, leaving him no room to flee. Quick didn't rush him. He ran his hand up Cayson's flat stomach and over his chest. He caressed the smooth skin beneath the top of his collar before he placed his entire palm over Cayson's throat. He didn't squeeze, just held it there, staring down into Cayson's shocked eyes. No fear. Only desire. He fit himself against Cayson, giving him his brawn to show he was still protecting him… always. But right now, he wanted to push Cayson and see how far he could pull him from his comfort zone before he retreated. He needed his surgeon to trust him, but how could he ask that when Quick hadn't told Cayson everything? He closed his eyes and breathed when he felt the fast thump of Cayson's pulse and the nervous dip of his Adam's apple. Quick breathed in through his nose and out through is mouth, feeling a coolness wash over the inferno that was his body. How did Cayson do that? He was calming him.

Cayson spoke and Quick felt each syllable under his palm. "Joe said he was going to do what I'd wanted him to do, and fuck me," Cayson spoke hurriedly.

That was when his self-control went to hell… literally. It felt like Cayson had tossed him in a lake of fire. Quick's body shook, but Cayson kept going. "He undid his belt and pushed me against the wall. I couldn't, um… I couldn't get loose."

Quick grunted, the beast within scratching and clawing to be let free. To get even. His fingers twitched against Cayson's damp flesh.

"I told him no, but he grabbed for my dick. I pushed him as hard as I could and when I raised my voice and mentioned sexual harassment, he left."

Quick wanted to beat on his chest. How dare that son of a bitch. He went to remove his hand from Cayson's throat while he processed what Joe did to his man. *His*. He'd kill him. This was fucking war. Before he could drop his hand, Cayson grabbed for it and put it back to his neck, pushing his fingertips closed firmly around the most vulnerable part of his body. He was showing Quick the extent of his trust in him. Cayson wasn't afraid, no matter how angry Quick got. That was going to be critical in their relationship, because one thing was for certain, Quick could get extremely mad.

"Look at me." Cayson's voice sounded far away, and Quick realized he had a decent grip on Cayson's throat. "It's okay. Look at me."

Quick eased up, pressing his forehead down on top of Cayson's head while he breathed through his gentle words. They were close enough that Cayson could pucker up his lips and kiss him right between his pecs. When he felt him pushing his throat against Quick's hold, trying to get his mouth on Quick's body, his nerves settled, and his ire fizzled to a simmering burn.

"I'm sorry he touched you. I hate that I wasn't there."

"Maybe it's best you weren't."

Quick couldn't help but agree. "I think you're right." He finally took his hand down only to stare at the faint handprint left there. *Jesus*.

"What?" Cayson must've read his expression. His delicate, expert fingers reached up and timidly touched the tender flesh over his throat. "Is there a mark there?" Cayson asked, almost wistfully.

"My handprint." Quick swallowed a thick gulp of worry. He was embarrassed. He and Cayson hadn't quite got that far in their courting yet. Before they could go there, they'd have to talk about boundaries and limits. Quick wasn't thinking in terms of a D/s relationship, but he liked to play rough. Who didn't sometimes?

"Good," Cayson whispered. "I hope he sees your marks if there's a next time."

*Calm.*

# CHAPTER TWENTY-NINE

*Cayson*

While he silently helped Quick clean up the dinner dishes, Cayson resisted the urge to touch the slightly inflamed skin around his neck. If Quick hadn't been so upset, he would've seen how turned on Cayson was by his strength. He got a little nervous when Quick was breathing and counting, and all the while, his hand was squeezing tighter and tighter around his throat, but he was able to reach him through it all. His voice, his touch had calmed him. He knew he'd needed to tell Quick the whole truth about what happened in his office, he just hadn't expected such a strong reaction. Quick acted like… like he lo—

"How about we get started?" Quick clapped his hands loudly, breaking Cayson from his thoughts. Quick wiped the last of the moisture off the kitchen island and hung the dishtowel over the handle.

Cayson swallowed nervously. He hoped he didn't make a fool of himself. He was semi-coordinated, which sounded silly since he was a surgeon. He could perform a successful bladder cystectomy, but he feared he couldn't execute a proper chokehold.

"Don't worry. You'll be fine. I'm not gonna show you anything difficult."

Cayson had changed into a pair of his alma mater's sweats and a white wife beater. As Quick pushed a few pieces of furniture out of the way, Cayson couldn't help but admire that amazing physique. The tight muscle shirt left nothing to his imagination. Quick's arms were thick and defined, like two over-ripe grapefruits covered with tattooed skin. His legs like goddamn tree trunks under his loose basketball shorts. Cayson was hardly containing his drool when a hard fist pounded on the front door a couple seconds before it opened.

"Knock, knock!" Cayson heard Duke's deep voice, then saw his handsome face peeking through the crack of the front door. He stepped in, pulling his own set of keys from the door. "Well, what's about to go on in here that you had to move the fuckin' furniture, dude?" Duke laughed. He was in a great mood, if his broad smile and teasing were any clue, and Cayson had a feeling it was the beautiful man coming in the door behind him who was the cause for his jovial temperament.

"Hey, Pops." Vaughan moved around Duke, rolling his eyes. He and Quick embraced, their love and wonderful relationship easily visible. Cayson realized how much he missed his dad when he saw what those two had.

"Vaughan. You look tired, Son. How was work?"

Tired? The man looked like a superstar in his designer suit. Did he really just get off a plane? Just because his tie was loosened at his neck and his shirt was a little wrinkled, Cayson would hardly say the guy looked worn. And Duke's hungry, dark eyes ate him up, no matter which way Vaughan moved. Cayson gave the young attorney a warm smile and he got a nice one and an even warmer hug back in return.

"Doctor. Duke was filling me in on the way home from the airport, and I insisted he bring me over. I can't believe you have a stalker ex." Vaughan looked genuinely concerned, and Cayson was glad they cared. Glad anyone cared.

Quick looked at Duke, annoyed. "You have the biggest fuckin' mouth, man. Didn't I say leave him out of this?"

Duke took off his skullcap and threw it, along with his coat, over the arm of the couch like they were staying a while. "He asked what's been going on. What was I supposed to do... lie?"

"No."

"No," Vaughan and Quick said, at the same time.

"Not lie. Just omit some things. Big mouth."

Duke shrugged, not caring what his best friend was beefing about. Instead, Duke ignored Quick's tirade and pointed at the large, open space they'd made in the living room. "Um, again. Do I wanna know?"

"I was going to show Cays a few submissive moves." Quick pushed his recliner back next, flicking off Duke when his friend started to laugh. "Don't laugh at him," Quick barked.

Duke straightened and retorted, "I wasn't." And sent Quick his own stern glare. After a while, Duke kicked off his shoes and rolled up the sleeves of his thermal. "Well, let's show him some moves, black belt." Duke winked, standing boldly in the middle of the room.

"It's been a while since you sparred, Duke, you sure you wanna dance with me? And Vaughan has a black belt." Quick tilted his head in Vaughan's direction. "I'm way higher than that."

"You make him sound like he's in a beginner's karate class, babe. My dad's an eighth degree black belt."

"Whose side are you on, prodigal son?" Duke frowned.

Cayson laughed, looking quizzically back and forth between the three of them. Eighth degree. What did that mean? It sounded badass, honestly.

"What's an eighth degree mean?" Cayson sat on the edge of the coffee table while Quick and Duke did some slow stretches.

Vaughan took off his suit jacket and settled into the couch like he was preparing for a good show. "It's an amazing accomplishment, Doc. Just like you being a surgeon."

"Not quite," Quick put in, looking a little uncomfortable at Vaughan's reference.

"You studied for years, trained for even longer. Yes, it's exactly like that." Vaughan looked so thoughtful when he spoke of his father. "It's practically unheard of in this day. Not many are disciplined enough to receive that degree belt. It takes a lot more than fancy moves."

"Now that your cheering squad is in place. You ready to do this?" Duke grumbled, taking a wide stance, his hands up in front of his face.

"Wait. As your doctor, Duke; I think I may have to disagree with this level of activity." Cayson stood, holding his hands out like he was the referee.

Duke gasped, feigning offense. "Seriously. Does no one have any faith in me? I'm not over the hill."

"Just shy a few years." Quick chuckled, but Duke wasn't seeing the humor.

"You know what, shut up. Come on, we should take this seriously." Vaughan chastised them both.

"You're right, son. Cayson, come over here and show us how he had you pinned. We'll go from there."

Cayson knew he was beet red. How was he going to reenact his humiliation? Joe was a punk bitch, and yet he'd gotten the best of him. Suddenly he was feeling too self-conscious in front of these well-trained fighters. He thought this was going to be a very private lesson, eventually ending with both of them sweating and grabbing on each other until it turned hot enough to take to the bedroom. Quick and Duke looked so serious. Vaughan stood up and placed a supportive hand on Cayson's shoulder. "My dad and Duke are the best at what they do. You can trust them. You can trust us. We're not here to make light of your situation. I really wanted to know you both were okay." Vaughan's light eyes were so much like his father's. He even squinted like him when he was concentrating on something. He didn't realize until it was too late that Vaughan was staring at the reddening around his neck. Cayson clutched his throat, looking back at Quick.

Quick stood directly behind Cayson and moved one of his hands away from his throat. He kissed his palm and turned him so they were face to face. His tone was low and only for him to hear. "I hope you're not embarrassed."

"No." Cayson put his hands down and lifted his chin higher. "I'm not embarrassed at all."

Vaughan continued as if everything was normal. If Cayson didn't want to elaborate, that was his business. The gorgeous man went back to talking up his father. "He'll protect you with everything he has, but wouldn't you like to be able to protect yourself, too? Now, using me, please show us exactly what he did."

Cayson was always shocked when Vaughan spoke. No man in his early thirties should be that mature. He'd still been hiding behind textbooks at that age. Vaughan was so much like his father. So in control and in charge. Cayson found himself doing exactly what he was told, by not only the father, but by his son, too. The moves he repeated became easy and the lesson very educational.

"If he comes at you again, he won't be expecting you to defend yourself. Attackers usually go after the unsuspecting, vulnerable types. Surprise is going to be a big advantage for you next time," Vaughan said, getting back into his original position. Duke and Quick had taken a step back and let Vaughan handle the lesson, since Cayson looked more comfortable working with him. Every now and then, they'd add a note here and there, or reposition Cayson's arms.

The next lesson was recovery moves, for use if he was grabbed from behind or around the neck. Vaughan showed him how to gain air and a couple attacks that could startle an assailant. The knuckle punch to the temple was harder than it looked, but the collarbone jab was easier to execute in that position. Next were frontal attacks, defense, and offensive maneuvers.

Vaughan was starting to sweat, so he unbuttoned his dress shirt, keeping his white t-shirt on. "Again," he barked, sounding like a real martial arts instructor. Vaughan stunned Cayson by quickly grabbing him from behind before he could get into position. Putting his forearm across his windpipe, and cutting off his air, his other hand wrapped over the top of his skull. He remembered he only had a few seconds before the body started to panic and demand air, causing a person to forget their training.

"Think, Cays," Quick yelled, cutting through his fear.

Cayson stopped uselessly digging at Vaughan's corded forearm and turned his head so that his Adam's apple was in the crook of Vaughan's elbow, that's where the air was. He sucked in a much-needed breath. "Good, Doc. Now get him off you," Duke added, circling around for a better angle to view what Cayson was trying to do.

By the time his three-and-a-half-hour lesson was over, he was drenched and sore. "Holy hell. How can you handle all that? Fighting is so strenuous. So taxing on the body."

Duke stripped off his damp thermal and went to grab an extra t-shirt out of Quick's laundry room. "I hope this is clean," he quipped, slinging it over his head, sniffing the pits after he did.

"You can go home shirtless," Quick teased his friend.

"That's fine with me." Vaughan winked.

Duke blushed, and Cayson found their relationship cute as hell. There was no other phrase to describe it. Quick looked like he wanted to puke when Vaughan smiled deviously at his father as he inched closer to Duke.

"I love you," Vaughan said sweetly, gazing into Duke's midnight eyes.

"I love you, too," Duke replied, leaning down to kiss Vaughan slowly.

"Yeah, yeah, everybody loves everybody," Quick murmured, rolling his eyes. Cayson shot him a disbelieving look, but then he remembered that Vaughan was Quick's son, so… yeah, maybe it was a little weird.

"Stop being a hater," Duke said to his best friend, turning to give Vaughan his full attention. "I want you to show me that move you did on the floor earlier as soon as we get in bed."

"Okay! Out! Lesson's over!" Quick jumped up out of his recliner, almost knocking Cayson off the arm, pointing at the door. "Right now. Good fuckin' night. One more word out your mouth, Duke, and I swear to god."

Duke was being shoved towards the door, hardly able to get his coat on because he was laughing so hard. "I was joking, Rome."

"Well joke your ass up out of my house and take your boy toy with you." Quick shoved Vaughan, too, and Cayson thought he hadn't seen anything that funny in a long time. It was so obvious they goaded Quick, knowing he hated to see them getting mushy, yet he fell for it every time.

"I'm glad you two are together," Vaughan yelled over his shoulder. Cayson stood beside Quick and waved at them, leaning into Quick's strong side, until Duke's taillights were at the end of his court.

"I would've told them thanks for the lesson if I had the chance."

Quick closed his front door and locked the deadbolt. "Yeah. Too bad they had to leave so suddenly."

Cayson was elated. He felt so good. Felt like he had real friends.

"Let's go to bed. We'll put the furniture back in the morning."

"Sounds good."

Quick hit the light switch and held out his hand, both of them climbing the stairs a little slower than normal. "Actually a hot bath sounds better… then bed."

"Now you're talkin'."

# CHAPTER THIRTY

*Quick*

When Duke and Vaughan had busted through his front door, his first thought was, he needed to set some new ground rules. He never used his key at Duke's house since he and Vaughan had been a couple, unless he knew they weren't home. He needed the same courtesy, because if he wanted to bend his sexy man over his couch and take him right then and there, he wasn't going to be worrying about anyone walking in on them.

Quick stripped out of his shirt, his muscles feeling good and stretched from his light workout. He filled the tub with hot water, dumping in a scoop of therapeutic bath crystals. He knew Cayson's sore muscles would appreciate it. He was looking forward to rubbing Cayson down with a warm cloth and massaging the oil into his spent body. He'd really taken his lesson seriously, given it everything he had. Cayson may not have been the strongest or the fastest, but it was sheer will and determination that won a fight many times, not only build and stamina. Cayson had caught on like the brilliant man he was and quickly learned where his strengths were. Tomorrow he'd build on the pressure points lesson. But for now, maybe he could revive Cayson enough to be interested in a different type of lesson Quick wanted to teach him.

His bathtub was partially concealed behind a wall in his remodeled bathroom. He'd torn out part of the second bedroom to build himself a nice-sized master bath with a large shower and a massive whirlpool tub. He made sure the water was perfect and took two fluffy towels out the linen closet, placing them on the towel warmer. Cayson was still shaving when he emerged from behind the wall. "Bath's ready."

"So am I." Cayson smiled sexily, dropping his boxers and stepping out of them.

Quick removed his own briefs, both of them standing and admiring the other. "You going to look at me all night, or do you want me to bathe you?" Quick asked, walking closer, and enveloping Cayson tightly. "I'm so proud of you. Vaughan didn't pull any punches on you. You did good tonight, baby. I know some of that stuff can be scary."

"Thank you," Cayson whispered. "I'm just a little tired now. I'm glad I have tomorrow off."

"I hope you're not too tired." Quick stressed the word *too*, climbing over the tub's edge, and held his hand out to Cayson.

"What'd you have in mind?" Cayson purred, easing down along with him, molding his back to Quick's chest. Ahh. It was absolute perfection. Dr. Cayson Chauncey was finally naked and in his arms… hopefully for good.

Quick picked up the thick washrag and began to rub it up and down Cayson's chest.

"Damn, this feels incredible." Cayson sighed.

Quick slid down so his face was next to Cayson's and he could nestle in the crook of his neck and lick at the mark that was still visible on Cayson's pale skin. Those three scary words were swimming around in his head again, taunting him, teasing him that he'd fallen in love way too fast and he was going to get his heart handed to him on a platter… or a trashcan lid.

"Feels good," Cayson moaned seductively. Quick could see Cayson's semi-hard cock bobbing in the deep water. He used his rag to rub over that tight stomach and down the thin trail of fine hair to Cayson's groin. He experimented with a few loose tugs on his shaft, wondering if Cayson was too tired or if he'd—

"You're making me horny."

—Rise to the occasion. Bingo. Quick smiled, gently thrusting his hips, careful not to jostle them too much. He didn't need a gallon of water on his floor. Cayson's ass had to be sore by now, especially after that last round of sex against his door back at his place. Quick's ass however, was tight, and ready to be breeched. He looked down at Cayson's long, thin cock. He could take it. Wasn't obscenely big or anything. Average size. The pain would be minimal, if any, as long as he was prepared properly. His heart hammered in his chest as he prepared to throw his suggestion out there, nervous he might get rejected, but fairly certain he wouldn't. "I was thinking maybe you could make love to… fuck… me this time."

Cayson stopped drawing circles in the oil that had congealed on the hot water's surface. He was very quiet, but Quick felt like rejoicing because the tip of Cayson's cock was sticking up out of the water. He was obviously turned on by the suggestion.

"You want me to take you?" Cayson spoke very low, like he was trying to be sure he'd heard Quick correctly.

"Mmm hmm. Yeah. I want to feel you. I want to feel you so bad." Quick squeezed Cayson close to him, trying to let his actions say what his mouth couldn't. It was too fast. He was pushing his timid doctor. He was still dealing with an unpredictable ex. Quick didn't want to make things more stressful. Hell, the man suddenly found himself needing to learn self-defense.

"Where'd you go?" Cayson had leaned back until the back of his head was resting on Quick's wide shoulder. His pretty blue eyes looked like they could see right through him.

Quick loosened his kung fu grip on Cayson's waist. "Nothing. Was just thinking. Look. We don't have to do anything tonight." He didn't know why he was back-pedaling. He just suddenly felt so raw and exposed. "We can just rest and relax in front of some late night bullshit reality show."

Cayson laughed humorlessly. "Um, okay. Sure. That sounds so much more appealing than being able to make love to you." Cayson turned back around and sighed sarcastically, wiping his brow. "Phew. I'm glad you threw out that other option instead – what'd you call it? Bullshit reality TV? Mmm hmm, that's way better than being able to penetrate a man for the first time." Cayson sat up. "Come on. Let's not waste another minute, let's get our asses in front of that TV now."

Quick yanked Cayson back to him, growling, and biting at his neck. "Real funny, smart ass. I was trying to be mindful of your situation. I don't want to rush you." Quick stopped making him laugh and squirm in his arms, his expression turning serious. "We'll be each other's first."

"That sounds…."

Quick smirked. "I know. As old as we are, huh? Talking about experiencing firsts."

"Speak for yourself." Cayson raised one brow at him.

"Okay, I will." Quick ran his hand over Cayson's wet hair. He loved how it looked dark brown when wet, making his bright blue eyes appear peculiar and majestic. "I want to experience a lot of firsts with you, Cays." Quick hoped that was close enough without actually having to say the words. He wanted Cayson to know that what they'd been doing, what they were about to do, was the most important thing to him since having Vaughan. This was so major in his life. He'd known he was bisexual for over twenty-five years and had never gotten to act on it until now. Until Cayson stormed into his life, he'd thought he'd be alone. He'd only been sure he didn't want another conservative, high-maintenance woman. He never actively pursued a man. Hell, he practically ran from Cayson when he first realized he'd found the man extremely attractive. Then, when he knew without a doubt that he wanted him, wanted the hot doctor underneath him, he tried to scare Cayson away. Thank god he had Duke and his son to talk some sense into him. Now here he was offering his body and his heart… and having no regrets.

# CHAPTER THIRTY-ONE

*Cayson*

They'd finished bathing quickly and were in Quick's large bed underneath his blankets, warming each other with light touches and hot, panting breaths along their damp skin. It was a chilly night and Quick's bedroom was large, and a little drafty. If it weren't for Quick's huge body, which he was quickly realizing doubled as a furnace; he'd be curled up, cold and uncomfortable.

Cayson knew what was coming, knew what he was getting ready to do, and he'd be lying if he said he wasn't over the fucking moon about it. Being able to top a man like Roman Webb. Holy shit. Cayson took a deep breath and pushed at Quick's shoulder until he was lying flat on his back. He could feel the erratic rise and fall of the big man's chest. Knowing he had to get him to relax, Cayson aligned his body with Quick's as well as he could with their height difference, and started a slow grind.

Quick pressed his head back into his pillow, moaning how much he was enjoying what Cayson was doing to him. With his long throat exposed, Cayson leaned in and sucked passionately at all the enticing stubble along Quick's jaw. He thought he'd loose his mind when Quick spread his large thighs wide and allowed Cayson to nestle in between, encouraging him to keep moving his hips. It simulated fucking, and Cayson clenched his teeth in concentration, careful not to rut until he came like a teenage boy. "Fuck, Rome. I know I'm gonna blow as soon as I'm inside you." Cayson thrust again, the head of his cock nudging against Quick's tight star. Fuuuuck.

Quick leaned over, his long arm reaching blindly for his nightstand. Cayson got the hint and opened the drawer, wishing for a second he'd find a huge dildo in Quick's drawer too, but unfortunately, he only saw a few envelopes, some miscellaneous tools or whatever, an unopened economy size box of condoms and at least five different tubes of slick. *Nice, he's prepared.* Cayson smiled shyly and pulled out the large box. When he looked at Quick, he simply winked back at him. Leaving the condoms for a minute, he opened one of the lubes and let some drizzle down his fingers.

He leaned back on his knees and coaxed Quick's legs wider. They'd left the lights off in the bedroom, the bathroom light providing plenty enough for Cayson to see the dark smattering of hair nestled alluringly between those plump ass cheeks. It was so tempting to bury his face right there and lick and taste Quick until he could truly say he knew the man personally. Instead, he rubbed his finger around the taut skin and sank his mouth over the head of Quick's cock, pulling a deep, delicious moan from him.

"Oh, god, yes. Damn, Cays."

Cayson sucked in more of Quick's length, slurping and making the most obscene noises to rival any porno.

"Fuck, that's perfect."

He hadn't seen perfect. Cayson didn't have firsthand experience on how to fuck, but he did know how to study the hell out of something. He'd read every damn thing he could on gay sex, especially in his early twenties. Those who couldn't do it… read and fantasized about it. He was feeling as confident as he would if he were taking his medical boards. He'd make this awesome for Quick, because he knew now what made it awesome for him. Patience.

Cayson slowly dragged his mouth all the way up Quick's shaft and kissed the tip of that fleshy meat, only to dive back down again. He tasted so rich and fulfilling. When he felt Quick's hips buck up into his touch, he knew that was the time to add something. Quick's body had to be screaming and demanding more, because that's exactly what his own body was doing. He noticed Quick was up on one elbow, his long, wet hair laying across his pillow as he watched with fascination. It was a sight right out of his wildest dreams. A huge, tattooed Adonis was staring down at him, waiting to be taken. Cayson kept his eyes on Quick's dark green orbs and swallowed him to the root while pushing his index finger in to the first knuckle. He was glad he didn't miss the look of blissful surprise cross that handsome face. Sucking harder, faster, Cayson turned his hand palm up and pushed in deeper, angling upwards.

"Ah! Fuck!" Quick bucked hard, throwing his head back and cursing, but Cayson didn't let up off his prostate for a second. A huge burst of precome landed on Cayson's tongue, and his own cock surged with need, leaking on Quick's dark brown sheets. He ignored his throbbing dick and lapped at Quick's balls, rolling them around on his tongue, slicking down the short hairs with his spit. Glancing back up, he saw Quick nodding his head at something, Cayson hoped it was what he was doing. He pushed in a second finger, pausing momentarily at Quick's hiss, then moving deeper and deeper into that hot confinement.

"You. I want you," Quick gasped, falling flat on his back. With one hand, he reached out and gripped a handful of Cayson's hair, pushing his head back into his groin, thrusting up into his face. Did he want to fuck Cayson's face or did he want to be fucked now? Cayson didn't take time to decide. He moved Quick's wide palm to the back of his head and sealed his mouth over his seeping dick again. This would be a good distraction while he got his lover ready.

Quick was a fast study. He held Cayson's head low as he pumped his hips, shoving his length down Cayson's throat while spearing himself on Cayson's slick fingers. He clamped one hand down on the base of his own dick in a tight grip, hoping it'd stave off his orgasm. His dick pulsed so hard, he knew he was going to erupt any minute. He hadn't had his face fucked properly in a long time… if ever. He took it, too. Took every bit of the strong, relentless pounding. Damnit. He had to get inside of this man. He wouldn't make Quick's first time that big of a disappointment by shooting all over himself.

"I'm gonna come." Quick's voice was gravely and rough. "Make me come, Cays."

Cayson leaned over and with shaking hands; he managed to get the condom on his cock and even lubed himself without spraying his spunk all over Quick's legs. He wanted to take him just like they were, but it'd be easier and more comfortable for them both if he settled in behind him instead of trying to lift Quick's leg onto his shoulder. Um, not likely to work since it probably weighed more than he did.

He inched over and nudged Quick's shoulder, urging him to roll onto his side. Cayson moved in behind him, pushing that thick leg up towards Quick's chest. He angled himself at Quick's entrance and gripped his hip to hold him still while he pressed inside.

With only the head in, Cayson thought he would lose his mind or explode. *Oh, my god, he's so damn hot.* He was very thankful that he was behind Quick, because he had a feeling he was making a face scary enough to use on Halloween. Quick's ass was tighter than he ever could've imagined. Squeezing his dick to the point of just this side of unbearable pain.

Fuck, fuck, fuck, fuck.

Quick was jerking every time Cayson eased in another inch, grunting and moaning in what sounded like ecstasy. It wasn't until he was buried all the way that he released a lungful of air.

Quick gulped in air too, exhaling roughly. Cayson tried to lean up far enough to see Quick's face. He turned to look at him, allowing him to see into the erotic green eyes of the most gorgeous man he'd ever met, and he knew at that moment, he'd fallen in love. He was glad his brain still had enough blood in it to tell his heart it was too cliché to say, "I love you," while he was balls deep inside a man for the first time, but he was going to say it, and soon.

"You okay?" he asked instead. Struggling to stay in control, and not start pumping without letting up until he overflowed the condom.

"Yeah. Slow. Go slow."

Cayson moved Quick's long hair off his face, pulling him to his mouth while he eased out a couple inches and just as slowly eased back in.

Quick moaned and Cayson swallowed it down. "Just like that."

"Baby, you're so damn tight."

"You're longer than I thought."

Cayson grinned. That was a damn good compliment. Rocking his hips, Cayson got into an easy groove. He didn't have the urge to go crazy with reckless abandon anymore, instead, he had the overwhelming sensation to keep the loving slow and sacred.

"Damn. Deeper."

Cayson wrapped his body around Quick's so he could comply. He pushed in until he was able to grind against that hairy ass. The electricity was instant and powerful. He couldn't resist pulling out almost to the tip, then gliding every inch back in, dragging his entire length against Quick's narrow channel, only to grind against him again.

"Ohhhhhh. Fuuuuuck you." Quick hunched his back, gripping at the edge of the mattress.

Cayson chuckled. Damn, his bad boy had a way with expressing himself. He had to let go, he needed to come. But he wanted Quick to lose it first. *Please, god, give me a little more strength.* He reared back, pushing his pelvis harder against Quick's ass, as deep as he could, and kept using slow, shallow thrusts. He saw Quick's arm moving frantically in front of him. He was already jacking himself. Cayson knew exactly what that craving felt like. He stroked everywhere his hands could reach. Massaging Quick's shoulders, his strong back, massaging those furry cheeks, using his fingers to touch and rub around their connection. Everywhere.

"Love your hands on me. You got me so fuckin' hard, Cays." Quick's breath was coming fast, his orgasm on the edge of peaking. "Oh, fuck."

Cayson upped the pace. Still not pistoning his hips, but driving in fast enough to tip them over the precipice now. "Yes, fuck me. Make me yours."

Cayson was just cognizant enough to decipher what Quick was mindlessly murmuring while Cayson drove his long cock in and out of his virgin hole. "Mine," Cayson whispered to himself, getting lost in the rhythm, lost in the pleasure. His toes curled tight enough to cramp, and his back went rigid before his cock hardened ramrod straight.

"I can't hold it," Cayson groaned. Thrusting a few more times. "You feel too good."

"Fuck, yeah. That's your fuckin' hole," Quick answered, his fist still flying up and down his own thick cock.

That did it. Quick couldn't talk like that. He couldn't tell Cayson his body was his. What was he going to do with all of this man? Could he keep him happy? Could he satisfy his needs? Hell, he could barely penetrate him for two minutes without blowing.

"Ugh! Ugh!" Quick's hand stilled while he squeezed the head of his hard dick until his come erupted from him, landing on the sheets in a milky puddle.

*Thank you, lord.* Cayson tumbled right along with him. He was completely on autopilot. He rubbed along Quick's back while he rode out his powerful release. He nestled his cock into that hot bottomless chamber and let himself go, let his come flow, overpowering him with a mixture of amazing euphoria and unyielding love. His body was wrapped tightly around Quick's frame while his dick throbbed inside his lover. Speechless. There were no words. Only their laboring breaths and sweet touches conveyed how they felt as they drifted off to sleep in each other's arms.

# CHAPTER THIRTY-TWO

*Quick*

It had to be the most relaxing sleep Quick had experienced in a long time. Life was absolutely perfect at that moment. The world completely silent and out of his face. Suddenly, the sound of a piercing alarm made him shoot upright in the bed, knocking Cayson off of him. His lover flailed his arms, scrambling at the covers tangled around their legs while he came fully awake. Quick didn't have time to settle him. The alarm on one of their watches was ringing angrily, louder than any smoke alarm he'd ever heard.

Goddamnit. They'd been so lost in each other's bodies they'd both forgotten to put their watches back on. Quick ran into the bathroom, skidding to a stop in front of the counter. He squinted, his sleepy eyes adjusting to the shock of being yanked awake and the assault from the bright light of his bathroom.

He silenced the alarm and waited a minute while it calculated who activated it and where they were located. Quick had the watch in his hand while he yanked on a pair of jeans and an Atlanta Falcons t-shirt. He was at his locked safe on the floor of his closet pulling out his black 9mm handguns when Cayson's frightened voice cut through his determination to get to one of his brothers in need of his help.

"Roman. What's going on?" Cayson asked, standing in the middle of Quick's bedroom, looking unsure.

"Just wait here, okay." Quick looked back down at the face of the watch. "It's Brian. Fuck! He's at the office."

It wasn't even four in the morning. What the hell was going on? Quick's brain screamed. Quick's cell phone rang on the nightstand and he hurried to pick it up. It was Duke. Cayson was watching his every move and Quick wanted to take the time to offer him some comforting words, but he couldn't.

Quick hit the button and Duke's voice blasted through his speaker.

"My alarm rang. Did yours?" Duke sounded like he was moving around just as frantically as Quick was.

"Yes. It's Brian. He's on bond duty. Did he get a call?" Quick asked, tucking his guns behind his back. He raced downstairs with his cell and watch in his hands, Cayson hot on his heels. Duke was still firing off orders while Quick grabbed his leather coat out of his closet.

"Get to the office now, Rome! Get there before Ford! If something's happening with Brian, Ford's gonna kill first, then ask what happened."

"I know. I know."

"I'll see you there. No one approach without my order."

He hit the speaker button and had his hand on the front door without a second thought. If someone had fucked with Brian, Quick and Duke would be down a team member, because Ford would be in jail for first-degree murder if he got there before they did. Quick had to get there first. Brian had activated the team's alarm. Cayson's didn't ring.

"Rome. Maybe I should come with you. What if you need medical help?"

Quick stopped on his porch and turned to Cayson. He wanted to pull him into his arms. The dark morning was cold and unforgiving, and his doctor only had on a pair of shorts he'd scooped up off the floor. "You can't. Too dangerous. If I need you, I'll call you."

No kiss, no hug, no nothing. Rome turned to dash down the two steps.

"Rome." Cayson rushed to get his attention before he was gone.

"Yeah?" he called over his shoulder, unlocking his truck.

"Please be careful."

Fuck. This was a pretty big reality check for Cayson. Quick didn't have time to say the right thing to take that worried look off his angelic face. He wondered what Duke was saying to Vaughan right now. Was his son used to this life already? Used to the life of a bounty hunter? Would Cayson be able to handle it? Maybe it was best they found out now, before Quick handed over his heart. Too late. He had a sinking feeling in his stomach that Cayson would be gone when he got back, but he still had to go. Had to force himself to nod at his lover and get inside the cab. He and Ford were about the same distance away from the office. Duke had a slightly longer drive. Looking at his watch, he knew it usually took ten minutes to get to their building, but he was getting ready to break every traffic law in Atlanta. He had to get there ahead of Ford.

# CHAPTER THIRTY - THREE

*Brian*

Motherfucker. Brian clenched his teeth when he was backhanded across his face. He'd been dragged across the floor after being stomped repeatedly by steel toe boots. They tried to get him up into one of the chairs, but he dropped his entire two hundred and forty pounds of muscle like dead weight. No matter how they strained, the three of them couldn't lift him. He acted like he was dazed from the blows, but he was very much alert. He'd managed to hold the alarm button on his watch while he was being kicked. Now he was propped against one of the steel columns in their lobby area with his hands duct taped behind his back. Four minutes and thirty-five seconds. Brian kept counting in his head. His brother would be there in about another four to five minutes. He said a little prayer for the souls of these men. They'd need it. They were about to meet their maker.

"Tell us your name! Tell us your goddamn name!"

Brian didn't speak. He never spoke, but these bastards didn't know that. They thought Brian was just being stubborn. He let his head dangle lazily. One of the three thugs who'd burst through their office door the moment he got back from posting a bond turned a chair around in front of him and lowered himself into it. Brian didn't look up, but he knew exactly how far the man was away from him.

Brian was Special Ops; military trained and used to watching his surroundings, so he'd made sure the parking lot was empty when he got out of his classic Mustang. He'd just got the key inside the door to their office when he heard hurried footsteps approaching, and a blunt object slammed across his back. He hadn't had the chance to counter when another blow landed hard across his temple, knocking him sideways, stunning him.

"Is that him?" One of the men asked, out of breath.

"Gotta be. He's huge."

"Make sure."

"The other owner isn't as tall. This has to be him."

Who are they looking for? No sooner than Brian thought it, he realized this had something to do with Quick. This was personal. These men didn't even know what Quick looked like, that meant they were sent as a favor. Sent by someone who had money.

"Roman… Quick. Whatever the hell your name is."

"Is that you?" One of the other men was smart enough to have a hoodie over his head and a black ski mask concealing his identity. He appeared to be the lookout man, because he fidgeted nervously as he stared out the window. "Just say your name and we'll leave."

Brian wanted to roll his eyes. These guys were idiots. If they were after Rome, then they should've at least known what he looked like. And it was obvious they didn't scope out the area, otherwise they'd know everyone who worked there, and they'd target the right man. For fuck's sake, his photo was on the company website. Now they were all going to either be seriously injured or die because of their amateur methods.

"Dude, call your nephew again and ask him what the guy looks like. Tell him we got him. He's freakishly tall, tattoos, and built as shit. This has to be him." The man who posed like he was in charge had an older model six shot revolver pointed dead center at Brian's chest.

The third one pulled out a cell phone and started dialing. Brian could hear the phone ringing, could hear a male voice pick up, barking angrily through the connection. He kept his count in the back of his head and tried to listen intently to the caller. Concentrating on his tone, accent, words or repeated phrases. The more intel he could gather the better.

"I know you said not to call you, but I wanted to be sure we had the right guy."

There was more angry shouting across the line, and the third guy began looking more and more frightened. "Shit. Oh, my god. I think… Wait a minute. I don't… I don't—"

Brian tried to keep his thoughts clear. Any minute they were going to figure out that he wasn't Quick. They'd tied his hands but not his feet, and they thought he was still dazed. If the guy with the gun came any closer, Brian could spring up and kick it out of his hand. He'd have a spit second to grab him while he was shocked, and have him between his thighs, choking the life out of him before the others could react. Hopefully, the others didn't have weapons, but if they did, he'd fight until one of them shot him. *Stay in fight mode. Stay in fight mode.* He couldn't let his mind go back to that cave. Not back to the hell he'd lived in for ten months. Couldn't let the fear claim any other parts of him, it'd already taken his voice.

Keeping his breathing even, he thought of what was important to him. He thought about his big brother. About his team, his new band of brothers. He thought about Jenkins. He owed it to him to fight every day. He'd given his life so Brian could live. When Jenkins took his last breath in Brian's arms, he'd promised him, promised he'd never give up in that cave, and he damn sure wasn't going to give up now and let some haughty doctor take his life because of a mistaken identity, not after everything he'd been through.

He could hear Dana's tricked out muscle car in the distance. If he was already here… so were the others. But where? Obviously, they hadn't pulled into the parking lot; they had to be approaching on foot. Now it was time to notify the cops. He used his thumb to push the button for 911, he held it longer than needed, making sure they got the call. Cops would come flying towards them with sirens wailing and scare the shit out of the wannabe hitman. He hoped he hadn't waited too long, but he was confident his brother and friends were getting ready to make a move any minute.

The gunman gripped Brian under his chin and knocked the butt of his gun into his jaw hard enough for him to fear it was broken... again. The pain was immediate and devastating, but he steeled his resolve. He'd taken worse blows than this pussy could give. This fake gangster wouldn't know torture if he gave him a ten hour lecture on it. Now the Taliban... they knew how to torture.

"Shit. Stop. Stop. That's not him." The third thug let the phone dangle from his fingers. Now it was someone else's turn to look sick. "This guy doesn't have a long ass ponytail, Jake."

"You idiot. Don't say my goddamn name," the leader yelled, pushing the guy hard in his back.

Okay, it was now or never. Brian couldn't wait any longer. Only one man was wearing a mask, the other had actually used his cell phone to call the person who hired them, and now Brian knew one of the men's legal names.

"What? What do you mean, it's not him?!" The gun holder yelled.

The phone was blaring an irritating dial tone, and the third guy looked like he was about to shit himself. "The guy, Quick, or something. Has long hair. Really long. This guy is almost bald."

"I'll make you fuckin' talk." The gunman sneered and squeezed Brian's already bruised jaw. Bile stirred instantly in his stomach and threatened to spew out from the pain. Brian spit the blood from his mouth onto the guy's shoe. *I'll pay you myself, ya punk, if you can make me talk again.*

"Answer me!" The man boomed, standing over him.

When he finally looked up into the man's eyes, ready to make his move, he noticed a red dot, bright and steady in the center of his forehead. Brian tried to brace himself, but nothing prepared you for death. Ever.

*Bye, bye.*

The sound of glass shattering, and the disgusting grunt of pain from the gunman's mouth right before his head exploded in the middle of their office, triggered an involuntary reaction in Brian. He tried to curl in on himself at the same moment the body was propelled ten feet away from him by the bullet's impact. The lifeless body hit the wooden floor with a punishing thud. His arms and legs bent and twisted in unnatural directions. When Brian chanced a look, the gunman's head was half off, practically split in two, and one wide-open eye stared back at him. He would've cried out if he'd been able. He needed his brother, needed him to save him… again.

Ford! Ford! Why couldn't he just yell? He wasn't sure, but it felt like his mouth was forming the words, but there was no sound. Like always.

Duke and Quick were busting through the door before realization had computed for the remaining assailants. The two men started to panic when they saw the state their partner was in. It would make even the toughest S.O.B. cringe in the instant right before his brain kicked in and told him to bolt. The one who'd made the phone call was already on the floor retching when Ford busted through the back door, both guns drawn and aimed. His sharp eyes took in the entire scene, including Brian's busted face. Still running, Ford went for the first man he saw, with his full momentum. He kicked the scared thug in his already convulsing stomach, knocking him into the wall. The impact hard enough to cause him to bounce off it, and Ford's huge boot was there and poised again. His next blow landed in the center of the guy's chest, sending him sliding across the bloody floor, putting him right next to his dead partner in crime.

Ford looked back at his brother, and dropped to his knees, gently cupping Brian's bruised face. "I'm here, Brian."

He knew his brother was there, could hear him, but he couldn't see him. His eyes were blurry and moisture leaked down his face. All he could see was Jenkins looking at him like he had in that cave. The visage wore a clear look of disappointment and was aimed at Brian for breaking his promise.

"I'll fuckin' kill all of you," Ford hollered, standing back up and going for the man Quick had already secured.

# CHAPTER THIRTY-FOUR

*Quick*

"Duke! Get him," Quick yelled, trying to shield the man from Ford's wrath. They already had one dead. They needed the other two alive for questioning. They had no idea why these three men were in their office beating the shit out of Brian. Was it a bond gone wrong? We're they trying to rob him? They knew nothing. But if they let Ford kill them all, it would stay that way.

Duke and Dana pulled Ford off of Quick's back when he tried to get to the other attacker. The man looked relieved that Quick was there, and he used his big body as a shield. "Help me."

"Shut up," Quick snapped at the guy, standing back up to his full height when Dana and Duke had Ford under control.

"It's you. You're... you're Quick."

Quick looked down at the guy and it was like a light bulb turned on in all of their heads at once. Ford scowled at Quick, and Duke was at his side in a heartbeat. Damn, he didn't want to have to fight Ford. But he understood his fury. His brother – a previous prisoner of war – had taken Quick's beating. While he'd been laid up under his loving doctor, Brian was taking his ass whupping. Shit.

Quick put his hands up. "Ford. I'm gonna fix this."

"*We're* gonna fix this," Duke added, staying close to Quick's side.

"They attacked my brother because they thought he was you." Ford's tone was sinister and angry. Ignoring the loud wail of sirens closing in on them, Ford stepped into Quick's space. He was prepared to take a punch if he had to. He deserved it. Quick was the one who had goaded a wealthy man and taken his prized possession, now his family was paying for his selfishness. "If you don't take care of it… I will. I'll eliminate any and every one who's a threat to Brian."

"I'm not a threat to any of you. You know that. You know me, Ford."

"Then it's that goddamn doctor of yours. Where is he?" Ford yelled.

*He better be home in my bed.*

"Are you threatening him? Are you threatening Cayson?" Quick didn't realize he was advancing until he felt Duke's palm against his sternum. Dana looked too confused to pick a side, so he stood there, his still-smoking rifle in his hand.

"Easy. Calm down, Rome." Duke was there in front of him, but Quick was still locked on Ford's stealthy eyes while he held his brother. Was he thinking about getting even? Rome realized he didn't know the lengths to which Ford would go to protect his blood. Duke, Dana, and him were nothing more than colleagues when it came down to it. Brian was something else altogether to Ford. If Ford hurt Cayson… Quick snarled, his body starting to shake from an adrenaline spike. "Rome, look at me. Look at me damnit."

Quick closed his eyes and then opened them again. Ford was still watching him carefully, but Quick looked at his best friend and listened to his words. Duke knew how to bring him back from the edge. If Ford thought he was angry, he hadn't seen anything yet. Ford reacted well, compared to what Quick could do. Ford could be pulled back and held. When Rome got angry and unleashed his specially trained beast, there was no holding him. There wasn't a submission hold he couldn't break. If Ford was promising retribution, he hoped he aimed it where it belonged. At Dr. Joe.

A fire engine and a paramedic pulled into their tiny parking lot, but the police stopped them from entering. Dana propped his rifle against his desk, raised his hands high in the air. The police entered with their weapons drawn, cautiously moving around them, taking in the dead body and the two subdued perps. None of them moved, waiting for the officers to feel safe enough to tuck their guns back in their holsters.

Duke checked to make sure Rome was calm enough to leave his side.

"I'm okay, Duke," Rome answered the silent question. "Go help Brian."

Quick went to stand behind his desk while Duke filled in the officer in charge. Quick wanted to go in Duke's office and have a stiff drink, while he called Cayson just to hear his voice. Cayson. Fuck. He was there alone. Well, hopefully, he hadn't left and gone home. It was definitely too dangerous now. He finally got his hands to stop shaking long enough to send Cayson a quick text.

*I'm okay. You still at my place?*

When Quick lifted his gaze, Brian was being checked over by the paramedics, while the fireman and cops stood over the dead body. Quick groaned under his breath. This was going to take all damn day. Paperwork out the ass, including a lengthy trip downtown for more official statements. Yellow police tape all over their property and the news cameras which were sure to follow, never brought the kind of publicity they were going for. Surely, it was a justified shooting. Dana was a licensed marksman, all he'd done was save SWAT from having to come down and do the job themselves. His phone vibrated in his palm.

*Thank god, I've been going crazy!! I'm still here. You coming back soon? Was it a false alarm???*

God, he wished. It was already daybreak, the sun just barely lighting up the gloomy sky. He looked at his watch.

"You got somewhere to be?" One of the young cops asked Quick, watching him cautiously, raising a cocky brow in his direction.

He wanted to flick the rookie off. His sculpted biceps were crossed over his starched blue uniform shirt and all the gel-spiked hair screamed "Fresh out of the academy." He had something to prove to his sergeant, so Quick ignored him. As soon as the paramedics got Brian on the stretcher, Ford walked out with him, his hand firmly inside his brother's. The driver was shaking his head when Ford tried to climb inside the back. All it did was set off another wave of anger. Surprisingly, Dana ran outside, wrapping his long arms around Ford's bulk, pulling him backwards while the medics slammed the doors and sped out of the parking lot. Quick watched out the window, not intervening, thinking it better to not add to Ford's stress. Dana was whispering something in his ear and it appeared to do the trick. It also looked intimate, from where he stood.

Ford turned to look at Dana, neither of their mouths were moving, but their bodies were so close that they could've been whispering in each other's ears.

"What's going on?" Duke asked, looking to see what Quick was watching so intently. "Oh."

"Is Dana?"

"I don't think so." Quick frowned.

"Is Ford?"

"Whatever. I don't give a damn. What'd you find out from the cops?"

"It's exactly what we thought."

"Goddamnit."

"Call Cayson. We all need to stick together right now. That distinguished, well-known, very rich doctor just put a hit out on you. We need to make moves."

"I know." Quick felt terrible. He watched as Dana ushered Ford into one of the EMS vehicles. They were getting a ride either to the hospital or to their vehicles, which they'd parked around the corner. He wanted to go check on Brian, too, but knew they had to go down to the station.

"Which one of you pulled the trigger?" The rookie cop asked, approaching them from behind with his notepad open.

Duke huffed. "I already told you. My sniper did."

"And where is he?"

"He just left with the paramedics."

"He was ordered not to leave."

"I have an injured man. He went to be with him. And he's not under arrest; it was a justifiable homicide. Besides, he went to the hospital, not the Bahamas," Duke argued, digging some papers out of Dana's desk. He needed to be sure they all had their licenses and credentials when they went to give their statements.

"Um, sir. That's all official police evidence right now." The rookie stood erect, his chest jutting out against the cheap blue polyester of his uniform.

"This is my office, probie." Duke sneered.

"It's my crime scene at the moment. I'm going to have to ask you to step outside."

This was new, but then again, there'd never been a homicide in their office. He wasn't in the mood to argue and hoped Duke wouldn't either. He was past ready to be out of the office. There was vomit, and even urine, on the floor where one of the perps had pissed himself. The tangy, metallic smell of blood was stifling in the closed space. He knew the smell too well. Couldn't stand it. But something worse was coming any minute, and he didn't need the added stench that would surely have him clutching his stomach and throwing up. Post-mortem defecation.

"I'm going to need you both to come downtown with us now." The rookie delighted in telling them what they were going to do.

Quick grumbled, "Call Judge. Tell him to call those friends of his in the Atlanta PD; we might need a couple allies on this one."

"We always think alike, brother." Duke pulled out his cell phone while they were being escorted out of their own building. They went to stand at the end of the sidewalk behind the tape another office was putting around their parking lot. It was brighter outside, and the Atlanta working class was waking up and heading to their jobs while Quick and Duke waited for Judge to answer.

"This better be good," Judge's groggy voice answered on the fourth ring.

"Wish I could call with good news, but it's not happening today."

"What's up?" Judge asked, more alert.

"Fast version. There's been a homicide in the office. Dana fired the kill shot. Brian's hurt and Quick has a hit out on him."

"Oh, damn. Everyone alright?"

"For the most part, yeah. Brian looks bruised pretty bad."

"I'm getting up. I'll be there in an hour. Let me make a few calls."

"Thanks. We're gonna be going down to the precinct soon, so meet us there. Call up your friends in the APD. We need some help. The cops are hinting at we may have used excessive force."

"God and Day? Hell. Shit's about to turn real ugly, now."

"I heard they're a little unorthodox, but just call them."

"You asked for them… you got them."

# CHAPTER THIRTY-FIVE

*Cayson*

He didn't get another text from Quick, but at least he'd gotten the one saying he was okay. Must've been a false alarm. He had no clue what time Quick was going to return, and regardless of the fact that he'd awoken before dawn, he couldn't possibly go back to sleep. He grabbed his messenger bag and went into Quick's office, shutting himself inside with his cell phone right next to him and his watch securely on his wrist.

He rubbed his tired eyes, and looked at his watch. It was after noon already. He picked up his cell phone and checked to see if he had any missed messages. Nope, none. He sighed tiredly, standing to stretch his back. Cayson needed to do something to pass the time, because he'd already caught up on the few files he'd brought with him, and since he wasn't at his home computer, he couldn't access any other files from the hospital. *Why didn't I grab my laptop? Maybe I can run home real fast and get it.* Working was how Cayson always dealt with stress. The hours would pass and before he knew it, Quick would be back and in his arms.

Cayson sent Quick a text and went to put on some warmer clothes.

*Running home a sec, be right back. Need my computer. Don't worry, my watch is on.*

He wanted to add a PS at the end of that message, but again, figured there'd be a better time to say what he felt for Quick. Cayson looked at his watch, then checked his cell phone again.

Quick didn't object to him leaving, assuming he saw his message, so he threw on his thick parka when he heard his cab honking at the curb. He'd drive his own car back so he wasn't stuck here later and forced to use a cab if there was an emergency.

Cayson sat back in the cab after he rattled off his address. He wasn't even halfway there when his cell phone rang in his pocket. He fumbled nervously, hoping it was Quick. His face dropped when he saw it was the nurse's station in the ER.

"Dr. Chauncey speaking." Cayson listened while the ER charge nurse begged for him to come in and help them with a rush. Something about a housing complex fire this morning. Patients were being rerouted to them from Regency South. First, he was miffed about not being able to spend his last day off with Quick, but he felt like a moron, because Quick wasn't able to spend the day with him, anyway. Cayson exhaled in disappointment and told the nurse he'd be there in five minutes, then asked the cab driver to drop him at Emory Hospital instead of home.

It was indeed a madhouse when Cayson rushed through the double doors of the ER. Patients were lined along the hallway, all the rooms already in use. Shit, why hadn't anyone opened the other triage area? One of the ER doctors on duty was taking a woman up to maternity; the other three were in patient rooms. Cayson looked at the chart and began crossing off and rewriting in new orders. If they didn't clear the waiting room, there was no way they could accurately assess how many patients they were able to take from College Park. A fast track acute center should already be running as well, to clear out the patients with minor scrapes and bruises.

"Dr. Chauncey. Thank god you're here. We're so slammed. Dr. Benton and Dr. Rajih are both in with traumas. No one else could come down. I really hated to call you on your day off, but I knew you'd come." Nurse Jenny smiled sweetly at him.

Cayson looked down and gave her his most understanding smile, lightly patting her shoulder. She was completely flustered; her usually tight bun was hanging loosely at the nape of her neck as she used a threadbare washrag to wipe the perspiration off her forehead. Her other arm was weighted down with files, and Cayson hurried to relieve her of them. "Here. Give those to me. Send three nurses to do acute injuries in the south wing, and send two to triage."

"That'll only give us four RNs in the main wing," she said tiredly.

"We'll make do. The faster we clear out the non-emergencies, the better you're going to feel." This was medical school 101. He didn't understand why he had to tell them that every time. He plucked the files from her and let her scurry off to do what he'd said. As he separated the files, a name caught his eye and he went back to take a closer look. King, Brian P.

Cayson let the name roll around in his head. It wasn't clicking. He'd heard that name, very recently. Well, it was a common name. Cayson had almost tossed the thin file into Dr. Rajih's pile, but his eyes caught the next of kin on his information page: King, Bradford, Sibling.

The King brothers from Quick's office. The big ex-military guys. Yep, it was them, because the file indicated a sign language interpreter was required. What were they doing here? Cayson's stomach dropped. Was that who the alarm was for? Is Roman here? Cayson took off in the direction of trauma room nine. He knew he should've finished his assignments first, but he had to know what was going on. Had to know Quick and Duke were okay, as well as Brian.

He tapped on the glass before he pulled back the curtain. As soon as he stepped inside, he was thankful for his years of experience, because he would've gasped in shock at the heavy bandages lying across the entire left side of Brian's face. The man's large frame wasn't able to fit on the standard-sized hospital bed. There were no casts or splints on his limbs, nor was he confined to the bed, so Cayson was able to see his injuries were confined to his face. A morphine drip hung along with a bag of saline. Had Brian been to X-ray, yet? Did he have a CT of his head to be sure he didn't have a concussion or brain injury while he lay there half-asleep from the pain meds? Damnit, Dr. Rajih irritated him with his lazy method of practicing medicine. You'd think the man paid for the tests he ordered out of his personal bank account. Someone always had to come behind him and order more workups.

Cayson was getting ready to address Brian when his big brother stood up, his face a contorted mask of anger and rage. "You," he growled.

Cayson paused, looking over at the third man in the small room, who he recognized as one of Duke's frequent visitors when he was in the hospital under Cayson's care. He think the guy's name was Dan… no, Dana.

"You do this and Quick will never forgive you," Dana said sternly against Ford's ear, standing just as fast and holding onto his forearm so tightly that Cayson could see the blood draining from Dana's nails.

"I don't care," Ford snarled, his large hands were on his hips while he gave Cayson a death glare like he'd never seen before.

"Duke won't either. This man is a friend and very important to all of them. None of this was his fault." Dana kept talking. Cayson wore a bewildered expression.

He had no clue what was happening. Why was Ford so mad at him? They'd just met. Literally, yesterday. The man had been talking about protecting him, now he wanted to kill him.

"I'm sorry. I didn't mean to upset you. I saw the name and recognized it. It's fine if you don't want me to treat your brother. But if you let me. I promise I'll treat him like he's the President of the United States." Cayson moved to peel back the bandage on Brian's face, but the way Ford tried to break free from Dana's hold was all the message he needed. Stay away.

"You touch him and you die!" Ford roared.

Cayson jumped back, terrified at the deep octave of the man's voice and the rage he heard in it. He slowly put the chart down on the counter and stepped away from Brian's bedside. "I only wanted to help. He needs more tests done than that." Cayson pointed at the chart. "He hasn't been checked properly for a concussion, he needs more neuroimaging. I know he doesn't talk, but has anyone interviewed him for signs of a heady injury using you as a translator?"

"No," Dana piped in, with Ford still boiling next to him. His mouth a thin, angry line. "No one has been in here for hours. The nurse said they were dealing with a trauma and they'd try to find Brian a room." Dana looked at his watch, identical to Cayson's. "That was three hours ago."

"Ford. Bradford!" Dana yelled next to him. "Let Brian get some help."

"It's his fault." Ford pointed at Cayson and he had to stop himself from looking behind him to see if he meant someone else. How were they blaming this on him? He'd been at Quick's worrying for all of their safety, now he was fearing for his own.

"Where is that punk motherfucker who did this to my brother? Where is he?!"

Cayson assumed security was busy too, because all the screaming and ruckus going on behind their curtain should've been addressed by now. Where was everyone? Not even a nurse came in to see what the noise was. "I don't know what you're talking about."

"Answer me!" Ford boomed.

Cayson turned and fled through the curtain, leaving the chart on the counter. He looked behind him to see if he was going to have to break into a sprint. If Ford came after him, he'd forget about the minimal self-defense training he'd had and haul ass. He was somewhat relieved to see Dana emerge first, looking left, then right before he saw Cayson at the end of the hall.

"Doc. Wait," he called out.

Cayson stopped, but he craned his neck to make sure Dana was alone.

"He won't leave Brian's side, not even to chase you, so don't worry."

"Don't worry." Cayson slumped against the wall, digging his thumbs into his aching eye sockets. "What the hell is going on? And where is Roman?"

"You haven't heard anything from Quick or Duke?"

"No. Not since early this morning. Quick said he wasn't hurt."

"Quick wasn't hurt. Luckily. They got Brian instead, thinking they had Quick. Three men jumped him after he came back from a bail release. They kept trying to get Brian's name out of him, but of course…."

He doesn't talk. Cayson felt the pain so deep he fought to keep from doubling over. "Wait." He pushed off the wall, and started pacing while he put together what Dana said. "Some guys were after Quick, but they got Brian. What guys?"

Dana looked like he didn't want to say anymore, but Cayson glared at him. "Just say it!"

"Your ex-boyfriend sent some guys to kill your new boyfriend, but they got Ford's brother instead."

Cayson slumped down the wall and landed hard on his ass. He plunged his hands into his hair, pulling at the length on top. He'd completely forgotten about the ER and his job. His head started to pound and his heart felt like it'd been stabbed repeatedly. He coughed and hacked, trying to catch his breath. What had Joe done? This was unbelievable. This didn't happen to people like him. This was real life criminal activity going on and he'd started all of it. Brian was... beaten. He couldn't call out for help. So he had to push the alarm. *Oh, god. What did I do? It is my fault.*

"Doc. You alright? Breathe." Dana was squatting next to him. "Hey don't do that. Chill out man. Breathe. Breathe. Everyone is alright now."

He'd fucked up. Big time. He'd dumped Joe and downplayed his anger, calling him a scared anesthesiologist. All the while, he had the capability of an organized mastermind. Quick and Duke would never want to see Cayson again. He was a troublemaker who had brought strife and chaos to their close-knit family. This wasn't who he was. He didn't cause problems – he fixed them. Well, now he was the problem, and Ford was going to fix him properly. He wouldn't be able to run forever. Cayson would pay for what happened to Brian. Maybe Ford would kill him swiftly. Surely, he knew how. He felt sick. Sicker than any patient in that hospital.

"No. No. Don't pass out. Shit! Quick is going to kill me for telling you." Dana sounded tired and extremely nervous, but Cayson couldn't form any type of response. "Doc! Doc!"

Cayson's world was tilting and fading to darkness. Was that the ground? His cheek was smashed hard against something freezing cold and he wanted to pull away from it, but his body was completely zapped of energy. He must've had his eyes closed, because he couldn't see a thing and it scared the shit out of him. He heard his name being called and he thought he answered, but if he had, they wouldn't keep calling out to him. He was jostled and pulled as he was hoisted up and carried away, he didn't know where he was taken because he couldn't figure out where he was.

# CHAPTER THIRTY-SIX

*Quick*

*Augh! I have to know what's going on with Brian.* Quick was in an interrogation room no bigger than his downstairs bathroom. He assumed Duke was in another just like it somewhere else in the building. He was slowly going out of his mind in the tight confinement, especially when there was so much more Quick needed to be doing. He needed to talk to Cayson and Vaughan. Let them know everything was going to work itself out. Right now, no one knew anything about where they were. And Brian. Was he okay? Quick massaged his temples, groaning at his ever-growing to-do list. They had bond calls that were probably going unanswered. People still got arrested on Sundays. Magistrate recognizance bonds were the easiest. He had a feeling Duke hated to miss those.

They hadn't officially been charged with anything, but it was clear they weren't free to go. They could be held for questioning up to thirty-six hours, ninety-six if they were suspected of a serious crime. Murder was quite serious. He hoped the APD checked their facts quickly, because he was ready to go.

They'd taken all his possessions: his cell, his wallet, his goddamn watch. Everything. He hadn't been able to contact Cayson and let him know to stay at his house with all the doors locked. He huffed again in frustration. At least he wasn't chained like an animal anymore. They'd removed the wrist and ankle cuffs an hour after he got there. He tried to do his breathing exercises to keep his anger at bay, but the more he thought of needing to hear from Cayson that he was safe, the less effective the techniques were. It wouldn't be long before he was up and putting his fist through that one-way mirror. He'd punched through way thicker objects.

Quick figured it had to be at least one or two p.m. by now. His stomach was growling loudly, having missed breakfast and lunch. If there was anyone on the other side of that mirror, he was sure they were getting a good laugh at his discomfort. He leaned back in the chair, was trying to pop a few kinks out of his neck when he heard a commotion and loud voices just outside the one door to the room. They were male and it sounded like the argument was escalating, because it wasn't long before Quick could hear exactly what was being said.

"He's my suspect, Lieutenant. A brutal murder has been committed." Quick recognized the voice of the smug rookie who had kicked them out of their office. Had he been watching Quick for hours?

"Looks like self-defense to me." A deep voice responded casually. He sounded important and he sounded in charge.

"A man's head was blown wide open from a distance by an expert marksman."

"Well I gotta meet this guy. Step aside." The third guy's voice was not as deep, and his comments were not as serious as his partner's. Everything this guy said sounded laced with humor.

"With all due respect, Lieutenant Godfrey, this isn't your department. I don't need your assistance. We're more than capable of building a case without the dynamic duo intervening."

"While I'm flattered you find us so dynamite... fuckin' move out of my way."

"Lieutenant Day! Do not speak to my suspect" The rookie was yelling at their backs as the door was forced open so hard Quick thought it'd been kicked, and a  huge, hulking figure appeared in the doorway.

Well, it didn't take rocket scientist to know the sarcastic, witty son of a bitch was the partner. He realized it was the notorious God and Day who Judge raved – well, more like bitched about, all the time. Supposedly, their team was off the charts crazy. But, because their team was so successful and made the mayor look good, they got away with a lot of borderline ethical crap. They weren't only partners on the police force, they were also lovers, and it was no secret. That in itself was badass, because couples were prohibited to work together in the same department in most any government job.

"And you are?" The man who stepped from behind his taller partner said by way of greeting. They both had on street clothes, accessorized by bright gold badges with Lieutenant etched in black across the top.

"You first." Quick stood to his full height, only to realize that the big motherfucker glaring at him with intelligent green eyes, packing two of the largest handguns he'd seen, was an inch or two taller. Damn.

"I think you know who we are."

"I think you know who I am," Quick said right back, tilting his head down at the file now in Day's hands. Day nodded once, a disturbing smirk on his – good fucking lord he was fine – handsome face.

"We don't have all day. Judge is in our office. You can walk over with us," God said with finality.

"Then can I leave? Or can I make a one-minute phone call? Is Duke still here? Did he call our lawyer?" he asked either one of them, rapid-fire.

"I don't answer questions, so stop asking. Let's go." God crossed his arms over his chest and moved a couple inches to the side so Quick could get out the door. There was no way in hell they'd both fit.

"Just a goddamn minute. You can't take my suspects!" The rookie yelled at their backs as Quick left the room with God and Day behind him.

"Take a right at the end of the hall and you're gonna take it all the way down to the double doors marked Homicide Division," Day said, keeping pace behind them. "As soon as you walk through them, I want you to yell that everyone there is under arrest for being a fucking idiot and wasting taxpayers' money, under authority of Lieutenant Leonidis Day." Quick frowned and stopped to face the two men. He couldn't be serious.

God was shaking his head, looking as if he was not amused. "Ignore him. Never do anything Day tells you to do. It'll either get you cursed out or laughed at."

Quick didn't speak, simply turned around and followed his two saviors' directions. They did have to walk through a few other departments, including homicide to get to the Narcotics Unit. It was interesting that they got a lot of curious, and more than a few unpleasant looks, but Day had no qualms flicking off other cops if they stared to long. He unnecessarily shoulder checked officers who walked by them in the hall instead of giving them room to pass. He swiped another cop's lunch bag off the end of his desk and rifled through it, all while not missing a step. He took out the apple, tossing the bag back to him. "Next time bring an orange. And stop eating PB&J, what are you, five? Did you come to work or day camp?!" Day yelled with his mouth full of a Red Delicious. He continued to tease his coworkers by plucking papers off their desks when he walked by. Anything to rile up the other officers. Quick hoped they didn't get jumped before they could get to their destination.

Judge had been right. Day was an annoying, gorgeous pain in the ass, whose sole purpose was to get drugs off the streets of Atlanta and make everyone else within its borders miserable.

He had to hide his smile by the time they got to the other side of the huge precinct. Day was one funny motherfucker. It helped to keep him thinking about something other than Cayson or Vaughan. That were both without protection as long as he and Duke were being held. Quick immediately noticed Judge and Duke standing around with several other men, who he assumed were members of God and Day's task force. The older gentlemen in suits stood out like a sore thumb amongst the casually dressed men.

Duke spotted him walking up and held the door that read "Special Task Force – Narcotics – Lieutenant Cashel Godfrey, Lieutenant Leonidis Day, Sergeant Corbin Sydney" open for him. It was an impressive set up. They gave each other a fast one armed hug, Judge stepping up to do the same.

"What the hell took you so long?" Quick grumbled, holding Judge's hand longer.

"Hey. Those guys aren't easy to track down." Judge flicked his long beard in God and Day's direction.

"I'm sure they're in real high demand," Quick said under his breath.

"Hey. If you're dissatisfied, I'm more than happy to let wonder-rookie, here, hold you for a few more hours until he figures out he doesn't have a goddamn case," Day said sarcastically, pointing his finger at the rookie cop who had followed them the entire way and was now standing in their department.

"Captain. I'm glad you're here." The rookie sneered, still looking at Day.

"Rome, sit down. Hopefully, this will be over soon." Judge motioned to the chairs positioned around a huge white board and conference table. "Captain Murphy is God and Day's boss. Captain Jones is from homicide. Technically, because this falls under his jurisdiction, he's the only one who can release you."

Quick got it. Day and God were good. But their authority was limited. They didn't have the power to just let Duke and Quick walk out of there, but at least they were able to get them in front of the right people, so they didn't have to be there all night.

Captain Murphy was standing back, observing. Captain Jones unbuttoned his suit jacket and sat down at the table, fingering through the file. "I usually let my cops handle their own cases, but God asked me to come over and speak to you personally, as a favor." Everyone was quiet while he read a statement Quick had written when he first got there. When he moved that paper aside, he saw another exactly like his, which he suspected was Duke's.

"Where is Dana Montgomery?"

"He's still at the hospital with the guy who was beaten," Judge answered.

"He was the shooter, sir. I'm sending a car to his house and the hospital. I want to charge him with first degree murder until—"

"Have you lost your mind? I ordered him to shoot. So if you wanna charge someone, charge me," Duke said angrily, struggling to keep from yelling. "That man had a gun trained on one of my guys, and after he'd beaten him half to death, he was definitely getting ready to kill him."

The captain put his hand up, a gesture everyone recognized as telling them to be quiet, while he flipped a few more pages.

"Missing quite a few reports, Officer Cambridge." The captain frowned, looking back at his officer. "Ballistics, forensics, do you have any more evidence that points to malice?"

The rookie didn't look so confident anymore. His eyes darted around to all the men standing around, listening. All of them were in some form of law enforcement, so this guy couldn't BS his way through his reasoning for holding them.

"I'm waiting on those reports, sir."

"And you were making them wait in interrogation rooms?" The captain was looking quite angry, and then he started to look a little embarrassed. "Cambridge, go and follow up on those reports, ASAP."

Day smiled politely and turned to open the door for the fuming rookie. Quick had a feeling Day wasn't willing to let the guy off so easy. When he was almost out the door, Day whispered not so quietly. "And make sure you stop by the bathroom and take a good dump before you get those reports, because you're full of shit." Day slammed the door hard enough to rattle the glass and draw the rest of the bullpen's attention.

Several of the guys hid their laugh under loud coughs while the captain wagged his finger at his Lieutenant. "That was unnecessary, Day."

"I don't like cops who abuse their authority."

The captain scoffed at Day. "Kettle, make sure I introduce you to pot when he gets back."

"Can we stay focused, please?" A man who'd introduced himself as Syn spoke through the noise with authority, calming most of the men... and Day. Quick was surprised. The man had been sitting in the corner, listening with a sharp ear and watching carefully. He only spoke in his grave, raspy voice when he had to.

"Fine." Captain Jones stood, taking the file with him. "I have your written statements. I need Mr. Montgomery to get down here within the next couple of hours to write his own, and he'll need to comply with a ballistic swabbing. I understand Brian King is currently receiving medical attention. I can send an officer who can translate to get his statement."

"I'm sure they'll both comply," Duke answered.

"I'll need a report from Dr. Cayson Chauncey as well."

Quick's head perked up at the sound of his lover's name, but the distinguished man wasn't looking at him as he kept speaking.

"Once the forensics reports come back, I'll hand this off to one of my lead detectives. Make sure none of you leaves town. As long as your story checks out, I don't know of a DA who'll prosecute. From what I've read." The captain looked up at them with a surprising amount of sorrow. "I hate it had to happen this way, and I'm sorry your man was hurt. I strongly suggest you get restraining orders while my officers locate and question the man whom you allege hired the attackers."

"I can let Dana know to get down here now." Duke sounded about as ready to leave as Quick was. "I have all his paperwork, but it was taken along with all the other stuff from my office."

"Yeah. Can I get my phone back now?" Quick looked back and forth at God and Day. He really needed to speak to Cayson.

"We're not your fuckin' errand boys, Marlboro Man. You can get your shit on the way out, like anyone else," Day snapped back at Quick.

Who did he think he was talking to? This was not the time to get on Quick's nerves. He'd been thrown in a tiny room and cut off from his loved ones for hours. He was struggling keeping his ire under control. When he looked at Day's smug smile, he felt an overwhelming desire to slap it off his face. Quick sizzled in his seat while Day watched him to see if he'd make a move.

"Rome," Duke hissed. "Settle down. They did help us."

Damn, his friend knew him well. Ignoring the warning, Quick was ready to throw up a challenge, but he felt more than he saw the heavy presence of Day's partner. God was watching Quick with the intense green eyes of a fierce guardian. It was a look that told Quick without words that he may want to think about his next move very carefully. God looked like a man who didn't appreciate his possessions being threatened, either. Quick's heart pounded in his chest, and his hands began to squeeze the arms of the chair, almost to the point of tearing them off. The look Day wore, it was like he took pleasure in making others squirm. As the captains talked and the rest of the team went back to work, no one was paying attention to their silent exchange.

Quick looked back at God, he didn't think the man had even blinked. If there was one thing a predator could immediately recognize, it was when he was in the company of another predator who was just as strong. Regardless of how well trained Quick was, he didn't want to go up against a man who actually called himself God. When two alpha lions fought, there was rarely a victor… just mutual destruction and a lot of bloodshed.

He turned away. His inner beast didn't like backing down from the challenge, but he had more important things to handle. Fighting God wasn't one of them.

When he finally turned back, Day nodded his head and whispered, "I thought so."

# CHAPTER THIRTY-SEVEN

*Cayson*

As soon as Cayson woke up, feeling groggy and unsettled, he saw Dr. Rajih standing there, looking up at the television, which was airing a special report about a local homicide. Cayson turned away from the typically inflammatory local news. It took him a minute to look around, his head pounding hard enough for him to grit his teeth. Did I fall? Cayson thought back to what had landed him on this bed in the surgeon's lounge.

"Cayson!" Dr. Masey came in, with a flourish of long blonde hair, with White Diamonds perfume lingering on her white coat. She was on the transplant board with him, so he'd gotten to know her pretty well. "Oh, my lord. I just got in and I heard what happened."

"Great," Cayson groaned, leaning up on one elbow.

"Hey, hold on, Doc. Your scary nurse friend said that you were not to move if you woke up, and to come get her as soon as you did," Dr. Rajih said, hurrying towards the door.

Cayson had no clue what time it was, but looking out the window, he could see it was fairly late. The sun had gone down, and the daylight was slowly creeping behind it. Dr. Masey laughed, sitting on the foot of the cot he was resting on. "He must be talking about Jenny."

"Sure, Dr. Rajih. Thank you for keeping watch. But I'm fine." Cayson's voice was full of exhaustion that he couldn't hide. He waved the doctor away, hoping he could be gone by the time he made it all the way back from the ER with a very busy Jenny.

"So what happened?" Dr. Masey asked, poking gently at the bruise on his cheek. "You got a little bump there. Did that happen when you passed out?"

"I guess."

"Did you want to run a few tests? I'll work them up myself," she asked, smiling sweetly while her expert fingers traced the bones of Cayson's cheek.

"I'm good, really. I was already on the floor when I passed out. It was blood pressure. I assure you. I remember now. I was upset about something and hyperventilated. I'm fine Gina, I swear."

"Only if you're sure. You're the specialist." She winked, still cupping his sore cheek.

Cayson held her eye contact for too long, feeling uncomfortable with her extra flirty bedside manner. Dr. Gina Masey was a beautiful woman. Young, and a brilliant urologist, but Cayson couldn't return her advances and she was fast to pick up on it when he gently removed her hand from his face. Maybe she was just testing the waters, but Cayson wasn't bi, he was gay.

He gave her an apologetic smile while he sat upright and began to gather himself. "I really need to get home." He stood up and swayed a little on his feet. She jumped up and grabbed ahold of his elbow. He barely resisted tugging it out of her grasp. When he checked his cell phone, he saw he had no messages from Quick and it was almost six. Cayson felt like he was going to pass out again. Surely, Quick could've sent a text or something by now, if he wanted to. This about confirmed it, Quick was done with him. He probably already had a medical records release request from Duke and Vaughan in his mailbox. He'd not only lost patients, but guys who he'd considered friends, and Rome… *Please don't give up on me.* Cayson felt tears stinging the corners of his eyes. He couldn't lose out on love now. He was almost certain he'd never find it again.

"I'm gonna use the bathroom, Gina. Then I need to make a phone call, if you don't mind."

She waved him off like he was being silly. "Of course. I'll be in my office if you need me."

"Thank you." He avoided looking at her as she left, not wanting her to see his morbid expression.

He went in the bathroom to relieve his bladder, and after finishing, spent an extra few seconds splashing cold water on his face to try to wake up, but all it did was aggravate his headache more. Cayson couldn't help but think about Brian, too. Was he alright? Had he gotten all his tests done? Was he discharged or admitted? He knew it wasn't a good idea to go looking himself, because running into Ford was the last thing he wanted to do. They were probably all down there now, if Brian was still here. Cayson's eyes stretched wide. He had to get out of the hospital before any of them found him.

Cayson peeked out the bathroom before he left; wanting to be sure he wasn't seen. He looked at the two computer terminals in the lounge and thought about pulling up Brian's record to see what had happened, but he changed his mind. No longer any of his business. He threw on his big coat and grabbed his personal items off the cot where he'd spent the last few hours. He walked as fast as he could, which wasn't fast at all, trying to escape unseen, but it was obvious word of his fall had spread fast. About thirty people offered to drive him home, but Cayson refused everyone. The walk was a short one, it was still at least somewhat light outside, and the fresh air would help clear his head, maybe even stop the pounding.

His brain was on overdrive. He was asking himself so many questions, so quickly; that he could barely answer one before another was on its heels. He began questioning everything, from his life and chosen profession, to his ridiculous behavior of falling in love with a man so far out of his league it was comical.

He thought they'd both overcome a major hurdle and had learned to trust each other. Cayson even made love to him. Quick had to feel it, right? Before he knew it, his walk to clear his head was over and he was at his gate, unlocking it. He let himself inside, pretending not to see his little old neighbor waving at him. He simply wasn't in the mood for a conversation about perennials. He wanted to get in his bed, close all the shades and put on some sad ass love ballads. He'd never got to experience real heartbreak, and he had to admit, they didn't exaggerate on those Lifetime movies, because this shit hurt worse than anything imaginable.

He didn't bother to turn on his television, instead heading straight to his vinyls. His chest ached right along with his head. He picked an Al Green album from 1975 and placed it gently on the turntable. It'd been his dad's favorite. As soon as the first sounds of crackling emerged from speaker, Cayson thought he'd lose it. Why couldn't he just be left alone to be happy? "Goddamnit!" Cayson picked up the ceramic bowl on his coffee table and threw it with all his might against the wall, shattering it into a zillion pieces, which he was too fucking tired to clean up. Smart, Cayson.

His stomach churned and convulsed like he was going to be sick, but he fought it. There wasn't a damn thing in there to bring up but stomach lining; he hadn't eaten since his English muffin breakfast. He couldn't imagine eating anything right now. *I'm just going to bed.* This was going to be it… this was his life… again. He shouldn't be that upset, because it was only a few weeks ago that it'd been his normal routine. And he was okay with it then. He could've done that forever. But now. Now look at him. He was alone, heartbroken, and probably wanted by the police for questioning, if what Dana said was right. He'd unleashed a madman into his friends' lives. There was no recovering from that.

He wasn't on the second step when his doorbell rang. Sweat popped up on Cayson's temples and leaked down his cheeks as he shook nervously all the way to the door. Was it the police? The knock sounded official.

"W-who's there?" Cayson stammered.

"FedEx with a package." A woman's voice answered.

Cayson opened the door, peeking his head out. He saw the large white truck parked outside his gate and opened the door a little wider.

"For a Dr. Chauncey. I need your signature, sir."

"Um, who's it from?" Cayson already had one return to sender package, and didn't need two. She could take it right back if it was from Joe.

"Last name, Webb. That's all I got on here."

Webb. Cayson breath hitched. It was from Quick. He squinted at her hand-held gadget and accepted the stylus, scribbling his illegible doctor's signature before handing it back to her. "You guys usually come earlier."

"Sorry, new to the route. Running a little behind. Have a good evening." She handed him the flat package and hurried back to her vehicle.

Cayson flipped the square envelope over and saw it wasn't from Quick, but from Vaughan. Why was he sending him a package? He inquisitively ripped the tab and looked inside, almost knocked off his feet. It was an actual record. An old vinyl record, but he didn't recognize the name. He barely closed his front door, still studying the cover. Jeffrey Osborne? Stopping Al Green, Cayson pulled out the record and placed it on his antique record player. He sat down on his couch and listened for the first few notes to start. He wondered what kind of album Vaughan would think to get him. They never discussed music together.

Oh, how he wished he hadn't put on that record. He immediately recognized what it was after the first few beautiful lines.

*I don't even know how to love you*
*Just the way you want me to*
*But I'm ready to love,*
*Yes, I'm ready to love.*

It was their song. The one Vaughan had chosen especially for them on their first official date out. He'd bought the record for them to have, to probably share together. Cayson rubbed his hands over his face, not realizing he was crying until he had to wipe his wet hands on his pants leg. He was torturing himself by listening to every note, every word. Punishing himself. He held his hand to his chest and tried to breathe through the pain. He was ready. He'd been ready. And before he could enjoy it fully, it was ripped away from him. The story of his life.

He must have fallen asleep on his couch, because he was woken up by thin, firm hands, holding him around his waist. It felt different, felt wrong. He fought through another groggy state, trying to understand why he was being held and where he was. As soon as he heard unknown voices, he shot upright, his head screaming as he did. "Oh, my god. Joe! Joe, what are you doing here? Get your hands off me. How'd you get in here?" Cayson jerked and squirmed until he was sitting all the way up. He looked behind him and saw two men who looked like they were well-dressed mobsters standing behind his couch.

"Your door was open. Look, Cayson. I need your help. I'm so sorry about everything. The way I treated you. Talked to you. And I know I don't deserve it, but I need you. I need a friend. I mean really, really need your help." Joe stopped trying to hug Cayson and started walking back and forth in front of him. "I swear to you. I'm innocent."

"I didn't accuse you of anything," Cayson countered, still peeking back at the large men, who had yet to speak.

"Don't worry about them. They're for my protection. I'm in trouble, Cayson. You have to come down to the police station with me and tell them I didn't do it." Joe's hair was a messy bird's nest on top of his head and he had dark circles under his eyes, as if he hadn't slept in days. He had on an Adidas tracksuit, like he'd just come from the gym. Cayson had to be careful not to let his worry show. He'd never seen the man in anything less than business casual. Joe looked like he really was on the run. *Maybe I should... definitely.* Cayson pressed and held every button on his watch, too scared to look down and make sure he was hitting the right one for 911. He wasn't concerned with Joe's innocence; he just wanted him gone. He didn't know this man. It seemed he never had. Cayson just wanted to be left alone, by everyone.

"Turn yourself in Joe. Tell the truth. Your dad has lawyers up the ass."

"I only told that idiot to scare Roman Webb. I didn't tell him to actually try to kill anyone, and I damn sure didn't tell him to hire more men. It wasn't supposed to get this far!" Joe's hands shook with his wild gestures.

"What?"

"Now my outcast nephew on my mother's side is at the police station fabricating a story to get himself a deal and frame me. I wouldn't try to have anyone killed!" Joe grabbed Cayson's arms, shaking him. "Cayson you have to know that. You have to help me."

# CHAPTER THIRTY-EIGHT

*Quick*

"My damn phone is dead. Do you have a charger in here, Judge?" Quick asked from the backseat of Judge's F350.

"Naw. Michaels broke it last week. Haven't replaced it."

"Fuckin' great! All of us in here with dead phones!" Quick punched the seat and Dana jumped in the seat next to him. Duke turned around and looked at him like he was crazy.

"That can happen when you're up at four a.m. and held in a police station for almost twelve hours," Judge said, ignoring Quick's anger.

"Stop me by a payphone or something," Quick ordered, his skin getting hot and tight the longer he sat.

"A payphone. What the hell is that?" Judge laughed.

"Stop playing around Judge. Does it look like I wanna fuckin' entertain you right now? I've had enough comedy today from your ridiculous cop friends to last me a lifetime." Quick was still simmering from having to deal with God and Day. No one should ever have to be subjected to their antics. And he was pretty sure that rookie cop had been put on desk duty by the time Day finished making him look incompetent.

"Look, Quick. I'm sorry, okay," Dana started again, but Quick threw his hand up and shot him another look that said "Shut the fuck up, or else." Dana sealed his lips and made himself small, inching over as close to the door as he could get.

"Rome. Knock it off. Cayson was going to find out anyway," Duke said, trying to get his cell phone to turn on.

"He didn't have to find out like that. And Ford. What the hell was he thinking talking to Cays like that? He threatened him, Duke. I want him fired, immediately." Quick fumed, trying to be careful not to rip apart the interior of Judge's truck. Quick growled deep in his chest and Dana looked like he would rather walk the long way home than ride next to him.

"We're going to get this resolved, Quick. But I need you to calm the fuck down," Duke said, and then turned to Judge. "Go to Quick's house. I doubt the doc is still at the hospital. Maybe he went back there after—"

"After he was picked up off the goddamn floor from passing out! Cayson could be anywhere, beating himself up for all of this!" Quick yelled. Before he could stop himself, he'd reached over and grabbed Dana by his collar. His large fist pulled the material up tight and pressed it hard against Dana's Adam's apple, cutting off his air. He could feel the truck beneath him swerving and skidding along the asphalt as Duke yelled for Judge to pull over. He could hear Dana choking and barely calling out to Duke for help, as he pounded and clawed at Quick's arms in a fruitless effort to free himself.

All Quick could see behind his closed lids was Cayson's face. His scared face when Ford yelled at him. He could imagine the pain inside his sweet doctor while he beat himself up for what had happened to Brian. Quick already knew Cayson was too empathetic. Probably no sooner had Dana opened his big mouth, than Cayson had tortured and blamed himself until he'd lost consciousness. A fierce roar erupted from Quick's chest and he knew his beast was taking over. If he didn't get control, he was going to hurt Dana, irreparably hurt him.

"Roman! Rome, stop!"

Strong hands were pulling at him, but he held on to Dana with all he had.

"Roman! Rome open your eyes? Rome, look at me. This isn't helping Cayson. He's alone and hurting. He's not going to understand any of this until you get to him and explain it."

Dana finally wrenched his neck free of Quick's hold, making him stumble back, dazed and confused. When Quick lost himself to his rage, his sensei used to call them episodes. Once he opened his eyes, he saw that Dana was clutching a protective hand over his Adam's apple and was looking at him like he needed an exorcist. Quick ignored the stare and instead concentrated on counting and breathing. They were on the side of the road, and the oncoming traffic was creeping by as they rubbernecked to see what was going on.

Duke was watching carefully, constantly talking in a soothing tone and reminding Quick to breathe.

"Goddamnit, what the hell did you do to my throat?" Dana coughed hard.

"It was throat clutch. It's very deadly, so Quick was still in control," Duke responded, putting a hand up to ward off any retaliation. Dana wasn't a lightweight; he could hold his own in a fight... with a regular person. Not an eighth degree martial arts expert.

"Control?" Dana rumbled, coughing again.

"Yes. Because if he wasn't, you'd be dead by now. Your tongue is just a little swollen, it'll go down. He's okay," Duke huffed, running his hands through his hair. "Judge come on, we gotta go, now. We gotta get him home."

"What the hell? Fuck no, Duke. I'm gonna have to call Uber or something. I'm not riding in back of this truck with him," Dana said, shaking his head vehemently.

"With what phone? Dana, just shut up, or get out and hang on to the damn bumper for all I care. I don't have any more tolerance for this shit, today! I need to check on Brian, and I'd like to get home some time tonight, too, ya know! They still haven't picked up the man who put out the hit, so let's fuckin' go! Now!" Duke yelled. By this time, everyone was angry and yelling. Damn, was this day from hell ever going to end?

Quick knew that he needed to get to Cayson, but if he didn't calm down, they weren't going to make it, because he'd end up causing an accident if he lashed out again. Only Duke understood what Quick was going through, and he hoped he was able to find a way to get the guys to forgive him one day, but for now, he had to get home. Needed to know his son and Cayson were both okay.

Dark hit fast, and Judge was already breaking the speed limit when the alarms on their watches blared deafeningly loud in Judge's truck. He swerved, just missing the guardrail as he took the exit off the interstate. "What the fuck is that? Shit! Turn 'em off." Judge tried to holler over the shrieking alarms.

The noise died off as they all pushed the buttons to turn them off. Quick stared at the watch face, praying silently that it wasn't….

"It's the doc!" Dana yelled first. "He's home. Go to his house."

Duke was turned all the way around in his seat, his dark eyes boring into Quick as Judge followed the directions Dana blurted out. He knew why his best friend was watching him, but he was hanging on to his sanity. Barely… but he was hanging on.

"He hit all the alarms," Dana informed them.

All of them. All of them. Quick was still coming down from his episode, so it took a while for him to comprehend what Dana was saying. All that was rattling around in his head was; what was happening to Cayson that was so bad he had to push all the alarms? Had Dr. Joe hired more guys? Did they go after Cayson?

"That means Ford will respond, too," Dana said solemnly.

Duke's eyes widened as realization set in. "Shut up, Dana. Judge, step on it," Duke whispered sternly.

Quick was silent, too quiet for even his own comfort. He didn't know what he was going to see when they pulled up to Cayson's house, but he hoped that if Ford had done something to his doctor, he'd forgive him in the afterlife. Because he was going to meet his soul in hell after he killed him.

# CHAPTER THIRTY-NINE

*Cayson*

Cayson sat very still while he listened to what Joe had to say. He was upset that it'd been seven minutes and he didn't even hear sirens yet, not to mention none of the guys with watches had shown up either. *Why would they come? They hate me.* Cayson wondered what was going to happen to him if he just sat there and waited. Waited for Joe to slap him. Waited for the cops to cuff him and take him away. Waited for Ford to eventually find him. Whatever the hell was coming, he'd welcome it. It'd be something he could focus on instead of his broken heart.

"Are you listening, Cayson?" Joe yelled.

"Vaguely," Cayson said. He was so distraught; he just didn't care anymore.

"Come on, we got to go. We're going to the police station. I'm going to turn evidence on my nephew and tell them it was his plan to take it a step farther and hire more guys who had their own agendas. It's not a crime to try to scare someone, right?"

"Then go," Cayson replied, flipping his hand in a shooing motion.

"I need you as a character witness," Joe said unbelievingly.

"Character!" Cayson was getting angry. Angrier by the minute. This guy had some nerve. Joe had cost him everything. While Cayson had been blaming himself, he realized that if Joe had just walked away in the first place, they wouldn't have had to go through all of this. He shot up from the couch and walked right up into Joe's face. "What character? You have none! You tried to buy me, asshole! Did you forget that? We never had a real relationship, and as soon as I get one, you fuck it up! For what? To save face. To prove you're better than Roman. Well fine! The dick measuring is over! You won. Roman Webb is officially out of my life forever."

Cayson could feel how hot his hand itched to strike another human being for the first time in his life, so that's exactly what he did. Cayson jolted his right hand out, palm up and flat just like Vaughan had taught him and slapped Joe in the center of his forehead, hard enough to snap his head back. He hollered out in shock, holding his forehead and looking at Cayson like he was insane. Damn, that did feel awesome. He'd never hit anyone before.

The two men, who hadn't moved a muscle the entire time they'd been there, had Cayson out of Joe's face and pinned up against the wall with his hands pulled behind his back before Cayson could think of another strike move. He hoped he'd done it right. It didn't look like it caused any real damage to Joe, but it did stun him. Good enough for Cayson. "Let me go. The police are on their—"

Cayson heard his front door burst open and the glass at the top shatter when it connected with the wall. He couldn't see who it was, because he was still pinned by one of the guys. The other had moved to Joe's side and was reaching into his waistband as he went into a defensive stance.

It wasn't the police; they announced themselves when they entered a house. Who'd gotten there first? Cayson heard slow deliberate footsteps on the hardwood floor in his foyer. If this had been Friday the 13th, this would be the exact moment Jason turned the corner and hacked them up.

"Dr. Joseph Wellington, I presume."

Cayson began to shake under the bodyguard's hand at the sound of Ford's voice. He knew it was him, even though he wasn't yelling like he'd been at the hospital. Cayson still recognized the rage in his tone. He was going to kill all of them. None of the other team was coming. Ford was going to take them all out and ghost before the cops got there.

"Joe, run! He's going to kill you!" Cayson hollered, fear griping him like a vise. He was livid at Joe, but he didn't want anyone brutally murdered in front of him.

"Look. I don't know who you are, but I'm sure we haven't met." Joe tried to reason with Ford, standing behind his bodyguard.

"This is for my brother." Ford's strike was swift and fast to the bodyguard's throat. If he'd wanted to reach for his weapon, he couldn't. The big man dropped to his knees, clutching his throat, his eyes bulging as he tried to take in a breath. Ford didn't give Joe a chance to run or react. He grabbed a handful of Joe's wayward hair at the back of his head and slammed his fist into his nose, not once but twice, in rapid succession. "My brother sends his regards," Ford snarled in Joe's bloody face.

Cayson was down on the floor watching everything in high definition. The sound of Joe's nose cracking had Cayson slamming his hands over his ears like a scared child. It sounded like ice breaking on concrete. The blood spewed from Joe's nose, even spraying Ford's white t-shirt as he stood over him, watching with what looked to be satisfaction as Joe screamed and wailed in agony at Ford's feet.

The doctor in Cayson wanted to run over and control the bleeding, but he didn't dare move. There was only one more bodyguard left between him and Ford. One throat or nose left to demolish before Ford got to him. Cayson had never been so afraid in his life. Men were on the floor, shaking and crying out in pain and they were all completely helpless. Cayson was mindlessly pushing any and all the buttons on his watch but nothing was happening. No one was there, and the sirens he could hear sounded way too far away to provide any comfort or relief.

The last bodyguard stood taller and pulled a silver handgun from his waistband, aiming it at Ford's chest. Ford cocked his head to the side as if he were confused. Like he was flabbergasted this man would stay there and try to take him on… and with one measly weapon.

"Leave him alone," the bodyguard said slowly, like he was talking down a serial killer. "I will shoot you."

"No, don't. Please." Cayson was still crouched down on the floor with his hands still over his ears, dreading the sound of a gunshot. "No, no, no, no."

Another loud bang resonated through the room. It wasn't a gunshot, but was just as terrifying. Cayson turned towards the wall and curled in on himself, squeezing his ears harder, trying to eliminate the shouts and curses. He could hear glass breaking and chaos ensuing all around him, but he kept his head down, his eyes squeezed shut so tight they ached, as he tried to mold himself into the corner.

*Just go away. All of you just go away.* Panic was settling in Cayson's soul, and he could feel himself slipping back to unconsciousness. He felt like he'd suddenly been drugged. His limbs were heavy as he slid down until he was lying on his side. It felt like it took so much strength just to crack his eyes open, but he managed to get a glimpse of several men in his living room, fighting each other, or fighting together… he couldn't tell. He was so tired and afraid. His body shook with terror until the sound of a gunshot made him jerk violently, right before his stomach began to convulse and heave while he spit pale yellow saliva onto his floor. He could've sworn he heard someone yelling Rome's name, but maybe it was his imagination, because there was no way Quick would be there for him after what he'd done.

Quick was out of Judge's truck before he even slowed to a stop, and he knew Duke and Dana were gonna be close on his heels. Quick leaped Cayson's gate like a hurdle and ran fist first into Cayson's home, taking out the first threat he saw. Ford.

"No. Rome, don't," Ford hollered, right before Quick leaped through the air and crashed into him. He'd only had a split second to survey the scene, but in that brief time, he managed to see a blurred image of Cayson's shivering form on the floor and Ford standing too close to him, his shirt splattered with blood.

As soon as they both hit the floor, Ford rolled them to try to get the advantage. Quick knew that trick and he threw his leg back, stopping the roll, and pushed off, throwing them in the other direction. Quick successfully blocked the first blow Ford threw at his head, but he took a couple body shots before he was able to throw his own. Once he did, he unleashed the full power of his beast onto Ford.

Rome grunted, throwing fast, precise punches and elbows at each sensitive part of Ford's body. His strikes were so fast that Ford eventually stopped trying to fight back, and went into survival mode. While animals were created with or evolved tons of defense mechanisms to protect themselves from fiercer predators, humans… all they could do was curl into a fetal position and try to protect their vital organs from attack. Ford's fists were balled tight and tucked close to his head, to protect Quick from breaking anything on his face. His abs and back muscles tightly contracted as Quick tortured Ford's kidneys by kneeing him hard in back while he rained down punches. In hand-to-hand combat, a fight could feel like ten minutes, when in actuality, it'd only been ten seconds. That's how long Quick had been on Ford before Duke and Dana got to him. He knew he could do some serious damage in that short amount of time.

"Police! Police! Nobody move!"

Quick was tackled by several hard bodies and was knocked off of Ford and slammed into the bottom of Cayson's stairs. He didn't feel a thing. Quick fought them all, going for pressure points on anyone who had the audacity to touch him. He didn't know who was on his back, but a firm squeeze to the crevice of their forearm made them let go immediately, the pained scream coming from next to his right ear was only slightly soothing to his beast as he went after every vulnerable spot on anyone who held him.

"Watch your fuckin' throat, Duke."

That was Judge growling for Duke to watch out. Was he fighting Duke? Quick stilled suddenly, his chest heaving from the exertion. His body pulsed with an overload of adrenaline as he tried to take a deep breath and failed. There were people all around, but he still couldn't see clearly. He tried to count to five, but only managed to get to two, when his body began to shake uncontrollably. An aftereffect of the adrenaline.

"Breathe, Rome." Duke was there, he hadn't hurt him. "Officers, please just stand back and give him some room. Please."

Quick had to get himself together. He went up to his knees and dropped his head down between them. He kept trying to count and breathe. Each count got higher and each breath got deeper. Sweat leaked into his eyes the moment he was able to actually focus them on something. The scene looked very similar to their office this morning. Quick looked around to see if there was anyone with their head missing, but was relieved to see the gun must've missed its target because there were no dead bodies. He'd heard the gunshot but it was no louder than the roaring in his ears had been.

He stumbled on his first few steps as he looked around the room like he was seeing it for the first time. He looked over in the corner by Cayson's record player, squinting at the bloody man in the tracksuit. Quick shook his head to clear the fog. His first thought was that it couldn't be Dr. Joe being worked on by those EMTs. Quick clenched his fists. Just the sight of Joe was making it harder to settle down.

"Forget about him. Cayson needs you, Rome." Duke stood close to him, leaning in to talk in his ear. "Make the right decision."

Quick growled and seethed beneath his curtain of sweaty hair as he kept his head lowered like a bull about to charge. He tried to let Duke's words sink in.

"You're a fuckin' Grandmaster, for shit's sake. Get yourself under control, before these cops think you're too big a danger to yourself and everyone in this room." Ford snapped right in his face.

Quick jerked back. Ford was there next to Duke, trying to help. What did he do? *What happened? I was fighting Ford, wasn't I?* Damn, he hated when his episodes – his beast – got the better of him. He was so good at keeping himself in check, ever since he was a teen, but he guessed when it came to Cayson – to the love of his life, all checking was off.

Cayson. Quick didn't know if his love was alright or not. He hadn't even stopped to see. What kind of partner would he be? He stood to his feet, pushing his hair back behind his ears, searching for one person in the room full of civilians and city authorities. Now he had a real mission. Find Cays.

Quick spun around, pushed between two police officers, both of them putting their hands on their holsters as he moved around. Duke and Judge were in a serious conversation with a group of officers, but Quick didn't miss Duke's eyes tracking him while attempting an explanation to all this.

"C-Cayson!" Quick croaked, his throat aching, on fire from the growling and yelling.

"Rome."

Quick spun back, moving another officer out of his way. Duke was pointing behind him, Quick had to turn again. All this spinning was not helping his head to clear at all. He could see three huge paramedics working on a man propped against the wall in the dining room. With a newfound focus, Quick moved through the crowd, officers were escorting the bodyguards out of the house. Two men in suits, who Quick assumed were detectives, tried to stop him, but the look he gave them said fight or flight… they chose the latter.

As soon as he was directly behind the paramedics, they turned and looked at him, and then scattered out of the way like Quick was a supernatural being. He ignored them and went down hard on his knees in between Cayson's spread legs.

"Baby." Quick knew he voice must sound like the devil's, but he had to try to get Cayson to forgive him. Forgive him for not being there. He needed that right now. The pain in his chest was unbearable; his heart shattering at the realization of what his leaving Cayson alone had allowed to happen. No one was ever there when Cayson needed them, and Quick had done the exact same thing. It didn't matter the circumstances why he couldn't get to him, the fact still remained. He wasn't a man of excuses. Cayson's eyes were just slightly open, like he was exhausted, they were hazed over and not their usual radiant blue. Quick raised his trembling hand and cupped Cayson's bruised cheek. "Cayson are you alright?"

"Roman. I didn't mean… I'm so sorry… Brian… God, I'm so sorry." If Quick wasn't concentrating so hard on Cayson, there was no way he would've heard what he was saying. Not only were Quick's ears still ringing from his episode, but Cayson was barely gusting out each word on very shallow, labored breaths. His voice sounded so small and he was apologizing. For what? Was this what Cayson usually did? Take on blame that wasn't his own? The blood pressure cuff inflated on Cayson's arm, and

Quick blinked, realizing the paramedics had moved back in and were calling out vitals.

"Sir. Sir, your blood pressure is slightly elevated, but your pulse is slowly returning to normal. How are you feeling? Are you nauseous? Dizzy?"

"It was a panic attack. I'm pretty sure I had one earlier and its lingering effects triggered this one. I'm fine, really. I'll monitor my blood pressure through the night," Cayson said, sounding winded.

The paramedics didn't look convinced, and honestly, neither did Quick. Cayson was still quite pale, and his lips not the normal soft pink color, instead they held a disturbing bluish tint, like he'd been deprived of oxygen too long.

"I'm a surgeon. I know the symptoms if my blood pressure and pulse start to elevate and things become more serious. Right now I'm just... just exhausted." Cayson slumped against Quick's chest and he thought he'd heard a chorus of hallelujahs over his head as he squeezed his love to him. He wasn't feeling any rage, only need. An extreme need to protect the man in his arms for the rest of his life.

Cayson was staring at Quick, his bloodshot eyes pleading for forgiveness. Quick needed Cayson alone. He couldn't deal with all the other noise going on. He rose up, his eyes squinting into the crowd. There was more noise, more commotion, as more police officers filed into Cayson's home.

Duke was standing off to the side with Dana and Judge. All three of them with their IDs out, speaking with the detectives, but Quick brushed them off. It looked like some uniformed officers were reading Dr. Joe his rights. No sooner had they finished, than he started to yell for Cayson.

Cayson rubbed his forehead against Quick's chest in frustration, his hands hovering over his ears. He barely heard the pained, "Get me out of here," from Cayson's mouth with Joe losing his shit as soon as the metal cuffs clicked around his wrists.

"Just go, please," Cayson whispered brokenly.

Quick didn't take another second to think of his next move. Cayson needed to get out of there and he was going to do that for him. Not paying any more attention to the paramedics who were packing up their huge duffle bags, Quick lifted Cayson in his arms like a man would carry a woman over a threshold, and squeezed him close. Pain didn't register in his mind as he hefted Cayson up higher on his chest and made his way through the crowd. He was at the base of Cayson's stairs when he heard the detectives calling out to them. They weren't Quick's concern or priority, nor were their reports.

"Sir. You can't leave yet. Not until we get a statement."

Quick climbed each step gingerly, careful not to jostle his tired doctor too much. Quick tuned out the angry men at the foot of the stairs and tucked his face into Cayson's neck, breathing in his scent, letting it continue to settle him down.

"Sir. You can't go until we've spoken to you." The detective was trying to radiate a little more authority, but Quick wasn't stopping. And it would be a pity for anyone who tried to force him to.

"Just give him a minute. The guy he assaulted is still standing here and he already said he's not pressing charges, so pipe down. Goddamn. There's not a fuckin' heliport up there, he'll come back down." Quick heard the end of Duke's bitching right before he turned the corner into Cayson's bedroom. It sounded like his partner was about out of patience and needed to get home to his man, too.

His best friend always had his back, no matter what. Sighing wearily, Quick knew he was going to owe everyone. He was glad to hear that Ford wasn't going to press charges and have him arrested, but the consequences of his actions hadn't even crossed his mind. Cayson was still occupying 99% of his brain space.

# CHAPTER FORTY

*Cayson*

Cayson blinked his eyes awake, squinting at the faint light coming through the open curtains in his bedroom. He didn't remember opening them. He fought to come fully wake and remember why he was in his bed still dressed and feeling like he'd been dragged behind a truck for a couple miles. His body ached all over and his limbs felt too heavy to lift. What was going on? As the memories flooded back to the forefront of his mind, a throbbing pain began behind his eye sockets and radiated to the base of his skull. Ugh! Tension headache. He'd loathed them in college. Used to get them frequently until he'd learned to manage his stress level.

The quiet was unsettling. Quick had been there last night. Had come to him, fought for him, held him, carried him, but he didn't remember anything else. Did he leave? Did he not forgive Cayson? He sat up slowly, easing his legs over the side of the bed. He took a deep breath and held it for a few seconds before blowing it out. It did nothing to ease the pain. Sighing in defeat, Cayson stood slowly, careful for his first few steps that he didn't get dizzy and fall. He was closing his bathroom door when he heard the sound of footsteps downstairs.

He moved a little faster to the railing, peering over the side. He saw Quick on his hands and knees, shirtless, in a pair of jeans, his long hair tied up into a loose man bun. There was a bucket of soapy, pink-tinged water beside him as he scrubbed the mess that'd been made on Cayson's hardwood floors last night. Even though there was blood on his wall and in several other places in his trashed living room, he couldn't take his eyes off of Quick. He was there. That was all that mattered.

Cayson smiled, his heart soaring. Even if Quick was there as a friend and no longer a lover... he'd take it. Every damn scrap or bone, he'd take it. "Rome," he said, his voice sounding like a frog croaking. He coughed and tried to clear it, making his way to the stairs, but Quick was already taking them three at a time up to him and was stopping him from trying to come down.

"Baby. What are you doing out of bed? You should be resting," Quick asked, dipping low to look into Cayson's eyes.

Without another thought, Cayson flung his arms around Quick's waist and held on. "I don't need rest."

"Yes, you do. Come on." Quick held Cayson in his big arms, moving him back towards the bed.

"No. I'm fine. What I need is a shower. I smell like the dead." Cayson grimaced. He also needed some answers, but he was scared to ask any questions. He fidgeted nervously, needing to at least say this before he made another move. "I, um. I also want to know where I stand with you. Have you cut bait and thrown me back in?"

"What?" Quick frowned.

"Nothing. Bad fishing reference my dad used to always say."

Quick held Cayson at arm's length. They stared at each other for several minutes and Cayson thought he might be getting ready to hear some disturbing news, until he saw a rapt determination spread over Quick's rough features right as he went down on both knees, tightly holding Cayson's hands in front of him.

"Marry me."

Cayson gasped, then blinked like maybe he hadn't heard right. Was that his answer to "Where do I stand with you?"

"Rome." Cayson's breath whooshed out of him. Holy shit! Was he for real? Yes! The answer's yes!

"Cayson. I'm not trying to terrify you by asking you to spend your life with me. But, this is real. It's what I feel." Quick stood up and walked them back until they were sitting side by side on the bed. He kept Cayson's hands clutched to his chest while he went into a long explanation of exactly what happened yesterday, from the time he left Cayson in his home before dawn, to the long stint at the precinct, to the misunderstanding between him and Ford. Laid it all out there. Even about his anger episodes. There needed to be no more secrets so there'd be no more confusion.

He was grateful that Brian was safe at his brother's home, recovering from a concussion and a fractured jaw. Cayson was left short of breath when he found out that Brian had been the one to convince Ford to leave the hospital and come help him when he pushed the alarm on his watch. Brian wasn't mad at him and didn't blame him for Joe's acions. Cayson was fine to let all of that burden rest heavily on Joe's shoulders while he sat in jail, for however short a time that turned out to be, facing a couple counts of conspiracy and extortion and a few more of harassment.

According to Duke's phone call to Quick that morning, Joe had already posted bond and was out on bail. He was not able to practice medicine or initiate contact with any of them. Quick's voice was stern when he told Cayson to call the police immediately if Joe contacted him in any way.

"I'm not sure if all those charges will stick, but one or two might, if we both testify. This was not your fault, Cayson, and I hate myself for not being here for you. Not being at that hospital when Ford went crazy on you."

"Stop," Cayson whispered. "I think maybe we should both stop trying to accept blame and just—"

"I know it seems rushed and too fast, but you don't have to continue to fulfill my life every day for the next two or three years before I realize you're the one. You're it." Quick interrupted, sliding off the bed and getting back on his knees. "I love you, Cayson. I do. And, I haven't said that to many people. My sweet Cays. I love you from a place so deep, that I feel like I've just started to live life. That a missing part of me has come alive, and it feels so good when I'm with you. I know I have my son, and my friends. But you soothe something inside of me that no one ever has. That's how I know." Quick pressed their joined hands over his heart. "You own this. Whatever your answer is. Yes or no. You'll always own this."

~~~~~~~~~~

"How many people have you told already?" Cayson rolled his eyes playfully, while he finished packing his bags. He was going to stay with Quick while he had a cleaning crew come in and clear the stench of blood, melee, deceit and any other disgusting shit that'd been left behind last night. Even though they were technically engaged – Cayson was still smiling from three hours ago – he wasn't going to move in with Quick. Having his own space would be good for them while they continued to date and learn each other during their hopefully not too long engagement.

"Only a few," Quick muttered, avoiding Cayson's eyes. Quick's fingers were flying over the keys on his cell phone, a wide grin sitting firmly on his face, the same way it'd been since Cayson said yes.

He'd been a little more than scared when he realized he was about to say yes, but he couldn't dispute that he was in love with Quick as well. Hook, line and sinker, his heart belonged to Roman Webb.

"I was texting Vaughan. He's at work, but he's going insane. He wants to help plan the wedding," Quick said, laughing as he read more of Vaughan's responses. "Oh, hell. He and Duke want us over this week for dinner."

Cayson finally started to ignore the slight twinge of pain in his bruised cheek from smiling so much, because there was no way he could stop. "How long do you think we're going to be at the police station?" Cayson asked, zipping up one of his suitcases.

"Hopefully not long. You have to meet the detective at one, so maybe an hour or two. You'll have to answer whatever questions they have, then write your statement." Quick helped Cayson lift the suitcase off the bed and set it on the floor. He took Cayson in his arms for the hundredth time that morning and kissed him passionately.

"Then I want to go home, help you get settled and then…."

Cayson walked behind Quick, carrying his garment bag while Quick carried the other luggage and his toiletry bag. They locked up the house and packed his things in his car. "And then what?" Cayson asked when he got inside and started the engine.

"Then, since you're on medical leave for the next couple weeks." Quick leaned over the console of Cayson's hybrid and seductively licked at his lips. "I want to make love to you for two weeks straight, where we only get out of bed to piss, shower, and eat, then it's back to bed."

If Cayson wasn't a law-abiding citizen, he would've blown off his appointment with the police detective and sped back to Quick's home, running every light that tried to slow him down, and been in Quick's bed, spread wide open for him.

# CHAPTER FORTY-ONE

*Quick*

Quick turned and held his hand out for Cayson's keys. "I'll drive, gorgeous. You still look tired."

"I am exhausted, a little. From being in there." Cayson clutched the back of his neck, pointing behind him at the police station. "It felt like they were asking the same question over and over, just wording it differently each time."

"Yeah." Quick started the quiet engine. "They try to catch you in a lie."

"But I wasn't lying."

"I believe you, baby. But they don't know you're not a liar."

"Now we have to go to court, right?"

"Yep. In a couple months. Joe will probably get a lot of suspended sentences, and maybe probation, if they can't make everything stick. He's got more lawyers than OJ had."

"Whatever. One of those cops was a dick. He made me feel like a slut."

Quick laughed, picking up one of Cayson's hands and kissing each knuckle. "I don't remember that part."

"He treated me like I was a bed-hopper. Like I went right from Joe's bed to yours in the same night, as if I drove him to act desperately."

"Um. Didn't you?" Quick winked, then flinched when Cayson slugged him in his arm, rubbing it exaggeratedly as if Cayson could really hurt him. "I'd go crazy if you dumped me, too."

Cayson slapped his hand on his forehead. "I didn't dump him."

"I'm just ribbing you. Get used to it in this family." Quick headed to his home, in Cayson's tiny clown car. First thing he'd request was for his doctor to get an actual vehicle that he could fit in, and that wouldn't crumple like a piece of paper in the slightest fender bender.

It was after five by the time they left the station. Cayson declined Quick's offer to go to a restaurant and surprised him by asking for a basic club from Subway. God, he loved a low maintenance partner.

When they got to Quick's place, they wasted little time putting Cayson's things in a couple drawers. Quick was happy to make plenty of space in his bathroom and anywhere else, so Cayson would feel so welcome, he never wanted him to leave. With that thought in his head. Quick was starting on Cayson's welcome right now.

After his shower, he put new linens on the bed while Cayson washed up. It was only dusk, but they were getting ready for a long night and hopefully morning, in bed. Quick had his weapons stashed and was waiting on top of the covers for his fiancé when he opened the bathroom door.

"I'm in love with your showerhead." Cayson was drying his hair with a large, fluffy, royal blue towel.

"I thought you were just washing up, you showered this morning."

"But the water felt so good, I wanted another." Cayson smiled. Quick would never get bored of seeing it. Most couples probably said that in the beginning of most relationships, but he truly believed it. Cayson pulled on a pair of white Hanes boxers and crawled next to Quick, settling in to his side. A perfect fit.

He and Cayson laid there with the curtains open to Quick's lavish backyard, watching the last of the daylight leave for its time of rest. Neither were asleep as Quick lazily rubbed soothing circles on Cayson's back and his sweet doctor ran his hands through Quick's long hair. There was no more talk of Joe's uninvited imposition on their relationship or police reports, no talk at all. They didn't feel the need to fill the calming moment with chatter. Quick was perfectly content lying there with his love in his arms, protected from the cold and bitter world.

~~~~~~~~~~

Quick slowly opened his eyes, adjusting to the pitch darkness of his bedroom. He stretched like a lion – having no clue what time it was, and not caring – and popped the few kinks in his neck, then burrowed back into Cayson's warmth. He wasn't surprised they'd fallen asleep in each other's arms. That was the way it was supposed to be. A real soulmate could sense his lover's inner conflict and soothe him with something as simple as a touch or a look. Cayson had been upset when he left the police station, but Quick's touch had put him right to rest.

He leaned over Cayson's back and began to kiss down the side of his face, not stopping until he got to those ripe lips. He couldn't believe he thought he'd never get to kiss Cayson again. If he never knew another thing, he knew he couldn't live without Cayson.

Quick moaned and responded to Cayson when he blindly reached behind him and urged Quick's hips to move. "Ohhhhh."

Damn, the sounds his doctor made.

Quick tucked his hair behind his ear, leaning in further to deepen the kiss. He slowly eased Cayson to lie flat on his back. Propped against him, Quick had to know one or two things before they started.

"You sure you feel okay? Are you still resting? There's no rush to do anything right now, ya know. We have all our lives to make love. I understand if you—"

"Rome. Be quiet and make love to me. Slow and deep," Cayson moaned, inching his boxers down his pale legs.

Quick was up on one elbow, leaning against Cayson. He let his head fall back the second Cayson wrapped his slim fingers around Quick's turgid length. "You like that." Cayson breathed hotly against his throat.

"You know I do." Quick held Cayson's hip while he ground his erection into the warm cleft of his ass cheeks. God, his ass was so perfect, so delectable. Quick couldn't help but worship it. He kneaded the soft, round mounds with the same intensity as his thrusting. "Cays, baby?"

"Hmmmm," Cayson moaned long and deliciously, matching Quick and pushing his ass back just enough to excite him.

"I'm clean. I haven't told you that yet. We have to have regular physicals for work. Mine was two months ago, but I wanted you to know, I'm negative for everything." Quick fumbled on his wording, because he knew what he was needing from Cayson was a big deal. Especially for a doctor. Having intercourse without protection was morally and socially irresponsible. That just wasn't Cayson.

"I'm clean, Rome." Cayson turned in his arms, looking him in his eyes. The silent acknowledgment of both of them wanting to go bare resulted in another round of heavy petting and panting. "Do it. I trust you, Rome. I trust you with my life, my heart, and my health. Make love to me. Come inside me."

"You're so fuckin' amazing. I love you, Cays."

Quick covered Cayson with his body, pressing him into the soft mattress beneath him.

~~~~~~~~~~

Cayson was ready. Ready for his life to change. There would be no going back. He heard the click of the lube cap right before he felt Rome's thick fingers nudging at his pulsing hole. Damn, he hoped he lasted longer than a few seconds, but he wasn't thinking he would. Hell, just looking at Quick with that gloriously thick mane, his sculpted body and tattoos, made Cayson want to come, so he eased back onto his stomach, raising his ass up to his fiancé.

"You are so beautiful presenting that gorgeous ass to me like that," Quick said roughly, slicking up his bare cock while he watched Cayson get into a comfortable position. Quick's voice was splintered and jagged, revealing how close he was to busting his nut.

"It's yours. Take it." Cayson ached with the need to be filled. He had to squeeze the base of his cock, trying hard not to come yet as Quick moaned louder with each inch of his broad dick he sank into Cayson's warmth. There was no hurrying, no concerns, no outside world. This was their time. Just for them.

Quick's strokes were bottomless and lazy as he lay on top of him, every inch of their bodies staying in contact while Quick slowly pumped his hips. Cayson craned his head to the side to let his big bounty hunter lick and tongue at his throat. "Fuuuuck. It's so good, Rome."

"You're so warm for me. So fuckin' warm and wet," Quick murmured drunken nonsense.

Every tortuously slow drag inside his ass with Quick's pipe-hard length drove him that much closer to nirvana. No matter how much he bucked his hips or clenched his hole, Quick kept it steady. There was only them right now. They rode that ride to pleasure together, holding each other close. Quick's bulging chest plastered securely to Cayson's back.

"Rome. You feel perfect… Ugh, fuck… It's too much." Cayson clenched his eyes closed, his body rocking erotically with each wave that Quick created. He felt like the bed was yanked from beneath him and he lay there suspended in Quick's arm, impaled on his dick. Helpless to the sensations racking his body, his heart. "I'm going to fall apart, Rome." Cayson whimpered, begging for stability.

"I got you. Let go, Cays. Let go. I'll never let you fall," Rome gritted out, pumping just fast enough to push him over. Sure enough, his big lover held him tight and rode him until all that was left of his orgasm was aching noises and light tremors.

He lay almost lifeless, completely sated and satisfied. He wanted Quick to come undone. To tumble and fall just as fast and hard as he did. With what little strength Cayson had left, he rose higher on his knees and clenched his hole tight, not giving his lover the option. Quick was going to give him every ounce of that nut inside his hungry ass. Cayson had waited his entire life for this. "Come inside me, Rome."

"Yes," Rome grunted. Cayson's body began to shake as the nerves tingling and wracking his body became too much to bare. Quick restlessly chased his orgasm with so much strength and power, all Cayson could do was hang on to Quick's hard forearms while his future husband showed him an in-depth glimpse of what his body, his mind, his soul was going to feel for the next forty plus years... he prayed.

"Goddamnit. You're so tight... I can't hold it anymore," Quick groaned.

"Fuck, yes."

"Augh! I'm coming... Cays, baby... Augh, fuck... I'm coming so fuckin' hard." Quick jolted violently on top of him and Cayson felt another orgasm slam into him unexpectedly as soon as his channel was flooded to overflowing with his fiancé's hot come. It was like nothing he'd ever experienced, nothing had ever remotely close. You might as well ask an angel what is heaven like. Is there a word invented that could describe it?

They laid there, tangled around each other, while they took their sweet time coming back to the present. Quick very carefully eased out of Cayson, and a contented grin spread across his face when the warm essence began to seep from his body. Back to back orgasms. He closed his eyes in an attempt to calm his racing heart, but he was just too fulfilled, and before he knew it, he was asleep in his man's arms again.

True to their word, they woke an hour and a half later ready for more, but this time, it was Cayson who got to slide his long, bare cock inside Quick's body. He entered and filled him as smoothly as the right key fits into its own lock. Absolutely perfect.

When sunlight began its first footprints across the bright blue Atlanta sky, Cayson woke again, his body still humming and firing on all cylinders. They got up to clean themselves after another hour of dozing and fondling. They'd held hands, walking downstairs to Quick's kitchen to find them some sustenance before they dropped dead. Quick hadn't lied about his plans over the next couple weeks. They'd made love again, bathed each other, now they were eating pasta with grilled chicken, needing those carbs to reenergize. Cayson was already looking forward to what was coming up next.

Quick pulled Cayson close to him and tipped his head back until his chin could rest between his pecs. They held each other for a few seconds, just looking in awe, wondering how the hell they both got what they wanted – a love so sweet and pure – amidst all that disarray.

"Damn, I love you. Thank you for believing in me, Cayson. I never knew what I was missing until I let you in."

"I love you too." Cayson smiled shyly, overwhelmed at how to respond to Quick's emotions. This deadly warrior standing there declaring his love for him. He no longer hid how he was feeling and neither did Cayson. They promised to be honest with each other for the rest of their lives. But for now, they had more learning and exploring to do. Neither of them had got to experience all the fun and exciting things that happened in the honeymoon phase of any relationship yet, and Cayson was elated to share all his new adventures with the man gazing down at him like he was something special.

Quick was right on schedule when he stepped back and held his hand out to Cayson, a wicked gleam in his brilliant green eyes.

Cayson leered sexily. "Should I take a wild guess what we're getting ready to do now?"

Quick's laugh was deep and genuine. "Oh, yes. We are getting ready to do that… but guess where, my sexy, white-collar doctor."

Cayson's mouth dropped open when Quick walked them through his office and opened up his patio doors to his backyard oasis. The weather was in the upper fifties today, which wasn't bad for Atlanta in February, especially when the sun was out. Towering spruce trees along the perimeter of Quick's yard blocked any nosy neighbors from being able to see anything going on. The grass was trimmed neatly and the vast colorful pansies, and bright yellow forsythia that lined the walkway and the deck made Cayson feel like he was right back in Atlanta's Botanical Gardens, dancing in Quick's arms and breathing in the strong perfumes of nature. He could easily see them entertaining, holding many summer barbeques together.

Cayson was shaking his head in surprise as he surveyed his fiancé's pride and joy. He spun in every direction, in love with everything he saw. When he finished taking it all in, he turned to look for Quick, only to find him completely naked inside a screened in porch just off the deck that wrapped around the back of the house. He was spread-eagled on an oversized patio couch with thick green and white cushions. Cayson's eyes had to be wider than saucers, while he watched Quick slowly stroke his thick cock, his serene face tilted up towards the bright sunshine. Cayson was moving towards Quick as if on autopilot. As soon as he stepped inside the screen, a blast of warm air hit him in his face. The large heater plugged in the corner would more than protect them from the slight nip in the air. If not, maybe they could work up enough of a sweat to not care.

"I'm going to be the first man to die of an ejaculate overdose," Cayson said, raking his eyes up and down Quick's body.

"That'd be a sweet way to go," Quick said. His big hand still stroking his fully erect cock, which was aimed right at him. "But before you do, get naked. Because the day's just starting and before it ends, I promise you I'm going to fuck you in every part of my house, baby." Quick pointed at the large ottoman in front of the couch. "Starting right here."

*The End.*

# BIOGRAPHY

A.E. Via is an author in the beautiful gay romance genre and also founder and owner of Via Star Wings Books. Her writing embodies everything from hopelessly romantic to spicy to scandalous. Her stories often include intriguing edges and twists that take readers to new, thought-provoking depths.

When she's not clicking away at her laptop, she devotes herself to her family--a husband and four children.

Adrienne Via has tons of more stories to tell, but she really would like to hear yours. Via Star Wings Books is currently accepting submissions for established and aspiring LGBTQ authors. I've contracted and successfully published a couple authors - whose information can be found on my website - who can tell you that my passion is giving other writer's stories the love and care it deserves so it could be a gift to another. Visit my site to learn more!

Go to A.E. Via's official website http://authoraevia.com for more detailed information on how to contact her, follow her, or a sneak peak on upcoming work, free reads, VSWB submissions, and where she'll appear next.

## Author A.E. Via

*"Only Thing Sexier than One Man, Is Two of Them Together"*

Author Official Website: http://authoraevia.com/
A.E. Amazon Author Page: http://amzn.to/1QW1Krk

A.E. Blog: http://authoraevia.com/blog---fabulous-authors---new-and-noteworthy.html
Facebook Author Page: https://www.facebook.com/aeviaauthor
Facebook: https://www.facebook.com/authoraevia
Twitter: https://twitter.com/AuthorAEVia

# ALSO BY A.E. VIA

## Nothing Special (Nothing Special #1)

THIS TITLE HAS BEEN REVISED AND REEDITED. An additional 6k words have been added to the original text.

Detective Cashel 'Cash' Godfrey is big, tattooed and angry so people typically keep their distance. He's fresh out of the police academy, however, no one is looking to partner with the six foot four beast with a huge chip on his shoulder and an inability to trust. When Cash scans the orientation room he wasn't expecting to find sexy hazel eyes locked onto him. Eyes of the handsome Detective Leonidis 'Leo' Day.

Leo is charming, witty, hilariously sarcastic and the only one that can make Cash smile. He's proud, out and one bad-ass detective.

Together Cash and Leo become the most revered and successful narcotics detectives Atlanta's ever seen. Able to communicate and understand each other, without even having to voice it, they quickly climb up the promotional ranks.

When Cash saves Leo's life in a raid that turns deadly, Leo begins to see something in the big man that no one else does…something special. But Leo fears he'll never break through the impenetrable wall that protects Cash's heart.

Nothing Special takes the reader through various emotions throughout the richly fulfilling plot that's full of erotic gay romance, heartache, passion, trials and tribulations, police action scenes, and an intriguing twist that comes to an amazing ending that's impossible to see coming.

### **Embracing His Syn (Nothing Special #2)**

Sergeant Corbin 'Syn' Sydney had dedicated his life to becoming the best detective. So when he heard there was an opening on the notorious Atlanta Narcotics Task Force, he jumped at the chance. But, what he wasn't ready for was realizing just how lonely he'd made himself, when he observed the loving and dedicated relationship between the two men he served under: Lieutenant Cashel 'God' Godfrey and Lieutenant Leonidis Day.

Syn prepared himself to accept his lonely fate until he walked into a small pub and met the long-haired, tattooed bartender, Furious Barkley. Before Syn can even understand why, he's overcome with feelings he barely recognizes: passion, yearning, craving. And if the dark, lustful gazes are anything to go by, Furious might be feeling the same things for him.

Just two thing needs to happen before Syn and Furi can give each other what's been missing from their lives for so long... Syn needs to find the evidence that proves Furi's innocence of murder, as well as protect him from a past that refuses to let go.

God, Day, Ronowski, and Johnson are still as entertaining as ever...

You'll swoon over God's massive take-charge attitude...

You'll laugh hysterically at Day's never-ending wit...

You'll fall in love with Furious' mysterious, sexy demeanor...

and...

You'll embrace Syn...

Disclaimer: The main characters of this book DO NOT participate in polygamous sexual pairings.

## Here Comes Trouble (Nothing Special #3)

Detectives Mark Ruxsberg and Chris Green are very good at their jobs. Being the enforcers for God and Day's notorious Atlanta PD Narcotics Task Force causes the crazy duo to get into more trouble than they can often get out of. The pair never misses out on an opportunity to drive their Lieutenants crazy with their dangerous, reckless, and costly stunts, landing them in the hot seat in front God... often.

Ruxs and Green love their jobs and they don't mind the very demanding schedule that leaves them little time for socializing or dating. It was fine with them, they enjoyed hanging out with each other anyway.

However, most of the men in their close circle of friends and colleagues are pairing off and settling down. God has Day, Ro has Johnson, and their Sergeant Syn has Furious.

For the past several years, Ruxs has only sought out the advice and company of one person, his partner and best friend Green, and vice versa. Both of these alpha males are presumed straight, but neither can deny the heat that's building in their once 'just friends' relationship.

## Don't Judge (Nothing Special #4)

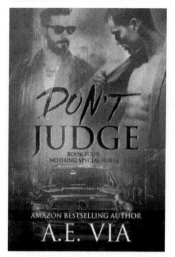

Detective Austin Michaels didn't think life could get any better after he was accepted into the most notorious narcotics task force on the East Coast, headed up by two of the baddest' Lieutenants with the Atlanta Police Department - Cashel Godfrey and Leonidis Day.

Michaels knew he would fit right in as the team's sniper, having received his fair share of commendations for marksmanship. He was just as badass as the rest of the twenty brothers that made up their team. But when Michaels lets their prime suspect get away from a huge bust with over a quarter of a million dollars in drugs, he's willing to do whatever it takes to make it right.

Left with no other options, God chooses to bring in outside help, calling on his long-time friend and bounty hunter, Judge Josephson.

Judge was considered one of the best trackers during his enlistment in the United States Marine Corps. After retiring, he used those skills to become one of the most sought out fugitive trackers in the country. When Judge gets a call from his old friend needing his help, he quickly tells God, yes.

Still embarrassed, and intent to prove himself, Michaels immediately volunteers to partner up with Judge to get their suspect back quickly and quietly. Neither man wanted or needed a partner. But, after Judge and Michaels get on the road, the hate/lust relationship they quickly develop between them will either make them heroes… Or get them killed.

## BLUE MOON SERIES

Angel DeLucca is one of the most sought after gay bachelors in Virginia Beach. He's smart successful, lethal, and more than anything he's drop dead gorgeous. Angel has his pick of the men that come to his popular Oceanfront night club, but lately the one night stands haven't been enough...Angel craves something deeper. When a one night hook-up goes terribly wrong, Angel comes into contact with the breathtaking Maximus (Max) Strong.

Max is a firefighter for the Virginia Beach Fire Department. Max is beautiful, charming, and also very straight. One meeting with the mysteriously, sexy Angel DeLucca and a whiff of that silky, jet black hair, Max finds himself questioning everything he's known to be true about himself. Max tries desperately to understand the new feelings he has for another man and turns to his gay, older brother...Ryker.

Ryker has always been Max's protector and his guide their entire lives, which has left him feeling uncared for and alone to handle his own life's problems. Ryker craves to be taken care of, he craves the attention and praise of a Master. No one knows the dark desires within him until Angel's Chief of Security, Sebastian 'Bass' Bagatelli, shatters that secret with their first intense encounter.

How will Angel win the heart of the straight firefighter that was tailor-made just for him? Will Max be able to continue denying his feelings for another man? Can Ryker and Bass get through their personal issues to take and receive what they both need from each other? Or will they each give up on a happiness that appears too good to be true?

These men's stories will unravel in a whirlwind of romance, bdsm, revelations, lots of action and very hot sex, co-starring very entertaining supporting characters.

### Blue Moon II: This Is Reality

THIS INSTALLMENT OF BLUE MOON CAN STAND ALONE

The Story of: HAWK, PIERCE, SHOT & FOX ALONG WITH THE OTHER BEASTMASTERS

Pierce aka Strategic Intelligence Specialist, Backhander is back to flush out some of the DEA's most notorious criminals, and he has one helluva' team backing him up. The country's most decorated

Navy Seals...the Beastmasters.

Pierce is more than capable of doing his job, but he has one insanely hot distraction that continuously causes him to second guess his hidden orientation.
Dane Aramis, call-sign, Hawk. Hawk can see what most people can't, and whether his sexy Pierce wants to admit it or not, he can see the brilliant man's desire runs deep for him.

However, when Pierce and the Beastmasters are on their final assignment, the last person they expect to encounter with the opposition is rogue assassin...Omega. The man is unstoppable, and when he comes too close to what Hawk holds dear, the Beastmasters call on the only man that can control the lethal assassin. Omega's faster, deadlier brother, Alpha.

Bringing Alpha back into society may be disastrous for everyone involved. But, Hawk is willing to take that risk to keep Pierce safe.

### Blue Moon III: Call of the Alpha (COMING SOON)

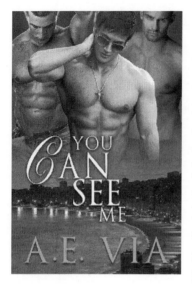

You Can See Me
(STANDALONE)

World renowned chef Prescott Vaughan was at the height of his career. Right before he's to leave for Paris to work alongside his idol, a horrific car accident leaves him completely blind.

His female fiancé leaves him in a state of desperation and depression. He pines for love, companionship, and so happens to find it in the form of his very sexy neighbor. Sexy male neighbor, Dr. Rickson 'Ric' Edwards.

Prescott's not gay - at least he never considered himself gay - until Ric saves him from a date, gone terribly wrong. The two neighbors hit it off quickly and waste no time exploring and learning each other. Things are great until Ric begins to have his doubts about meeting Prescott's many wants.

When Ric insist he and Prescott take a breather, Pres finds himself lonely and lacking again. Enter, male escort and aspiring chef, Blair McKenzie to fill the void.

In the meantime, Ric works on his issues that prohibits him from displaying the love he knows he has for Prescott. When Ric is finally ready and returns to claim Prescott he's not sure that Pres can let go of the sexy, southern, hotness that is Blair McKenzie. After Ric has his own personal encounter with the sinfully sexy man, he can't help but become entranced and crave more as well. Pres soon realizes that there's no need to choose between his two men, because when all three of them finally come together - grab a cold drink - the heat is going to go all the way up!

## Also By
## Via Star Wings Books

Vegas is a hot phone sex operator who knows just how to make your deepest, darkest fantasies come true either with a gentle whisper in your ear or with a rough growling command. When he's in control, you know you're in good hands. Vegas can tickle or scratch whatever itch or fetish a caller can throw at him.

But his job at the exclusive 'Black Vanilla' has its dark side, which becomes all too clear when Vegas receives a call one night that hits a little too close to home.

Somewhere out there, someone's watching him. Someone who's taken their fantasy one step too far. It isn't long before Vegas finds himself entangled in a web of dark and dangerous obsession. An obsession that can only end one way.

"Dirty Talk" will take you deep into the world of stimulating oral desire and blur the lines that exist between our ultimate fantasies and harsh reality.

(While this book does contain dirty talk.... it DOES NOT contain...'disgusting talk', Joey does a great job of giving you some kink but not making you uncomfortable)

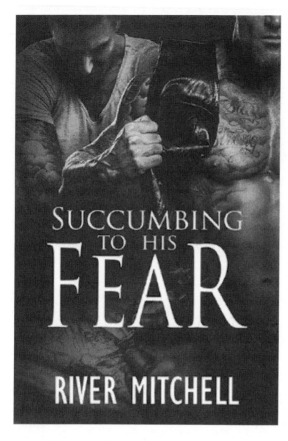

After a life changing event makes Alfie the legal guardian of his estranged half-siblings, as well as a chance meeting one drunken night, he finds his world turned upside down when he discovers that everything he thought he knew about himself was catastrophically wrong.

Before meeting Alfie and his family, Fear was content with his casual hookups and one-night stands, purposefully keeping everyone at an arm's length. As Alfie comes into his burgeoning feelings, a curve ball shakes the two men, threatening to destroy Fear and his new found chance at happiness with Alfie.

With everything thrown into turmoil, Fear decides to fight for those he loves, Alfie and his family included. Will they be able to survive the collateral damage around them, or will they lose everything?

Printed in Great Britain
by Amazon